"*John Dies at the End* has a cult following for a reason: it's horrific, thought provoking, and hilarious all at once. This is one of the most entertaining and addictive novels I've ever read."   —Jacob Kier, publisher of Permuted Press

"The book takes every pop culture trend of the past twenty years, peppers it with fourteen-year-old dick and fart humor, and blends it all together with a huge heaping of splatterpunk gore. . . . Successfully blend[s] laugh-out-loud humor with legitimate horror."   —*i09* on *John Dies at the End*

"Kevin Smith's *Clerks* meets H. P. Lovecraft in this exceptional thriller that makes zombies relevant again. . . . From the dialogue to the descriptions, lines are delivered with faultless timing and wit. [Pargin] never has to reach for comedy; it flows naturally with nary a stumble. . . . The most pertinent story of the genre since George Romero's *Dawn of the Dead* . . . A tighter, more concentrated read than *John Dies at the End* . . . [Jason Pargin] is a fantastic author with a supernatural talent for humor. If you want a poignant, laugh-out-loud funny, disturbing, ridiculous, self-aware, socially relevant horror novel, then *This Book Is Full of Spiders: Seriously, Dude, Don't Touch It* is the one and only book for you."   —*SF Signal*

"The comedic and crackling dialogue also brings a whimsical flair to the story, making it seem like an episode of AMC's *The Walking Dead* written by Douglas Adams of *The Hitchhiker's Guide to the Galaxy*. . . . Imagine a mentally ill narrator describing the zombie apocalypse while drunk, and the end result is unlike any other book of the genre. Seriously, dude, touch it and read it."   —*The Washington Post* on *This Book Is Full of Spiders*

"[A] phantasmagoria of horror, humor—and even insight into the nature of paranoia, perception, and identity."   —*Publishers Weekly* (starred review) on *This Book Is Full of Spiders*

"One of the great things about discovering new writers, especially in the narrow range of hybrid-genre comedic novels, is realizing that they're having just as much fun making this stuff up as you are reading it. Sitting squarely with the likes of S. G. Browne and Christopher Moore, [Jason Pargin] must be pissing himself laughing at his own writing, even as he's giving fans an even funnier, tighter, and justifiably insane entry in the series. . . . The humor here is unforced and good-naturedly gory. Anyone who enjoyed the recent

films *The Cabin in the Woods* or *Tucker & Dale vs. Evil* will find themselves right at home. . . . A joyful return to the paroxysms of laughter lurking in the American Midwest." —*Kirkus Reviews* on *This Book Is Full of Spiders*

"[Pargin's] wildly mind-bending third installment (after *This Book Is Full of Spiders*) of the adventures of protagonist David Wong is filled with the humorous horror readers have come to expect. . . . While the story gleefully wallows in absurdity, thoughtful themes of addiction, perception, and the drive to do the right thing quickly emerge beneath the vivid and convoluted imagery. The plot's rapid pace holds the reader's attention to the truly bitter end."
—*Publishers Weekly* (starred review) on *What the Hell Did I Just Read*

"[Jason Pargin] burst onto the horror-comedy scene with his phantasmagorical novel *John Dies at the End* and has been steadily ratcheting up the madness ever since. . . . A frenetic, welcome return to Dave and John's grotesque but funny grind house nightmare."
—*Kirkus Reviews* on *What the Hell Did I Just Read*

"Introduced in *John Dies at the End* and last seen in *This Book Is Full of Spiders*, [Pargin's] irreverent protagonists return in another action-packed horror adventure full of crude but effective humor. For fans of the humor website Cracked.com." —*Library Journal* on *What the Hell Did I Just Read*

"*What the Hell Did I Just Read* is reminiscent of Douglas Adams's work, stuffed with layers of absurd pastiche." —*The Washington Post*

ALSO BY JASON PARGIN

John Dies at the End

This Book Is Full of Spiders: Seriously, Dude, Don't Touch It

What the Hell Did I Just Read

Zoey Punches the Future in the Dick

FUTURISTIC VIOLENCE AND FANCY SUITS

JASON PARGIN

ST. MARTIN'S GRIFFIN
NEW YORK

Published in the United States by St. Martin's Griffin, an imprint of St. Martin's Publishing Group

FUTURISTIC VIOLENCE AND FANCY SUITS. Copyright © 2015 by Jason Pargin. All rights reserved. Printed in the United States of America. For information, address St. Martin's Publishing Group, 120 Broadway, New York, NY 10271.

www.stmartins.com

Designed by Steven Seighman

The Library of Congress Cataloging-in-Publication Data is available upon request.

ISBN 978-1-250-04019-0 (hardcover)
ISBN 978-1-250-83054-8 (trade paperback)
ISBN 978-1-4668-3543-6 (ebook)

Our books may be purchased in bulk for promotional, educational, or business use. Please contact your local bookseller or the Macmillan Corporate and Premium Sales Department at 1-800-221-7945, extension 5442, or by email at MacmillanSpecialMarkets@macmillan.com.

Second St. Martin's Griffin Edition: 2021

10 9 8 7 6

For Rico the Bunny, RIP

FUTURISTIC VIOLENCE AND FANCY SUITS

The near future, somewhere in rural Colorado . . .

If Zoey Ashe had known she was being stalked by a man who intended to kill her and then slowly eat her bones, she would have worried more about that and less about getting her cat off the roof.

Said cat was on said roof because it was terrified of the Santa Claus hologram in the front yard, a tacky Christmas decoration Zoey's mother had brought home from Walmart two weeks ago. Everybody else in the trailer park had them, so she apparently had felt pressured to demonstrate her Christmas spirit with this dead-eyed apparition that unenthusiastically said "HO-HO-HO-MERRY CHRISTMASho-ho-ho-Merry-Christmas" in a flat robotic voice to anyone who approached. Zoey thought it was a little unsettling herself, but every time the cat saw it blink to life, he would hiss and go streaking off to some high place where he thought the translucent bearded devil couldn't reach him. So that's why on the evening of December 16, Zoey was standing in the snow trying to coax the cat off of the roof while, just a block away, a man was waiting to abduct her and stream her slow mutilation to half a million viewers.

ONE

For eight hours, Zoey's pursuer had been staking out the trailer where the twenty-two-year-old lived with her mother, waiting for the most dramatic moment to make his appearance. Catching Zoey in bed or the shower would be optimal, but he got the sense that this particular young woman had no rigid schedule for doing either of those things. All day he had been watching her through a dirty bay window that put their trailer's whole, sad living room on display. Zoey had begun her day promptly at one PM by waking up on the sofa and initiating a "morning" routine that involved going to the bathroom, returning to the sofa, and then staring blankly at the ceiling for an hour. Then she read for a bit, ate a bowl of cereal, and did something with her hair that involved wrapping part of it in tinfoil while a nature documentary about pack hunters played on the TV behind her. Now the sun had gone down and Zoey, still in her pajamas, was standing in her yard and yelling up at a cat that had jumped onto the roof. Her stalker had intended to send the news media a video of his entire pursuit of the girl, but he knew that this part would have to be edited way down.

He was out of patience. He resolved to move in for the kill and even switched on the tiny camera he kept pinned to his lapel, so his fans could watch it live. But then, at the last moment, he had second thoughts. Mainly about branding.

The man had called himself "The Jackal" for most of his short but prolific career, but had decided to switch to "The Hyena" after watching a pack of them tear apart a moose during the documentary that had played on Zoey's television earlier. He thought it was more fitting—hyenas were wild, unpredictable predators and had the most powerful jaws in the animal kingdom (that last part was what had really sold him on it). But then again, the documentary seemed to show them only hunting in groups (where he was definitely a loner) and, unless he misunderstood, the female hyenas had penises, and even gave birth through them. That was a problem—when he became famous and the press started speculating on why he chose that moniker, he didn't want pundits throwing around a bunch of wild theories about his genitals. But if he amended his manifesto to address the issue, or included photographic evidence that he had a normal penis, then that would just make *him* seem like the weirdo for bringing it up. Maybe "The Wolf" was a better name. Or "The Shark."

As he sat in his rental car and wrestled with this decision, Zoey went inside the trailer, then returned dragging a kitchen chair through the door. She tried to use it as a step stool to reach the cat on the roof, at which point she immediately overbalanced and fell off, landing hard in the snow. She gathered herself, brushed snow off her butt, mounted the chair again, and searched in vain for a cat that, unbeknownst to her, had already jumped down the other side of the trailer. This went on for a very long time, before Zoey finally noticed the cat was not on the roof, but rather lying in the snow under the very chair she was standing on. Exasperated, the girl trudged back inside cradling the cat with one arm and dragging the chair with the other. The Shark ("The Piranha"?) decided he would wait for her to get settled again, then make his move.

Instead, Zoey reappeared at the door and headed for the old and busted Toyota Furia in her driveway. Her stalker wasn't worried about losing her if she left—the advantage of self-driving cars for a man in The Piranha's line of work was that their navigation systems were very easy to latch on to. He could just set his own to follow the same route and the car would do the tailing for him—he could literally stalk the girl while relaxing and playing a game on his phone. He watched as Zoey scraped frost from the Toyota's windshield with what appeared to be a spatula, and then pulled out of her driveway, leaving behind a dark rectangle in the snow as if the car had forgotten to take its shadow with it. The Piranha gave her a ten-second head start, and then told his rental car to follow. He tried to picture the headlines that would tick along the bottom of the news feeds next week, like, "The Piranha Claims His Sixth Victim." Hmmm, maybe "The Leopard" would be better. It needed to be some kind of biting animal, otherwise the surgery would have been a waste.

He rubbed the itchy line of stitches that ran from one temple to the other, looping under his jawbone like a chin strap. He'd had his entire lower jaw and upper teeth augmented with a motorized black market implant consisting of a graphene lattice frame and titanium chompers that could bite through metal. As soon as he had gotten home from the surgery, he had turned on his camera and announced his new powers to the world by biting through a hunk of copper pipe. He thought it made for an ominous demonstration of his new abilities, even if he'd had to quickly turn off the camera at that point because he had cut up his tongue pretty badly. No matter—the jaws worked, and his next test would be on Zoey Ashe's fingers. Then he'd just chew his way up from there.

This, he thought, was what he had always been missing: a gimmick.

She made a left turn, then another. Circling the block. Did she suspect she was being followed? The Leopard would have to be careful—prey animals were weak, but alert and wary. The girl surely could sense the malevolent predator that lurked behind her in the darkness.

TWO

Zoey Ashe had forgotten to tell the Toyota's navigation to stop for food, so she had already missed the turn by the time she was able to convince it to deviate from its route by screaming repeatedly at the windshield. The car reluctantly circled the block and pulled into a food-distribution center that people in the future call "the Wendy's drive-thru." Her Toyota's heater had stopped working weeks ago, which was bad news in a Colorado winter, so she needed something hot inside her. Zoey pulled up to the window and ordered a small container of a semisolid, protein-rich foodstuff that the people in her time call "chili," hoping it would warm her up a couple of degrees (at least before the heat left her body a few minutes later in the form of several dozen hot farts). She then urged the lethargic compact car back onto the deserted streets, where the autopilot took over once more. The Toyota whined its way through the darkness, heading directly toward the Zombie Quarantine Zone, which was the name of the topless bar where Zoey's mother worked.

The radio had stopped working years ago, and so Zoey made up for it by singing a hit pop song from her time called "Butt Show (and I Don't Charge Admission)" while she plugged in the strand of Christmas lights she had tacked around the top of the car's interior. She peeled the lid off her chili, watched steam waft into the frigid air, and decided that things really could be worse. Zoey always tried to appreciate the little things in life, like the fact that just a generation ago you couldn't devote both hands to eating a bowl of fast-food chili while the car drove itself (how did people use to eat car chili? With a straw?). She had also recently upgraded her phone to one that displayed a little holographic image of the caller, but so far she had found this feature was only useful for terrifying her holophobic cat, which hardly justified the cost of the upgrade. However, a moment later that feature did allow her to see that the call that saved her life came from a man who was fond of wearing fancy suits.

When her phone rang, Zoey was only a few blocks away from the trashy, zombie-themed bar where she was supposed to pick up her mother at the end of her shift (that is, the point in the evening when the younger girls were rotated in for the lucrative nighttime crowd). When the phone's hologram blinked to life it startled the crap out of her, as she had forgotten the phone was in her lap and for one terrified moment thought a tiny ghost had emerged from her crotch. Zoey flinched, cursed, and splattered chili everywhere before she figured out that she was not in fact going to have to undergo an incredibly awkward and invasive exorcism. She groaned and tried to scoop hot chili off her pajama pants with her fingers, and panicked when she saw she had also gotten it all over her new phone. She licked chili off the screen and, in the process, accidentally swiped the "Answer" slider with her tongue.

The little hologram man floating above the phone looked puzzled and said, "Hello? Is this Zoey Ashe?"

"Hold on. I got chili all over my car."

"I—Are you there? What's that sound?"

"It's the sound of me eating chili off my phone. Who's this?"

"Zoey, my name is Will Blackwater. You are the—I'm sorry, are you still there?"

"Yes, I'm listening. Are you actually wearing that suit or do you just have your phone set to display you wearing it?"

"Please pay attention. You are the daughter of Arthur Livingston, correct?"

"No. I mean, yeah he is my biological father, but we have nothing to do with each other. Is he in jail again? Are you his lawyer? Is that why you're all dressed up?"

"No. Listen to me, Zoey. A man is coming to abduct you. Right now. His car is one block behind you."

"Wait. What? Who is this again?"

"I'm going to take control of your car. Don't touch the wheel or the pedals, or do anything else to disengage the self-drive. Do you understand?"

"No, I *don't* understand. How can you—"

"Please buckle your seat belt."

Headlights loomed in her rearview mirror. Zoey, her hands shaking, tried to latch the seat belt as the Toyota abruptly lurched to the left, jumped the curb, flattened a row of shrubs, and plowed across a lawn.

"HEY! JESUS CHRIST!"

Zoey grabbed the dash and held on for dear life as her car smashed through two fences and a child's swing set before it thumped over another curb and turned left onto a residential street.

The hologram man on her phone, Will, said, "I apologize for that, I'm not driving the car. My associate, Andre, has the controls and I'm afraid he's had several drinks."

From somewhere in the background she heard another voice in the phone say, "Hey, I drive better when I got a few in me."

Zoey was thrown against the door as the Toyota went power sliding around a turn. She twisted around in her seat and saw the headlights of her pursuer streak through the yard they had just left, sweeping onto the road behind them. Zoey's Toyota abruptly turned into a too-narrow alley, missing a brick wall and a Dumpster by half an inch on either side. Her side-view mirror exploded when the car clipped the corner on the way out.

The man on the phone said, "I'm terribly sorry to tell you this, but your father was killed. It happened last week."

"So? I didn't even know him! I assumed he died years ago. Who are these people?!?"

"Hold on."

The Toyota jumped off the road again and plunged into a grove of pine trees, branches raking the doors with a noise like frantic predators clawing to get in.

Over the phone, Zoey faintly heard Will say, "Cut the lights."

The headlights blinked out, along with all of the dashboard lights and the navigation overlay on the windshield. Zoey was now hurtling through the darkness of the trees, completely blind.

She screamed.

The little hologram man on her phone, which was now located somewhere on the back floorboard, told her to calm down. The car emerged from the trees onto a lawn, fishtailed in the snow-covered grass, then shattered somebody's solar panel array with an explosion of sparks. Another hard left turn, and they were on a paved street once more. Exactly four seconds later, the tailing sedan was behind them again.

Will said, "Don't let this question alarm you, but do you have any weapons in the vehicle?"

"No! Why would I—Wait, I have a spatula . . ."

"Well, we have no indication your pursuer is a pancake, so we'll abandon that angle for the moment. Now I will need you to stay calm. We can't out-run him in this vehicle. I'm going to have you get out."

"How is that possibly going to help?"

"We need to pick a spot where he'll be forced to follow on foot. Other-wise he could simply run you over with his car, obviously."

"Obviously. Who is he again?"

"It's a hired thug. You don't know him."

"Hired by *who*? What does he want?"

"I can explain later. I can assure you that knowing the fine details won't enhance your survivability and it certainly will do nothing to ease your panic. Let me just say that this particular thug took the contract for a reason, which is that he likes when the targets are women. And he likes to take his time. He's calling himself The Hyena, according to his feed."

"Does he give birth through his penis?"

"What? Zoey, listen to me—our map shows a pond about two hundred yards ahead, but does not show us if it's frozen over. Is that a safe bet this time of year, where you are?"

"It . . . I don't know! I don't go ice skating! I know the kiddie pool our neighbors left out in their yard is frozen, but—"

Zoey was thrown against the door again. Another hard right was taking her off the road once more, this time through a pasture. The car swerved to miss a single cow that was lazily grazing in its path. It mooed at her, probably telling Zoey she should turn her headlights on.

Will said, "It's our only option. Hang on."

"What's our only option? What are you going to—"

Zoey was thrown forward against her seat belt as the Toyota slammed on its brakes, skidding across the rough carpet of frozen grass.

Will said, "Go! Get out onto the ice! It will support you but not his car, if he wants to follow he'll have to get out on foot."

"But then wha—"

"GO! NOW!"

Zoey grabbed the phone, threw open the door, and ran toward the frozen pond. Before her was a moonlit sheet of snow that Zoey thought was like the thin frosting on a cake made of filthy water and dead fish, the bitter wind having frozen the part of her brain that thought up metaphors. She didn't even know she had made it to the ice until her sneakers slipped and sent her down to her knees, the surface below her crackling and popping a warning in response. As Zoey climbed to her feet, her shadow suddenly stretched across the ice—headlights looming behind her. She tried to move quickly but gingerly, but after three steps, she slipped again and this time fell hard on her butt.

She heard a car door close behind her. She risked a look back and saw only a silhouette backlit by the twin bluish shafts of headlights. Zoey pushed herself up, her hands swiping aside fresh snow to reveal black ice underneath, her stumbling path across the pond leaving a row of haphazard streaks like Chinese calligraphy. Two more steps—now the ice was making wheezing complaints like a squeaky door hinge each time she lowered her foot. She thought she could hear liquid water sloshing up ahead—she had no idea how thick the ice beneath her was, but knew that not far up, that thickness became "zero."

She had stuffed her phone into her coat pocket at some point and, from inside, she heard Will say, "Are you still there?"

Zoey dug out the phone with numb fingers and whispered, "He's coming. He's coming and I can't go any farther. What do I do?"

"Let me do all the talking. Just hold out your phone."

Through the wind, Zoey could barely hear her pursuer say, "I've reached the edge of the pond." Then after a dramatic pause, he declared, "She has nowhere left to run."

Zoey asked Will, "Who is he talking to?"

"He's streaming this live, he has a Blink camera pinned to his jacket. You don't want to know how many people are watching. Let me talk to him."

Zoey held her phone out toward the menacing shadow in the headlights. The foot-tall holographic ghost of Will Blackwater said, "Stay on the shore, Lawrence, the ice isn't thick enough to support the weight of both of you. You're a beefy guy and you'll notice Zoey here is not what one would call 'willowy.'"

The shadow took a few strides onto the pond and said, "Come back off the ice, sweetie. You're going to come with me one way or the other, and you won't like 'the other.'"

Will's hologram replied, "Talk to me, not to her. We both want Zoey for the same reason, with the minor difference that I do not want to also eat her flesh on a live video feed. Your advantage is that she is worth more to us than she is to you. Our advantage is financial. It appears this leads to easy compromise—we're more than happy to compensate you for what you lose by forgoing the contract on Zoey here. No authorities will be notified. You know my word is good, Lawrence."

"Call me by my true name." He paused, as if thinking. "The . . . Bite . . .

Master. And you left out several important points. First of all, there is the fact that I'm here in person, where you appear to still be in the city, six hundred miles away. Second, there is the fact that you and I both know the girl is worth much more than that contract. And third, as you mentioned, I have a *personal* use for her afterward, which means more to me than any financial reward."

"I am actually aware of all of those factors. I am, however, still confident that an arrangement can be reached. Mr. Livingston had substantial resources, as you well know, and again we're more than willing to ameliorate whatever perceived losses you may incur by turning Zoey over to us. As for your . . . personal predilections, surely some dollar amount could be assigned to the loss of visceral pleasure. Perhaps, even, we could offer a substitute for Ms. Ashe here. We dare say we could produce a subject you would find even more satisfactory."

The man laughed. A fake laugh, Zoey thought. For the camera.

"You are a piece of work, Will. But let me ask you—if you were to take a gazelle from the jaws of a lion, could you satisfy it by substituting a hundred and fifty pounds of Cat Chow? No, because as an apex predator, the lion doesn't just want to eat. It wants *the prize it won in the hunt.* That is why you are to call me The Lion from now on."

Will's hologram, appearing completely unperturbed by this conversation with a serial killer, said, "I understand perfectly, and I see no reason we should permanently deprive you of your prize. We only need Ms. Ashe's services for about forty-eight hours. And after all, is there no greater pleasure than that sweetened by delayed gratification?"

Zoey tried to process what Will had just offered the man, but the howling, frozen wind and the sound of ice clicking and wheezing under her made it difficult to think of anything but a sudden splash followed by endless darkness and paralyzing cold.

The silhouette in the headlights said, "If I was amenable to such an arrangement, I would of course need guarantees that my property would be returned to me at the agreed upon time. And I would need compensation immediately to make up for *delaying* my gratification."

Will said, "I would suggest nothing less. How about a nice used Toyota Furia?"

Zoey's driverless car came flying onto the ice, smashing into the man and throwing him onto the hood. A split second later, man and car went crashing through the ice, sinking into the frigid pond so close to Zoey that the splash threw freezing droplets onto her stunned face.

Will said, "RUN!"

Zoey did not need those instructions. She took off in the opposite direction of the car-sized hole in the ice, praying there was a solid path between her and the bank of snowy dead grass that marked the shore. She took a step, fell, crawled, stumbled to her feet, nearly fell again, then slid and skidded her way incrementally forward. She made frustratingly slow progress, like one of those nightmares where you run and run but the light at the end of the hall just stretches farther and farther away. She was about ten feet from the shore when she heard the ice below her shatter once and for all.

She was in freefall, the world gone beneath her feet. It happened in slow motion—first she felt the stabbing freeze of the ice water swallowing her feet, then her calves, then her knees. Then the bitter, frigid depths engulfed her knees, and then her . . . knees. This was when Zoey realized the water this close to shore was only knee-deep. She sloshed through the broken ice and climbed onto dry land, and only then turned back to see her poor Toyota gurgling as it pushed its nose deeper into the depths, taking the psychopath with it.

From the phone in her hand, Will said, "Are you all right?" Zoey faintly heard the other voice in the background, the man remotely operating the car, say, "I can't believe that shit worked."

Zoey said, "I'm hanging up. You offered to let that guy eat me to death."

Will said, "That wasn't a genuine offer, it was a delaying tactic. Half of negotiation is about dealing with people on their level. Speaking of which, we need to have a word."

"I'm not *negotiating* with you. Go piss a centipede."

"Right, overcoming resistance to negotiation is the other half of negotiation. Can you get somewhere where we can talk?"

"I'm freezing and I'm stranded. I have no idea where I even am."

"Circle around the pond and take The Hyena's car. He won't be needing it."

THREE

Zoey sat shivering in the serial killer's Changfeng sedan, a cheap rental that nonetheless had a wonderful working heater that was pure bliss against her soaked pajama pants. She had driven away from the pond and parked in the shadowy rear of a building downtown that was marked as a real estate office but, by its shape, had clearly once been a Pizza Hut. Zoey put her head in her hands and tried to gather herself. The hologram man in her phone was now sipping from a glass of scotch, while under him scrolled a notification that her mother had tried to call.

Zoey said to her phone, "All right. Who are you again?"

"Will Blackwater. I worked for your father."

"Right, and he's dead? Did I hear you say that?"

"Yes. In an accident. There was . . . an explosion."

"What, was it a meth lab or something?"

"No, nothing like that. Or maybe it was, no one is quite sure. I'm terribly sorry for your loss. He was . . . a great man."

"Mr. Blackwater, I only met that man like two times in my entire life. The first time I ever saw him was when I was eight. It was my birthday. He gave me a football, because somebody told him I was a tomboy. The last time I was sixteen, so it's been . . . six years at least. He was a total stranger to me. So why would him getting exploded to death cause people to come after me?"

"It's just a misunderstanding. But there is a contract out on you and you'll be in danger until we clear it up."

"A contract? As in, whoever kills me gets paid a bunch of money?"

"They actually need you alive."

"Oh, well, at least there's that."

"But the contract specifies that after you've served your purpose, they can have their way with you. It's difficult to explain and also moot, as long as we're both in agreement we don't want you falling into their hands. Zoey, we you need to come to the city. Have you ever been to Tabula Rasa?"

The actual spelling of the city's name was Tabula Ra$a, with a dollar sign instead of an "S," because that's what happens when a bunch of rich douche bags build a brand-new city in the desert and reserve the right to name it themselves.

"I've never been, and I'm not going now. I'm going to the police. And then I'm going to bed."

"That would be a mistake. We've already made plans for accommodations here, we already have a car on the way. It will be there in a few hours. We'll give you a location and a limousine will—"

"Wait, a limo? How many drugs did Arthur Livingston have to sell to afford one of those?" She was never going to refer to the man as her "dad," since the connection was genetic only and she would disavow even that if she could.

"Listen, Zoey, this must be done quickly, for everyone's sake. There could be other bad guys en route right now."

"I . . . I'll think about it. I have to talk to my mom."

"It's dangerous to involve her. You shouldn't even go back home."

"I'd need to pack a bag. And I have to tell her *something*."

"Tell her that your father unexpectedly passed and his estate has requested that you make an emergency trip to meet with his associates. Tell her you were so stunned by this news that you drove your car into a pond. Tell her that to compensate you for the inconvenience, the estate is prepared to pay you fifty thousand dollars. That last part is true, by the way." He paused, to let that sink in, then added, "That should cover the damage to your car plus pay you the equivalent of a year's salary in addition."

Zoey had a solid line of reasoning in her brain that demonstrated with perfect clarity why she should refuse, but it was quickly obscured behind a chorus line of dancing dollar signs. Fifty thousand was actually way more than one year's salary—she worked at a coffee bar, after all. It was the kind of money that could get her and her mom both out of the trailer park, or to a nicer trailer park, anyway. It could get her back into school. She could get a degree in some lucrative field, like nanotechnology. Then she could open a quaint little nanotechnology boutique in Fort Drayton, next to the bait shop. Still, Arthur Livingston was a criminal, which meant this man who "worked" for him was also a criminal, regardless of what kind of fancy little suit he wore in his holograms. That meant the chase that had just occurred was really between two factions of bad guys—he had, after all, just told her not to go to the police.

She asked, "If I leave, how do I know more bad guys won't come after my mom while I'm gone?"

"If you leave, they'll have no reason to. The contract is on you, not her. But if you stay, then *I guarantee you that more of them will come,* which means that just by delaying, you're putting both you and your mother in danger. Making this trip is literally the only safe option."

Zoey remembered the psycho's soft call—*come back off the ice, sweetie*—and shuddered.

She said, "All right, how do I know you're not just more bad guys trying to collect on this 'contract' yourselves?"

"Honestly? We don't need the money. And if we meant you harm, couldn't we have just driven your car into an abutment earlier?"

That made sense, she supposed. Still, she wasn't getting into a car with any of these people. Even if she decided to make the trip to Tabula Ra$a—which on some level she knew would be incredibly stupid and reckless—she'd find her own way there.

Will said, "Are you still there?"

"Prove the money offer is real."

"Hold on. All right, check your account. I just sent you five hundred dollars."

Zoey logged into her bank account and found he wasn't lying—she now had a total of five hundred and seventeen dollars in her savings. Zoey sucked in a breath and thought, *We can get the refrigerator fixed.*

Will said, "The rest I can put into an escrow account, give me twenty minutes and I'll set it up . . . if you agree to make the trip."

"I'll think about it. But don't bother with the car, if I go, I'll take the train."

"Ms. Ashe, I would strongly, strongly advise you *not* to—"

She hung up.

It was seven PM; if she took the train out of Denver, she could be in Tabula Ra$a by midnight. She pulled into traffic, not realizing that a tiny camera The Hyena kept on his dash had recorded her entire conversation, or that more than 1.5 million people were watching.

FOUR

Zoey didn't want to be paranoid, but there was something about the man in the loincloth made of charred doll heads that made her nervous.

He was at the opposite end of the train car, standing in the aisle muttering to himself, his only other item of clothing a pair of blacked-out welder's goggles that made him look like he had bug eyes. When he had boarded at Salt Lake City—the last stop before Tabula Ra$a—Zoey had immediately assumed he was another crazy who had come for her, but then he had just silently taken a standing spot at the other end of the car and she felt bad for prejudging him. Still, Zoey studiously avoided looking in his direction; as any mass transit commuter can tell you, the only way to counter the dark powers of the mentally ill is to avoid eye contact. She gazed out of the window at the scrub brush blurring past at 250 miles an hour. She wondered if her head would go flying off if she stuck it out the window. Her cat meowed a complaint from inside the plastic carrier on her lap.

Zoey's nerves were eating her alive. For the tenth time she pulled out her phone and logged into the escrow account, mostly just because she liked seeing the $49,500.00 displayed on the screen. She dropped her phone back into her purse and nervously started scraping black polish off her thumbnail with her bottom teeth. It was her first time on the high-speed rail and for about five minutes she had been awed by the speed, and then she had quickly gotten bored and started to notice how much this particular car smelled like pee. She had bought her ticket at the gate and the only open seat was this one at the very rear of the car, next to the restroom. Whoever designed the train had put the seat about three inches too close to the restroom door, so it bumped her seat every time somebody went in or out. It had happened exactly nineteen times so far, and what was worse was that each person who did it would stop and look down at her like, *Whose idea was it to put this weird girl in the way?*

Someone said, "What's your cat's name?"

Zoey gave a start, because for a moment she thought the male voice was the crazy homeless guy with the doll heads on his crotch. But it wasn't; it was the stranger in the seat next to her, a fancy young man in an old-fashioned suit who had spent the entire ride constantly checking his e-mail via a pair of wired-up eyeglasses. She looked him over and got the sense that this kid had taken vacations that cost more than she made in a year.

Zoey forced what she hoped was a friendly smile and said, "Excuse me?"

"Your cat. What's his name?"

"Stench Machine."

"Really? That's mean." He grinned, flashing perfect teeth.

"Have you smelled him?"

"No, but still."

Zoey finger-petted Stench Machine through a slot in the crate. He was a Persian, white except for his face and chest, which were black fading to brown. He looked like somebody had thrown a cup of coffee in his face and the fur around his mouth gave it a downturned expression that made it look like he wasn't at all happy about it. He wore a black leather collar encircled with silver spikes. It made him look like a punk rock cat, Zoey thought.

Jacob asked, "Does he answer to that name?"

"Cats don't answer to anything."

"My name is Jacob, by the way."

"Good to meet you." Zoey realized she was supposed to give him her name at that point, but even when she wasn't a target for abduction, she didn't go trusting train strangers that easily.

Jacob asked, "Is this your first trip to Tabula Rasa?"

"Yes, and I'm already a little freaked out. I grew up in Colorado, a tiny place called Fort Drayton. It's way out in the boonies. Just to give you an idea, at the entrance of the—" She almost said "trailer park" but caught herself in time. "—uh, subdivision where we live, there's this big statue of an elk, made of concrete. And the whole thing is chipped with bullet holes where over the years drunken hunters have shot it by mistake."

Jacob laughed, showing those perfect teeth. Zoey squashed the jealousy she always felt toward people whose parents had actually taken them to the dentist as a kid. She was missing a lower canine due to a skateboarding accident when she was eleven, and had a chipped incisor due to an encounter with a drunken stepdad. She suddenly wished she had more than just the one amusing anecdote about Fort Drayton to share with Jacob. She could tell him about that time the high school basketball team made it to the state finals and one of the players got diarrhea during the game . . .

Another person shuffled down the aisle toward the restroom, and they *also* glanced down at her, an act that was starting to seem intentional—Zoey swore everyone who passed was doing it. Did she still have chili stuck to her face? This time it was a black teenage girl with wired-up glasses like the ones Jacob was wearing, which meant for all Zoey knew the girl had the built-in camera on and was broadcasting a feed, maybe one called *The Worst Hair Dye Jobs on Mass Transit Daily* (today's episode: "The Cat Girl in the Back Row with Cyan Bangs").

Jacob said, "Well, you're about to enter a whole new world out here. How much do you know about it?"

"I know it didn't exist twenty years ago, that it was just an empty patch of desert in Utah. Then a bunch of rich people started putting up skyscrapers and suddenly there's a city there. There's no government, right? That's all I know. Oh, and every picture I see of Tabula Rasa looks like the Blade Runner universe is holding a Mardi Gras parade."

Jacob laughed again. "Yeah I'd say you're in for a bit of culture shock. There is no place like it on earth. Your phone will never die, though, there's wireless power coils under everything. Charges the cars as they drive."

"Great, maybe I'll get cancer while I'm there."

Zoey glanced at Doll Head Man again, and thought she had caught him staring at her—it was hard to tell behind his bug-eye goggles. She watched as the man stuck a filterless cigarette between cracked lips. He then casually lifted his hand, touched the end of the cigarette with his finger, and lit it. *With his finger.*

Jacob said, "There's construction everywhere. After dark, it looks like the half-finished buildings are full of fireflies, all the crews in there working through the night, welding the metalwork—"

"Did you see that? What that man just did?"

Jacob glanced toward Doll Head Man. "Yeah, there's no smoking on these trains. You want to tell him or should I?"

"No, he . . . nevermind." Zoey decided the guy must have had a match hidden in his palm or something.

Jacob stared at the guy in amusement and asked, "Are those tiny heads glued to his crotch?"

"You know what the scariest part is about people like him? Everything he's doing makes perfect sense in his own mind."

"Ha! Though I guess that's true of all of us."

No one else had noticed the Doll Head guy doing his cigarette trick. Yet just in the time Zoey was looking in that direction, two other passengers had craned their heads around to look at *her*. She knew she wasn't just being paranoid now—one at a time they would glance around their seat or raise up a bit to see over, peer back, then quickly turn around again when they saw she was meeting their gaze. The bathroom door bumped Zoey's seat. The black girl shuffled past and she made a point to look down at Zoey *again*. She felt to see if there was something in her hair, but then remembered she was still wearing the knit cap she had pulled down over her ears during the bus ride to Denver. Were they making fun of the hat? Or maybe they were looking at Jacob? Was he a celebrity?

"Anyway," Jacob said, "it's amazing how fast they can build them now. You leave for vacation, and when you come back a week later there's one less gap in the skyline, you have to stare at it for a minute to figure out what they added. They're amazing to watch, the way they work. They never stop."

"'They'? What, like robots?"

"No, Mexicans. All of the crews are immigrants on work visas. Great workers, though."

"Oh . . . that's kind of racist, isn't it?"

"Is it? I mean, I guess some of them are probably bad workers. Anyway, it's kind of mesmerizing to watch them go, they have these huge fabricators right there on the job site, like big 3D printers that just ride up the side of the building and stamp out whole sections of wall, ready to assemble."

Zoey tried to figure out if Jacob was hitting on her or if he was just bored from the train ride. She imagined the scary doll guy coming back and pulling a weapon or something, and Jacob punching him out like one of those old-timey boxers.

Jacob continued, "One Friday on the way home from work, I made an offhand comment to my friend about how I wished we had a Falafel Fusion joint in our neighborhood. Then, when I was on my way home from work Monday evening, there it was! They had built it over the weekend, almost like they had heard me say that. It went from vacant lot to open business in less than seventy-two hours. That's Tabula Rasa in a nutshell—you blink and the landscape changes around you. It's like an American Dubai, back when Dubai was Dubai."

Zoey mumbled, "Yeah, that's weird," and she knew Jacob picked up on the fact that she wasn't really paying attention. He fell silent.

Thinking desperately of something to fill the lull in the conversation, Zoey said, "Do you like your glasses? My ex-boyfriend couldn't live without his, but they always give me a headache when he let me put them on."

Occasionally Jacob's eyes would dart up and to the right and she knew he was refreshing an inbox that was only visible to him, otherwise she had no idea what he was actually seeing out of the glasses. They made games where you could bounce a little rubber ball off the faces of the people in the room (the ball was only visible to you, of course) or that would obscure everything with a fantasy world and leave you blind to your surroundings, which if you did it on the bus, was a good way to get your purse stolen. But either way, any time you talked to a person who was wearing the glasses, you never knew if they were actually seeing you.

Jacob said, "You get used to them. They leave kind of an afterimage when you take them off, and you find yourself constantly looking around for your notifications."

"My boyfriend downloaded an app that would superimpose a cartoon mustache on anyone he was talking to. He'd laugh and laugh. The glasses got broken when he got hit in the face with a football and I was kind of glad." She realized she was now talking about her ex-boyfriend a little too much, and in fact had forgotten to add the "ex" just then. She quickly added, "He was stupid. We broke up two months ago." That was pretty subtle, right?

Jacob said, "If you're free over the weekend I'll show you around the city. There's tons to do."

Huh. So he was probably another serial killer. Still, this was Thursday night, she wondered if she could lose twenty-five pounds or gain four inches in height by Saturday. Then she realized that, while she was thinking about it, she had neglected to actually answer his offer and had created an awkward moment by leaving him hanging.

Jacob, trying to cover for it, said, "So what brings you into the big city, Zoey?"

"My father—my *biological* father—died." Wait—when had she told Jacob her name?

"Oh, I'm sorry. When's the funeral?"

"I'm, uh, not sure. They said they needed me for some other stuff, legal paperwork or something. It's pretty weird."

"What happened? He couldn't have been very old, you're only—"

"Twenty-two. It was an accident. I don't know anything yet. They said something blew up."

"Oh, was it that warehouse explosion?"

"Yeah, I guess so. Unless there was more than one. You heard about it?"

"Everybody did, it was big news. So you're Arthur Livingston's daughter? I'm so sorry for your loss."

"Was he famous?"

"Around the city, yeah. Probably could have run for mayor, if the city had a mayor."

"Well, good for him."

Jacob picked up on her cold tone and went quiet, creating the second awkward silence in Zoey's five-minute relationship with him. She pictured bringing him home to her trailer in Fort Drayton, this kid in his three-piece tweed suit with the silk tie and dainty gold pocket-watch chain dangling across his vest. She imagined him pulling up in a restored classic car that rolled in silently on battery power, then getting out with a walking stick and striding to the door. Then Zoey would invite him to sit on a sofa that was covered in cigarette burns and frayed wounds inflicted by cat claws. At that point she pictured him either running for his life, or staying and offering to rescue her from the squalor. She didn't know which would be worse.

Zoey noticed a tiny pinprick of blue light at the corner of his glasses near the hinge, and said, "Oh, is that on? Were we live this whole time?"

The wired glasses all came with forward-facing video cameras that could be left on around the clock, broadcasting everything you did. If you didn't want to wear the glasses but still wanted to livestream your life to the world, you were in luck—you could get those tiny cameras in any accessory you could imagine—pocket watches, necklaces, earrings, tie clips, hats, little copper dragonflies that teenage girls clipped to their hair, whatever. You didn't need a viewfinder, the camera captured a panoramic view of everything in front of you, with software that automatically zoomed and focused on faces and other points of interest—you just turned it on and it recorded your life. The kids these days never left the house without a live feed running (and ever since she got out of high school, Zoey had thought of everyone under twenty as a "kid").

So who was watching their broadcasts? Nobody, or everybody—if they left the feed public, anyone could jump in and watch. The cumulative cloud of all of these millions of connected camera feeds was referred to as the Blink network, or just "Blink." As in, "Did you see the fight between Ayden and Madison at Isaac's party?" "No, but I saw the Blink." Occasionally you'd hear someone use it in past tense, saying they "Blunked" their whole vacation and that you should totally watch it. If you obstructed their feed they'd say you "Blanked" them, and they'd refer to their Blink followers as their "Blinkers," at which point Zoey usually felt the urge to stab them. The point being that the little blue light on Jacob's glasses meant a thousand people could have been listening in on their conversation this whole time. She tried to remember if she had said anything embarrassing.

Jacob put a hand to his glasses and said, "Oh, yeah, I'm so sorry. Jesus, I should have told you it was on. I don't even think about it. Don't worry, I don't have any followers, and lately it's just my mom and a couple of guys from Pakistan who want to see what America is like. The only people watching right now are an old couple who jumped in when I boarded, they're planning a trip and wanted to see how clean the train was."

"Oh. Did you tell them it smells like pee?"

"I did not, but I assume they heard you say it just now."

He tapped his glasses and the little blue light blinked off. The light was mandated by law, so pervs couldn't sneak them into locker rooms without everybody knowing they were part of a live broadcast. But Zoey didn't think the light was near prominent enough, considering she hadn't noticed it until just now. Her eyes drifted toward the window again. The scrub brush and occasional mountains had been replaced by a dirt field growing rows of wood frames that would eventually bloom into a housing development. Black ribbons of newly paved roads undulated between the rows in gentle curves, sometimes ending abruptly where they met an empty space that would probably be another development a year from now. Zoey noticed that as they got closer to the city, the houses became more finished and had less motion blur—the train was slowing down. She looked around for the Doll Head guy. He had moved a few rows closer; he had finished his cigarette and was now smashing the butt under a bare foot, grinding it into the carpet.

Eager to restart the conversation with Jacob, Zoey said, "So, what's it's like living in Tabula Rasa?"

He thought for a moment and said, "Overload."

"What does that mean?"

"You'll see. The population sign comes with an epilepsy warning. Oh, and you can fight a bear, if you want."

"You can what a what?"

"You can pay twenty bucks and a guy will let you fight a bear. In the park, there's a roped off area and you get five minutes to fight a grizzly bear."

"How is that legal?"

He shrugged. "Everything's legal when there's nobody to enforce the law. Three months ago half the cops went to jail in this big bribery scandal. Most of the rest walked off the job. Paychecks were bouncing. It's a huge mess. They've got such a backlog that nothing gets prosecuted."

"Wait, really? Who do you call if a psychopath breaks into your—"

"Look."

He was nodding toward her window. Zoey looked and thought, *overload*.

On the horizon was a cylindrical skyscraper with a gigantic serpent curling around it. The snake writhed and twisted and turned menacing red eyes toward the train. It opened its mouth and hissed. Below it appeared the words "COMING DECEMBER 23." The building, Zoey realized, was wrapped in crystal-clear video screens from roof to foundation, every single window flashing one continuous animation—an ad for a movie. The huge, computer-animated snake snapped around and writhed off *onto the building next to it*, twisting its massive emerald body around letters five stories high that said "JADEN SMITH IN . . ." The serpent slithered along the skyline, and Zoey realized that every structure in downtown Tabula Ra$a was synced to carry a continuous video along every inch of its surface, the snake sliding smoothly from one building to the next, the ad playing to the people on the arriving train. The serpent then crawled onto the front of the domed roof of the train station they were about to pull into, wrapping its body around red block letters that spelled "JADEN SMITH FIGHTS A GIANT SNAKE."

Jacob said, "I like how literal they are with the titles now, you know exactly what you're getting."

The animated snake then *burst out of the ceiling of the station*, climbing into the night sky—Zoey gasped, startled for a moment before she realized it was just a hologram set up on the roof of the building, positioned to give the illusion the snake had broken free of the ad. A couple of people on the train gasped and laughed and took pictures. Zoey noticed Jacob had a big stupid grin on his face. He had seen her jump. She elbowed him and told him to shut up, but she knew she was smiling too, and had to remind herself to keep her lips closed so as not to show off her substandard teeth. And then the train slipped between skyscrapers and suddenly downtown Tabula Ra$a was puking gaudy colors all over her window.

Looming over them was a crystal canyon of towers in various stages of construction—they passed a hotel that blasted a Sony ad into the heavens, then a building that was just a darkened framework of girders topped with cranes that stuck out like a spiky haircut. Zoey looked down and saw that below the rail was a gleaming, blinking river of cars. Swimming in the slow current of cabs and fleet vehicles were the flamboyant, tricked-out rides of the kind of people who were (a) rich enough to drive and park in the city and (b) hadn't been rich long enough to develop any taste. There was a bright red motorcycle whose body had been molded in the shape of a dragon, the rider an Asian guy in a green suit with a six-inch-tall pompadour wig. Hulking in the next lane was a monster truck on tires as tall as a man, a jet of blue flames pouring out of completely unnecessary chrome pipes. Behind it was a Ferrari from the 2020s with an LED paint job flashing undulating colors that rippled across its body in beautiful psychedelic patterns. Behind it, a massive retrofitted 1960s Cadillac convertible, sporting a white leather interior and a huge black man in a white cowboy hat.

Just off the pavement on one side of the street was a deep trench where work crews in orange vests were laying some kind of underground cable. Their project was slicing right through a construction site where someone else was trying to dig out a foundation for yet another building, pallets of brick and bags of cement scattered like islands in the dirt, a flow of tire tracks swirling around where forklifts and Bobcats had scurried to and fro.

And swarming over all of this: the people. With no finished sidewalks to speak of, pedestrians leaked out into the gridlocked traffic, shuffling between bumpers. There were drunk girls in tiny dresses and fake hair giggling and leaning on each other, packs of burly guys off to construction jobs, Japanese kids in sunglasses and glue-on sideburns, Indian families with double-digit packs of kids. Every fifth person wore one of those irritating blinking shirts, fabric that flashed brand logos, obscene sayings, or cartoon characters performing the same looping animation over and over. Flickering, pulsing torsos floating around taillights, everyone screaming for attention in a cloud of light and noise. Zoey had to remind herself that this is what the city was like at eleven PM, *on a Thursday*.

Zoey asked Jacob, "Do you *like* it here?"

He laughed. "That's a complicated question. All I know is that now I can't tolerate living anywhere else."

The train was gently penetrating the station now, brakes whining against the rail. They passed a parking garage bearing glowing signs promoting all of the standard car rental franchises. Standing on each side of the entrance were men in black trench coats and ties, which Zoey thought brought a nice touch of class to a parking garage, until she noticed they were carrying machine guns.

Zoey said, "Tell me those guys are cops."

Jacob leaned over to see out her window, casually pressing his body against hers, and said, "Private security. Those guys are probably Co-Op, you can tell by the trench coats. A bunch of the bigger companies pooled their money to fund their own security when it became clear the city's police were worthless. It's a good thing, you call the cops here, you get voice mail telling you to leave a message."

"Oh, wow. So you get in trouble, you call those guys instead?"

"You probably can't afford those particular guys, Co-Op is more for corporate customers. But yes, private security is who you call. There's a big board online where you can post jobs and they bid on them. It gets kind of crazy, half of the guys are freelancers who either got their private security licenses by taking a five-day gun-safety class, or by paying forty bucks for a fake one. It's a little bit Wild West out here. That's what I was saying, somebody like you shouldn't walk around alone."

Jacob was still leaning against her and she smelled aftershave and hair gel. He let out a breath that Zoey felt on her neck and then settled back into his seat. He reached into an inside pocket and pulled out a sterling silver flask, and took a sip.

He held it out to Zoey and said, "It's going to be cold out there, this'll warm you up."

As far as she knew, she had never in her life taken a drink from an unmarked container from a stranger. She didn't like germs and she didn't like getting slipped date rape drugs, but how often do you meet a rich, handsome stranger on a train? She took a drink and felt lava ooze down her throat. Whiskey. She coughed and they both laughed, and she felt like she was in some dumb movie. They were in the station now, a half-finished geodesic dome that Zoey thought, when completed, would be absolutely stunning, or the ugliest building in America—it was too early to tell. The finished parts were all glass arches with art deco flourishes, alternately futuristic and old-fashioned. The rest was a tangled mess of exposed steel skeleton and bundles of wiring that dangled like innards, as if the building had been in a knife fight.

Just off the platform, behind the hundreds of waiting travelers, was a row of fast-food and drink franchises Zoey had never seen before. She was a little ashamed of how excited they made her, but Fort Drayton only had five places to eat, and one of them was a gas station. Tabula Ra$a's train station alone had twice that many. Just from her seat she spotted an AwesomeChanga franchise, where according to the ads you could get just about anything as long as it could be wrapped in a thick tortilla and deep fried to a crisp. Next to it was a Waffle Burger, which is just what it sounds like, and then a Go-Juice bar serving a long line of exhausted passengers waiting to pay nine dollars for a mixed fountain drink containing four hundred milligrams of caffeine and twelve percent alcohol. Next to it was a From-the-Oven cookie stand with a clear glass oven under the counter where you could watch them bake chocolate chip cookies right in front of you. Then they'd pull them out and shove them into your hand, still warm, the chips melting all over the wax paper. Zoey decided after she got off the train she would stand over there and just smell that place for half an hour. At the end there was a beverage joint called Spiked Ice, selling sugary fruit smoothies that, according to their sign, were laced with "fuel shots" that sounded illegal as hell—Codeine, Lithium, Hash Oil, DXM, Modafinil. She half wondered how such a place could just operate in the open, cops or no cops, but mostly she just wondered how much the drinks cost and which one she would get. The line in front of it was the longest of all.

Stench Machine meowed and stuck a paw through a slot in the crate, getting restless. He had never been put in an enclosed space for this long and he was probably wondering where the stink was coming from. The train finally bumped to a stop and Zoey heard the passengers up by the door stand and start wrestling carry-on bags out of the overhead bins . . .

And easily half a dozen of the passengers glanced back at her as they did it.

And yes, they were looking at her, not Jacob. She had an urge to stand up and ask them what they were staring at, but decided she was being silly. She needed to find her hotel, and was about to ask Jacob for a ride. But right as she opened her mouth, a new voice said, "You know what's the difference between you and me?"

It was Doll Head Man, shouldering his way through the departing passengers. Looking right at her.

"You," he said, to Zoey. "With the blue streaks in your hair. Do you know what's the difference between you and me?"

He edged up until he was looming over them in the aisle. The rest of the passengers were shuffling away behind him, grateful to be on the other side of the crazy man's attention.

Jacob said, "Come on."

He made as if to stand and bring Zoey along with him, but Doll Head put a hand on Jacob's shoulder and pushed him firmly back into his seat. The man was not huge, but had a body like leather stretched over bundles of steel cable.

Jacob said, "Buddy, we don't want any trouble, just move along or we're gonna have to call the—"

"Shut up. I'm talking to her." He rested his hands on a pair of seat backs, arms and torso forming a bridge across the aisle. He squeezed the seat cushions and veins throbbed under his biceps. Zoey saw her own pale face reflected in the man's pitch-black goggles. "And I asked her a question. Do you know what's the difference between you and me?"

Exasperated, Zoey said, "I don't know. What?"

Doll Head Man smiled. "The difference," he whispered, "is that *I* would never have let a stranger intimidate me into answering such a question."

Jacob said, "Now you listen here—"

Doll Head Man, without looking at him, raised his right hand to Jacob's face. He snapped his fingers and there was a crackle and a piercing flash of bluish white light, like the man had just spawned a tiny lightning bolt from his fingertips. Stench Machine hissed and thrashed inside the crate.

Jacob recoiled and said, "What the—"

The man shushed him. "I am *talking to her*. There is a long, long line waiting to feed off this chubby little piglet. Please *wait your turn*."

Yep, her first instinct had been right. This psychopath was here to finish the job that had been left undone by the last psychopath, both presumably sent by someone who had an endless ready supply of them. And here she thought she was being open-minded by not judging him. It hit Zoey all at once that she had just traded a gruesome death for fifty thousand dollars—not even enough for her mom to buy a nice car later, even if Livingston's people followed through with payment, which they almost certainly wouldn't.

Zoey peered around the man to see if there was a guard, or conductor, or burly passenger, or *anyone* paying any attention to what was happening in the back of the train. But no one in uniform appeared, and none of the shuffling passengers wanted any part of whatever was going on with the crazy naked hobo and the young couple he was tormenting. This man, Zoey realized, now had absolute power in this tiny corner of the world.

She was going to die on this train.

"Do you know what these are?" He gestured toward the doll heads. Zoey didn't answer.

He said, "It is rude not to answer direct questions."

"They look like doll heads that you've melted with a lighter or a blowtorch. Because you thought they would make you look scary."

The man grinned. "They are souls. Each represents a soul I have taken. I am the Soul Collector. They will serve me in eternity."

Before Zoey could even begin to formulate a reply, a bored but authoritative voice said, "You need to clear out the car, pal . . ."

Finally. All three of them looked up to where a balding man in a gray uniform was leaning in the sliding door. His eyes met Doll Head's inhuman black goggles and all the color drained from his face.

"N-now we don't want any trouble here. Whatever business you got with those folks, just clear out and take care of it elsewhere, all right? No need to hold up the train."

Zoey glared at him. *"Are you kidding me?* Call the cops!"

Doll Head Man turned away from the uniform to face his hostages again.

He smiled and said, "I agree with the blue-haired piglet completely. Call the police. Call Co-Op. Call the black vests. Call the LoB. Tell them all that the Soul Collector has Arthur Livingston's daughter. If anyone tries to enter this train, or if she does not give me what I want, I will add her to my collection."

FIVE

The platform was now crowded with onlookers recording the scene from dozens of tiny cameras, people probably watching their viewer counts skyrocket as word spread across Blink that someone was about to be lightninged to death by an escaped mental patient. No one made to intervene, they just watched in detached curiosity as if Zoey, Jacob, and Homeless Zeus were behind the glass at a zoo enclosure. Doll Head stalked up and down the aisle of the train car, glaring out of the windows at the crowd. Zoey realized he wasn't trying to scare the onlookers away, but was instead making sure all their cameras had a chance to get a clear shot of him in all of his menacing glory. At one point he stood in the open doorway, raised his hand, and with a crackle that made the whole crowd flinch, did that lightning trick with his fingers. The audience was impressed. Zoey wondered if she had lost her freaking mind.

Something else that was weird, which had almost gone unnoticed by Zoey due to the other, weirder things happening in her life at the moment, was that there were *a lot* of armed people in that crowd. Scattered among the gray-jumpsuited rail staff, white-shirted security guards, and hundreds of gawkers, Zoey could see half a dozen of the Co-Op guys in their black coats and ties, looking like Secret Service agents with their little machine guns pointed at the air. Then she counted at least five more men and women in black vests full of pockets, wearing amber wraparound shades and black backward baseball caps, clutching assault rifles with fingerless gloves. And then there were the armed loners—the odd man or woman who didn't seem to be part of any team. There was one guy in a tank top with two pistols in shoulder holsters, beside him was a bald Japanese guy in a leather jacket with a katana on his back, then a woman with pink hair and a short double-barreled shotgun strapped to each thigh. They hadn't shown up in response to the developing hostage situation—they hadn't had time. They must have been waiting there, but why?

"I have to say," thundered Doll Head, striding up the aisle, "they were wise to hide you on the train. But I found you, as was my destiny. Now you have seen the power inside me. You know what I can do to you."

Zoey replied, "Okay, don't, uh, go into a psychotic rage here or anything, because I'm more than happy to cooperate. But right now *I have no idea what you're talking about.* Okay? I know there's some kind of contract. But here's the thing: I don't know who wants me, or what they want me for, or anything else. And I *don't want to know.*"

Doll Head grinned. "You are truly Arthur Livingston's daughter. I should have expected nothing less."

"Did he owe you guys money? Is that what this is about? Did he screw you on a drug deal or something? Whatever it is, I don't care—if you want me to call the guy I talked to earlier and tell him to pay, I'll do it. But I *didn't know Arthur Livingston.* He tried to give me a car for my sixteenth birthday, I gave it back. His money was dirty, I wanted no part of it."

"Good. So you will open his vault for me."

"I would absolutely do that, if I knew where it was, or *what* it was, or how to get into it. But I swear, this is the first I'm hearing of it."

"I want you to know that I am not surprised, nor disappointed. In fact, I would have been disappointed in anything less. After all, you have no reason to respect me. Like all who have power, you only respect others who have it. You need me to demonstrate my power to you. So that you can respect me, and deal with me as an equal."

"No, no, you really don't—"

Doll Head reached out with his left hand and grabbed Jacob by the throat.

Jacob thrashed and tried to twist out of the man's grip. His perfect hair tumbled down into his eyes as he choked out the words "Hey! No! What are you—Let go!" Doll Head was not choking him. Just keeping him in place. "Zoey!" hissed Jacob, tendons straining in his neck, face turning red with panic and exertion. "Just do . . . what he says . . ."

Doll Head said, "Shhhhhhhh," and, continuing to pin Jacob to the seat with his left hand, reached out and laid the other hand gently on Jacob's forehead. He held his palm against Jacob's brow, pressing his thumb against one temple and his middle finger against the other, gripping his skull like a bowling ball.

"Zoey . . . tell him . . . how to . . ."

"Shhhhhhhhh."

"Please."

"Shhhhhhhhh. The only human destiny is to succumb to one stronger."

There was a pop, and a sizzle, and smoke. Jacob's body went rigid, his hands clenched and flew to his chest, his feet kicked the seat in front of him. One shoe flew off. There was a stink like steamed broccoli. Zoey's cat howled and hissed and tried to claw his way out of the crate. Doll Head withdrew his hand and Jacob slumped back, his eyes open but blank, his mouth hanging slack. A low gurgle escaped from deep in his throat, a line of drool ran from his mouth, a pool of urine spread across his lap. In Jacob's temple was a smoking hole left by the electrical current that had fried his brain.

Zoey screamed. "WHAT DID YOU DO? WHAT DID YOU DO?!?!"

In a theatrical voice, Doll Head Man said, "I have freed him from that weak husk. He has joined me, become part of something far more powerful. Only the limp vessel remains. I have added him to my collection."

It was chaos out on the platform. A TV camera crew was now covering the situation live, and Zoey heard the soft drumming of helicopters outside the station. A huge screen that ran along the rear wall had flipped away from the local weather report and switched to live coverage of the scene. The headline that crawled along the bottom was not, as Zoey expected, "Crazy man holds up train" or "Hobo harnesses the power of lightning." No, what it said was: "LIVINGSTON DAUGHTER HELD HOSTAGE"

Zoey clinched her teeth and wondered how many times she was going to have to pay for her mom having chosen a scumbag for a sperm donor. Jacob, his half-closed eyes twitching aimlessly around the cabin but seeing nothing, slumped over against her. Zoey pushed him off and screamed through her window at the people on the platform.

"HELP ME! HE'S GOING TO KILL ME!"

Once more, they just stared. Up until that point in her life, Zoey had lived every moment with the unspoken assumption there was always *somebody* she could call if things went to hell. Her mom, a teacher, the police, God. But now she was trapped in this giant steel tube—just her, and this man, and death. Maybe everyone feels like this at the end. The ice breaks under your feet and you realize that there had never been anything below you but cold and darkness. It was the point at which things could not get worse.

There was a stir in the crowd. People started to turn, to look back at the main entrance of the station. Then the crowd parted, slowly, as if a wild animal had wandered in and no one wanted to startle it with sudden movements.

From the split in the crowd emerged first a huge black man, with a perfectly bald, polished head Zoey thought looked like a Whopper, the chocolate candy. She didn't know if that was racist or not, but all of the progressive attitudes in the world wouldn't change the fact that his head looked exactly like a Whopper. Behind him was a stunning but stern-looking Chinese woman, walking with the gait of someone whose skirt is too tight to be practical, but who is quite used to it. Behind her was a man in a cowboy hat with bushy eyebrows and a red nose who looked like he had popped out of a cartoon. Looming behind them was one more man she couldn't see clearly. But the crowd knew who he was, who they all were, and wanted no part of them. No one in the group was visibly armed, but not even the men with machine guns would make eye contact with them. Everyone just stood down.

Doll Head Man, aka The Soul Collector, reached out a hand and pressed it against Zoey's brow, digging finger and thumb into her temples.

He whispered, "I can take your treasure, or I can take your soul. I desire no outcome over the other. You choose. You have three seconds. One."

"No! Listen!"

"Two."

"PLEASE! I'LL TAKE YOU TO THE SAFE OR WHATEVER IT IS WE'LL FIGURE IT OUT I'LL DO WHATEVER YOU—"

"Stop. I'm here."

At the door stood a striking, pale man in an overcoat and fedora. He had cold blue eyes and sharp cheekbones. His suit jacket, vest, shirt, and tie were all shades of gray and silver—Zoey thought it made him look like a robot. There were no wrinkles, it was as if the suit was part of the skin he was born with. Zoey immediately thought that she could not imagine this man wearing anything else.

She had seen him once before, projected through her phone.

The Soul Collector turned to face the man, arms loose at his sides, blocking the aisle with his body, putting himself between the silver suit and his prey.

Will Blackwater glanced around the train car as if assessing the situation, then calmly said, "First thing's first—are you all right?"

Zoey was about to answer, when she realized Will was asking that of the Soul Collector, not her.

He smiled and said, "I wondered when you would arrive, Will."

Will stopped where he was and removed his hat. His hair was a black helmet that looked ready to withstand a hurricane.

"How are you doing, Brandon? Are you still taking your medication? You're not, are you?"

"I'm free of all that now. Thanks to Molech, I have become my destiny. I am the Soul Collector."

"Yes, I can see that. The boy in the back there, is he dead?"

"His soul is with me now."

Will nodded thoughtfully, as if doing some minor math in his head. "All right. That complicates things. I can get you out of here. But we have to go *now*. The girl looks unharmed. Is that correct?"

"Yes."

"All right. That's good. I'm sure you've noticed we've drawn quite a crowd here."

The Soul Collector cast a scornful glanced toward the platform. "I possess a power that can reduce all of them to ashes."

"Well, I don't want to get ashes all over my suit, so let's go ahead and do this as cleanly as possible. We have a car outside and we can get you through this crowd without incident if we move *soon*."

He looked past the Soul Collector and said to Zoey, "You're coming with us. We're taking you to your father's estate. That's where his vault is. Do I need to tell you that your best—and only—course of action is to comply?"

Zoey glanced at the brain-dead man slumped next to her, thin tendrils of smoke still drifting out of the burn holes in his temples, stinking like piss.

She said, "Please. Just . . . let me go. Whatever shady business Arthur Livingston was into, whatever money he had, the vault, I don't care about *any of that*."

"It doesn't matter. You're involved because your father involved you, and now you're a hunk of meat in a kennel. If you don't do what I say, things will get bad in ways you cannot comprehend."

Will stood straight, placed his hat back on his black helmet of hair, straightened his sleeves, and addressed them both.

"Now, the situation is this. You see what's happening out on the platform. In the absence of an actual organized police department in this city, what we have instead is a gaggle of grossly unqualified and often mentally unstable hired guns. Every single one of them knows Livingston's daughter is here, each of them thinks they can get a payday out of this. It's a lot of very stupid people, pumped up on adrenaline, who know their every move is being broadcast to a live audience. We have to make it clear to them, and to everyone who may be lying in wait between here and our destination, that we are now in charge of this situation. Now, I'm going to walk out that door first. Zoey, you'll be next. The Soul Collector will be right behind you. The moment we step out, we will be swarmed. Zoey is going to address the nearest camera and say the following. Listen carefully. Are you listening?"

Zoey nodded. Beside her, Jacob let out a guttural sound while his cloudy, unblinking eyes shifted lazily around the car. In a flash, a whole alternate future played in her head, one in which Zoey and Jacob arrive at the station without incident, the two of them shuffling off the train together . . .

He carries her bag for her. On the platform, she gives him her number. They agree to meet on Saturday night. The day comes and Jacob picks her up at her hotel. Her handsome stranger has a convertible and even though it's December they put the top down and cruise through the chill air, the fifty-story video screens flashing ads and brand logos overhead. They go to a fancy restaurant, maybe one at the top of a tall hotel that looks out over the new city, and there's a long line but of course Jacob can get right in because he knows people. They eat and drink and laugh. She sees the way he looks at her, Jacob knowing he can get someone thinner, and prettier, but he sees who she really is. He sees what's inside, and wants it. And afterward, they're waiting for the valet to bring the car around and the night air is cold and she's a little bit drunk and Jacob drapes his coat over her shoulders . . .

Zoey said, "I'm listening."

"You're going to say, 'My name is Zoey Ashe. I am Arthur Livingston's daughter, and I am being held hostage. I have—'"

"Held hostage by the Soul Collector," said the Soul Collector.

"Right. 'I am being held hostage by the Soul Collector. I have been told that if anyone tries to intervene, he will kill me. Please do not interfere with this process. All other bounties have been rescinded.' Got it? It doesn't have to be those exact words but the idea has to come across. Everything is under control, there is no money to be made if they interfere."

Zoey nodded. She stuck a finger into the cat crate and scratched Stench Machine's head. "Let's get out of here."

She stood, and realized Jacob's silver flask had fallen into her lap. It was wrong to take it, she barely knew the guy. But she took it anyway, and stuffed it into her purse. Something to remember him by, if she lived through this. The moment Zoey stood, a buzz went through the crowd outside, everyone trying to muscle into position to get a shot of the hostage and captor emerging from the train. Will wrestled her carry-on from the overhead bin and stood by the door. Zoey followed as instructed, carrying Stench Machine's crate by her side.

Zoey felt a hand on her back, and flinched. Even through her jacket she thought she could feel a buzz from the Soul Collector's fingers, a jittery vibration like ants crawling between her shoulder blades. The door slid open and the noise hit her like a wall—reporters crowding around and screaming questions, gray uniforms trying to shove back the rubberneckers. All of the screens on the back wall were now tuned to the local news, and the local news was showing the three of them, creating a jarring House of Mirrors effect. Zoey watched their situation play out on the monitors a split second after it occurred in real time—the tall man in the overcoat and fedora, followed by all five feet two inches of Zoey, looking pale and frazzled with black and blue bangs dangling out of her wool cap. Behind her, the strapping savage in the loincloth. The crowd backed off at the sight of him.

No, that wasn't right. They were backing away from *Will*.

The trio edged out onto the platform, into the massive unfinished building that Zoey had only glimpsed from inside the train. She saw another train on the next platform over, the line from Las Vegas. All roads lead to Tabula Ra$a, a place that didn't even exist when she was born. A TV news crew rushed up, and then another. She was famous. It sucked.

Behind them, the guys in black vests and sunglasses prowled into position. The Co-Op men in overcoats with their little machine guns edged toward the door, to block the path. Will glanced back at Zoey and nodded. There were cameras all around now—hell, even the random onlookers were essentially walking cameras—so Zoey didn't look at any particular one.

"Um, can everyone be quiet? I'm supposed to say something."

She gave the commotion a moment to die down. She glanced back at the train car and saw paramedics rushing inside to tend to Jacob. She wondered if his family was here in the crowd, or if they even lived in town.

"Okay, um, listen. I am being held hostage, by—" She couldn't bring herself to say his stupid name. "The scary-looking man behind me. He has told me that if anyone tries to interfere, he will kill me."

A stir went through the crowd. Gasps. What the hell did they think was going on here? Zoey looked back at the TV screens again and saw that the cameras had zoomed in on the Soul Collector's face. He was baring his yellow teeth, inscrutable eyes behind the bug-eye goggles, TV monitors along the back wall reflecting back his own face in their pure black lenses. He was soaking up the attention. Zoey realized she was watching the greatest moment of this man's life. She bit her lip so hard it bled.

Zoey cleared her throat and continued, "His name is the Soul Collector. He has magic powers."

Zoey turned to face the man and said, "Show them." She held up her thumb and forefinger. "Show them the trick with the lightning. So they know you're serious."

The Soul Collector thought this was a fantastic idea. He bared his teeth again and raised the hand, letting all cameras focus in. Zoey, feeling like now would be the perfect time for some liquid courage, unscrewed the cap on Jacob's flask and tipped the rest of its contents into her mouth. The Soul Collector leered at her, held his hand in front of her face, fingers spread, and let the piercing arc of blue electricity leap from thumb to forefinger.

Zoey spat half a flask of whiskey at him, the mist flying through the arc and igniting into a fireball. She had aimed at his face, but the ball of fire instead descended and engulfed his crotch. The Soul Collector shrieked like a man whose nuts were on fire, and fell hard on his ass. Zoey grabbed Stench Machine's crate and sprinted through the crowd.

SIX

Zoey flew through a gauntlet of elbows and tumbled through a revolving door. She emerged onto a noisy sidewalk full of rumpled people waiting for cabs to drift past in the molasses ooze of traffic outside the terminal. She thought about flagging down a cab herself, but in this traffic, her pursuers could just lazily stroll up and yank her out of the back seat.

Instead, Zoey ran into the street, weaving and juking across six lanes of gridlock, clutching tightly her box full of annoyed cat. She dodged behind a steampunk van covered in copper tubes, wooden panels, and clockwork gears, only to almost get run over by a Coca-Cola delivery truck, its side panels playing a looping video of animated polar bears frolicking in the snow and urging everyone to drink Coke on Christmas. She shuffled between a customized pickup with a naked holographic woman dancing in the bed and a Vespa scooter that was straining under a trio of young Middle Eastern men. She finally emerged on the other side of the street and hurdled a stinking pit where men were trying to repair an oozing sewer line, only to have her left foot land in a patch of wet cement, marring a stretch of unfinished sidewalk. She stumbled and fell and Stench Machine thrashed and hissed as his crate bounced, no doubt realizing how much better off he'd be on his own. Zoey ignored the yells of an enraged work crew, clambered to her feet, and pushed through the first door she saw.

She smelled grease and curry, and found herself in a packed McDonald's bearing signs in both English and Hindi, glossy ads on the doors promising beef-free burgers made of fried vegetables and Indian spices. She shouldered through the EMPLOYEES ONLY door to the kitchen and bumped past harried

Indian teenagers working a row of deep fryers, then crashed through another door and emerged into an alley that served as an open market of street vendors selling knock-off purses, prepaid phones, and AK-47s. She wove her way through chattering customers and vendors haggling in sprays of rapid foreign words.

She took a corner and saw a crowd up ahead, thick enough to disappear into. The people were milling about in a city park, clumping around a scattering of steaming food trucks. There was a bandstand nearby and somebody was packing up gear, the aftermath of a concert in the park that must have just ended. Zoey cast nervous glances over her shoulder and headed for where the crowd would be dense enough to swallow her. She ran, sweat freezing on her face, feeling like her lungs had sprouted razor blades. She shouldn't be in this bad of shape, she had quit smoking when she was fifteen.

Zoey excuse-me'd her way through a bunch of laughing black people around a picnic table having what appeared to be a birthday party, and tried to blend in. She scanned the crowd. A dozen college kids ran back and forth in wired-up glasses, playing some open-world video game, throwing magical fireballs at each other that only the other kids in glasses could see, dodging real makeshift tents where homeless people lived. She saw giggling Japanese girls in parkas who looked like tourists, a group of Indian kids around a park bench eating fried curry balls from insulated McDonald's boxes, and a pair of old homeless men arguing about something. Most of the rest of the crowd was lined up in front of food carts selling kebabs, pizza cupcakes, and ice cream churros. Nearby there was another cart selling baggies of weed, to help perpetuate the cycle of junk-food commerce.

Zoey decided to keep moving, putting more crowd between her and the street. She passed a group of drunk guys circled around a roped-off area where a chubby frat boy was menacing a confused, heavily sedated bear. She eventually found an empty park bench that was displaying a video ad along the back featuring a man in a skull mask holding a huge knife, advertising his services as a vigilante for hire, hostage negotiator, and bail bondsman. She plopped down on the bench and sat Stench Machine's crate at her feet. She tried to think.

She had no ability to leave the city, short of just walking—obviously she wasn't getting back on a train (ever, again, for the rest of her life) and she had no means to rent a car, not with her credit. She also had no place to stay—she literally didn't have enough limit left on her credit cards to pay for a room, even with the cash advance Will Blackwater had used to lure her out here (and they were probably having a good laugh about that, too—for a measly five hundred dollars they had gotten their hostage to come right to them). She could try hitchhiking along the highway out of town, hoping some stranger would get her out of the city without also murdering her or demanding sexual favors as payment, but the odds of that were even worse than usual—her face was all over the news, and she had some kind of a bounty on her head. She had an urge to call her mom, but what would *she* do? Drive the ten or twelve hours from Colorado, on a suspended license, in a beat-up Toyota that, oh wait, was now a fish habitat under a frozen pond?

Zoey let Stench Machine out of his crate. He prowled the area around her bench, hoping to find a bird to eat. He wasn't much of a hunter, so when he saw that no birds had died of natural causes within five feet of the bench, he just gave up and lay down in the dirt. Zoey picked up the cat, hugged him, and tried to think of what to do. She glanced around. The Bank of America building that loomed over the park was wrapped in a thirty-story-tall animated weather forecast, showing cartoon rain drifting down over the next week. The Hilton next to it was one big promotional video boasting about their heated rooftop pool. The office building next to it carried a feed of the local news, which first covered the aftermath of some kind of small explosion (shots of shattered glass and debris surrounded by startled onlookers) but then cut to video of Zoey's big, dumb face. Zoey groaned and stupidly tried to pull the knit cap down further, as if obscuring her eyebrows would make her anonymous. She glanced at the people around her, seeing if anyone was paying attention.

The building was showing a clip of her walking off the train, just minutes ago. Then it cut to her doing the trick with the whiskey, then to video from *inside* the train car, the news grabbing the Blink feed from one of the people who had walked past her and Jacob on the way to the restroom. There were some cheers nearby in the park, and Zoey thought for a moment they were cheering her up on the screen, but she turned and saw the frat boy had the bear in a headlock. The bear seemed mildly annoyed—

Zoey froze. The feed up on the screen was now showing her, sitting on the park bench. Then it cut to another view, from behind. Then another, closer. It suddenly dawned on her that she had just tried to disappear into a crowd in a world where half of the crowd was wearing live cameras.

Every stranger was staring at her now. Clutching her cat and leaving its crate behind, she ran.

Through the crowd, across the street, and into an alley full of pantsless women in heels, wigs, and imitation fur coats. She rounded a corner pawn shop with a sign boasting that they would pay $75,000 for a human kidney, and headed toward the only spot on the landscape that wasn't bathed in light: a roped-off construction zone around a low, oddly shaped building. She climbed over orange barriers and ducked behind a huge metal roll-off bin full of construction debris. She peered back the way she came . . .

Lights, hovering about ten feet in the air, creeping toward her. It was a whizzing device the size and shape of a flying barbecue grill, with twin blue beams piercing the darkness, sweeping the ground for its target.

The lights hit Zoey's hiding spot and she ran, the drone tailing her, probably already reporting back to her father's mob, or the vigilantes, or the hobo wizards, or some other faction of thugs who also wanted to capture her and do unspeakable things. She plunged into the darkened construction site, tearing through yellow caution tape, shoes alternately sinking into sucking mud, then crunching through shards of broken glass that coated the ground. Looming ahead of her was a brick structure that looked like an apartment building that had been tipped onto its side. Exactly that, in fact, right down to useless sideways balconies and an ornate main entrance mounted fifty feet off the ground, its shredded awning flapping in the breeze.

Zoey saw faint light coming from an unglassed window low enough for her to climb into. She clambered her way through, entering what she thought was destined to be the most inconvenient building in the history of architecture. Stench Machine had finally had enough and thrashed out of her hands, darting toward the light at the end of the hallway that Zoey had climbed into. A sideways hallway—Zoey was standing on a painted wall, to her left was a tiled floor, to her right, light fixtures and acoustic tiles. She moved gingerly down the hall, stepping around open doorways at her feet. Above her was an identical row of numbered doors that only a gymnast could enter.

From behind her came the glare of lights and the angry bee hum of four rotors—the drone was following her in. Zoey jogged deeper into the absurd sideways building, kicking debris that had landed on the floor/wall—chunks of furniture, broken table lamps, a shattered toilet. She tripped over a fire extinguisher box and nearly plummeted into one of the floor doors. The drone was right on her now, and Zoey scrambled back to the emergency box, yanking the fire extinguisher free. She advanced on the whirring drone and, letting out a karate yell, swung the fire extinguisher. She knocked the little bastard right out of the air in a shower of sparks and chunks of shattered plastic.

Something burst out from the guts of the machine as it crashed to the floor, bundles wrapped in foil. Curious, she picked up one of the bundles. It was warm, the size of a burrito.

She unwrapped it.

It was a burrito.

She kicked over the broken drone, one rotor still whirring uselessly in its plastic housing. In bright yellow letters on the side it said:

HELITACO!

FINE MEXICAN FOOD

DELIVERED TO WHEREVER YOU'RE STANDING

Below that was a phone number and a Web address to place orders. The drone itself was painted the red, green, and white of the Mexican flag. It had a festive sombrero glued to the top of it.

She heard voices from down the hall.

Zoey turned, seeing no one. The faint words were echoing from the direction of the lights at the end of the hall. Zoey moved cautiously along the wall, which sloped increasingly to her left as she went, as if the whole structure had a slight twist to it. She whispered a call for Stench Machine, which she knew was useless even while she was doing it. She found the source of the light, pouring up from an open doorway in the floor below her. The top of a ladder was visible, obviously having been propped up there for someone to go down into the sideways apartment without falling in and breaking their neck. Stench Machine was perched at the edge of the doorframe, peering down inside.

Something grabbed the cat. In a blur, he disappeared into the opening below.

Zoey ran to him, glancing back one more time to see if anything or anyone else had followed her into the building. She reached the open door, crouched, and peered into a lit chamber full of harsh shadows and debris. She yelled for the cat again, which again was stupid, because even if he responded he wasn't going to climb a ladder (even if cats in general could climb ladders, she was pretty confident that *hers* couldn't). So, she climbed down and found herself in a broken, sideways dining room. There were shattered windows on the floor, showing off a view that consisted of nothing but impacted mud and dead weeds. Furniture was tossed around the wall. Above her, to the right of the door she had just dropped through, was a sideways kitchenette with a bar. Two large, filthy Latino men used the bar as a bench, their muddy work boots dangling over the black marble countertop. Zoey turned and saw four more men standing behind her. One was holding a sledgehammer, another a pickaxe, another a regular axe. The fourth, a stocky man with Spanish words tattooed on his forearms, cradled Stench Machine in one hand and held an unlit blowtorch in the other. They all stood in silence for a moment, under the dim glare of a work lamp that lit the room like a medieval torture dungeon.

The man who was holding her cat said, "You lost, Chica?"

She was just so, so tired. She gave the ladder a look but she wouldn't make it up two steps before they grabbed her. As if she could leave without Stench Machine anyway.

Zoey sighed exhaustedly and said, "People are after me. I just need a place to hide. You guys got this . . . area here and that's fine. It's a big building, I'll find another room. But that's my cat. I'd like him back, please."

The stocky man said, "We can't let you do that."

One of the other men said something to him in Spanish, and he answered in kind.

Zoey said, "Just let me have the cat. Please."

"And then where you gonna go?"

"Somewhere else. *Please*—"

Her phone rang. Thinking that somehow this could be a rescue, she pulled it out. The hologram of Will Blackwater blinked to life once more, floating above the phone in the dim light of the room. Everyone around her reacted, and started bantering with each other in Spanish. The stocky man with Zoey's cat let out a harsh laugh.

Zoey hung up on the call.

The stocky man looked her up and down.

"You're not from around here, am I right?"

"No."

"And you got no place to stay? No friends, no family? That why you're tryin' to squat in a horizontal building?" Zoey didn't answer. Instead she wiped tears from her face and thought about how much she just wanted to go lay down somewhere. *So tired.*

He said, "Make you a deal. I'll give you a ride wherever you want to go. Maybe even give you something to eat. But you got to do something for us, first."

Two of the men started talking to him in Spanish, talking over one another, insistent. The stocky man gestured with the blowtorch and said, "*Callate.*"

He turned back to Zoey and said, "And you got to do it for *all* of us."

SEVEN

Behind the sideways building was a row of mobile homes parked haphazardly in the shadow cast by the dancing lights of downtown Tabula Ra$a. Inside one of the trailers, five of the men were standing around the cramped living room. Zoey and the stocky one with the tattoos, named Rico, were in the bedroom.

Rico sat upright on the bed and Zoey said, "Now the head. Hold still."

She set the phone to scan and held it next to the man's right ear. She slowly moved it in an arc around his face. She checked the scan, and tapped the screen and told it to save.

"Okay."

Rico said, "So that's it? It's got me in there? So I call somebody, it'll look like I'm standing there in front of them, right?"

"Well, you'll look like you're a foot tall and standing on their phone. It's not like *Star Wars*, it can't project you into the middle of the room. You'd need a projector on the floor for that. Or the glasses, the glasses will make it look like the person is right in front of you. But they'll make *you* look like a dork."

They'd been at this for half an hour. It had turned out, after a lengthy and embarrassing discussion, that Rico and his crew were not, as Zoey had thought, a roving gang of rape bandits. They were the first wave of a demolition crew hired to recover anything and everything of value from the sideways building—copper wire, plumbing, undamaged fixtures—before the structure that had once been the Parkview Luxury Apartments would be demolished without having ever seen a single tenant.

"A-Ron! Get in here. We'll do A-Ron next, then we'll be done. Thanks for doing this. Bought these for the crew a month ago but the hologram thing never worked. Made everyone look deformed, like funhouse mirrors."

Rico dialed from his phone, and A-Ron answered as he was walking through the doorway. A hologram of Rico's squat frame popped out of A-Ron's phone and A-Ron said, "Yay. It works. See, now you just got to hire Zoey to hang around you twenty-four hours a day for when you inevitably break it again a week from now." To Zoey he said, "Yo, why does your cat smell so bad?"

Before she could answer, Rico asked, "If I'm sitting down then why am I standing up in the hologram thing?"

"It plays your face in real time but your body is just a standard animation. When you call somebody, your mouth and face will move while you talk but you'll always be wearing what you're wearing now."

"Oh. Why?"

Zoey started to answer but A-Ron cut in. "So if I call you while you're takin' a dump, I don't got to watch you."

Zoey made A-Ron stand in the center of the room just as she had done with Rico. She stood back a few feet and started scanning A-Ron's body.

Rico said, "Suck in your gut, *ese*. You see how fat I looked in mine? This thing adds twenty pounds."

"It ain't the phone, *ese*."

Zoey said, "So, I don't understand. That building just fell over? Perfectly intact?"

"Could have been way worse. If it'd fallen the other way, it'd have taken out the Rand Hotel, like dominoes."

A-Ron said, "Inspectors in this city are a joke. Everybody's dirty, nobody's taking time to do it right."

"Hey, Parkview was built to code, it's what they did next door that doomed it. They started digging out the basement but they were too close to the foundation here, they dig and dig and one day you got twenty stories just falling gently on its side, like it got drunk and stepped in a ditch. Concrete pilings snapped like toothpicks, sounded like cannons going off."

Zoey finished with A-Ron and he called Rico's phone to test it. His hologram popped up and A-Ron said, "Yo, it does make you fatter."

Zoey said, "You can actually download any body or outfit you want. Make yourself into a muscle man, put a little tuxedo on it to class it up."

A skinny guy with a mustache, the oldest of the group, popped his head in the bedroom and said, "Why is it taking so long for the burritos to get here?"

There was an awkward silence. Zoey finally said, "Oh. That was for you. I might have . . . crashed it. I thought they had sent it after me."

"You thought somebody sent a burrito helicopter after you?"

"I thought it was a security drone or something."

"What did you do?"

"Nothing! Well, I helped drown a man and set another man on fire and vandalized that restaurant's toy helicopter but all of that was after. My biological father died and I'm in town to settle his affairs but now they're trying to get into his safe or something, it's a big mess. He was a . . ." Zoey trailed off as the expression on every face in the trailer froze. "What?"

Rico said, "Get Cesar."

Confused, Zoey said, "This town has a *Caesar*?"

"No, that's just his name. You know the whole world's lookin' for you, right?"

EIGHT

The Blink network encompassed some 120 million cameras in the United States alone. Along with the millions of live feeds broadcasting from glasses and pinned-on cameras, Blink also included hundreds of thousands of indoor and outdoor security cameras, in addition to most car dashboard cams (standard on every new model since 2020), and a swarm of aerial drones owned by police departments, TV news channels, and tens of thousands of random voyeurs. At any given moment, ninety-eight percent of these feeds were broadcasting absolutely nothing of interest.

But "Blink" wasn't just a bunch of cameras. The nerve center of this sprawling mass of electronic eyes was a software algorithm that made sure the viewer always had something to watch. So if you logged into Blink from your phone or computer, it greeted you with three general categories: People, Places, and Events. Once you were in "People," you could jump into your best friend's camera to see what he was up to, or log in to see what pop star Latrell La'range was doing with his Thursday evening. If you had wired-up glasses, you could overlay your view with their feed—literally see the world through their eyes, blotting out your own reality completely. If you chose "Places," you simply told Blink where you wanted to be and it'd give you the most popular view of it—if you wanted to see Mt. Everest, you'd jump into the feed of whichever climber had the most interesting view at the moment—or whichever one was having the most dramatic near-death experience.

"Events," however, were the real star of the show. For example, if the aforementioned pop star got high and stabbed a dancer at a nightclub, as had happened four times in the previous year, then "Latrell La'range Has Stabbed

Another Stripper" would appear as an Event on Blink within a few seconds. Then Blink could drop you into whatever feed had the best view of the situation, and would continue following the event from camera to camera as the mostly nude man with the massive orange afro fled from the club, stole a car, led police on a chase, and attempted to board a private jet to Mexico. As long as there was a working camera in range, you could watch the drama unfold in real time, the view hopping from one feed to the next. If things were moving fast and there were a lot of cameras around, the view jarringly switched every few seconds, which was disorienting to new viewers (and why everyone had started calling it "Blink" years ago). The result was that the network had become a massive breeding ground for spontaneous reality shows that organically popped up within that worldwide nebula of camera feeds. The "Event" listings updated in real time with everything from drama in your social circle ("Catfight at Rob and Jina's Wedding Reception") to worldwide news ("Hostage Standoff in Kyoto Burger King").

A lot of this was new to Zoey, and had to be explained to her as she sat there on the sofa in the construction crew's trailer. She didn't own a Blink-enabled device, as it seemed absurd to imagine anybody would want to watch her serve lattes and mood-enhancing teas to rednecks. She didn't really keep up with the feeds, either, as she thought Blink was still just for creepy people to broadcast upskirt videos of women on the bus, as it had been when it was new. This is why Zoey didn't realize that for the last eighteen hours, she had been the star of a viral Blink Event that at the moment was being followed by more than twenty million people.

The work crew in the trailer knew, however, because of Cesar. He was the youngest member of the crew who, according to Rico, had been following Zoey's story religiously from the start. Rico called Cesar away from his task of ripping copper wire out of another part of the building, and when he walked through the door and saw Zoey, there were a few seconds of confusion followed by pure, starstruck awe.

Cesar uttered some kind of Spanish curse and clapped his hands and said, "So who gets the five million?"

Zoey said, "Wait, what? Is that the bounty they have out on me?"

Cesar said, "Girl, you don't even know what's going on, do you?"

"I've been traveling since seven, I'm out of the loop apparently."

Cesar took over the controls on the wall screen and scrolled to an Event listing called "The Hunt for Livingston's Key." The icon for the show was a picture of Zoey's face.

She sighed and said, "Already this is ridiculous."

"Okay," Cesar said, "it all started when that warehouse blew up last week. Right after that, this rumor floats around that Arthur Livingston had a vault, okay? But here's the thing—nobody can find the key, because he hid it somewhere. There's talk that there are all these clues hidden around and everybody's obsessed with this mystery. Now, nobody even knows what's in the vault, okay, some say it's bodies of people he's had killed, some say it's gold, some say he's got a woman trapped in there and she's only got twenty-four hours' worth of air. It's all crazy rumors—you know how Blink is. Or maybe you don't. Anyway, so then this huge offer pops up on the skin wall—"

"The *what?*"

"The, uh, board, the underground one where people post illegal bounties for freelancers. So an offer goes up, okay, a million for the key to the vault. It's from Livingston's own people, which is huge, because it confirms that the whole story is true and that they don't got the key. Blink goes totally wild with this—for days the crazy stories are flying around, all these treasure hunters promoting feeds claiming they know where the key is, saying it's in some abandoned cathedral or a cave out in the desert. But it's always just a big show, nobody ever comes up with a key. And meanwhile, the hype over this thing just keeps building and building, millions of us watching, everybody talking about it. Then finally, this morning, *pow*, big plot twist, okay? The key ain't in town. The key is in *Colorado*. With the daughter that nobody knew Arthur had."

"So this whole thing is over some Blink rumor? Can I just look into a camera and tell everybody I don't have the key?"

"You *do* have it." Cesar pointed at his temple. "Up here."

"What, like a combination? Because I don't have one of those, either."

"No. The vaults the rich people got now, they don't open for keys or combinations or nothin' like that—they open for *people*. Okay? Fingerprint scans, eyeball scans, that sort of thing. Livingston's vault is one of a kind—it has a scan that goes right into your skull. Reads your brain neurons and synapses, all that. And Livingston set his vault so it would open for one person and one person only. You."

"And he did this knowing it would make me a target for every greedy psychopath in the country." Zoey thought about all of the strangers giving her glances on the train, and the crush of reporters as she was being escorted to a gruesome death. She shook her head and said, "That man was cancer on two legs. So you were watching this the whole time?"

"Everybody was. And all eyes were on you, all these treasure hunters and crazies all heading your way, and the rest of the world watching them to see who gets to you first. Everybody on Blink forming up into teams, fans rooting for their guys to win. And then it gets really good. This other contract goes up, outbidding Livingston's people, okay? Three million. Some other crime family, they want the key for themselves. So now you've got a whole other faction of scumbags in on the action, and everybody's heading off to Colorado, and then that motivates all these white knight types who want to save you. All head out to converge on your location."

Zoey thought, *And that whole time I was on my sofa watching wildlife documentaries and failing to dye my hair.*

"But the problem is," he continued, "they got the wrong town. They think you're out in some suburb around Boulder, okay?"

"Ah. Nobody knew I'd moved."

"So everybody's trying to nail down your current address, but this wrongcock with mechanical jaws figures it out before anybody. So while everybody else is turning over every stone in the wrong town, this guy is staking out your trailer, just waiting, and watching. And then he turns on his feed and then there's that crazy car chase and the thing with the ice . . . well, you know. You were there. So the next time it picked up was when you boarded the rail. So then all the hunters and crazies swarm the train station here waiting for you to show up, but a few guys get smart and go to Salt Lake, thinking they could get on the train with you. Two of 'em made it."

"Two?" Ah, right. The Soul Collector, he was one. The other was, of course, Jacob. He hadn't been hitting on her. He had been there to collect the bounty, and to shoot an impromptu reality show about it.

She said, "So explain the thing with the people who can shoot lightning out of their hands."

Three different people in the room said, "The *what*?"

"The bad guy on the train? He could shoot electricity from his fingers. Is that something people just *do* here?"

Rico said, "Nobody *I* know. Seems like it'd be dangerous to take a leak."

Zoey said, "Nevermind, forget I asked. So, whoever turns me in to Livingston's scumbag mob gets a million, but whoever turns me in to this other group of worse bad guys gets three?"

"Make that five," said Cesar. "Look."

He brought up a list and at the top, just above the one million–dollar offer from Livingston Enterprises, was an updated offer of five million dollars. The name next to the bid was . . .

"Who's 'Molech'?" Zoey asked.

The response was a series of nervous glances.

"Let's put it this way," said Rico. "Even if the people in this city didn't need that cash, they'd turn you in just to get on his good side. You don't want to know what he does to people who get in his way. Though if you do want to know, I can bring up the videos. He likes to do it for an audience. Got a creepy fanbase on Blink, these Team Molech guys were cheering the loudest when the Hyena started broadcasting from outside your trailer. Throwing up a lot of suggestions about what he should do to you."

"Do I want to know how many people are on Team Molech?"

Cesar said, "It's a lot. But ya know, not all of 'em are psychos, probably, some just doin' it for the shock value. Still, if they saw you in public, they'd report your position without a second thought. Then they'd pop some popcorn and watch Molech's people tear you apart on cam—"

Rico cut him off. "*Enough.* Cesar, you got to learn when to stop talking."

Zoey went cold, but remembered that whoever got to her first, it was really her father who had murdered her.

Rico squinted at Zoey and said, "And you, get that look off your face. I got a wife and four kids, I'm gonna bring home a suitcase full of blood money? Where do I tell them I got it from?"

A-Ron said, "I'll take your share."

"Man, your momma would string you up. And she'll know where you got the cash, because I'll tell her."

Cesar said, "I hate to tell you, but it's either gonna be us, or those guys."

He gestured at the screen, where the feed had switched. They were now watching a half dozen flamboyantly dressed men packed into the back of a van. One guy had a red Mohawk and was covered in tattoos, and was sharpening a scimitar. Another had what looked like a bazooka with war slogans painted on the sides. The guy next to him looked like he had covered his body in glue and rolled through a knife store. At the bottom of the feed was a logo that said "LEAGUE OF BADASS."

Cesar said, "They're in their van, on their way to Parkview. Right now."

The feed on the screen cut to a dash camera on the van, which showed they were rounding the park, the collapsed apartment building sweeping into view ahead. Then suddenly, the feed went black.

Cesar said, "They're jamming us, so we can't watch how they approach. Smart."

Zoey scooped up the sleeping Stench Machine from the sofa and said, "Where can I hide? Is there a place they can't get to in the sideways building?"

Rico said, "We told you, you can't go back in there. It's not safe, the place is fallin' apart. We don't even let the crew go off unsupervised. If you stay here we can—wait, Zoey—"

She was already heading for the door. These people seemed nice but she thought there was no way they'd walk away from five million dollars when it was between that and fending off a bunch of high school dropouts with military-grade weapons looking to create a shootout for their Blink show. She yanked open the door of the trailer—

Standing there, blocking the view of everything beyond, was an enormous bald, black man in a suit that was an expanse of dark pinstripes around a white shirt and a bright purple tie. She had seen him before—he was part of the entourage of fancy suits who had showed up at the train station with Will Blackwater. He was one of her father's men.

NINE

"My name is Andre Knox, and I'm alone and unarmed," he said, politely but with some urgency. "If you want to frisk me, I'll let you, but you got to hurry because there's a lot of me and we don't got much time. And don't be alarmed if I get aroused."

Zoey made no move to do this, so instead the man opened his jacket, showed there were no guns dangling in holsters, then lifted the tail and gave a twirl, to show no weaponry was stuck down his pants. The interior of his suit jacket was the same garish purple silk as his tie. He faced Zoey again and looked past her, at the nervous men standing behind her. He nodded and splayed his hands, as if to confirm that everyone agreed he was unarmed.

He straightened his lapel and said, "Now, I know that assurances mean nothing from a stranger, even one with as honest a face as mine, but I got reason on my side. You do know why we need you, right?"

"The thing with the vault. It has to scan my head to unlock."

"That's right. And it only works if you're alive, it will not unlock for a dead brain, by design. That means that my associates and I care more about keeping you alive than perhaps anyone on earth, aside from you and your momma. As far as assurances go, that's about as good as you're gonna get in this town."

Zoey met the huge, brown eyes of the man, then glanced back at Rico and his crew.

She said, "I'll go along on one condition. I want it made official that the guy behind me caught me and brought me in. His name is Rico Hierra. I want him to get the bounty."

"Done."

"The five million, I mean."

"Done. Come on."

Rico started to voice a nervous objection behind her, but she was already moving, Andre ushering her along toward an elegant black sedan. He opened the passenger-side door for her and she plopped into a leather seat that immediately conformed to her lower back and butt, like sitting in a punchbowl full of jello. Without her touching a thing, the seat raised her up and forward two inches. The dashboard lights blinked on and a navigation overlay on the windshield made it look like the road in front of her was glowing yellow, tracing the route they would take. Zoey nervously looked behind her—through the rear window she saw headlights bouncing across the construction site, headed right toward them. The van of the heavily armed freelancers who called themselves the League of Badass was coming to collect the bounty that would make their careers.

Andre glanced back at them and said, "You mind if we lose them first?"

"I . . . guess not?"

"Hold on." Andre picked up a coffee cup from the console and sipped it, then said to the car, "Bentley, lose these guys."

The Bentley was way, way better at car chases than Zoey's half-dead Toyota had been. The sedan launched itself down the dirt lane wrapping around the rear of the toppled building. They were rolling across ruts and gravel and debris, but no bumps or even noises made it into the interior of the car. Floating along, a bubble of luxury isolated from the world. One of the crazies behind them leaned out of the van and fired a machine gun, little gleaming brass shells twirling away into the night. Zoey yelped but Andre just sighed and sipped his coffee. A spray of bullets left a row of little spiderweb marks on the rear window. As Zoey watched, the wounds in the glass healed themselves, the circular cracks shrinking to white pinpricks before disappearing completely. The Bentley found the street along the park and merged into traffic, dodging in and out of taxis and scooters and garish custom vans.

Andre sniffed and said, "What's that smell? That your cat?"

"He has some kind of skin problem."

"You don't look hurt, but I should've asked you anyway. Are you hurt?" She shook her head. Andre continued, "Now, this is perfectly understandable, but I'm thinkin' you misconstrued what occurred on the train. Will is the best negotiator I've ever known, and you got to understand that to have any chance, he needed to get on the scumbag's side."

"Right. Just like you're trying to get on my side now."

The Bentley smoothly took a corner at top speed, the rear wheels sliding, then regaining traction and launching them forward again. Andre had to momentarily pause his coffee drinking.

Behind them, the van tried to take the same curve and flipped over, smashing through a storefront. Zoey was disappointed that the van didn't explode into a fireball like in old action movies, but that was one of the downsides of electric car technology. Andre glanced back, satisfied at the outcome, then settled back into his seat and rubbed his Whopper head.

He said, "My point is, none of that stuff on the train was supposed to happen. We sent a car, like we told you on the phone. We couldn't come up with a limo, but we sent a nice sedan. Not as nice as this one but still a better ride than the train. Car showed up, you weren't there."

She shrugged. "I didn't know if I could trust you. Still don't. I wanted to find my own way."

"I guess there's no point in tellin' you why we didn't want you to do that? Seems pretty apparent now, right?"

"Because you offered every violent nutjob in America a huge pile of money to find me?"

"Well, in fairness to us, the moment word got out about the vault situation, some of the city's shadier characters put out a contract to bring you in. Our contract was simply us tryin' to outbid them. We were telling the truth, though. The city really is the safest place for you. You saw for yourself, the bad guys own cars and maps and your daddy's place has a hell of a lot better locks than your trailer."

"Why not leave me out of it completely? Why couldn't that man just leave me alone?"

"The only one who could answer that question is no longer with us. And his passing, well, it has thrown things into turmoil. More than you know, even. If on the day of the Lord's judgment you want to find your daddy and punch him in the gut, I'll hold his arms back while you do it."

"So this vault has, what? All his money in it?"

"Rich people don't actually have big physical piles of cash they keep around. Especially somebody like your daddy. He's got stocks, bonds, commodities, and land on top of land, far as the eye can see. Plus there's offshore accounts, shell corporations, Lord knows what else. And I mean literally, only the Lord knows. What's in the vault are . . . other assets. That's probably all I should say."

"So it is criminal stuff."

"You really didn't keep up with news about your daddy at all? He was a pretty famous dude."

"No, I avoided all mention of him like the plague."

"Well, he wasn't as bad as you think. Mostly he just owned land. Got in on the ground floor of Tabula Rasa, he owns a lot of them towers downtown, half the casinos, all of them housing developments out east—we're talkin' land that doubles in value every six months. And it's all legit. He was kind of the Bugsy Siegel of Tabula Rasa."

"I don't know who that is, but don't bother trying to sugarcoat Arthur Livingston. I know he ran prostitutes. It's how he met my mom. I know he skated on prosecution over and over because the witnesses disappeared."

"All that was true in his youth, I don't deny it. But he was tryin' to get out of all that. He was a big political donor, ran a bunch of charities. We're mostly just the real estate now." There was a pause, and Andre sipped his coffee. "Mostly."

"So you get enough dirty money and you can just spend yourself clean?"

"Well . . . yeah. This suit is Hugo Boss. That's not just the name of a brand, it's the name of a dude—a German dude who got his start making uniforms for the Nazis. Ferdinand Porsche—as in, the fancy sports cars—same thing. I could take you back home to South Carolina and show you the fancy homes of rich folk who got rich six generations ago off slave labor. And guess what—they're still rich."

"It's weird how you think those examples are supposed to make me feel better."

"System don't care how you feel about it. It is what it is. Bentley, take us home."

The car confidently followed the glowing path in the windshield and soon the city gave way to suburbs and the suburbs gave way to the rich people enclave of Beaver Heights, which featured a golf course and palatial mansions with sprawling lawns and imposing fences. They followed a winding road designed to prevent anyone from driving faster than fifteen miles an hour, until they arrived at a massive wrought-iron gate set into stone pillars carved into the shape of dragons.

The moment they rolled to a stop, a holographic woman in stripper garb appeared outside Andre's door. Ornate glowing letters appeared across the gate that read "Casa de *Ass*-a."

Andre rolled down his window and the holographic stripper said, "Welcome, visitor! I'm Candi! Sorry I'm not decent, I accidentally locked myself out of the house wearing nothing but *this tiny thong*. Mr. Livingston says he wants to know who's here, and what size kimono you wear."

To Zoey, Andre said, "It's a recording." To the stripper he said, "Andre Knox with Zoey Livingston."

"Ashe."

"Sorry. Zoey Ashe."

A moment's pause. The stripper looked into the air as if she was hearing instructions, and then said, "Arthur says he will see you now. And he wants to see *all* of you, if you know what I mean. Please leave your inhibitions at the door."

The stripper vanished and the gate slid open. Zoey said, "This is going to seem like kind of an odd question, but was Arthur Livingston thirteen years old?"

Andre grinned and said, "Take a look around the world, girl. Men don't never grow up. Get a bunch of us together with no ladies around and it's all boner jokes and headlocks. Your daddy just had enough money that he didn't have to hide it like the rest of us."

The Bentley drove itself through the gates and instantly a million points of colored light exploded into view. The cobblestone drive wound through a sprawl of manicured landscaping that at the moment was nothing but a support system for a constellation of Christmas lights. Every twenty feet or so along the path was a statue of a knight holding a sword, each wearing a red Santa Claus hat. The path was circling around a sprawling enclosure housing two white Siberian tigers, one gnawing on some huge hunk of meat that Zoey hoped was not a human being. As they neared the end, they passed a life-size Christmas nativity scene in which the traditional figures had been replaced with characters from *Die Hard*. Finally the Bentley floated to a stop in front of a huge, dignified mansion that had clearly been designed and built by someone other than Zoey's father, a sprawling Gothic thing that would be referred to as Something Manor in one of those old movies about English aristocrats.

"This house is a hundred years old, but has only been sitting on this plot of land for five. It was originally on the north shore of Long Island, the Gold Coast. Arthur had it shipped across the country and reassembled here, brick by brick."

Andre led the way up to a pair of massive charcoal gray metal doors that were decorated with an etching depicting a tangle of nude women.

"Those doors are solid bronze. They weigh seven tons. Each."

The huge doors swung squeakily open for them as they approached, Zoey following Andre and cradling Stench Machine. Standing at the door was a terrifyingly thin, balding man in butler clothes who look about two hundred years old.

"Welcome back, Andre. A pleasure to meet you, Ms. Ashe."

Andre nodded toward the man and said, "Zoey, this is Carlton."

They entered a cavernous foyer, at the center of which was a Christmas tree easily four times as tall as Zoey. Carlton led them around the tree, shoes clicking on the marble tile, toward a dual grand staircase that split off to opposite wings of the mansion. On the landing at the top of the stairs they were suddenly accosted by a ghost, rising from the floor in an eerie bluish glow. Zoey almost tumbled backward down the stairs, and Stench Machine thrashed in her arms. The ghost was a hologram of Jacob Marley from *A Christmas Carol*, clanging his chains together and saying "*Scroooooge!!!* I wear the chain I forged in life . . . I made it link by link, and yard by yarrrrd . . ."

Andre said, "I'm gonna apologize right now, your daddy had a thing for holograms. He knew they were tacky, but said they made him feel like he was living in the future."

Carlton the Butler led them up the stairs and to the left. The house smelled of pine and varnish and floor wax. They reached an open door and passed into a room full of rich, brown leather furniture arranged in front of a fireplace large enough to roast a horse. Above the mantel was a gigantic stuffed and mounted buffalo head, wearing a Santa hat and a white fake beard.

Carlton stopped at the doorway and said, "Ms. Ashe has arrived."

Up until that night, Zoey had no experience being either famous or infamous, and as such, she was unfamiliar with the feeling of meeting a group of people who didn't know her and yet hated her. In this alien realm that seemed to have been entirely handcrafted in rich wood and leather, she was greeted by dismissive eyes, condescending smirks, and sideways glances that said, *This ought to be good.* It was clear that no matter what she did or said, everyone in this room intended to laugh about it later. Zoey was suddenly aware that her nose was running. She sniffed. The sound was deafening.

There were three of them in the room, besides Zoey and Andre, all of whom were already standing when she entered. She spotted the silver suit and lacquered black hair of Will Blackwater right away, holding a glass of scotch because, of course, he was that kind of man.

Next to him was the beautiful but annoyed-looking Chinese woman Zoey had seen on the platform with him earlier, wearing a pitch-black outfit that straddled the line between smart business suit and business-themed sex fetish costume. Hair pulled back to show off her neck. Pearls, brazenly short skirt, calf muscles, heels.

Leaning against the far corner with an empty scotch glass was the guy who earlier Zoey thought looked like he'd stepped out of a cartoon—jowly face with grin lines between a white cowboy hat and a suit that had been tailored to not fit quite right. His body language said that corner was his leaning spot, that he'd spent many a long meeting or brainstorming session there, always with a glass in his hand. A spot where he could see the whole room and take it in, while listening to the fireplace crackle and pop to his left.

Zoey, on the other hand, had arrived there wearing a pair of muddy tennis shoes, the left one ruined by wet cement that was rapidly drying to a crust. She wore too-long jeans that were frayed at the bottom, which were also too tight in the hips even though they hadn't been when she had bought them last summer. She was carrying her denim jacket and wearing a black cardigan she inherited from her mother over an orange T-shirt bearing the logo for a band called Awesome Possum. A gray wool stocking cap was hiding a rats' nest of black and blue hair. She was clutching an angry, smelly cat and was wearing half a pound of its shed fur all over her torso. Fortunately, no one in the room knew she was also wearing a pair of pink underwear that said "BUTT SHIRT" across the back.

The moment Andre stepped through the door, soft music faded in—a wokka-wokka guitar that Zoey somehow recognized as the theme from *Shaft*. Like it was Andre's personal theme song.

Will looked annoyed and waited for the music to fade before he said, "Zoey, glad you could make it. This here is Echo Ling, in the corner back there is Budd Billingsley. You've met Andre. We all worked closely with your father and—I'm sorry, please have a seat."

Zoey let Stench Machine down and shuffled over to sit in a vast leather armchair that probably claimed the lives of twenty cows in its creation. But no one else sat, so she was now seated with her hands knotted in her lap like a nervous little girl, while the four suits loomed over her. She saw Andre had acquired a scotch on the rocks. She wondered if there was a chute somewhere that just fired them into your hand the moment you walked in. She stared down at her ruined tennis shoes. These were the only shoes she had brought and, in fact, were the only tennis shoes she owned. Her nose started dripping again and she sniffed and wished everyone would turn their backs so she could wipe it.

The butler, Carlton, said, "Can I get you anything, Ms. Ashe?"

"Could you get me a new pair of shoes?" She tried to laugh but everyone just pursed their lips and shared their quick sidelong glances. In the distance, a wolf howled.

Finally Carlton asked, "Is there anything else?"

"No, I'm fine. Or, maybe some water." She felt like she needed to ask for *something*, and that was the only thing that occurred to her.

"Very well."

Carlton exited. Zoey tried to remind herself to breathe.

Andre said, "Look, we made a terrible first impression. Specifically, *Will* made a terrible first impression. We all owe you an apology, your departed daddy included. So let me say it, for everybody here—it was good of you to come down and help us take care of this, and we'll make sure you're compensated for every terrible thing that has happened today. More than compensated. Right, Will?"

"Absolutely."

"Nobody should have to go through what you went through back in Fort Drayton, and on the train earlier—"

"What *was* that? Who was that guy? I mean, I know he was after me because of, well, all this, but what *was* he? He could . . . summon electricity or something."

More glances. A silent decision was made to let Will explain. Or rather, to decide what *not* to explain.

"We don't know. That's actually the issue at hand. Would you mind if we asked you some questions about that?"

"I doubt I know anything useful."

"Did you see any kind of device hidden on him? Even something small, like something that could fit on his belt?"

"No, I don't think so."

"How many times would you say he did it? Made the electrical current arc between his fingers like that?"

"I don't know. He liked to do it, to show it off. I'd say at least five times."

He shot a glance at the Chinese woman, Echo. This was important, apparently.

"So?" Zoey asked. "Who was he? *What* was he?"

"Just a man, with some kind of gadget, a weapon, we think he had it augmented into his hand." He shrugged, as if this was an unimportant oddity that was worth no further thought. "All of that—don't concern yourself with it. He's certainly not going to bother you anymore, and this room, right now, is the safest spot in the city for you. Maybe the safest spot in the whole world. Your father had enemies, as you know, but he spared no expense in protecting his home. The moment a foot bends a blade of grass anywhere on the grounds, a dozen armed guards spring into action. You will not be disturbed."

Carlton emerged from behind her and placed onto an end table a sterling silver tray on which was arranged a pitcher of ice water, a glass, a bowl of lemon wedges, some sprigs of mint, a candy cane, and a box of Kleenex. He poured her a glass of water. The ice cubes were perfect spheres.

Will continued, "So, you know what you're here to do."

"There's a vault and only I can open it. It scans my brain or something."

"That's correct. There is no way to fake it, it has to be you."

"And once I open the vault, it's all over, right? All the contracts and bounties and stuff disappear? I'm just a regular person again?"

There was a pause—ever so slight—from Will before he said, "Absolutely."

He was lying. Zoey knew she wasn't going to get the truth by just asking, so instead she said, "And we have no idea why he designated my brain as the key instead of yours, or hers, or . . . literally *anyone* else's? ?"

Will shook his head and said, "Trust me, no one is more surprised than we are. In fact, as far as we know this is your first visit, so we're not even clear how the vault can be set with your brain's imprint if he never brought you in to let it scan you."

Zoey started to say, "I have no idea . . ." but trailed off halfway through, when a memory suddenly popped into her head. "In the fall my mom made a doctor's appointment for me, she said it was something they had to do for the life insurance. But it was weird, they put me in something like an MRI machine and I was in there for a solid hour. They told me they were checking for early Alzheimer's or something, but . . . I don't know. It seemed fishy. Like they wouldn't answer direct questions. Could Arthur have arranged that?"

Echo glanced at Will and said, "Well, there's one mystery solved."

Will asked, "And *how* long ago was this?"

"September, early October, around there."

Glances. Traces of confusion and alarm. This was a bombshell, apparently. Zoey tried to think of why, then it occurred to her that this meant she wasn't here due to some drunken last-minute decision or a mix up with the vault's programming. Her father had planned all of this months in advance—in other words, *he had known he was going to die.* Or at least, he was making preparations for the eventuality. And no one in this room had known.

Echo shook her head and muttered to Will, "I keep imagining him up there, laughing at us while we scrambled around the country trying to figure out exactly which trailer park he spilled his DNA in."

Budd adjusted his cowboy hat and said, "'Up there'? Echo, I don't know exactly what religion you believe in that has Arthur Livingston makin' it to Heaven, but I reckon I wanna join."

Andre said, "Eh, probably just bribed his way in."

Will, raising his voice to cut off the banter, said, "It doesn't matter. The daughter's here, let's get this over with."

The daughter. Zoey realized he had already forgotten her name. She sniffed, wiped her nose with her sleeve and took a drink from her water glass. She glanced around the room—a wreath on every wall. The stuffed and mounted buffalo, wearing its stupid Santa hat and beard. Yet another Christmas tree in the corner. Zoey and her mom had a plastic artificial tree they put together every year. It had a bare spot where two of the branches had broken off, so they had to keep that part facing the corner. Her estranged father, she observed, apparently had a real tree in every room. Zoey suddenly realized that her yearly salary would not even pay to decorate this place for Christmas, and that her entire trailer wasn't big enough to serve as off-season storage for all of the ornaments, lights, and holiday tchotchkes that encrusted the walls of this place.

Once, as a teenager, she had spent all of Thanksgiving and Christmas with a cracked tooth. She endured the throbbing molar for six weeks, due to the wait list to get into a dentist that accepted Medicaid. Every day at work with this pain stabbing like a shard of glass when she bit down on anything harder than pudding. The cost of one bottle of whatever scotch these people were drinking would have paid for her appointment. And now, here were Arthur Livingston's people, in suits that could probably put her through college, looking at her like she was a muddy dog running through their wedding reception. Her ears were getting hot. She pulled off her cap and shook her bangs out of her eyes.

Zoey let out a breath and said, "And then what?"

Will answered, "Then for us begins a very long and tedious task of sorting out the contents of the vault, whatever they are. But that's our problem, not yours. We will release the fifty thousand dollars from escrow, and send you back home in whatever mode of transportation you prefer. Hell, we'll rent you a private plane. Or let you take the company helicopter, if you like. After that, we will never bother you again."

"And what if I see something in that vault I'm not supposed to see?"

Glances. Will clenched his jaw a little tighter. Echo pressed her lips together. The oilman in the corner—Budd—grabbed a bottle from a nearby cart and poured himself another glass of single malt or bourbon or whatever it was. He seemed to be trying to suppress a laugh.

Will, who was trying very hard to hide the fact that he clearly wanted to strangle Zoey, said, " 'See something'? Like what?"

"Arthur Livingston was a mob boss. You're the mob. Maybe the rumors were right. Maybe there's bodies in there, or stolen stuff, or drugs. Maybe *just knowing the vault is here* is dangerous information."

"Don't let your imagination get away from—"

"*Bzzzt!* Stop. Don't play the 'hysterical woman' card here. I've been through three attempted kidnappings in the last five hours. I mean, I'm the vault key, right? Well, why are you any different from all the other crazies that keep coming after me? Because you're wearing Armani? Maybe you don't want the key to your vault just walking around out there."

Andre said, "Come on, now. It's not like that . . ."

"And despite the fact that you people all supposedly worked with my father, I still can't get over the fact that he didn't make any of *you* the key. Why not, if you're so trustworthy? Hey, for all I know, you're the ones he was specifically trying to keep *out* of the vault. For all I know, *you're the ones who had him killed.*"

She wanted to see what Will's reaction would be to this. The reaction was barely suppressed rage.

"Maybe," said Will, "all of this is the result of nothing more than the fact that your father, despite extreme wealth and power, had a history of making terrible decisions."

Echo smirked at the inference that Will was in fact looking at one of Arthur's terrible decisions right now. Zoey literally bit her tongue, and took a moment to gather herself.

"So," she said, evenly, "my question is, how do I know that after I'm done, the sedan I climb into isn't going to take me out in the woods where Tex over there will pull out a little gun and shoot me in the back of the head? See, I know for a fact you won't do that *right now*, because I haven't opened your vault yet, and as you said, it doesn't open for a corpse. As long as it stays closed and you want what's inside, I'm safe. But the moment it opens, the value of my life drops to zero. And I, unlike you, care nothing whatsoever about what's in there. So. Mr. Blackwater. I need you to sit down and explain to Arthur Livingston's *bad decision* how you're going to make it worth my while to open that vault for you, and how you can guarantee my safety after."

Silence. Something popped in the fireplace.

In the corner, Budd laughed from around his drink and said, "I like her!"

Echo Ling, on the other hand, made an expression that could suck the laughter out of a child's birthday party. She turned on her heels and said, "Well, she's definitely Arthur's daughter."

Zoey stared into Echo's back and said, "If I hear anybody say that again, I'm *never* opening that vault."

Zoey grabbed a tissue from the tray and loudly blew her nose.

Will gathered himself and said, "I understand your concerns completely—"

"I said I want you to *sit down* and explain it to me. Stop looming over me. It's rude."

Will took a breath and seemed to count to ten in his head, then took a seat on the leather sofa in front of her. Probably a hundred cows murdered for that one.

"Let's just approach this logically. What you're asking is impossible—you want me to negotiate with you while you maintain the assumption that I'm operating in bad faith. After all, if we were the kind of people you just accused us of being, then my role would be to say whatever it takes to placate you, knowing we'd never have to follow through on whatever offer is made. So instead, how about you tell me what you want in the way of assurances, and I'll see what I can do to accommodate you? But keep in mind, time is very short."

"Why is time short? I don't have to be back at work until Monday."

"You don't under—"

"No. Listen. Everything you said is right—the problem isn't what you're offering or failing to offer me. The problem is *you*. I don't trust you. So before I can even begin to think about this, I need to convince myself that you're on the level."

"All right. And . . . how will we go about doing that, precisely?"

"I don't know. But it's late. And I'm tired. Is there a spare bed in one of the thousand rooms of this house?"

"We were really hoping to have this resolved tonight."

"Well, to get over this disappointment, you'll just have to console yourself with the fact that you have absolutely everything else you want in life."

Will started to speak again, but Andre put a hand on his shoulder and said, "How about you don't piss her off, eh? The world will still be here when the sun comes up tomorrow." He turned toward the doorway, where Carlton had materialized at some point, and said, "Can you get a room ready for Zoey?"

"It is already done, sir. Her suitcase is up there as well."

"Of course it is. See? It's all good. Zoey, we even retrieved your bag—you left it on the train platform when you set that dude's dick on fire. So get a good night's rest, have Carlton make you some waffles in the morning, and we'll figure this all out tomorrow while I nurse the hangover I'm about to cause."

Andre smoothed his lapel and walked out, while Zoey silently planned how she was going to escape this terrible place.

TEN

The guest bedroom suite they set Zoey up in had its own bathroom, media room, and minibar. The covers were turned down on a king-size four-poster bed that would not have fit in her bedroom back home unless it was folded up like a taco shell. There was a touchscreen on the end table that, after tinkering with it, Zoey realized controlled the firmness, texture, and temperature of the mattress. Her suitcase was placed neatly on the bed next to a stack of white bath towels, the one on top folded into the shape of a swan. Carlton had found a cat bed, somewhere, and had sat it in the corner of the room. Stench Machine was curled up asleep on the floor next to it.

Zoey sat on the bed and stared at the door. She got up and locked it, but that was stupid because surely they had a key—it was their house. She scooted over an end table that had an expensive-looking table lamp on it so it blocked the door. The table wouldn't delay someone breaking in for long, but would maybe give her a few seconds to try to escape out the window. Plus she would die knowing she had made them break one of their expensive lamps, so screw them. She looked around the room for a weapon, the closest thing she could find was a bag of golf clubs that was propped in one corner. She pulled out the heaviest-looking driver and sat on the bed with it across her lap. It didn't make her feel any safer.

She had let Andre bring her here to get her away from the crazies in the van and the much larger group of crazies known as All of the Citizens of Tabula Ra$a. But she had no illusions about opening Livingston's stupid vault and then riding off into the sunset with the escrow money. She wasn't some little princess from the suburbs who just graduated college with a humanities degree, she knew what people were really like. They'd kill her just to save the price of a plane ticket. So her plan was to wait for everyone else to leave or go to bed (did they all live here?) and just slip out of the house.

She sat there, gripping the club, and listened. There was something very off about the sound this place made, and Zoey eventually figured out that the weird sound was what other people knew as "peaceful silence." Zoey had been living in her mom's trailer, because she'd had to move out of Caleb's place when they broke up (Caleb being the guy she thought at one time she was going to marry and have babies with). So for two months she had been sleeping on a futon next to an aluminum wall, near a window that had been cracked by an errant fist and repaired with Scotch tape. All of the trailer park noises bled through into the room as easily as if she had been sleeping in the yard— always somebody revving a gasoline motor, a couple arguing or having loud sex, a barking dog or, more likely, twenty barking dogs. But the Casa de Ass-a was dead silent. She could hear her own breathing. So this was what a house sounded like when it had solid walls and, beyond them, acres of gated land onto which the poor were not allowed.

Zoey hated it.

She didn't have much of a plan beyond escaping the grounds of the estate. Maybe she would get out and find some hole to hide in, maybe find the Tabula Ra$a slums and make some friends. "Lay low," like they say in the movies. Maybe the mob would eventually decide it was more trouble to go after her than to just get somebody else to break into their stupid safe. She hadn't witnessed them do anything illegal—they didn't have anything to fear from her running to the FBI or whoever was still enforcing the law around here.

Zoey grabbed Stench Machine and curled up with him on the bed, feeling warmth and annoyance radiating off him as he meowed and made half-hearted attempts to wriggle free. She closed her eyes and immediately saw Jacob, his brain fried in his skull, staring blearily and drooling. She felt so stupid. Handsome rich kid flirting with dumpy trailer trash, to win money and a day as a Blink celebrity. Millions of people listening in while she swooned and giggled and tried to impress him. A vast constellation of strangers she'd never meet, laughing at her.

That prompted Zoey to turn on the wall feed in the bedroom (they had one of those projection units rich people have, a fist-size dome in the ceiling that could project the feed on any wall you wanted) and tune into the "Hunt for Livingston's Key" Event, to see what was going on in the fascinating lives of the various people who were trying to capture, kill, or torture her. The most popular feed at the moment belonged to the League of Badass—the ragtag group of morons who had chased them in their van earlier. They were back at their headquarters, which appeared to be somebody's garage—leaning over a table in front of their busted-up van, going over strategy. Their leader—the muscle guy with a red Mohawk and sleeves of tribal tattoos—was explaining to the camera that Zoey was safely in her father's estate and, as far as they knew, could be opening Livingston's vault as they spoke. But then he explained why this was by no means the end of the Hunt.

Sure enough, Will Blackwater had lied.

The five-million-dollar contract this "Molech" guy had put out on her, it turned out, was not just about abducting her so he could stick her into the keyhole of Arthur Livingston's vault. No, it was also about getting revenge for Doll Head guy. He had been an employee of Molech's, and he was now dead. Zoey was startled to hear this (could a person actually die from a small whiskey-fueled crotch fire? Maybe he had a prior medical condition), but more importantly, it meant that escaping the estate would change nothing about the fact that there was still a multimillion-dollar bounty on her head—in fact, it would only double the number of people who were looking for her. Her whole plan had fallen apart in ten seconds.

Zoey closed her eyes and rubbed her forehead. She supposed someone with more experience dealing with this kind of thing would know how to work this to her advantage—after all, if Molech's people wanted her dead, but her father's people needed her alive to open the vault, then her father's people had motivation to protect her from Molech's. But how long would she be able to keep that up before they decided it wasn't worth the trouble? If she was alive but refusing to open their vault, then she was no more useful to them than if she was a corpse.

Zoey flipped around the "Hunt" feed and found someone had assembled a highlight reel of the "players" involved. She brought up one labeled "Arthur Livingston: The Suits." There was a video of the four of them exiting a black sedan in slow motion, while ominous music played.

A gravelly voice said, "Arthur Livingston's death has left behind a power vacuum, with four members of his ruthless inner circle vying for control. In the criminal underworld, they are known as The Suits. Andre Knox, aka, Black Mountain—Livingston's deadly enforcer. Michelle 'Echo' Ling, the Chinese computer expert and sexy seductress. Budd 'the Regulator' Billingsley. And finally, Will Blackwater, The Magician—Arthur Livingston's cold-blooded right-hand man.

"Seven years ago, when a cartel hit man went rogue and made an attempt on the life of Andre Knox, the dismembered corpse of the guman was found on Arthur Livingston's doorstep twelve hours later . . . along with an apologetic note from the head of the cartel. When a Ukrainian mob tried to horn in on Livingston's territory a year later, Livingston asked for a face-to-face to avoid all-out war. Witnesses say the Suits met behind locked doors with a dozen mob captains. After only four minutes, both groups filed out of the room. By nightfall, the Ukrainians had left the city, never to return. Not a single shot was fired.

"But, strangest of all, when a federal indictment came down for a fifth member of Livingston's inner circle named Logan Knight, Arthur Livingston gave a press conference in which he made the bizarre assertion that no such man had ever existed. With no further explanation, all charges were dropped soon after."

Well. That was terrifying, and not at all helpful. Zoey noticed they had made one of these profiles/trailers for her, and she couldn't resist. She told it to play:

"Twenty-two-year-old Zoey Ashe, a devious and busty—"

She quickly swiped it off the screen.

Zoey fell back onto the bed and covered her eyes. She had no idea what do now, and couldn't think straight. The long trip, the roller-coaster adrenaline rush, the cold night, the warm bed. She lay on her side and felt herself melting into the mattress. Stench Machine was now prowling around the room, then Zoey finally realized he was looking for food because she hadn't fed him, because she was horrible at everything. She dug out two cans of cat food from her suitcase—yes, she traveled with cans of cat food in her luggage, like the crazy cat lady she was destined to become—and looked around for a fork. Stench Machine ate a mixture of two different brands and she had to mash them together. She was pretty sure it was some kind of chemical reaction from the combination that made him smell so bad, but it was the only thing he would eat without following the meal with two hours of disapproving looks that would devastate Zoey in her current emotional state.

The room was forkless. Logically she could just mix the stuff together with her fingers or whatever random object she could find in the room, but she had no desire to put her fingers in cat food and, to be honest, there was something else tempting her out of the bedroom, and that was curiosity. So, telling herself she was doing it for her cat, she scooted the table and lamp away from the door and stepped cautiously into the hallway, trying to imagine how a person would find a common eating utensil in a sprawling palace like this. She thought about going back for her golf club and decided if the situation deteriorated into a golf club duel to the death, she probably was already screwed. She tried to see in the darkened hall and took a step, wincing at the sound of the squeaky floorboards trying to rat her out. As stealthily as possible, she took a left toward the stairs and immediately crashed loudly through a low pile of boxes.

Shoes went spilling everywhere. She squinted in the darkness and saw nine boxes containing nine pair of shoes—three different styles similar to the pair she had ruined, each in three different sizes ranging from 6½ to 7½. She found a note from Carlton the butler apologizing for not asking her size first, but saying that he had tried to give her a range of choices and that she should let him know if none were satisfactory. Zoey imagined a pair of goons forcing some Foot Locker manager to open his store at gunpoint in the middle of the night, to get their boss's daughter a new pair of sneakers.

Zoey picked up the cat again and padded down the stairs, then almost screamed when once again Jacob Marley's ghost came oozing out of the floor when she reached the landing.

"*Scroooooooge!!!*"

Stench Machine jumped out of her arms and bolted down the stairs, across the foyer, zipping through an arched doorway on the ground floor. Zoey followed him through the arch and found herself in a long dining room with a table that could seat probably fifty guests. The cat darted through chair legs and prowled cautiously through a doorway at the other end. Zoey followed him into a hallway.

At one end of the hall was a boarded-up door with red tape crisscrossed over it that said "WARNING: MOLD—DO NOT ENTER." She headed in the other direction, but Stench Machine wouldn't follow. Instead he prowled around the Mold door, sniffing and pawing at it, as if there was a mouse or something behind it. As Zoey went to go pick him up, Stench Machine took a step forward and *passed through the door.* Partly, anyway—his butt and tail were sticking out. Zoey went to the Mold door and passed her hand through it—the door was yet another hologram. She could see the little projector on the ceiling, and waving her hand in front of it could make entire vertical slices of the "door" vanish where she was blocking the beam. The illusion had been hiding a real door, another heavy one made of bronze, a foot beyond the fake one. She tried the handle but it was locked, because of course it was. Was this the vault?

She didn't care to find out. She picked up Stench Machine and headed down the hall, then the big door clicked and squeaked behind her.

A stern voice said, "Who are you? How did you get in here?"

A guy she had never seen before had leaned out through the hologram, looking like a disembodied head had been nailed to the Mold door like a hunter's trophy. Then the man stepped out toward her, a bald guy with a gun in a shoulder holster over a tight black turtleneck. He had cop eyes.

A voice from inside the room behind him said, "That's the girl. Arthur's daughter." That voice was Will. Zoey had assumed everyone had left, but apparently Will had business in their secret room. The bald guy retreated back inside the room and Will leaned out past the hologram, his posture suggesting he was holding the door closed behind it. They were probably having an orgy back there. Again, Zoey had no intention of knowing either way.

He asked, "What are you doing here?"

"Nothing. I was just trying to find a . . . it doesn't matter. Is that . . . is that the vault?"

"Yes, this is the vault, that's why we're all standing inside it and the door is open."

"I don't—"

"The vault's in the basement. This is a private conference room. Finish doing what you're doing and go back to bed. We'll come get you in the morn— *Hey!*"

Stench Machine had twisted out of Zoey's grasp and darted through the hologram and through the gap in the real door beyond. Zoey ran in after him, shoving past Will, through the metal door.

Will yelled "STOP!" then grabbed her wrist and twisted. Zoey went to one knee. The room had flown into chaos, as the cat had jumped up onto a table, trying to make off with what looked like a hunk of gray meat. The bald guy who had met Zoey at the door snatched the cat by the scruff of the neck and looked like he was going to tear him in half with his bare hands. Zoey screamed at Will to let go of her, but he was dragging her backward, back out of the door. Her wrist felt like it was going to break.

From her knees, Zoey twisted her body around and bit the first thing on Will she could find—his thigh. He cursed and let her go. Zoey got to her feet and was about to demand her cat back, then she saw what was sitting on the table, and everyone saw that she saw, and everything ground to a halt.

Lying on the table was a severed human hand.

ELEVEN

Everyone in the room stood silently in place, staring at Zoey, as if the universe had finally created a moment so awkward that it had stopped time itself. Echo Ling was there, wearing glasses and holding a long metal probe, as if she had been interrupted in the process of prodding at the severed hand. The wall behind her was covered in projections of X-rays and schematics. Zoey's eyes bounced around the room, involuntarily etching what was surely incriminating information directly into her brain, seeing things these people would not allow to be shared with the world. Stench Machine meowed and that sprang Zoey into action, running over and grabbing him from the clutches of the bald guy with the cop eyes. She edged back toward the door, slowly, as if nobody in the tiny room would notice her leaving if she did it gradually enough.

She heard herself ask, "W-whose hand is that?" but she didn't actually want to know, knowing would only doom her, as if she wasn't doomed already. And what possible difference did it make?

From behind her, Will answered, "You don't recognize it?"

That did it. In a blind, spastic panic, Zoey spun and shoved past Will again, through the hologram door, down the hall, through the dining room and into the foyer with the skyscraper Christmas tree. She ran right for the huge front doors, pulled a cold bronze handle—

Locked.

Candi the holographic stripper blinked to life next to her, pouted dramatically, and in a babytalk voice said, "Ooh, I'm sooo sorry but house security isn't allowing exits through the front doors, for your own safety. To make up for the inconvenience, Mr. Livingston will compensate you with a free bottle of champagne or a sexual favor of your choosing!"

Candi giggled and blinked away. From behind Zoey came the steady click of footsteps on the marble floor. Will was in no hurry as he emerged into the foyer, his face an uncanny valley of calm. Trying to scare her, Zoey thought, with how calm he was. It was working.

Zoey's voice trembled as she said, "Unlock it. I'm leaving."

The bald guy in the black turtleneck strode up behind Will. Two more men in black overcoats and hats appeared behind them, carrying guns that looked laughably overpowered for a Zoey-scale threat. Will Blackwater had henchmen.

Will said, "No, you're not."

"I-I won't tell anybody. I don't care about this place, I don't care about you, I don't care about what happens here or who you kill. Just let me go, let me go back home, and I won't tell anyone, I won't tell the police, my mom, anybody. I don't even want the fifty thousand, just *let me go*."

"And we will do just that. As soon as you open the vault."

And all at once, Zoey was sure she would never see the sky again.

"Zoey," Will said. "Think. What are your options here?" As he spoke, two more overcoats appeared—some silent call had been sent out to the house guards. "This is not your world. Now I agree that your father could be a real abscess and dragging you into this was unconscionable. But there is literally nothing else to be done but for you to open that damned vault and stop wasting our time."

But you see, Zoey thought, *what is wasted time to you, are my precious last moments on earth.*

Zoey never answered, and Will took it for consent.

He nodded to the bald man and said, "Kowalski, escort her to the vault room."

The man took Zoey by the upper arm and pulled her along like a little kid. He was dragging her toward another arched door, leading to the opposite wing of the estate. She did not resist. Zoey, her bald escort, Will, and an entourage of armed men in trench coats filed down a hallway, taking her into what under other circumstances would have been the most relaxing room she had ever been in—it was some kind of library or reading room, walls of leather-bound books surrounding ancient leather armchairs and, right in the center of the floor, a crystal-clear koi pond. Fish bearing iridescent scales of orange and white zipped around in the water, the room filled with the soothing trickle of a babbling brook.

From behind Zoey, Will said, "Grab the gold one." Zoey tried to process those four words into some kind of meaningful command and finally noticed a single, gold fish darting around among the others. "The fish, Zoey. Reach down and grab it. It's not real."

She tentatively stuck her hand into the water and once again found that it was just a three-dimensional projection. She tried to grab the golden holographic fish as instructed, which turned out to be exactly as hard as catching a real one. She flailed at it and was starting to think she was the victim of an elaborate prank, but eventually she closed her hand around the image of the fish, at which point it instantly disappeared, along with the rest of the pond. The now-empty basin split apart, revealing a spiral staircase straight down.

Zoey said, "Okay, I did it. Just let me—"

"That's not the vault. That's just the entrance to the vault room." Will gestured toward the stairs. "After you."

Zoey descended, clanging down the spiral of stairs with one hand on the curved rail, the other clutching Stench Machine to her chest. A sprawl of gold coins came into view, as if the room below her was just piles of treasure, like Scrooge McDuck's vault. Then she reached the bottom and realized that was just the flooring—it had been tiled with actual coins. Forget the vault, you could come down here with a chisel and scrape up enough money to retire on. And in Arthur Livingston's world, this was how you decorated the entrance to the room the *real* riches were stored in. The vault itself was set in the wall in front of her, a perfect circle of ornate brass from floor to ceiling, the door probably weighing as much as twenty cars. There was no handle or hinges, just a giant, cartoonish keyhole in the middle about three feet tall and a foot wide.

The spiral stairwell had finished draining everyone into the room. The bald man, Kowalski, grabbed Zoey again and shoved her toward the vault door, the site of a future bruise throbbing a ring around her upper arm. She imagined some medical examiner noting it in her autopsy.

Will said, "See the keyhole? You're the key. Go unlock it."

"But . . . how? I don't—"

"Stick your head in the keyhole. Keep it still, it has to scan your brain and match it to the print it has on file."

Zoey walked tentatively up to the door, let out a breath, and stuck her head in the lock. A mechanism inside whirred and clicked. There were annoyed murmurs behind her. It hadn't worked.

Zoey pulled her head out. A monitor off to the side of the door had blinked on at some point. In red letters it said: OVERRIDE: COERCION.

A female voice behind Zoey said, "Told you." It was Echo. Zoey didn't even realize she had followed them down. "You can't coerce the vault's owner into opening it. The software is programmed to stay locked if the owner shows emotional distress, so they can't be made to open it at gunpoint. See, Will, because that would completely defeat the point of paying eight figures for a vault."

Will rubbed his eyes, gritted his teeth, and said, "Zoey, we are not forcing you to do this. You *want* to leave here. You want this to be over. You are sticking your head in that giant keyhole willingly. Just . . . think that thought, in your mind."

Echo said, "It doesn't work like that."

Zoey said, "I know you're not going to let me leave the city alive."

Will growled, "I *promise* you will be allowed to leave if you make that vault open. In fact, I will throw you over my shoulder and fling you over the goddamned border—"

Echo said, "Will . . ."

Zoey said, "You have no reason to let me go and every reason to shoot me and toss me in the river."

To Echo, Will said, "Is there something we can give her to calm her down?"

"What, like a joint? Some Valium? It won't open if it detects she's intoxicated, either. This is *Arthur Livingston's* vault we're talking about, the first instructions he gave to the contractor was to make sure it wouldn't open for him if he was drunk or stoned. Otherwise some call girl would have wound up owning the contents years ago."

Zoey said, "It won't open until I have some reason to think I'll be allowed to leave here. I need some guarantee. If this thing can read my thoughts or my emotional state or whatever it does, it knows I think I'm going to die."

"Well, *what can we do to reassure you?*"

Zoey turned toward the bald man, Kowalski. She eyed his shoulder holster and said, "Give me a gun."

Will had heard her clearly, but still said, "*What?*"

"Give me a gun. I point the gun at you, I open the thing, and then I *keep* pointing the gun at you as I walk out."

Will said, "There are six other guns in this room, you'd still have no chance against them if it came to a shootout."

"I wouldn't try to win a shootout. I'd only try to shoot *you*."

Will clenched his jaw. Zoey let go of Stench Machine and held out a hand. She said, "Consider it a gesture of good faith."

"We're obviously not doing that."

Zoey crossed her arms. "Great, the longer we put this off, the longer I live. We'll all stand in this room and grow old together."

Zoey thought she could actually hear the man's jaw clench. She said, "I can see it in your eyes. You *so* wish you could just torture me into this. Slap me around. Threaten me. Put a gun to my head. But you can't. The harder you push, the more locked that door gets. And Arthur *knew it*. He knew you would try this, and he knew the vault would stop you. It's so funny watching you try to match wits with a dead man, and *losing*. Well, you want me to trust you with my life, you trust me with yours. What's it going to be, Clenchy?"

Will met her eyes, let out an annoyed breath, then glanced at Kowalski and nodded. Kowalski raised an eyebrow as if to say "Really?" but then pulled his pistol from his holster, pulled back on the top of it to cock it or load it or whatever, and spun it around on his finger so the handle was pointed toward Zoey. He looked amused.

As Zoey took the gun, Kowalski said, "There's no safety. You pull the trigger, it goes bang."

"How do I know it's loaded?"

He shrugged. "Point it at the ceiling and shoot. And hope nobody is standing up there."

Zoey pointed it up, flinched, squeezed the trigger, and was shocked at how loud it was. Plaster rained down on her head. A little brass shell clinked off the coin floor and rolled away. Her ears rang. Everyone in the room looked like they had just soiled their pants.

She took a deep breath, turned, and pointed the gun at Will's face. She saw something strange in Will's eyes. Not fear—he looked like he had been on this end of a gun before. Not anger, either—the frustration that flared up earlier was gone. What she saw in his eyes, above the quivering sights of the gun, was a mind that was reconsidering her. Or maybe just considering her for the first time.

All four of the trench coats immediately raised stubby little machine guns at her, the men apparently having gotten a grossly exaggerated report of Zoey's combat skills. Kowalski whipped another pistol from the back of his pants and brought it to bear, and she wondered how many guns he kept on his person at any given time. Will did not draw a gun. He only adjusted his cuff links and gestured toward the vault.

With the pistol still pointed at Will's uncanny valley stare, Zoey took a calming breath, leaned over, and stuck her head into the vault once again. For a moment there was only silence. She took another deep breath, and let it out.

Finally, there was an approving chime, then a click and a squeak of hinges.

Everyone in the room but Zoey let out a gasp. Zoey pulled her head out and moved out of the way of the swinging vault door. She put her back to the opening and told herself not to turn around, since once again seeing what was in there would only shorten her life span.

The gun still trained on Will, she kneeled down and picked up her cat and said into his ear, "If they kill me, *run*."

But no one was looking at her anymore. Will had forgotten about Zoey and even the gun, and was staring into the vault, mouth agape (which in his case, meant there was an opening between his lips of about a quarter of an inch). He rushed forward, brushing past Zoey. And that's when she made her mistake: she turned to follow him with her eyes, looking into the vault.

It was empty.

Or at least, it was empty of treasure—the metal room was perfectly vacant save for a single, silver coin lying on the concrete floor, mockingly. Just behind the coin, was a man. In his late fifties, in a pinstripe suit with an elaborate mustache, standing placidly in a vault that had been locked airtight for days. It took a moment for Zoey to recognize that it was, in fact, her biological father, Arthur Livingston.

TWELVE

Zoey never heard Kowalski coming.

It took him all of two seconds to close the distance, and one second to wrench the gun from her hand, ripping the skin from her index finger in the process. In one continuous, practiced motion he then twisted her arm and shoved her to the floor, pressing a boot to her back. Zoey's face was mashed painfully into the carpet of gold coins. She noted that the one right next to her eyeball had been minted in 1918.

"Hello there," said the voice of Zoey's biological father from inside the vault. She craned her head around just in time to see Will walk through the man. When Arthur Livingston was alive, he had sure loved his holograms. Will was looking around the vault, as if hoping something else was hiding in one of the clearly empty corners. He accidentally kicked the single, sad coin across the floor, then picked it up, staring at it as if hoping he could make it start multiplying with the power of wishful thinking.

"If this recording is playing, then I am either talking to Zoey Ashe, my daughter by the lovely Melinda Ashe, or to a person or group of people who have found a way to subvert the security of one of the world's finest vaults. If it is the latter, you should know that I admire your skills, and such a breach in fact entitles the estate to a full refund from the Fisk Vault Corporation. But you will be otherwise disappointed with the contents you have worked so hard to gain access to—as you can see, this vault contains but a single coin, one which cannot even be redeemed as legal tender, whose significance will be apparent only to those closest to me. As for the purpose of this recording, well, I assume by now there is some anxiety over the fact that I did not leave behind a Last Will and Testament. But I have, and you are watching it. From here on out, I am going to address this message to my daughter, and only offspring that I know about, Zoey Ashe. Zoey, I am going to begin with a phrase I have always wanted to use: if you are watching this, it means I am already dead.

"Hopefully I died in my sleep, after a nice evening with a lovely lady, and hopefully I did not foul the bed at the moment I expired. But, if I have assessed the situation correctly, then that is not how I passed. I have, instead, died in some violent manner before my time, at the hands of brutal and greedy men. If so, then you should know that this event is not wholly unexpected and in fact is the reason why I am making this recording now, though I am only fifty-eight and have been told I am in perfect health. As such, my first wish is that my killers be found, and that this hologram projector be placed outside of their bedroom window at night so that they will think they are being haunted. But I digress.

"Zoey, about six years ago I got drunk one night and started doing what men like me do when we get drunk and lonely, which is hunt around social-networking Web sites to track down old girlfriends. There I found your mother and all of her proud photos of you. Little Zoey Ashe, my daughter, turning into a woman. I saw you smiling into the camera and striking poses, your mother's hips and my eyes. I saw birthday parties in tiny apartments and run-down trailers, you smiling over store-bought cakes and generic soda, your mom in the background, with a different boyfriend each time. Three different stepfathers, if I'm counting right. So, I made some drunken phone calls and, full of myself as I often was, I decided I would be a hero to little Zoey. On a whim, I bought you a hundred-thousand-dollar luxury car, and paid the dealership to deliver it to your home in Fort Drayton. I flew in, imagining myself rolling up to your trailer with my shiny gift, and you coming out and giving me a big smile and a bigger hug. I'd give you the keys and we'd take it for a spin and you'd decide that maybe I wasn't such a bad guy after all.

"But as you know, that's not what happened. Instead, you stood in the driveway, your arms folded across your chest just like your mom used to do, and you gave me absolute hell. You told me you'd rather walk to school every day than to be the stray I rescued. You said one expensive gift sixteen years too late didn't buy me the right to walk around thinking I had done right by you and your mom. You put a finger in my face and yelled and made so much ruckus that your neighbors came out to see what the commotion was. I was furious, as you surely remember. I said some terrible things and left that place with my tail between my legs.

"But I was only angry because deep down, I knew you were right. In your anger, I saw myself as I truly was when I wasn't surrounded by ass-kissers and yes-men. You must understand that in my world, I buy and sell people for the price of nothing more than shiny toys and lavish vacations. A bribe here and a beautiful escort there, that's all it takes to make people turn a blind eye to misdeeds, or do secret favors, or tell me what I want to hear. To abandon everything they know to be right. And these are comfortable people, who aren't hungry or desperate but who'll still sell out in a second for the right trinket. But then there was you, standing there among the weeds and dog turds and rusting cars, throwing my gift back in my face, because you wouldn't sell out. I saw all of the fire that made me crazy for your mother all those years ago, and that has made me unable to forget her since. All of the backbone that I like to pretend I have. Of course, years passed and I never saw you again, but I found myself thinking back to that day, more and more.

"So, in these tumultuous final days, I saw the writing on the wall and I thought, who can I trust? I'm surrounded by a core of capable people. Some of them are even loyal. But they're also ambitious. They like playing the game, acquiring power, the way men like me do. So who could I trust with my fortune, and my secrets? If I made it known that any of my inner circle would be in control of my assets, or even what those assets truly were, then it would begin—the jockeying for position, the jealousy, the under-the-table deals. No, it had to be someone on the outside. Someone worthy of the riches and the awesome power that even my inner circle does not yet fully understand. It had to be someone they'd never suspect in a thousand years, someone who would not be corrupted by the power. And so, Zoey Ashe, the daughter I never really had, I say to you, and to the world, the following:

"I, Arthur B. Livingston, being of sound mind and disposing memory and not acting under duress or undue influence, and fully understanding the nature and extent of all my property and of the disposition thereof, do hereby make, publish, and declare this document to be my Last Will and Testament, and do hereby revoke any and all other wills and codicils heretofore made by me. The entirety of the property owned by me at my death, real and personal and wherever situate, I devise and bequeath to my only daughter, Zoey Marceline Ashe, minus any estate taxes and the cost of the kick-ass memorial celebration I have detailed in my Last Will and Testament, a full text copy of which has been electronically transmitted to my attorney as of right . . . now. Ms. Ashe is also given full control of all offshore accounts, landholdings, stock, corporate holdings, and assets associated with all of my entrepreneurial endeavors under the umbrella of Livingston Enterprises, again as detailed fully in the text copy. All current employees will continue in their present roles until notified otherwise, at Zoey's discretion.

"If you examine the floor of the vault you should find but one object—my lucky coin. A rare, one-sided 1911 Chinese Silver Dragon, the roaring dragon on one side, the other completely blank due to a minting error. I won this coin in a poker game when I was sixteen, from a man who told me it was worth a hundred thousand dollars. It turned out to be a worthless counterfeit. I have always kept it, as a reminder. That coin was always on my person, from that day until the writing of this will. Years ago, Will Blackwater gave a job interview that consisted of nothing more than borrowing that coin and doing a magic trick with it. I hired him immediately. Zoey, the final provision in this will is that you have him show you how the trick is done. Oh, and tell Gary he can keep the golf clubs, I don't think Zoey plays.

"And . . . that's it. If anyone gets any bright ideas and tries to bring bodily harm to Ms. Ashe in hopes of acquiring some or all of my estate, they should be aware of the following. In the event of her demise, all assets will be liquidated and donated to the Church of Mormon, minus thirty million dollars, which will immediately be placed as a bounty on the head of whoever brought said harm to Ms. Ashe.

"Good luck, Zoey. I'm sorry I wasn't there for you. This is the best I could do. What you do with your inheritance is up to you. I only urge you to make sure you grasp exactly what it is you have been left before deciding what to do with it—the money and the land are trivial in light of the real treasure. Beyond that, my only advice is what my father gave me before running out on us when I was ten years old. Figure out who you can trust, and let them do the work for you. Arthur Livingston out."

The hologram man stood awkwardly for several seconds and then said, "Is it still on? No, it's the black button. The black one. Here, let me—" Then he walked out of his own hologram, and it blinked off.

There was silence. Zoey struggled to breathe, her chest pressed between the cold gold coins and Kowalski's heavy boot. And then Will started laughing.

Echo Ling, sounding near panic, said, "What just happened?"

Will wiped his eyes, straightened his tie, and walked out of the vault. As he passed Zoey, he said to Kowalski, "You might want to take your foot off my boss, before she fires all of us."

The foot lifted from Zoey's back and she sat up, clutching the hand that was bleeding freely from when Kowalski ripped the gun away. Her head was spinning.

All she could think to say was "Somebody get me a towel. And tell me what's going on. Did he . . . did he leave everything to me? The house and . . . everything?"

Will said, "Yes. You've seen *Willy Wonka and the Chocolate Factory*, right? Well, you're like Charlie."

Echo elaborated, "Only instead of a golden ticket, it was Arthur Livingston's aversion to condoms."

"Wait . . . really?"

"Another way to put it," said Will, "is that your father just killed all of us. Including you."

He pulled out a silk pocket square and tossed it to her. She wrapped it around her finger. Feeling light-headed, she looked around the room, and saw everyone looking back at her, waiting. Eager to hear what the boss had to say.

Zoey said, "You guys with the guns? You were Arthur's henchmen or whatever?"

One of the men said, "We're contractors. We're twenty-four-hour grounds security."

"So you heard his ghost say you work for me now?"

"Well . . . we've been told to assume the contract remains active until informed otherwise, and as far as—"

"Good." She looked at Kowalski and said, "You're fired."

"I never worked for you, babe."

To the guards she said, "Escort this man from the grounds. Tell him to take his severed hand with him."

Kowalski stuffed his gun back into his shoulder holster and headed up the spiral stairs. "I can see my own way out."

Zoey turned to find Will and to the guards said, "Him, too. He's fired. Everybody is fired. Whoever else is here." To Echo, "You, too." To the guards, "As for your contract, it expires the moment you finish that final task. Escort these people off the grounds, then escort yourselves out and close the gates behind you."

Will and Echo exchanged a look.

Will said, "Zoey, I want you to think carefully about—"

"*Get OUT!* You're trespassing. All of you are."

"Listen to me. If you leave this house unprotected, you will not survive the weekend. Word is going to get out and when it does, the predators in this city *are going to swarm this place like piranha.*"

"Guards, if this man doesn't leave this house in the next ten seconds, shoot him."

The guards clearly did not want to do that. But one of them—the oldest—cleared his throat and said, "You, uh, have been asked to leave, Mr. Blackwater."

Will stared long and hard at Zoey, like he was trying to read something in her face. Whatever it was, it convinced him to turn on his heels and follow Kowalski up the stairs. Echo followed him, and the four henchmen went last. Seven sets of heels clanged up the spiral stairs and then knocked faintly across the floor overhead. And then it was silent, and Zoey was alone. She sat there on the golden floor with her cat, bleeding in her dead father's cavernous palace, which she apparently now owned.

THIRTEEN

At two in the morning, Zoey sat on the bottom steps of the grand staircase in the foyer, petting Stench Machine as he ate cat food off of a piece of china that, for all she knew, was an antique worth more than everything she owned. Zoey was starving, and the house was presumably full of all kinds of rich-people food—caviar or whatever—but she was too exhausted to go looking for it or to figure out how to cook it. Instead, she got out her phone and found a pizza place that delivered late at night. There were dozens, if not hundreds, of them in Tabula Ra$a (there were zero such establishments back home in Fort Drayton) so Zoey did what she always did when shopping, which was to sort them by customer ratings. She called the top place and ordered their special: "The Meatocalypse." She got the large.

And so she sat there, waiting for the delivery guy, not even sure how to let him through that front gate when he arrived. She stroked her cat, her skinned finger throbbing, trying to come up with a plan. This was what she had so far:

Step One: Eat a giant pizza.

Step Two: Go to bed.

Step Three: Get up in the morning, call home and ask Mom what to do.

Zoey's mother had a lawyer who had done all of her divorces, maybe they could get him on the phone and figure out exactly what Zoey needed to do to extricate herself from the vast crime empire she now apparently ran. Didn't the government just seize everything in cases like this? For unpaid taxes and such? If so, she wondered if she could get a car out of the deal, something to drive herself back to Fort Drayton if nothing else. She'd also like to keep the shoes . . .

Candi, the house security A.I. stripper hologram, blinked to life by the door.

Stench Machine skittered up the stairs in terror as Candi said, "There is someone at the front gate, and my sensors show they are *incredibly aroused.*"

The hologram seemed to be waiting for some kind of instructions but Zoey wasn't sure what she was supposed to do. Could she talk to it?

"Uh, can you tell me who it is?"

There was a pause and then a male voice said, "Boselli's Pizza, delivery for Zoey Ashe."

Candi said, "Scans indicate the vehicle contains one pizza and no weapons. Shall I open the gate?"

"Sure."

A minute later there was a knock on the door. A monitor blinked on next to the doorframe, showing that it was in fact the pizza man. He was bald but with a thick, jet-black beard, wearing an old-fashioned navy pea coat with, of all things, a red boutonniere on his lapel. Even the late-night pizza delivery guys in this neighborhood were pure class.

Zoey opened and the man said, "Good evening, ma'am. That'll be thirty-eight fifty. You have a beautiful home, by the way."

"Oh, thank you. I just got it. Let me run up and get my purse."

"No problem, sweetie."

She climbed the stairs and headed for her bedroom. The feed was still playing on the wall, the "Hunt for Livingston's Key" event still hopping from one view to the next, continuing to follow the exciting race to see who could destroy Zoey's life first.

She dug through her purse for her wallet and mumbled to the TV, "You guys do what you want, I'm eating a giant pizza made entirely of meat."

She gave the feed a glance and saw a grainy nighttime shot of a camera bouncing down an alley. Two guys in black vests and guns were running toward something on the ground. It was a person, lying there, thrashing and squirming.

Zoey stopped what she was doing to watch.

One of them reached the writhing man and said, "Buddy, are you okay? Can you hear me?"

The man on the ground only grunted. One of the guys pulled out a flashlight and illuminated a bleeding man who was bound hand and foot, his mouth duct taped shut. Two things registered with Zoey immediately:

1. He was wearing a red T-shirt that was playing a looping animation of a "Boselli's Pizza" logo;

2. Several of his fingers had been bitten off.

Before Zoey could work out what this meant, the feed blinked away—one of the abrupt jump cuts that Zoey still wasn't used to—and what appeared next was a very clear shot of the stairwell she had just climbed, the view bouncing gently up toward the second floor.

Zoey stopped, and stared.

Text scrolled down a sidebar on the screen—video comments, posted by viewers, almost moving too fast to see. She caught one that said, "Hyena show us her tits before you eat her, bro," and then that one was quickly driven off the screen by dozens more that simply said "Team Molech."

Zoey dropped her purse and said, "Oh, *come on.*"

She turned and was not surprised to find the psychopath known as the Hyena standing in the doorway of her bedroom, blocking her way out. She had never gotten a clear look at the guy before, when it was dark and he was busy getting driven into a frozen pond by her Toyota. But there was no doubt it was him—he had ditched his "beard," revealing an ugly surgical scar that looped around his jaw, looking like work that had been done in some back alley. He was no longer holding the pizza, and Zoey now noted that the little red flower pinned to his chest had a blue pinprick light in the center—that was his Blink camera. He was broadcasting live to the massive "Hunt for Livingston's Key" audience, along with a dedicated base of Hyena fans who simply got off on watching women get tortured in real time. She again wondered how big that audience was, and again decided she didn't want to know. Out the corner of her eye, she saw herself appear on the monitor, from the POV of her assailant. The room was a little too dark for the camera, so the Hyena found the light control on the wall and dialed it up to his satisfaction.

Zoey looked at herself on the monitor and actually had the crazy impulse to fix her hair, but then saw on the screen that the golf club was still on the bed behind her. She quickly snatched it, holding it out toward the Hyena like a sword. A fraction of a second later, the video version of herself up on the wall feed did the same.

He smiled and said, "Bet you never thought you'd see me again. I've had a whole train ride to think about this moment. To get it just right. First, let's get this out of the way."

He yanked the club from her hands, like he was taking it from a baby. He held it out in front of him, letting his camera get a good view of it.

"Now watch."

In a series of smooth, casual motions, the Hyena bent the golf club into the shape of a pretzel. He didn't strain, or grit his teeth, or even appear to be flexing with the effort. He just pulled the metal rod into loops, like it was a silver licorice whip.

He held it up and said, "Eh?"

Zoey's mouth went dry. She muttered, "What *are* you people?"

"Wait! I'm not finished!" He held the steel pretzel up to his mouth, and took a bite out of it. Again, with only a trivial amount of effort, like chewing some mildly tough beef jerky. He spat out a twisted hunk of metal and grinned. Then he tossed the golf-club pretzel aside.

The Hyena spat blood, then said, "That fear, that paralysis, that you're feeling right now? That's a primal memory, bubbling back to the surface. It's the realization that first and foremost, you were born to be food for something stronger. That as an organism, you were destined to end your existence with the sensation of teeth tearing flesh and crunching bone. So, here is how this is going to go. I'm going to bite you eight times. Those bites will sever eight tendons, and they will render your legs and arms both inoperable. Then, over the course of days and weeks, I will slowly, and completely at random—"

"No."

Zoey crossed her arms.

"What?"

"No. I'm not doing this. I'm not running and screaming, I'm not letting you put on a slasher-movie chase for your creeper fans on Blink, I'm not giving you a show. I'm sick of it. I don't know what you are, or how you people can do the things you do. But I've been doing nothing but run for the last eight hours. I'm done with that. I don't run anymore. Anybody out there watching this hoping that's going to happen, go ahead and zip up your pants."

"You've got quite a mouth on you. And I'm going to cut out that tongue and eat it in front of you. But first I'm going to—"

"*No.* You don't get to monologue for your audience. You're not cool, you're not menacing."

"I don't think you're in any position to tell me what—"

"LA LA LA LA LA NOBODY CAN HEAR YOU! LA LA LA!"

"Shut up!"

"DOO DOO DOO DOO NOBODY CAN HEAR YOUR EVIL MONOLOGUE AND CREATIVE RAPE THREATS! BUTT SHOW, BUTT SHOW BABY—"

The Hyena lunged at her. Zoey tumbled back, hitting the floor while her on-screen doppelgänger was still singing "Butt Show." They landed with the Hyena straddling her, trying to pin down her arms. She quickly reached up and snatched the boutonniere camera off his jacket. Before he could put together what she was doing, Zoey worked her right arm free and chucked the camera toward the bedroom door. The view on the wall monitor blurred into a boring shot of the hallway ceiling.

The Hyena screamed, "*BITCH!*" but he was now at an impasse—he had lost his audience, and therefore had lost not only his entire reason for being there, but also his ability to prove he had fulfilled the contract. He climbed off Zoey and ran into the hall to get his camera and—

BANG

—took a single bullet to the head.

A red mist of blood hung in the air. The Hyena flopped to the floor like a sack of dog food. Zoey yelped and crawled backward on her hands.

Into view stepped a Latino man in his thirties, in a black suit with a bright red shirt underneath, open at the collar. He had contrived beard stubble, and was keeping a smoking pistol trained on the dead man on the floor. He crushed the boutonniere camera under his shoe, then checked for a pulse on the Hyena.

Satisfied the man was dead, he stashed the pistol inside his jacket and in a deadpan tone muttered, "Stop, or I'll shoot." He turned to Zoey and said, "Are you injured?"

"No. I don't think so. Who are you?"

"I apologize for entering your home without permission, and I will leave immediately if that is your wish. My name is Armando Ruiz, and if you will pardon my lack of modesty, I am the finest bodyguard in Tabula Rasa. If you look up my credentials, you can easily confirm this to be true and, in fact, I insist that you do so at your earliest convenience. I came to ask for a job but decided to intervene when I saw what was about to occur. So with your permission, I want to secure the front entrance and main gate, so that I am not forced to deal with additional intruders. This is actually not my preferred method for neutralizing threats, if for no other reason than the cleanup is very unpleasant for everyone involved."

"Uh . . . sure. How did . . . how did that guy do that? He bent metal with his bare hands. Then he ate it."

Armando shrugged. "I am going to guess that it is due to some combination of being very strong, insane, and high on hallucinogens. As of now, that is only a concern to whoever is saddled with the unenviable task of writing his obituary. Wait here, and lock the door to your room. I will be back within twenty minutes."

He whipped out the gun and a moment later could be heard stomping down the stairs. Zoey sat on the bed, staring at the bleeding corpse on the hallway floor, then decided she preferred this new stranger's company to that of the dead man. She followed Armando down to the foyer and watched as he worked out the gate controls on the front-door monitor. He tapped through menus and the system assured him that no other threats were on the property at the moment, though Zoey thought it was strange the system didn't at least mention the presence of two tigers.

When Armando noticed her behind him, she said, "Sorry, I didn't like being that close to the dead guy. He came back to life once already."

"He did?"

"Well. Sort of."

"All right. Well, Ms. Ashe, I can tell you that the security on the grounds is top of the line, but it will do you no good if you allow strangers through the front door. And my services will do you no good if you do not listen to my instructions. Did you look me up?"

"Oh. No. Hold on."

Armando headed back upstairs, maybe to make sure the Hyena was still dead. Zoey looked him up on her phone using the exact same method she'd used to find a pizza joint an hour earlier, and found he was lying about one thing—when she ranked bodyguards in the city by review score, Armando actually wasn't number one. He was number four. But to be fair, two of the guys above him were dead, and the other one had a really weird goatee. Armando charged—wait, really?—$300 an hour, but his highlight reel showed him escorting politicians and pop stars, tackling crazed fans and disarming gunmen. In the videos, he always wore some variation of that black suit and red shirt, like it was a uniform he had created for himself. If the clips were in date order, he had also gone through a phase where he wore a bright red fedora pulled down over his eyes, but apparently he had outgrown that. On the whole, he appeared to very much be on the level, and somewhat famous among people in his field.

When he returned, Armando said, "If you do not wish to hire me, I will give you some recommendations for other options. But I assume you know now that you cannot leave the grounds unguarded, correct?"

Zoey said, "Sure. You're hired, or whatever." She looked around and said, "Did you see a pizza down here somewhere?"

"As your bodyguard, my first instruction will be for you to not eat any food delivered to you by a serial killer."

"Yeah, that makes sense. I've kind of lost my appetite anyway."

"I'm going to contact the police to come get the body. It's a nonemergency, so it will take them four to six hours to arrive, if they arrive at all. In the interim I will be appraising the security situation and we will have a serious discussion about it in the morning. There's nothing for you to do, other than get some sleep."

"I'm not sleeping with that body right in front of the door."

"I'll drag him away, if that will ease your mind. But he took a bullet to the brain, which even by zombie rules should eliminate him as a future threat."

"Move him anyway. Oh, and I haven't figured out how to access Arthur's money yet but if I can't get into the accounts then you can just take a bunch of furniture or something as payment. It all looks pretty expensive."

He smiled. "I'm confident we can work it out. Do you have any problems or questions?"

"Yeah. I mean no, that sounds fine. I'm too tired to think."

"This is what you are paying me for. In the morning, you will have some big decisions to make."

"And then you'll tell me just how screwed I am?"

"Most people in your situation would be pondering just how screwed their enemies are. You're safe now, Ms. Ashe."

"Zoey."

"Armando." They shook hands. "Good night, Zoey."

When he let go of her hand, she lunged in and hugged him. He reciprocated the hug about as much as a tree trunk would, and clearly wasn't a fan of the way she spent the next ten minutes crying into his lapel. But he waited it out in silence, which Zoey thought was polite of him.

Finally she pried herself away and apologized, and by the time Zoey was closing the door to the bedroom Armando was already dragging the dead psychopath down the hall, leaving a red smear on the hardwood floor in his wake. Zoey locked the door and shut off the wall feed. She kicked off her shoes for the first time and crawled into bed. Stench Machine jumped up and pressed his back against her face, as he usually did. She had time to think that after this nightmare of a day, she'd never get to sleep again. But halfway through the thought, she was out like a light.

FOURTEEN

The first two things Zoey discovered after she woke up sore and stiff Friday morning was that she was apparently now a huge celebrity in Tabula Ra$a, and that the toilet in the guest room talked.

It was, on the whole, an extremely impressive toilet. It had a self-warming seat (which apparently automatically lowered itself when it detected a female approaching), played gentle music the entire time she sat on it, and had two nozzles inside the bowl to wash and then dry her private parts when she was done. That list was presented in ascending order of how alarming Zoey found each of them.

Topping them all, however, was the fact that in the middle of this process a male voice with a British accent asked her if she wanted to watch the morning news update while she peed. Zoey's answer, a sleepy yelp of terror, apparently was interpreted as "Sure, toilet, show me the news to drown out the sound of my farts." A screen blinked to life and automatically hopped around from coverage of Zoey's hostage situation on the train, to the intruder getting shot in her house, to rumors of her inheritance, to a recap of the chase for the "key" that had led up to it. Zoey thought for a moment that the whole world had ground to a halt to cover her situation, then figured out that the feed was set to deliver a custom feed of just the news that pertained to her. It was the kind of thing that could mess with a person's head.

The British toilet-bot interrupted to give a startlingly detailed report of her health, informing her that she was not pregnant, currently did not have any drugs in her system, was not diabetic or suffering from kidney disease, but was at risk for a urinary tract infection due to slightly elevated levels of leukocyte esterase in her urine. She thanked the toilet, but it did not respond. That was good—if she started to think of it as a sentient being, it would probably be much harder to poop in its mouth.

Zoey knew she should go out and get a status report from Armando, or at the very least find out if Armando had been killed by a second wave of psychopaths who were now waiting to ambush her outside the bedroom door, but she kept finding reasons to not leave the guest room or even get off the toilet. She decided she liked it in there, a little room with a big, heavy door and soundproofed walls. Outside was the big, crazy house and outside that, the bigger, crazier city. For all she knew, the corpse of the Hyena was still slumped out there somewhere, drawing a cloud of flies.

The toilet voice came back to ask if she was okay, apparently if you sat on it too long it started to assume you had died. She told it she was fine, but a few minutes later it asked again. She needed to figure out how to turn off that feature if she intended to sit there the rest of the day, which at some point had apparently become her plan. The part of Zoey's brain that thought up ways to procrastinate from unpleasant tasks—honed to perfection through years of exercise—reminded her that she should call her mother, who was probably worried sick about her. Especially if she had watched the news, though she normally wasn't in the habit of doing that ("Honey, don't you know they're just giving you all of the stories of people being ugly to each other and ignoring all of the good?"). The call went to her voice mail, because Zoey's mother also wasn't in the habit of answering her phone.

"Hi Mom. I just wanted to let you know I'm okay. I don't know if you watch the news but it looks like I inherited like a billion dollars in drug money or something. Can you find a lawyer? Just tell him I'm in danger of getting murdered or going to jail for having a bunch of heroin warehouses and mafia money that I didn't even ask for, so whatever he can do to fix that would be great—SHUT UP! Sorry, I wasn't talking to you, Arthur's robot toilet is hassling me. Oh also my bodyguard shot a guy last night, hope that's okay. He had super powers, they all do. I don't know what's up with that. Anyway, call me."

Well, that should set her mind at ease. Zoey hung up and summoned the tremendous force of will it took to stand. She glanced at the shower and tried to decide if she felt safe enough to get naked in this house, then decided she smelled so bad that she just had to risk it. Also, it would be another good excuse to not leave the guest suite. She went out into the bedroom and scooted the table and lamp in front of the door, just in case.

The shower, she discovered, had fifty nozzles and a touchscreen with dozens of settings bearing unhelpful descriptions like "Jungle Massage." After trying a few it became clear that each was set to fire the water from various patterns and temperatures in order to create some kind of transcendental showering experience, while some unseen aromatherapy module pumped the room full of scents ranging from "Fresh-Cut Grass" to "Baking Cinnamon Buns." Zoey could not find a setting for just "regular shower" so she picked one at random and set about trying to decipher which of the dispensers on the wall oozed shampoo (at least one of them seemed to have been filled with scotch). Then, a few seconds in, the walls of the shower stall vanished and were replaced by a crystal-clear view of an emerald rainforest, the four screens simulating the experience of being outdoors bathing under a tropical water-fall. This freaked her out, because even though she knew it was just a video feed, she still couldn't shake the fear that a group of savages would come along and find her inexplicably standing naked in a stream. She hurried up and finished bathing, then spent twenty minutes trying to figure out how to turn the shower off.

By nine, Zoey found herself sitting on her bed, staring at the big door, and steeling herself to go outside. At nine-thirty she was still sitting there, Stench Machine getting hungry and impatient. Time and time again she mentally resolved to go out, and time and time again, her butt would not leave the bed. Finally there was a knock at the door, and Armando was asking if she was okay. That broke the spell and, bracing herself to see the pale corpse of a serial killer, she yanked open the door and found that not even a bloodstain remained from last night's horror.

She said, "So what did you do with the dead guy, just toss him out to the tigers?"

"No, ma'am, everything was done through official channels. Though the TRPD and the coroner required two separate bribes, for some reason. I'll put it in my expense report."

"They didn't need to talk to me?"

"Welcome to the world of Tabula Rasa. Or rather, welcome to the world of *being wealthy* in Tabula Rasa. Now, the first decision I have to burden you with this morning involves access to the grounds. You've had a number of house staff try to report to work this morning. I've been turning them away—"

"Yeah, I don't want to bother with any of that."

"Well, you have fifty thousand square feet of mansion and fifty acres of land here, it takes a small army to keep it looking like this."

"Right, otherwise the people who drove past might not feel quite as miserable about their own lives when they see it." Zoey headed toward the stairwell and said, "I'm not staying here, all that stuff is somebody else's problem. Keep everybody out for now. Not just to keep the serial killers from leaking in, but to make sure none of Arthur's old cronies decide to get revenge."

"If you're referring to the house staff, I'm not sure how much hunger for vengeance lies in the hearts of the landscapers or cleaning crew."

"I'm mainly worried about—"

"*Scroooooooge!!!*"

They had reached the landing, and Jacob Marley's ghost had been lying in wait. Stench Machine went streaking down the stairs in terror.

"Oh my god, will you unplug that stupid thing? What I was saying was, I'm mostly worried about the Suits—the, uh, creepy henchmen Arthur worked with—"

"Oh, I know who they are."

"Well, will they come back with a bunch of thugs and try to kick down the door?"

"That would be an exceptionally poor strategy on their end. The security system would give me ample advance warning. The most difficult part would be neutralizing them before the crossfire created too much damage to the décor. I believe there are vases in that foyer older than the New Testament. No, the danger posed by those men is of a . . . different nature."

"So what do you—" Zoey stopped, startled by the sound of clinking noises from down the hall. "Wait, is somebody else here?"

Armando looked confused. "Just Carlton, the butler."

Zoey had completely forgotten about him.

Armando, growing alarmed, asked, "Was he ordered to leave? He said he never heard from you after he retired for the evening. The gunshot woke him up."

"I didn't even think about him. It's . . . fine I guess. Can I trust him?"

Armando shrugged. "I did a background check. He has been a butler for fifty years. You can't trust anybody one hundred percent but . . ." he shrugged again. "These are the decisions *you* have to make. It comes with the inheritance."

"Wonderful."

Zoey left Armando where he was and followed the busy sounds, which took her through the dining room and into the hallway where she had gone the night before, only instead of heading toward the holographic Mold door, she went the opposite way and soon found herself in a vast kitchen suited for a restaurant. She saw two huge stainless refrigerators with touchscreen controls, a flat-top grill like they have at Benihana, a deep fryer, and a row of three ovens topped by fifteen burners (Zoey marveled at all of the instant macaroni and cheese she could boil on that thing). She saw rows of copperbottomed cookware dangling from racks over two huge sinks. Off in one corner was the arched brick opening of a wood-fired oven.

She wandered around the room, past a fragrant wall-size rack of fresh herbs sprouting from tiny little pots under grow lights. On the opposite wall was a bar—mirrored shelves of liquor and a beer tap, next to a coffee bar setup boasting an antique brass espresso machine that looked ten times as expensive as the professional one she used at work. She went over to give it a look, finding it comforting to be around tools she had mastered—grinders, steamers, even a little jar of toothpicks for drawing designs in the foam. The lingering scent of coffee oils was wonderful, even if it did remind her of long days, sore feet, and one particularly awful steam burn.

"Mr. Livingston would have his beans delivered weekly," said Carlton's voice from behind her. He had walked in silently from the other door, carrying Stench Machine.

Zoey spun and said, "Oh, I'm sorry. I was just . . . looking."

"You're apologizing for looking at your own kitchen? Your cat was wreaking havoc in the pantry, I had to go chase him down. I do believe he is hungry."

"Oh. Right. I'm . . . sorry."

Carlton nodded toward the coffee bar and said, "Your father, he found a service that ships the beans the day after they are roasted. Flies them in from Colombia. Have you eaten? Would you like something?"

She was starving, but said, "Oh, don't worry about me. I'll . . . order something." Then she thought and said, "You don't keep cat food around, do you? Not for me, obviously. I put some in my suitcase but I didn't pack enough, I thought I'd have a chance to stop at a—"

Before she could finish, Carlton sprang into action, opening the nearest refrigerator.

"If you're asking if I can prepare a meal a cat would find satisfactory, well, how difficult can it be?"

"You'd be surprised."

Carlton pulled a tuna steak, eggs, and a stick of butter from the refrigerator, then continued loading his arms from a walk-in pantry. He emerged with flour, a bag of rice, a jar of peanut butter, a plastic bear full of honey, a box of brown sugar, and a single, perfect banana.

"Do you like bananas, Ms. Ashe?"

"Oh, you don't have to—"

"Your father compensated me quite well to do precisely this, in precisely this situation. Am I to assume that my employment continues under the previous terms? It is my understanding that some staff were let go last night."

"Um, sure, that's fine."

"Well, then, for you to refuse to allow me to perform my duties would turn me into a thief. Please have a seat."

The nearest stovetop was suddenly a flurry of activity. Knobs were turned. Blue flames whooshed to life and a saucepan and two skillets were banged into place above them. Zoey took a seat at the bar and soon the intoxicating scent of melting butter joining the smell of fresh herbs and coffee. Armando stared intently at the process, but it wouldn't occur to Zoey until days later that he was making sure Carlton didn't poison her.

Zoey said, "You, uh, pretty much know what goes on around here, right?"

Carlton shrugged. "I try to keep to myself, but of course a man hears things. We humans don't have lids on our ears, as useful as that would be at times."

He grabbed a loaf of crusty bread off of a wire cooling rack on the counter, the bread presumably having been pulled from that brick oven hours earlier.

Zoey asked, "Those men. Or rather, those three men and that one girl—Will and Andre and the rest. What do they do? Or what did they do, for my dad? Are they, like, hit men?"

"They solved problems that your father needed solved."

"So hit men, then."

"I can only say that if they did kill anyone, they did not do it in the house."

A banana was peeled, laid on a cutting board, and sliced lengthwise. The crusty bread was expertly cleaved into thick slices. The tuna steak was laid gently into the sizzling oil of one skillet, brown sugar was stirred into melted butter in the other. Boiling rice was pulled from its burner and covered.

"You know what I'm asking. Are they dangerous?"

"If you are looking for specifics, I can say only that I was not made privy to any illegal activity. That would have put me in a difficult situation should I ever have been called to testify. That was made explicit in the terms of my employment."

"So you knew Arthur was a criminal."

Carlton dropped the bananas into the butter and brown sugar mixture. Flour, salt, baking powder, and eggs were whisked together in a bowl.

"'Criminal' is something of a nebulous concept in this city, I'm afraid. But yes, your father dealt in many large-scale, cash-only transactions off the books and had . . . *colorful* associates. And I heard tales, particularly of things he did in his youth, and during the war. He was not a man you wanted as an enemy. But, behind every great fortune . . . you know the rest."

A quarter inch of white had formed along the bottom of the pink tuna, and Carlton flipped it with an effortless, elegant motion. He turned toward the counter, and quickly the two slices of bread were smeared with a wad of peanut butter, then drizzled with honey. Armando's eyes followed his hands every step of the way.

"So you know Arthur left me everything? And you're just . . . taking it in stride? I'm your boss now, that's it? You don't think all of this is weird?"

"I assure you, this does not rank even in the top ten strangest weeks I've had during my time in Arthur's employ. I'm sure your needs will be different from his, but I am confident I can adjust, even at my advanced age. Otherwise, employers come and go. Some better than others."

Carlton pulled the tuna off the heat and set it aside. He pulled caramelized banana chunks from the pan and laid them atop the peanut buttered slice of bread, then laid the other slice of bread on top and dunked the whole thing in the egg and flour mixture. He then dropped the batter-coated sandwich into the deep fryer. Zoey thought there was something vaguely obscene about it.

"And you're not curious at all as to why he left everything to me?"

"I had a friend pass recently, who left his home and life savings to a Waffle House waitress. Said she was the only person who was ever kind to him. I once read about another woman who slept in a tent under an overpass, who it turned out had a coffee can full of gold coins buried underneath it, worth two hundred thousand dollars. She left it all to a local church that she had never attended."

"So you're saying he was just crazy? That's why all this happened?"

"I believe 'eccentric' is the word they use when one acquires a certain level of affluence. But in Arthur's case, perhaps it was simply regret."

Carlton sat the barely cooked tuna on a cutting board, diced it, and piled the chunks in a small bowl. He poured in some of the rice, mashed it all up with a fork, and set a fresh batch of homemade cat food on the floor for Stench Machine.

Zoey said, "Regret? What, like he had a crisis of conscience?"

"In my youth, I used to loathe being told I would understand something when I was older, but I'm afraid I must find myself saying it here."

He pulled the deep-fried peanut butter and banana sandwich from the fryer and let the oil drain from the basket.

He said, "At your age, life is full of possibilities. But as the years pass, those possibilities vanish, one by one, like doors closing in a hallway. You feel time slip by, and your energy slip away. One day, you realize you're too old to be a famous musician, or change careers, or have more children. And each of those closed doors represents a regret. As you get older, well, those regrets come to define you. Perhaps the lack of a family life was Arthur's regret. But honestly, what does it matter? If you're asking what you should do with your inheritance, that is up to you, Ms. Ashe. If you're asking what Arthur Livingston would have wanted you to do with your inheritance, well, the man is dead. So who gives a shit?"

He set the sandwich gently on a plate, the batter having formed a perfect golden brown crust. He sliced it diagonally, melted peanut butter oozing out as he carefully arranged the two halves. He garnished it with a fanned-out sliced strawberry, sprinkled it all with a light dusting of powdered sugar, then slid the plate to Zoey, followed by a glass of milk.

"Your father's favorite brunch and, on occasion, midnight snack. Elvis Presley's, too, I'm told."

Zoey took a bite, felt the gluttonous rush of fried fat and sugar spilling across her tongue, and decided that the world was a wonderful place.

From behind her, Armando said, "A car full of your fathers' associates is on the way. They just turned down the inlet road, heading for the gates. God, I love the security system here."

Zoey asked, "They can't get through the gates unless we let them, right?"

"Correct."

To Carlton she said, "Here's what I think. I think this whole thing stinks of one of Arthur's scams. I only talked to that man twice in my whole life. He knocks up my mom, vanishes into thin air, then eight years later shows up at our apartment out of the blue, with a wad of money and a football."

"A football?"

"I think he saw a picture of me my mom posted on the Internet, as a kid I was kind of a chuck wagon and I had short hair, and I was holding a football in the picture so I guess he decided that was my thing. Anyway, then he disappears until eight years after *that*, when he shows up on my sixteenth birthday as if it's the first time, like every eight years he suddenly remembers he has a daughter. This time he turns up with a luxury car. And another football. Had it delivered on a flatbed truck, with a big red bow on the top—the car, not the football. And all my unemployed neighbors are standing around gawking at it . . . I've never been more angry and embarrassed in my life. I always assumed it was some stupid tax write-off or something. And that's what I think this is—it's all some legal thing to hide assets from the feds."

Carlton hesitated, as if deciding whether to share what he was about to say next.

"Your father . . . he had a routine. He would bring home a different, very beautiful woman every Friday night. Then every Saturday morning, he would have me *mostly* prepare a brunch—eggs, crepes, fresh fruit, homemade whipped cream, leaving only the final assembly and plating of the dish undone. Then I would exit the kitchen and your father would come and finish putting it all together, so that when the Lady of the Week walked in, she would see your father wearing his big, ridiculous chef's hat and preparing a five-star meal for her. And she would smile. They all did, every time."

"I'm sorry, but that's kind of gross. Not this sandwich, by the way. The sandwich is miraculous." On the floor, Stench Machine was eating his fish and rice just as hard as he could.

"My point is, I cannot tell you that your father was a good man. To those who went against him, I'm sure he was not. But even to his friends . . . it's not that he didn't want to be a good man. It's that he didn't really know how. So, he liked to impress people. To dazzle them. That was as close to good as he could get."

Candi the bimbo hologram blinked into the middle of the room and said, "Turn on the hot tub jets and open four bottles of champagne, Andre Knox and Budd Billingsley are at the front gates. Ooh, it looks like we'll have enough people to form a spank gauntlet!"

Armando said, "They're not armed. They never are. I don't judge them to be an immediate threat to your personal safety. As to whether or not they are a threat to your *financial* safety or are otherwise trustworthy, well, again that's what *you* have to figure out."

Zoey chewed, then said, "All right, let them in. But if they so much as reach into a pocket without permission, shoot them both in the head."

FIFTEEN

Armando opened the huge front doors with one hand, the other pointing his gun at the ceiling. Zoey stood behind him, kind of hoping the visitors would try to make a move. Carlton was lurking nearby, presumably to see if he'd be needed to clean up a bunch of blood or something.

Budd Billingsley took off his cowboy hat, looked past Armando to make eye contact with Zoey and asked, "Do you mind if we come in, miss?"

If he was mocking her, Zoey couldn't detect it. "Sure, why not."

Andre followed Budd through the door, looking very hung over and eating a giant chili dog.

Budd said, "Took some work to roust this vagrant but I reckoned he needed to be here, too."

As he passed Zoey, Andre said, "Yeah, I'm eatin' a chili dog at ten in the morning. Only God can judge me."

"Carlton made me an Elvis."

Andre squinted at Carlton and said, "You gave her a bunch of Quaaludes and made her eat them on the toilet? That's a new low, Carlton." He looked at Armando and said, "Who's this?"

Zoey said, "Oh, this is—"

"Armando Ruiz," finished Budd.

Armando said, "You have seen my ads."

"I knew of you when you worked for Pinkerton. Also met your daddy a time or three. Is he still the chief in Reno?"

Armando smiled. "I think my father will still be in that uniform when *I* retire. He'll probably wear it to my funeral."

To Zoey, Andre said, "Budd knows everybody."

Zoey was already heading back toward the kitchen, as she still had a quarter of a sandwich left and would rather die than leave it uneaten. They all followed her, and the moment Budd entered the kitchen music faded in from out of nowhere, a man singing of a woman named Black Betty Blamalam.

Andre saw Zoey's expression and said, "The house is programmed to play your personal theme music at random times, when you walk into a room, like you're making an entrance. Arthur's idea, obviously."

"Can we turn it off?"

Budd said, "Trust me, ma'am, if we knew how to turn it off, we'd have done it years ago."

Zoey took her seat at the bar and resumed her sandwich. "All right, you've got five minutes to say your piece, then Armando starts shooting."

Armando looked alarmed and said, "That's . . . really not one of the services I provide."

Budd said, "No, we completely understand. I just want to tell you a story, if you'll indulge me. Now this city, it can be real confusing for an outsider. I don't care where you're from, Tabula Rasa can make you feel like you've taken a train to Bizarro world. I remember my very first night here—and this is goin' on fifteen years ago—I was takin' a walk downtown, tryin' to get a feel for the place. And I'm walkin' through a construction site—and it was all construction sites back then, you understand—and I come across this hole in the ground, 'bout ten feet in diameter. I look down and I can't see a bottom, so I pull a quarter out of my pocket and toss it down, and listen for a clink or a splash. Nothin'. Coin just tumbles into the darkness and disappears. So now I'm real curious, and I look around for somethin' else to throw down there. And teeterin' right on the edge of the hole is an old refrigerator. So, I circle around and I give it a good kick and it tumbles down into the hole. I hear it bang off the side a few times but once again, there's no crash, no splash, like it just kept fallin' forever. It was the strangest thing. So I figure this is the first of this city's many unknowable mysteries and I start to go on about my way. But then I see the *second* strange thing—this goat, it goes flying past me, in midair. Like it was fired from a cannon. And now I think I'm losin' my mind, like maybe it's not just tobacco in my cigar, if you know what I'm sayin'. So I walk along and I come across a guy sittin' on the curb and I say, 'Holy cow, partner, did you see that goat?' And the fella says, 'Well, that's my goat.' And I say, 'Well, I hate to tell ya, but I think it's gone. It took off flyin'.' And the fella says, 'That's impossible. I had him chained to a refrigerator.'"

Zoey stared for a moment, then snorted a laugh that almost caused her to choke on her sandwich.

"Ha! Wait, was that a threat? Am I the goat in that story?"

"No, ma'am. I know it ain't fully sunk in yet, but to someone with assets like you now possess, a threat from a man like me wouldn't amount to more than a hiss from an angry kitten. No, ma'am, we're here, hat in hand, to ask if we still have jobs."

Andre swallowed a wad of chili dog and said, "Is *that* why we're here? Jesus, Budd, I would have sobered up first."

Zoey said, "I don't even know what your jobs were. And you know what, I don't want to know. This whole thing happened because I got up last night, because my cat got hungry and I had to go find a fork, and I stumbled into that conference room and saw Will and Ling and their cop friend messing with a severed hand."

Budd said, "A severed *what*?" and Andre said, "*Your cat eats with a fork?*"

"It was a severed hand. Don't ask me if I mistook something else for a severed hand because no, I didn't. It was a hand. They had it on the table, prodding it."

Budd said, "I'll ask Will about this hand situation, but I can assure you that I have no personal knowledge of any recent dismemberments by any members of the staff."

Stench Machine was finishing his fish and rice. Andre heard him clinking the bowl around, glanced down at him and muttered, "Well, that's disappointing."

Budd said, "The point is, Livingston Enterprises, it's a big ol' machine, with thousands of moving parts. And those parts are people, and investments, and transactions bein' made, day and night. And that machine is hummin' along even as we're sitting here havin' breakfast. But at the moment, there ain't nobody at the controls. See, because that's what the four of us did, managed various aspects of the day-to-day. Your daddy, he wasn't one to micromanage. And Will Blackwater, well, he was your daddy's right-hand man."

"I can see why, he's delightful."

"I'm happy to admit Will has the personality of a robot programmed by an asshole. But that don't change the fact that your daddy was like a fath— Well, the two were very close, is what I'm sayin'. Arthur was a mentor to Will and I'm here to tell you that whether you keep him or fire him, Will will never allow any harm to come to you or the business. Because it's not what Arthur would have wanted. Carlton and Andre both can confirm that. Armando, too,

I bet. Everybody knew of your father, and everyone who knew your father, knew Will."

"I'll take your word for it."

"So, that brings us to the main reason for our visit. Will wants a meeting. In a neutral location. He was hopin' that—well, that if you'd had a night to sleep on it, you'd see things different. Now what I'm about to say, it's not a threat, so please don't take it that way. That's why I'm delivering this message instead of Will, on account of he's got that peculiar speech impediment that makes *everything* he says sound like a threat. The message is, monsters like what came after you last night? Both times? They're not gonna stop. We can help you, Zoey. But you got to trust us."

Zoey turned to Armando, looking for a reaction. He asked Budd, "Where does he want to meet?"

"The crater. The, uh, blast site, where the warehouse used to be. Where Arthur died. Will says there's somethin' there he needs to show you. Both of you."

Andre said, "Well now *I* don't wanna go. That makes it sound like he's gonna get us out there and whip out his flop-hog."

Zoey sighed. "All right. Let me finish my sandwich."

SIXTEEN

Zoey asked Carlton how to get to the garage, assuming they had one. He led Zoey and Armando to a library, where pulling a certain book caused a shelf to slide over and reveal an elevator, because of course it did (though Zoey noticed the spine of the secret book had been covered with masking tape onto which "GARAGE" was scrawled in Magic Marker). The elevator took them down one floor to a cavernous showroom that contained at least fifty cars. There was nice variety of long luxury cars, SUVs, and low, crouching sports cars with tinted windows and paint jobs so glossy that you could have used the reflection to apply mascara. As they made their way down the aisle, Zoey found she had left Armando behind—he was carefully examining one sinister flat black sports car. It had bulbous fenders that curved around and down the front like a pair of scowling eyebrows, with a blood-red triangular vent in the center of the hood, like the car had sustained a fatal wound. Armando looked like he wanted to cry.

Zoey said, "Is that an expensive one?"

"This is a 2020 Bugatti Chiron. Fifteen hundred horsepower, widely thought to be the apex of the gasoline-powered automobile. Only thirty of them were manufactured. At top speed it gets three miles to the gallon, which means you could get a five-hundred-dollar ticket just for being caught driving it today."

"Looks pretty cool."

"This, Zoey, is a twenty-million-dollar car."

"Oh. Wow. I bet the insurance is outrageous."

Armando realized he had picked a terrible partner for this conversation, sighed, and glanced around the room.

Zoey said, "You want to drive it?"

"I would die a happy man. But for the situation we're walking into, we're taking that."

He nodded toward a big, black sedan with tinted windows, parked next to a bigger, blacker box truck like you'd use to deliver furniture. Zoey actually wasn't sure which vehicle he was referring to, but Armando walked to the sedan, opening the doors and trunk. He seemed to approve of what he saw.

"Bulletproof glass, half inch thick. Titanium shell around the whole body, carbon fiber inner shell, silica and polyethylene glycol core to catch shrapnel. Emergency oxygen system, run-flat tires. Threat detection A.I., emergency pathfinding navigation. Refrigerator in the trunk for a blood supply should an emergency transfusion be needed."

"Is that good?"

"A direct hit with an antitank rocket would not stop this vehicle. If somehow the driver was killed, the car would drive itself to safety."

"Cool. You can tell all that by looking?"

"I recognize the model. It's the same one the president uses. Get in."

He was nodding toward the back seat when he said it, but Zoey took the front. Armando slid in, threw the briefcase Zoey hadn't noticed him carrying into the backseat, and began tinkering with the windshield display. They had to pass through two separate garage doors to get out, the first closing behind them before the next opened, which Zoey assumed was to make sure nobody could wait outside the door and rush into the house while they were pulling out.

The scenic rich people enclave around the Casa was positioned to give the illusion that it was way out in the country, but only five minutes of driving put them back in view of the flickering forest of glass and girders that was downtown Tabula Ra$a. As she watched, a huge animated car raced across the skyline, an ad that spanned five buildings announcing a Christmas sales event at the local Changfeng dealership. They weren't even all the way downtown and Zoey was already getting a headache. They took an off-ramp and before long, the scenery changed to hangar-sized buildings, warehouses, and silos. Zoey wondered if she owned any of it.

Her phone went off and the word "MOM" hovered over it.

"Hey, Mom. Can you hear me?"

"Heeeey, Z! Saw you left a message. You having a good time in the city?"

"You didn't watch the news, did you?"

"No . . ."

"Well, when you do, don't have a panic attack. Everything is fine. I was accosted by a man on the train but it turned out okay. Then I was accosted by another man but he's—Everything's fine now, that's what you should take away from this."

"Oh my god! Where are you now? Did you talk to the police?"

"It's all taken care of. I'm driving around the city now, in one of dad's cars. Or my car, I guess."

"Did he bequeath you a car? Are you going to keep it?"

"It's a long story. But I think he left me some money."

"Hey, we can get the refrigerator fixed!"

"Sure. It's, uh, kind of complicated."

"I was just joking about the refrigerator, honey. The money is yours, buy yourself a vacation and leave a little to get something practical for yourself. You're a big girl and you can decide, but you know what I say, experiences are worth way more than stuff."

"It's a lot of money, Mom. In fact, I think he left me all of it."

Silence. Trucks were rumbling past outside, and they passed warning signs along the road depicting stick figures suffering various industrial accidents.

Finally, Zoey's mother said, "What a bastard."

"I know, Mom, he should have left it to you—"

"Oh no. He knew better than that. Zoey, I hope you're grown up enough to know that all he did was dump his burden on you. You shouldn't have to suffer from his stupid addiction."

"He was an addict?"

"Honey, you don't make that kind of money unless you're addicted to making it. These stockbrokers who work hundred-hour weeks piling billions on top of billions, you think they could stop, even if they wanted to?"

"It really did seem like he was having a good time . . ."

"Of course, because one hundred percent of his energy was devoted to building up appearances. You remember Elba the cat lady, used to live in the blue trailer? When she died they found she had over fifty cats in there, and they ate her face?"

"Ew. Gross. Yes, I remember that."

"So why do we call her crazy for piling her trailer full of more cats than she could take care of but applaud when somebody accumulates more money than they can spend? They're both hoarders."

"All right, all right, I shouldn't have brought him up. I know how much you hated him."

"Don't ever say that. I never hated that man for one second. He gave me the most beautiful, perfect daughter in the whole wide world."

"I have *a sister*?"

"You definitely inherited his smart mouth, missy." Armando was steering them around orange cones and a flashing sign that was trying to tell them the road ahead was closed. "My suggestion is you just bail out and let them take care of it. I'm betting that within the next week a swarm of lawyers and creditors and loan sharks and lord knows who else are all going to show up at the door. In my mind, you are under absolutely no obligation to put up with any of that. Life's too short."

"Like I said. It's complicated."

"I say just keep enough to do something fun. Heck, take a few thousand dollars, ride the train down to Vegas and just blow it all. Get one of those fancy hotel rooms with the big bubble bath, pick up some handsome boy, make a bunch of mistakes, and then come home and tell me all about it."

"Okay, I should go."

"Just make sure he uses protection."

"*Mom!* God."

"Good-bye, honey. See you Sunday."

She hung up and Armando said, "We're coming up on it here."

Zoey saw what was ahead and said, "Oh, wow."

The car stopped at a barricade flashing an announcement that the inlet road was closed and that no one was permitted beyond that point. Beyond it, Zoey could see the aftermath of the explosion. It was a giant perfect circle of black—it looked like God had reached down and taken out a football field–sized hunk of earth with a huge ice cream scooper. Arthur Livingston had gone out in spectacular fashion. Almost as if he had planned it that way.

Armando said, "It broke windows fifteen blocks away."

Andre and Budd pulled up alongside them in Andre's Bentley. Zoey stepped out and they all walked past the flashing barriers and made their way toward the blast crater. Within ten steps she was walking precariously on a jagged pile of debris—busted cinder blocks and shards of glass and twisted metal beams—that got more treacherous as she neared the black bowl where the warehouse had been. There were yellow bulldozers and backhoes and other vehicles scattered around the crater like toys, making it look like a giant sandbox some enormous toddler had been playing in. Everything smelled like burnt toast.

From behind her, Budd said, "You see that black gunk splattered all over them bricks there? That's glass. When this place blew, it melted in an instant and sprayed every which way."

"What could do this? I mean I know it was a warehouse, but what was in it?"

"You figure it out, be sure to let the rest of us know, all right?"

Andre said, "That's Will, out there by the crane."

Andre tromped off into the charred wasteland, and Budd followed. Zoey glanced back at Armando who said, "It's not a good ambush location, if that's what you're wondering. No choke points and no place to hide gunmen."

Zoey nodded toward his little black briefcase. "Is that full of guns?"

"Not *full*, no. But we've got a few things in here we might find useful should things go sour."

They trudged out into the crater and Zoey asked, "Should I have a gun? Just in case?"

"What kind of training do you have?"

"I've seen a lot of movies. As far as I can tell, as long as you're the good guy the bullet just goes right into their heads. It's only the bad guys that miss."

"I can sign you up for a six-week course, and after that we can talk about you carrying. But otherwise, no."

"Six weeks? I don't intend to be here six *days* if I can help it. So what if a psychopath jumps me in an alley when you're not there?"

"The gun without the training just means you've given your attacker a free gun."

They crunched through the charred landscape until they got close enough for Zoey to see that Will was standing next to a ruined truck. It was a pickup with a Livingston Construction logo on the side, and it had been twisted completely around—the rear wheels were upright, the cab was upside down, everything in between looking like it had been wrung like a wet rag. Echo was crouched near a bumper, examining it like a crime scene tech. Zoey wondered how in the hell she had traversed the crater in those heels.

Zoey said to Will, "I'm here, show me what you got to show me."

Will just gestured toward the twisted truck.

Zoey shook her head. "What am I looking at? The truck? It looks like it made it out of the explosion better than the building did."

Will shook his head. "This didn't happen in the blast. The truck belongs to the cleanup crew. They left it parked here last night, this is what it looked like this morning."

"I don't understand."

Echo said, "Look at the bumper."

Zoey walked around to the front and Echo said, "You see those dents? Two of them, each about as wide as a hand, about four feet apart on the bumper? One on top, one on bottom."

"All right."

"Now imagine in your mind a person grabbing the bumper so that they could twist a truck in half with their bare hands. That's where the dents would be."

"Oh. *Oh.*" A freaking *person* had done this. Zoey felt a sinking in her gut. Suddenly the five of them seemed very exposed, standing out here in the open. "Jesus."

Will asked, "Now do you understand?"

"Not in the least."

"It's a threat. Intended for us. Or rather, you, since now these are *your* trucks. It's from Molech."

"There's that name again. What's this guy's deal?"

Will pulled out his phone and brought up a video feed. "This is from a drone, above us right now. Look."

It was an overhead view of the dark circle of the blast crater, zooming in until Zoey could see the six of them standing around the twisted truck. The ruined vehicle was, she could now see, part of a message that could only be viewed from the sky—the truck they were examining formed the lower part of a capital "L." Scattered around the crater were the remains of probably a dozen other vehicles that had been torn apart and rearranged to form four letters: G O L D.

Zoey said, "What, he wants Arthur's gold? He can have it. Tell this Molech he can pick it up, or we'll drive it to him, whatever is convenient. Throw it in the trunk, we'll take it right now. I totally don't care."

Will shook his head. "It doesn't make any sense."

"Are you saying we don't have any gold?"

Andre answered, "Oh, I'm sure Arthur had some, somewhere. Gold and platinum and several hundred other commodities that made up a portfolio that even he barely kept track of. If somebody stole all the gold Arthur owned, he probably wouldn't even have noticed. Probably kept it in a cigar box in his basement."

Budd said, "It's like if somebody kidnapped your family and their only ransom demand was a jar of mayonnaise."

Zoey said, "Okay, and why do these people seem to have superpowers, again? Are they magic?"

Will said, "No. But the reality isn't any less alarming."

"Tell me."

"Information like that, Ms. Ashe, is precisely the kind of helpful insight I bring to the table as one of the chairmen of Livingston Enterprises. Unfortunately, I am not currently employed in that capacity, as you know."

"Ah. That's what this is about. You want a share of the money."

"I want to not get torn in half by one of Molech's carnival freaks. Whatever our differences, I think you and I have that in common. And if you look at this twisted wreck behind me, you will understand why *I am growing alarmed*. I'm sorry if I haven't exactly had time to be polite about this."

"Ah, and this is the point where you try to convince me you're really a nice guy after all."

"I'm not a nice guy. But I am on your side. Don't confuse the two. You hate me because I'm blunt and have no patience for wasted time or wasted words. Because I'm not *nice*. Well, a lot of nice people are nice because they've figured out it's a great way to get things from other people. Some of the slimiest snakes I've run across have been nice. So let me tell you now, if you ever see me resort to being nice, *run*."

"Forgive me if I'm not a genius negotiator like you, but my fragile little woman brain is telling me that just because the other guys are monsters *doesn't automatically mean you're not*."

"You'll change your mind when you hear what I have to say."

Armando was nervously scanning the lip of the crater, and then the sky, as if something was going to swoop down and spit fire at them at any moment. "Zoey, I no longer consider this a safe meeting location. I was thinking guns earlier, not . . . whatever did *that*."

Will said, "I agree. There's a nice meeting room in Livingston Tower, it has walls, chairs, and alcohol. Hell, we'll take you up to the roof and you can go for a ride in your own helicopter."

Zoey asked Armando. "You know where that is?"

Armando smirked. "People on airplanes flying thirty thousand feet over the city know where Livingston Tower is. It's pretty hard to miss."

"Is it safe?"

"It's a crowded building full of armed security. So I guess the question is, safe from *what*?"

SEVENTEEN

Livingston Tower was the tallest and weirdest building Zoey had ever seen in person. The structure that loomed in the windshield of the sedan was banana-shaped, and flat black (at the moment—Armando noted that it could turn any color, the black was for mourning) and the banana curve caused it to lean over the street below, as if it was in the process of being blown over by a hard wind. There was something vaguely obscene about it. Actually, no. It wasn't vague at all.

As they approached, Zoey asked Armando, "So that's my building? I own that whole thing?"

"And it's full of your employees, too."

"Weird." So she could walk in there and just fire them all. Ruin their lives, just like that.

They arrived at the circular drive in front of a row of revolving doors.

Zoey said, "Don't stop. Pull back out to the street. Keep going."

"To where?"

"Somewhere other than here. If this is where they want to meet, I want to go . . . whatever the opposite of this place is."

They rounded a corner, and Zoey saw the two trailing vehicles—driven by Will and Andre—follow them. She looked around for a sleazy bar or maybe a Chuck E. Cheese they could meet in. They passed a high-end massage parlor, a three-story-tall shop advertising military-grade weapons for sale, and another fast-food franchise she had never heard of, a place called Korea Streets that boasted dishes called bindaeduk and mandu. Undulating across the windows above them all was a row of text that shouted, "LIVINGSTON

MEMORIAL AND DROP PARTY TOMORROW! 5:00 PM UNTIL EVERYONE HAS PASSED OUT."

And then she saw it.

It was a ragged, half-finished building that looked like forty stories of stacked garbage—tarps, sheets, cardboard, plywood.

Zoey said, "Ew. What happened to that place?" Smoke poured from dozens of haphazard gaps where windows should have been. "Is it on fire?"

Armando said, "That's just people trying to keep warm. And I think you own 'that place.' This whole plaza is yours, unless I'm mistaken."

"What happened to it? It looks like the front was blown off by a bomb."

"This is as far as construction got. It was supposed to be upscale condos. Broke ground five years ago, they got the frame up and the concrete down, then it got stalled over some legal thing. Over time, the homeless started squatting there until it just . . . filled up. Everybody calls it Squatterville."

"Pull over. This is where we're meeting."

Armando looked alarmed. "I'm going to advise against that, for reasons I should not have to state out loud."

"We're driving a rocket-proof luxury tank, I think we can risk getting within fifty feet of poor people."

Armando reluctantly did what he was told, and Zoey remembered that he didn't really have a choice. This whole employer/employee thing was intoxicating. The car pulled onto a patch of weed-riddled concrete in the shadow of the battered structure. Zoey gawked up at it. It looked postapocalyptic.

Andre's Bentley and Will's sports car pulled up behind them.

Armando nodded back toward Will's vehicle and said, "Aston Martin Vanquish. 2023, I think."

Zoey and Armando got out of the car. Zoey looked up and was met with faces leaning down from every floor of the crumbling tower, rumor of the luxury sedans with the tinted windows having made it all the way to the roof. The place had a grapevine that could transmit information faster than wireless. The first floor was almost entirely open, even the framework of the unfinished walls having been torn away at some point, presumably for scrap.

A crowd of people were milling about in between exposed concrete pillars that Zoey thought looked ready to buckle at a moment's notice, everyone lining up in front of folding tables packed with food. If Zoey was famous in Tabula Ra$a, her fame hadn't reached this group—all she got were annoyed stares from people ready to fly into a rage if it looked like she was about to cut in front of them in line. She walked toward the crowd, then felt a hand clamp down on her shoulder before she could make it inside.

Armando said, "Let's keep our distance."

Another, more deliberate set of footsteps approached. Zoey turned and saw that only Will had exited his vehicle, presumably to ask them what the hell they were doing. Before he could reach them, he was accosted by a huge guy who had tattoos instead of hair on his skull—bundles of snakes, like Medusa. The man seemed to be muttering a series of demands and threats at Will as he passed. Will, never even glancing at the man, reached into his inside pocket, pulled out his wallet, and handed it to him without breaking stride.

When Will reached Zoey, she asked, "Did you just get mugged?"

"What are we doing here?"

"I changed my mind. This is where I want to meet."

Will glanced up at the smoking tower and let out an annoyed sigh.

Zoey said, "Armando says I own it."

"This," said Will, "is one of ten thousand headaches you'll be taking on if you insist on staying in Tabula Rasa."

Five floors above them, a filthy naked man was standing in front of an open section of wall, washing his crotch with a bottle of water. Will turned and motioned to Andre, Budd, and Echo to join them. All three faces looked terrified. Workers were hustling nearby, hauling containers out from the backs of a pair of box trucks in the parking lot, carrying them to the tables.

Zoey asked, "Who are those people?"

"You're paying them. This whole thing, it's a property line dispute with the people building the parking garage next door. The courts eventually ruled in their favor, which means this building has to come down and be moved thirty feet that way. But that will mean running out all your squatters up there and that didn't sit too well with your father. He had the Livingston Foundation set up a soup kitchen down here and contracted with a catering company to come in three times a day, every day, while he stalled with the court order."

Zoey watched filthy people continue to pile up in front of the folding tables, lines becoming undefined clumps, stage two of a process that seemed destined to progress to "unruly crowd" and then "riot." Half of the people in line were kids, most of the rest were women. A morbidly obese man in a beard was arguing with a wall. A toddler was picking off pieces of his sandwich and feeding them to a bony dog. There were a lot of smokers.

Will said, "See that lady over there, the one with dried diarrhea down the back of her pants? You could put her up in a mansion and hire servants to wait on her the rest of her life. Or, you could leave her here, to drink herself to death in her own filth. Same for every person in this building. Every person in the city. You have the power of life and death. How's it feel?"

Zoey was scanning the food table. From what she could see, the selection wasn't great. There was some kind of thick vegetable stew, and loaves of generic bread, lunch meat, and cheese they were making sandwiches from. Plastic tubs of apples that no one was taking, plastic tubs of bananas and oranges that were going faster. Bottles of water, bottles of imitation juice, generic soda.

Zoey said, "Maybe I'll just give away the whole estate. Sell all the land and give it to these people. What would you think about that?"

Will cocked an eyebrow and said, "Because you're a good person, right? Unlike me? But why do you consider yourself to be a good person? Back in the trailer park, how many times did you think, 'I'd rescue all of these people, and feed all of the sick children, *if only I had the money*.' It's real easy to say, isn't it? But then you actually get the money, and you find out some things about yourself. You realize how much of what you used to consider morality was just powerlessness—you took for granted the enormous comfort that comes with knowing that none of your choices could hurt anyone outside of your own four walls. And that, Zoey, is when you find out the terrible truth of every downtrodden person who has climbed to the top—that if put in the same shoes as the bullies, we'd be just as bad, or worse."

"God you must love listening to yourself talk."

"Look around. Do you want to have to make the final call on this building? It'll have to happen soon, the structure will become unsafe if it sits much longer. So what happens to the families if you give the demolition order? What happens if you do nothing but gravity does the demolition for you?"

The other three had arrived, everyone standing in a tight group as if huddling together would create a bubble that would keep out the poverty. A drunken elderly man tried to join them, shouting something about their mothers. Armando simply opened his jacket to show the man the gun in its holster. The man shuffled away.

Zoey said, "First item on the agenda, Will Blackwater has thirty seconds to somehow make me feel better about the severed hand in my house."

Budd said, "Oh, was that Sanzenbacher's hand?"

Will nodded and said, "Kowalski was able to get it from the coroner's office after the autopsy. Not like they were going to convict anyway."

Zoey said, "Who?"

Budd answered, "Brandon Sanzenbacher. The crazy fella with the doll heads who you dong-roasted to death. The Soul Collector."

"Who cut his hand off?"

Andre said, "No one. It happened on its own. Did you not watch the news coverage of your own hostage situation?"

"Why would I? I was there."

Budd said, "He exploded, into little pieces, just as you were leaving the train station. Like he had a stick of dynamite up his ass. I wasn't playing dumb back at the house, I honestly didn't know they were gonna bring chunks of the guy in for examination." He shot an admonishing glance at Echo. "*I eat on that table.*"

Andre said, "To me, looked like a transformer blew. You ever seen that happen? I mean a transformer like you have on utility poles, not them robots that turn into cars. Looks just like that, a flash of white and blue, bright enough to leave spots in your eyes."

Zoey said, "And . . . *why* would he spontaneously explode?"

Will answered, "The device he had inside him—the thing that was generating the electricity—it failed. Overloaded, shorted out, whatever. I'm going to speculate that if it had discharged properly, that you, Zoey, and everything within ten feet of you would have been charred to a crisp. I don't know how much juice this guy had inside him, but . . ."

"*Inside* him?"

"Do you really want to know this?"

Zoey threw up her hands. "I apparently have to!"

Echo said, "Here. This is what we were looking at when your cat tried to eat the hand."

She laid her phone on the hood of the armored sedan and tapped through menus until a holographic projection of a hand floated above it, rotating slowly. Echo tapped the phone again and the flesh vanished from the hand, revealing the bones underneath.

Andre grimaced at the ghostly skeleton hand hovering menacingly over the car, then glanced up at the vagrants in the building above him and said, "Man, these people are gonna think we're doin' some kind of voodoo ritual down here."

Echo said, "See these white lines running down his fingers? Along the bone here? Those are wires, conductive graphene braids, to be exact. This is how he did the lightning—they all run back to a device in his palm, that's this square here, which was wired up to . . . we're not sure what."

Zoey said, "So he had something implanted in his body."

Will said, "Something incredible. There's a device the military uses, called a laser-induced plasma channel. It fires a beam through the air, a pulse so strong that it creates plasma by separating electrons from air molecules, basically unleashing a bolt of lightning. To me, this looks like a micro version of one of those. But here's the thing—the military version has to be able to generate a pulse of around fifty *billion* watts. That's why their version is so big it has to be carried on the back of a tank."

"But this guy," said Echo, "seemed to have the equivalent stashed in the palm of his hand."

Zoey said, "How does a crazy guy on a train get something like that installed?"

Echo said, "Presumably the same way an even crazier guy would get strength implants added to his limbs, or jaws that can bite through steel. That's not even the question we're asking right now. The issue at the moment is that the device *shouldn't even be possible.*"

Andre said, "There were weird rumors, over the last couple of months. Dead bodies with freaky injuries, or their brains fried. Couple guys spontaneously combusted. One guy managed to get himself lodged into the engine of an airliner at thirty thousand feet, somehow. At first it came off like a viral Blink hoax, but . . . yeah. It turns out some of the shady characters in this city now have . . . *powers.*"

Zoey grabbed her hair and growled in frustration. "Okay, just *how much more information are you people withholding from me?* Because every new layer of this thing is more terrifying than the last."

Will said, "So now you understand the state of mind we were in when you arrived."

"Oh, yeah, you've convinced me. I want no part of this nonsense. This whole city is a butt that farts horror."

Another of the vagrants had wondered over, this one also shouting about someone's mother. Either he was copycatting the first guy, or else the mother thing was some kind of popular insult in Squatterville.

Zoey looked to Armando, who was standing between them and the unruly masses, looking ready to draw several guns.

She said, "I've got a bodyguard question. There's this huge bounty on my head, is there a way to buy myself out of it? If I just pay off this Molech and leave town, will his henchmen follow me?"

Will interjected, "Zoey, that's not the question. The issue is if you stay—"

"Hush. I asked Armando."

Armando gave careful thought to it and, without taking his eyes off the crowd, said, "Remember what I said, about how if a threat gets close enough to you that I have to physically deal with it, that I have already failed at my job? That's because my job is to deter adversaries long before conflict even begins—to make it clear that any attempt to harm you is so futile that it doesn't warrant leaving the house. In a city where there's no authority, that fear, that reputation, is all you have to keep the wolves at bay. A name that follows you like a black cloud. Do you understand?"

"It's the same reason the crazy guy on the train glued doll heads to his crotch."

"Exactly. A while back, a snitch started working with the prosecutors, back when this city still had them. Said he was going to give up Molech's identity, and tie him to this mass shooting at a nightclub. That snitch was dragged out of his home by Molech's men. They strung him up in the park by the fountain, upside down, hanging by his ankles, and poured molten glass into his nostrils. It burned through his sinuses, and ran out his eye sockets, before it finally burned through his brain. See, they do it upside down, so the man can continue screaming the whole time, right up until it finally cooks the part of his brain that controls that particular function. And of course, there were cameras there for the whole thing. If you wish to see the video, go to Blink and search for the name Marvin Hammett."

"Jesus."

"*That* is the reaction they seek. One you feel in your gut more than your brain. So now we apply that to your situation. There was a highly publicized chase to find Arthur Livingston's daughter. Molech's man won. All of the cameras were there to see it. Then, with everyone watching, well . . ."

Budd said, "You couldn't have known this, but in this part of the world it's considered a grave insult to set a man's pecker on fire."

Armando said, "You made him look weak, in front of the whole world. So. You tell me, Zoey. Do you think Molech can let that slide, even if you gave him *everything*?"

"Even though it wasn't my fault? Even though he caused the whole thing?"

"It is not about fairness. It is about building a brand." Armando looked back at the group and asked, "Do any of you disagree with anything I said?"

Will said, "If she stays here and keeps the inheritance, then she'll be a high-profile target with ten figures in assets for an aspiring kidnapper to ransom. If she goes on the run and leaves everything behind, makes it clear there is no financial gain to be had from going after her, then maybe she has a fighting chance."

The impact of what they were saying finally hit Zoey, all at once. She bent over, and tried to breathe.

"I think I'm going to be sick."

She was, quite simply, going to die. She would probably not see Christmas.

She would likely never see her mother again. Stench Machine would get stuck with some owner who probably didn't understand him. Or he'd wind up getting euthanized in a shelter.

Armando put a hand on her shoulder and said, "Come on, let's get you out of here."

She shook off his hand.

"Just . . . let me summarize. One of you says I'm dead if I stay and the other says I'm dead if I go, but reading between the lines, it's pretty obvious that I'm dead *no matter what I do.* You people—you've given me a terminal diagnosis with like two days to live, and you're all just so *casual* about it. Because apparently in this awful town, this sort of thing just happens all the time? Is that how it is? Girls come here and just get chewed up and spat out as part of this dick-swinging game you rich gangsters play with each other?"

She was drawing attention now. People from the crowd were actually giving up their place in line to come see the drama with the rich folks in the parking lot. A teenage girl with a shaved head shouted something about her mother.

Zoey met Will's eyes and said, "You just look *annoyed* by this, you know that? Like I've messed up your weekend plans. I'm imagining you in that room, with the stupid buffalo head on the wall, with all of your other suit buddies, saying 'Sorry we had to reschedule the golf game, this thing happened last week, my boss died and his daughter came into town and inconvenienced everybody, but that's okay because yesterday she was dragged screaming from her bed and gutted like fish while millions of people cheered on the Blink feed. So it's all better now, guys, that little glitch, that little bump in the road is gone forever, and now the *men* can get back to work.'"

Zoey found a wadded-up tissue in the pocket of her cardigan and tried to dry her eyes and wipe the running mascara.

From behind her, Armando said, "Zoey, whatever decision you make, stay or go, you must factor in one thing. You are not going to be hurt as long as I am on the payroll. Period."

Armando glanced back at the crowd. Many of them were recording the scene with their phones—if they hadn't known who Zoey was when they pulled up, they certainly knew now.

He said, "Come on. We should go."

Zoey stared at the crowd. A little girl was sitting cross-legged at the base of one of the concrete columns, trying to pick through the vegetable stew for the parts she liked. Her older brother was standing over her, he had discarded the bread from his sandwich and rolled the cheese and meat into a tube he was trying to play like a horn.

Zoey turned and found Echo, who was already heading back to Will's fancy sports car, eager to get away from a situation that was about to turn ugly.

"Hey, Echo. How many pizzas would it take to feed the building?"

She stopped. "How many what?"

"Pizzas. It's Pizza Day in Squatterville. You want to come back to work for me? Well, this is your first job. Call Boselli's, and order enough pizzas to feed everybody here. And get me a Meatocalypse."

Echo scrunched her brow. "I'm not totally clear as to whether that second part is a separate request or if it's elaborating on the first. And there are over two thousand people in that building, you'd need seven hundred pizzas. That restaurant would need a week to—"

"Then you'll need to call multiple places, won't you? Figure it out."

Will said, "That's a nice gesture, but what those people need isn't pizza. They need real housing, and heat, and running water. And diapers, and doctors, and daycare. And job training. And those kids need to be in school."

Zoey nodded. "Right, right. Echo, are you writing all that down?"

Echo asked, "Are you serious or are you being sarcastic? I honestly can't tell."

"Dead serious."

"And do you have any concept of what that will cost?"

"Will it cost *less than a billion dollars*? Just do what you can and let me know if we run out of money."

Andre said, "Zoey, I think what those people need most of all is some condoms and a time machine."

Zoey said, "Congratulations, you're now partnering with Echo on the Squatterville charity."

Zoey rounded the sedan and opened the passenger door. A huge man approached from the crowd—the tattoo-headed guy, the one who had taken Will's wallet. The man had an expression of one headed for the guillotine. He held out the wallet to Will.

"Mr. Blackwater, I am—If I'd had any idea it was you, I'd have never have—"

"I know."

"You should have said somethin'. I thought you were one of them lawyers that are always comin' by. I would've never—"

"I know. Forget about it."

"Mr. Blackwater . . . I got a wife and two kids up there. And I don't know what they'd do if—"

"You're fine. Walk away."

Will headed back to his car, the man stood frozen, watching him go.

Zoey closed her door but by the time Armando started the sedan, the dam had broken on the crowd, as if seeing the bald guy approach one of the Suits had breached some invisible barrier that gave permission to the rest. They spilled out around the cars, led by a few instigators who were shouting and laughing, too drunk for a Friday afternoon. Armando rolled the sedan forward, then stopped, finding his path blocked.

Zoey asked, "What are they saying?"

"I'm going to take a wild guess and say they're asking for money."

"No. Listen."

They were chanting something. Zoey cracked a window, and heard dozens of people in the crowd shouting the same phrase, over and over:

"Say hi to your mom."

They were intentionally blocking the car now, hands on the hood, chanting at the windshield. Chanting at Zoey.

Armando said, "Roll up your window. We're going to do some crowd control."

"Don't run them over!"

He tapped some controls and an electronic voice boomed from the car, telling the crowd to disperse, and that countermeasures would be used if they refused. The crowd didn't react, everyone having fallen under that riot spell that convinces normal people to turn cars over and set them ablaze, invincible as long as they do it en masse. Armando punched another button and there was a hum, winding up in pitch. And then, the crowd was running. They slapped at their limbs as they fled, as if on fire.

"What did you do? What did you do to them?"

Armando hit the accelerator and the sedan charged through the now wide-open gap in the crowd.

"They're fine, it's a nonlethal microwave blast. Heats up the water in your skin, makes you feel like you're getting cooked from the inside. Just a little nudge, that's all."

"What was happening back there? Why were they chanting about my—"

And then the nearest hotel came into view, and Zoey was looking at her mother's boobs.

The building—and the one next to it, and the next one down—was carrying a Blink feed from someone sitting in the Zombie Quarantine bar in Fort

Drayton. They were at a table, peering over a pair of empty beer mugs, chatting up Melinda Ashe, in her waitress uniform that consisted of a pair of camouflage hotpants, gray zombie makeup, and nothing else. She was holding a tray and it was clear she was doing the fake laugh she did with customers to drive up tips (there was no audio on the feed, but Zoey could tell she was doing her giggle from the way she . . . bounced).

There was a scroll of text at the bottom that said, "ZOEY, SAY HI TO YOUR MOM."

Armando squinted at it. "Who's that?"

"That, Armando, is my mother. She's at work."

"Wait? Are you joking?"

"No."

"They must have hacked the skyline feed."

"Molech?"

"Or his fans."

Zoey tasted blood, and had to make herself stop biting her lip.

"Take me home. With a route that avoids the buildings. And tell Will and the rest I want to meet them there."

EIGHTEEN

Both of the other vehicles had beaten Zoey back to the Casa, since they weren't taking a circuitous route that avoided any tower carrying the skyline feed. Zoey stormed off the elevator in the library and Carlton told her he had seated everyone in the salon, which made Zoey think she would find Will and the rest sitting like old ladies under a row of hair dryers, but apparently that was the name for the fancy room with the fireplace and mounted buffalo head where she'd met everyone the night before. Armando trailed behind her as she flew through the door in a rage, meeting the gaze of Will, Andre, Budd, and Echo. A nearly identical scene to her arrival just twelve hours earlier, with the circumstances having changed radically.

"Is it still up? The feed?"

Echo said, "We got it down from the skyline, but the Blink is still live, and is very . . . popular. It's coming from one of Molech's men, in Fort Drayton. We think he got there a couple of hours ago."

"Stalking my mom. Where is he now? Is he still at the bar?"

"No. He's inside a house, it looks like."

Echo brought up the feed to play on the wall across from the buffalo head. The wearer of the camera was moving slowly and casually through a dirty living room, past a sofa that had been tortured with cat claws. Down a short hallway . . .

Zoey tried to breathe.

"That's my trailer."

Zoey tried to ignore the column of comment text streaming down the bar to the right of the screen, but she couldn't miss that same phrase repeated over and over: "SAY HI TO YOUR MOM." It was a Team Molech meme.

Will said, "We have to stay calm, here. This isn't about your mother, this is about you, and getting your attention."

The person wearing the camera was lazily browsing around the trailer, picking up framed photos, making a point of touching everything. Acting like he owned the place. He stopped by the kitchen and started eating from a package of Oreos. He continued down a hall and arrived at a room at the end—Zoey's bedroom.

Zoey bit her lip again.

"And we can't . . . block this somehow? Cut off his feed from the rest of the world?"

"No. You can jam a device if it's close to the source, but you can't just pick a feed and cut it off."

The man with the camera knew he had found her bedroom, and was freely poking around her meager possessions. He went to the chest of drawers, opened each one, and then found the underwear drawer on the bottom. Over the next five excruciating minutes, Zoey and her new employees watched a stranger slowly pick through her bras and panties, then arrange them on the floor to spell the word "GOLD."

Then he added an exclamation point to the end, in the form of Zoey's pink vibrator.

The fans in the comment stream were going wild.

Zoey closed her eyes and was pretty sure she was going to be sick this time.

Will said, "I know it's difficult to see the, uh, positive in this, but whatever the 'gold' is, it's something Molech wants, and something he thinks we can give him. That's actually a good thing: it means we have a bargaining chip. Now what should happen next is—"

Zoey's phone rang. It was her mother.

"Mom! Are you okay?"

"Hi, baby! Can you hear me, it's noisy in here. We're getting six inches of snow today, are you guys getting anything out there?"

"Mom, do you have any idea—"

"I can't hear you, babe, they got the music way up. Hey I got a message from a guy who came in, he said he couldn't get through to you so asked if I'd pass it along."

Zoey's mouth went dry.

"What was it?"

"Hold on I wrote it down. Can you hear me? He says he's going to be at Arthur's memorial service tomorrow, and for you to meet him there. He says to bring the gold."

Zoey closed her eyes.

"You there, Z?"

"Got it. It's . . . it's just more stuff about the arrangements. It's no big deal."

"I can't hear you, Z. I'm gonna go, have fun at your thing tomorrow."

The line was dead before Zoey could even say good-bye.

Zoey started dialing again.

Will asked, "Who are you calling?"

"The cops. Our cops. We still have those where I'm from."

"Zoey. Think it through. You call Fort Drayton and tell them your mother is being stalked, and they'll send out one of their patrol cars to drive past your trailer once every couple of hours. That's it. And even if they dedicated every single officer they had on the payroll, would they be sufficient to protect your mother, knowing what we know about Molech's henchmen, and what their capabilities are?"

"*So what the hell do we do?*"

"We calm down and figure it out. Together. Assuming we have our jobs back."

"Consider this your tryout period. Your interview involves finding Molech and crushing him like a grape."

"Then I suggest we adjourn to the conference room."

Candi blinked into the room and everyone jumped. In her bubbly voice she said, "We have a visitor at the front gate and, ooh, it looks like he's been doing squats!"

A voice said it was the delivery from Boselli's, and Armando volunteered to just go accept it at the gate this time.

Andre said, "Bet you feel silly for almost buying pizza for those people back there."

"What do you mean, 'almost'?" Zoey spun on Echo. "Have you not ordered the Squatterville pizzas yet?"

"For . . . the people who swarmed your car and screamed veiled threats about your mother?"

"*Yes,*" she said, as they filed out of the room. "What is it with rich people thinking they can starve the poor into good behavior?"

They headed down to the Mold door and this time it opened at Zoey's touch—the mansion's security system had apparently been set to answer entirely to Zoey, the whole thing having switched over automatically as part of the terms of Arthur's will. Not much had registered about the conference room when Zoey had been there the night before, other than the strange schematics on the wall monitors to her left and the severed hand that had been sitting on the table. Some thoughtful person had put the hand away since then, and she wondered where it had gone, but then saw a red cooler marked "BIOHAZARD" on the floor and figured it was in there. That would be a helpful detail to remember for when she had nightmares about it later.

The center of the room was dominated by a long wooden table, its varnish ruined by cigarette burns and coffee cup stains. Surrounding the table were five well-worn leather rolling chairs. The wall to her right held a corkboard with dozens of photos pinned to it—mostly dead bodies, most having suffered gruesome injuries. At the opposite end of the room was a refrigerator and a counter with a coffee machine nestled behind a mountain range of piled junk food. Next to it was an open door that led to a bathroom. The toilet seat was up. The whole room smelled of ancient coffee and the ghosts of cigars.

Music filled the room—it faded the moment Will walked through the door, his personalized theme, apparently. It was a man singing about how he'd like to hear some funky Dixieland. The Suits fanned into the room and guided themselves to their designated chairs, all landing simultaneously, like four billiard balls rolling into their holes after a trick shot. The Suits, back to work, doing what they did. Well, not quite—the chair at the end of the table remained empty. Zoey decided she would just stand.

She nodded toward the bathroom and said to Echo, "You ever fall in that toilet?"

"I would never use that bathroom, it's disgusting."

Will waited for the music to fade, then surveyed the room, seeming to . . . *come alive*, somehow. His people, picking up where they'd left off.

"All right, let's tally up the score so far. Zoey, you didn't warn your mother she was being stalked. I take it to mean you don't think she's resourceful enough to slip away on her own?"

Zoey shook her head. "I wouldn't have put it exactly like that, but . . . she'd go and try to reason with the guy or something. Or just call a boyfriend to come protect her. Whatever she did, it would make things worse. Can we send somebody?"

"That's an option, but you wouldn't want to send one guy, you'd want to send a team. And they don't know who the stalker is or what he looks like. Or even if it's a he."

Budd said, "It is. Had man-hands, saw them when he was rooting through Zoey's unmentionables. Had a wedding ring, but no wristwatch. White guy, not much body hair, probably not Italian or Greek . . ."

Zoey said, "So what, we're just helpless? Molech can just say the word at any moment and his guy kills my mother five seconds later?"

Will said, "Yes, but you should be asking yourself why he hasn't done that yet. It's not conscience—it's because there's something he wants from you, apparently very badly, and the mother killing thing is a card he can only play once. So that means we now have two cards in *our* hand—the fact that we have something Molech wants, and that we know exactly where Molech is going to be tomorrow night."

Armando appeared at the door with a pizza box. Andre sprang to his feet and said, "It could be poison!" He took a piece and started eating it as he headed calmly back toward his chair. He chewed and said, "Nah, it's fine."

Zoey leaned against the wall with an eighth of a Meatocalypse in her hand and said, "So just to be clear—we don't even know who Molech is, right?"

Echo pointed to the corkboard behind Zoey. "That pretty much sums it up."

A series of photos were pinned together in a pattern, like the Suits had been trying to trace the members of a criminal organization the way detectives did on old cop shows. Only here there was no pyramid-shaped structure to mark levels of lieutenants and made men, just a row of crazy-looking people—many of them dead or dismembered—with one single picture above them. It was a black photo with a white question mark, with "Molech" scrawled below it.

Zoey said, "I take it he doesn't walk around dressed as a giant question mark."

Echo said, "I think that would cause trademark issues."

Andre said, "He's been playin' up the mysterious angle since he hit the scene, wants us to think of him as something larger than life. Mystical. Keeping us in the dark about what his capabilities are, or aren't. We've been working it, but he's the most Blink-savvy player we've ever dealt with. Always keeping the name out there, never showing the face."

Budd said, "Now, men like that, we've found they usually don't stay in the shadows forever, they get to where they crave the spotlight. But when this guy decides to go public, I'm thinkin' he'll do it in a way that's spectacular. And I mean spectacular in the bad way, like a collision between a fuel tanker and a school bus."

Zoey swallowed pizza and said, "Well, we've been told the memorial service tomorrow is going to be crashed by a guy who controls an army of mentally ill people with wizard powers. That sounds pretty spectacular."

Will said, "And do you understand why he's going through this whole dog-and-pony show, rather than just sending a thug to threaten you with a shotgun the next time you go out to get the mail?"

"He wants an audience."

"Now you're getting it. There'll be several thousand people at the memorial tomorrow, and probably a hundred times as many watching it via Blink. Now that the threat of a spectacular assassination taking place has been made—and trust me, he'll make sure word gets out—you can multiply *that* number by a hundred. Big showdown, heiress versus supervillain."

"Wait, are we talking like I'm actually going to go to this thing?"

Will, without breaking eye contact with Zoey, asked the room, "How hard would it be to get a Zoey lookalike?"

Budd said, "You're talkin' about an assassination double? It'll cost us, but we could find someone who passes."

Will, still looking at Zoey, nodded and said, "Yeah, lots of desperate people in this city. Go out to the trailer parks outside town, find a girl with the same build. You'll surely find someone happy to take the risk, for the money."

Zoey said, "Ugh, you are *the devil*. You know that? You are the literal devil. All right, I'll go to the memorial service. I'll act as bait for the magical sociopath who wants me dead."

Will said, "I was suggesting no such thing. It would be extremely dangerous for you to go yourself. Besides, with the kind of wealth you have now, you shouldn't have to take those kinds of risks. Not when there are plenty of impoverished women who would gladly—"

"Stop. Shut up. Just . . . pour some more scotch in your mouth, whatever it takes to make the words stop. I'm going. Better than just spending the rest of my life looking over my shoulder. Let's just do it and end this, one way or the other."

She turned toward Armando. "Is there any hope at all of keeping me safe during something like that?"

"As safe as anyone can be, doing what you are about to do."

Andre said, "You'll have help."

Zoey said, "So . . . is this just the type of thing you people do?"

Will said, "You mean staging elaborate traps for psychopaths, just to see what happens? All so we can get a look at their strengths and weaknesses, at tremendous danger to everyone in the vicinity? Yes, actually. With some regularity."

He turned and tapped the wall monitor. An overhead view of a patch of land appeared on the screen.

"Here's the park. Echo, we're going to start running down hardware, there's a lot of open perimeter here—that part is going to be an all-nighter for both of us. Budd, start vetting hired guns, work with Armando on that. Andre, you're already on party preparations. But of course, a lot of your hard work has just gone out the window, you have to completely rethink where you're channeling the crowds. The whole shape of this situation has changed substantially in the last few minutes or so. Don't plan on much sleep."

Andre grabbed another slice of pizza and said, "Now *there's* an understatement. I mean on top of everything else, we got to get Zoey something to wear."

NINETEEN

That night, Zoey dreamed about Jezza.

The dreams weren't an uncommon occurrence over the last eight years, dating back to when Zoey was in high school. She and her mother had lived in an apartment in a public housing complex, a cramped two-bedroom place with sticky linoleum floors and walls that smelled like old grease. But by far the worst thing about the place was that none of the interior doors locked—not the bathroom, not her bedroom. Zoey had never understood how fundamentally she had relied on the ability to lock out the rest of the world until Jezza Lewis had moved in with them during her freshman year.

Jezza was her mother's boyfriend at the time, a sleazy British guy whose hobby was "accidentally" walking in on Zoey every chance he got. On the toilet, in the shower, when she was changing. He wouldn't do it every time— she'd be safe for a week, or a month. It was just often enough that it was always lurking in the back of her mind. And then, during some vulnerable moment, he'd burst through the door, playing it off like a hilarious faux pas (because *hey, we're all just family here, right?*), then he'd get a good look before he backed out. Zoey had told her mother, who had just laughed and talked about how one day they'd get a bigger place with two bathrooms and locks on the doors, and how Jezza was getting more and more DJ work all the time.

The whole thing ended when, one day, Zoey stepped into the bathroom to take a shower and immediately noticed cracks in the plastic housing of the ventilation fan in the ceiling—like somebody had messed with the fan but was too stupid to know how to get the cover off without breaking it. She figured there was a better than even chance that there was now a little wireless camera up there, because she had been expecting Jezza to do something like this and that was the only spot to hide a camera that could see down past the shower curtain. That meant that everything she was doing was likely being fed wirelessly to Jezza's ancient laptop, the same one he used to play music at his DJ shows while he stood there and flapped his arms around as if the computer wasn't doing all of the work.

Zoey could have waited until her mother got home and then showed her the camera, or she could have stood up on the toilet and ripped the thing out of the ceiling. She could have done a lot of things. Instead, she undressed and took her shower. She took her time, and dried herself off slowly. Then she got dressed, found the laptop to confirm her suspicions, then called the police. Zoey was fourteen, which meant the video file on Jezza's laptop was child pornography. Jezza had two prior offenses, surprise surprise, which explained why he had such a strong reaction when he realized what Zoey had done.

She still had the scars.

When the cops dragged him away, Jezza swore he would come back and find Zoey, and finish making her pay. He described his payback in graphic detail—it was clearly something he had spent considerable time thinking about.

Six days later, someone at Zoey's school found the shower video on the Internet—it had been a live feed, it turned out—and within twenty-four hours, every single one of her classmates had seen it. A week later would mark the first and only time Zoey tried to commit suicide. She swallowed a bottle of over-the-counter sleeping pills, but vomited them back up after she passed out.

Regardless of his gruesome promises, Zoey had never seen Jezza again. Outside of her nightmares, that is. In her sleep, he visited her time and time again, magically appearing at her most helpless moments. Yanking back a shower curtain, ripping off a blanket, swapping in his body for Caleb's halfway through a sex dream.

This particular time she dreamed she was back home, sleeping on her futon, and woke up to see him looming inches over her with his stupid, greedy eyes and hot garbage breath. And once again Zoey felt those hands clamp down. His impossible strength, just as she'd felt it that day in the kitchen when he came after her, the sounds of muffled sirens in the distance. Until then, she hadn't known a human could be that strong—this scrawny little tattooed

DJ, crushing her under his hands, amped up with a power that courses through every predator upon the sight of quivering prey.

He grinned a grin so wide it threatened to sever his face and said, "Come back off the ice, sweetie."

Zoey's eyes snapped open and she found she was alone, in the tomb-silent guest room, Stench Machine busily licking himself at the foot of the bed. She sat up and pulled on her jeans and decided she needed to get out of this room. She headed out into the hall with Stench Machine in tow, trying to decide if her situation had gotten better or worse since she had done the exact same thing about twenty-four hours ago. She thumped down the stairs and upon sight of the massive bronze doors, she thought, *just go.*

She would be able to, this time. The mansion's security system listened to her now. She could stroll right out, across the grounds and through the front gate. She could walk to a Mercedes dealership and drive off with a luxury car to take her back to Colorado. Sure, it was the middle of the night, but she was rich—she could probably just take one and leave a note telling them to put it on her tab. The next day they'd send her a bouquet and a card apologizing for not being open.

But then, for the rest of her life, she would be right back where she was at fourteen, in that place without locking doors. Always waiting for some monster to come smashing in after her.

She arbitrarily decided to head right, through the arched doorway to the East Wing, the same way she'd gone the night before. Might as well get a look at the house she owned. She found that a lot of the first floor seemed to be dedicated to entertaining guests—in addition to the dining room and kitchen she'd already seen, she found a movie theater, featuring twenty leather recliners and a professional popcorn machine. The most impressive thing about that room, she thought, was that it had clearly been *used.* Having your own movie theater sounds like the kind of gaudy feature a rich person demands in their mansion and then never sets foot in, since it's not like you can't just kick back on the sofa and stream a movie to the wall, or your phone, or your glasses. But this room smelled of cooking oil and artificial butter and cigars, and the seats looked worn, several bearing stains and cigar burns. There were scuffs on the seat backs, where guests in the rear row had casually propped their feet up. She saw people relaxing, laughing, eating popcorn. Movie Night at the Livingston Place.

Next door to the theater was a room that had been turned into a massive ball pit, like they have at Chuck E. Cheese, about twenty feet by twenty feet of plastic balls that were chest-deep on Zoey when she dove in. When she climbed out a half hour later, she found that across the hall was a room with padded floors and walls full of harmless fighting gear—foam batons and overstuffed boxing gloves. The entire floor was a black mesh, and Zoey almost fell over when she tried to step on it. It was bouncy—the whole floor was a trampoline. A lot of the gear in the room was little kid–size, and Zoey immediately pictured a dozen adults all retiring to the theater to watch a movie over beer and popcorn, while everybody's kids went and screamed their heads off in the play areas.

Farther down the hall, in a private area around a bend, there was a black-tiled room with a massive Jacuzzi in the center, surrounded by live plants to give it a jungle feel (at least half of the foliage was hemp), and a waterfall along one wall. There was a wet bar at floor level along the Jacuzzi, so you wouldn't even have to get out to get yourself a drink. A woman's bathing suit top was still draped over one brass rail.

An invitation to Arthur Livingston's estate didn't mean black ties and cocktails, Zoey realized. People had the time of their lives here.

She doubled back to the foyer and headed up the stairs, past the buffalo room. The rest of the second floor seemed to be mostly bedrooms. Some of them had personal items and toiletries lying around, stuff she assumed belonged to frequent guests who knew they'd be back. People who hadn't known that the last time was in fact the last time, people who no doubt had been crushed by the news about Arthur. A whole constellation of friends and acquaintances that Zoey could barely comprehend. She had fifteen contacts in her phone and nine of them were friends and family of Caleb's, people who if she tried to call them, would see her number and roll their eyes before sending it to voice mail. Arthur could summon twice as many within five minutes, any time he didn't feel like watching a movie alone.

She was headed back toward the West Wing when she ran across a life-sized statue of Arthur Livingston, set back into the wall of the second-floor hallway. Zoey actually laughed out loud—the statue depicted Arthur with a walking stick, one leg raised onto a mound of earth, as if he was in the process of scaling a mountain. The statue had an elaborate mustache, just as she saw Arthur wearing in his hologram, and close inspection revealed that it had been added later—she could see the tiny welds where it had been attached to his upper lip, and it wasn't as tarnished as the rest. Zoey wondered if some poor artist would have had to come cut the facial hair off the statue again if the real Arthur had lived long enough to shave his.

Etched into the base of the statue were five words: There Is Always a Way.

As she was reading it, a mechanism clicked and scraped and the statue slowly rotated away, revealing a staircase that went straight up. Zoey didn't even realize the house had a third floor.

She cautiously climbed the stairs, half expecting to find a torture dungeon, or piles and piles of cocaine. Instead, she found a master bedroom, another space haunted by the ghosts of ancient cigars. The first thing that registered was that there was a car parked in the middle of the room. The second was that it was raining outside this room, and *only* this room.

The car, it turned out, was a grown-up version of the little plastic race car beds that kids have, only this one was made from an actual car, some kind of old-timey, very expensive-looking sports car that had the entire middle cut out and replaced with a king-size mattress. It had real tires and everything. As for the rain, Zoey moved over to the one giant bay window that overlooked a courtyard she also didn't even know was there until that moment. Raindrops were drumming against the glass with a perfect soothing, sleepy rhythm. There was a brass switch near the window, and when she hit it, the rain stopped. It was some kind of sprinkler device outside, supplying an instant lazy, rainy day with the flip of a switch.

Zoey wandered around the dead man's room, feeling like she was intruding. One wall was dominated by framed photographs—Arthur Livingston with the president, Arthur Livingston with a player from the Utah Jazz, Arthur Livingston at a casino with an old guy in a suit who Zoey didn't know but was sure she had seen on the news. There were dozens of these pictures—Arthur and famous people, Arthur in tuxedoes, Arthur demonstrating what a big shot he was. Under the photos was the obligatory wet bar and in the corner next to it was a punching bag—well-used, with a pair of gloves hanging on a nail nearby. Next to it was a massive bookcase full of antique, leather-bound volumes, all of the classics of literature. Zoey went to pull one of them from the shelf, and found they were all glued in place.

There was a vanity topped with bottles of aftershave and a single comb with a few loose gray hairs woven through. There was a narrow door to a surprisingly small bathroom with an old-fashioned tub and sink with brass fixtures, a lone toothbrush lying on the counter. Zoey had to force herself not to wonder where exactly Arthur's teeth were right now. On the opposite wall from the bathroom was an identical door that Zoey assumed led to a closet, but when she stepped through it she was suddenly in a Brooks Brothers store—the "closet" was an entire separate room, packed with suits. There had to have been five hundred suits on the racks covering the walls. At least. In the corner was a pedestal and mirrors for fitting—altogether, more floor space dedicated to the "closet" than the entire bedroom.

Zoey turned back to the bedroom and it registered with her that the room looked rumpled and harried—drawers partially open, some clothes tossed onto the floor, a box of old letters having been pulled out from under the bed and rifled through. The room had been ransacked, though gently and respectfully. Arthur's own people had surely done this, of course, in the frantic search for the "key" immediately after his death.

Zoey heard footsteps on the stairwell and froze, actually having a ridiculous moment when she frantically looked around for a place to hide. But of course this was her master bedroom now—she could squat and pee on the floor and nobody could say a word.

Armando appeared in the door and said, "There you are. I thought you were in bed, then I heard you laughing at something. Did you know this was up here?"

"No, I just stumbled across it. I couldn't sleep, so I figured I might as well take a look at my house before it winds up getting bequeathed to somebody else after I die tomorrow."

"So that's how it is? You're going to insult my bodyguard skills right to my face?"

"Sorry. If it makes you feel better I'm sure you'll also die, trying to save me."

Zoey went and sat on the ridiculous race car bed. On the nightstand next to it was an antique-looking bronze Buddha figurine that looked like it was in the process of blessing an ashtray full of cigar butts. There was a half-empty water glass, sitting on top of a Christmas card from somebody named Gary that had been used as a coaster. She pulled open the top drawer. Aspirin. Antacids. Chapstick. Reading glasses. A revolver.

Zoey asked, "You have any problems with the plan tomorrow? Me acting as bait?"

"Well . . . you know I can't just shoot Molech on sight, right? Tabula Rasa is lawless but not *that* lawless. But we're going to staff up the event, make sure that if he does make a move, we're there."

"I thought you'd tell me to stay home."

"That's actually the one thing I can't ever tell a client. Personal security would be an easy job if we could just make the client stay indoors."

Zoey pushed the drawer closed and something just happened to catch her eye, in the split second when the shadows fell over the contents inside: a tiny, blue pinprick of light, at the corner of the reading glasses.

Zoey opened the drawer again, studied the glasses, and then put them on.

She expected nothing—maybe an empty inbox floating over her field of vision, figuring the glasses were an unused gift from a younger friend or girlfriend that Arthur had tossed in a drawer and forgotten. Instead, a burst of code flew down the screen, appearing to her eyes to be scrolling down from the ceiling. Then the room disappeared, as Zoey's vision went black. A line of white text appeared in front of her:

"Welcome, Zoey."

TWENTY

Suddenly Zoey was looking down at the city from above, through a filthy window. The camera was recording from inside a helicopter, judging by the thwupping noise that drowned out all other sound. A timestamp at the bottom showed it had been recorded more than fourteen months ago, the night of October 4 of the previous year.

A hand came into view and glanced at a watch that seemed to have been crafted from about six pounds of gold. The view panned around from a side window to the windshield, where Livingston Tower was growing larger on the horizon. On this particular night the tower was a screaming shade of purple, rather than the dour flat black Zoey had seen in person. The color wasn't a paint job—the screens that covered the tower's surface blasted it in every direction, casting a royal shade across the neighboring buildings and the street below.

Zoey heard Armando say, "You all right? What's happening—"

"Quiet. There's video. In the glasses."

She watched the helicopter shakily descend toward what from the air seemed like a miniscule landing pad atop the glowing purple tower, and Zoey decided then and there she did not want to be a helicopter pilot when she grew up. The aircraft finally jolted to a stop on the rooftop and the wearer of the camera hopped down from the passenger side, then turned and watched the helicopter abandon him there, softly thwupping away into the distance until the only sound was the soft rustle of wind. The view panned around again and found that not far from the helipad was a man sitting in a wheelchair. Crouching calmly next to him was a chimpanzee, wearing a pair of sunglasses. The wearer of the camera advanced on the pair.

The man in the wheelchair—an Indian man in his forties—said, "Glad you could make it, Mr. Livingston." As Zoey had already guessed, she was seeing the world through the eyes of Arthur, as if she had gone back to inhabit his body, a living person possessing a ghost. "I am Rupert Singh. Please put on these goggles."

The man held out a pair of black welding googles and Zoey noticed this was actually what she was seeing on the face of the bored-looking chimp sitting next to the wheelchair, rather than sunglasses. She was mildly disappointed. The chimp was picking its nose and looking around, as if trying to figure out why the night was so much darker than usual.

The camera panned around and found that, across from them on the roof stood three department store mannequins, wearing military uniforms for some reason, complete with heavy bulletproof vests. Zoey wondered if the guy in the wheelchair—Singh, he said his name was—had set those up, or if the chimp had done it. It couldn't have been easy either way.

The camera looked back and forth from the mannequins to the chimp and Arthur Livingston's voice said, "I'm not making it off this rooftop alive, am I?"

He wasn't serious. The man in the wheelchair, Singh, laughed. "I am an engineer, Mr. Livingston, and one who is paralyzed from the waist down at that. Besides, murdering you would be somewhat detrimental to my goal of getting you to invest fifty million dollars in my project."

"You have five minutes, Mr. Singh. I do not enjoy having my time wasted."

"I watch the news, Mr. Livingston. You love having your time wasted. As long as it is wasted in a way that amuses you."

"Yeah, that's true."

"Put on the goggles, please. They are for your own protection."

Arthur took the goggles and put them on, but they didn't blot out the view from the Blink camera—Zoey deduced that this meant what she was watching had been recorded from a device other than the eyeglasses. One that was, presumably, more easily hidden—she got the sense no one else in the world knew this recording existed.

Singh muttered a command at the chimpanzee in a language Zoey didn't understand, and the primate waddled about halfway up to where the three army mannequins were standing, the chimp stopping about twenty feet away from where Arthur and Singh were watching. Singh pulled out a little control pad about the size of a phone, and tapped the screen. The chimp extended his right arm—or rather, the arm was extended for him, as if Singh was controlling the limb remotely.

Singh tapped the screen again.

There was a flash so bright that it blinded the camera, and a clap of thunder.

The chimp hooted and screeched.

When the camera was able to focus again, it found that the mannequin on the far right was now a handful of smoking chunks of black melted plastic. The chimp looked mildly confused.

Singh said, "Impressed, Mr. Livingston?"

"I . . . think I need some context for what I just saw there."

"That, Mr. Livingston, is your tax dollars at work. You're looking at the result of over twenty billion dollars in research and development by your Department of Defense."

"To make a weaponized monkey? Or just a lightning gun? Because I'm not seeing the practical applications of either, to be frank."

The chimpanzee had now sat down, and was looking at its right hand curiously, as if impressed by his own talents. Zoey wondered just how heavily the animal had been sedated. Singh tapped his control pad again and began his presentation.

"Let me ask you, Mr. Livingston—what separates a man from a god? What stops you or I from smashing a boulder with our fists, or turning a building to cinders with our eyes?"

Arthur clearly thought this was a rhetorical question, but Singh waited for an answer.

"Um, we're not powerful enough? I guess?"

"Power is an abstract concept. A politician has power. The word you are looking for is 'energy.' If you can store and release enough energy, all is possible. Limitations in energy storage is the only reason, for instance, that you cannot fly without a bulky aircraft around you, or that we cannot build a ship that can traverse the galaxy. Even if we can build an engine small enough for the task, the fuel—that is, the stored energy—adds too much weight, and bulk. Do you follow me so far, Mr. Livingston?"

Arthur, in a tone that made it clear he was ready for the man in the wheelchair to get to the point, said, "So this is about . . . batteries or something?"

Singh forced a smile, impatient with the rich douche who wasn't appreciating the marvel that lay before him.

"This is about the next step in human evolution, Mr. Livingston. You see, several years ago, something radical fell into the lap of your government. An eccentric Russian defector named Resnov appeared one day with a prototype device he called an exoquantum hypercapacitor, which you may recognize as a name that is made up of two nonsense words. He claimed the energy density of the device approached infinity. You may recognize infinity as a thing that cannot actually be 'approached.' He promised it could turn a man into a god. You may recognize that as a claim made almost exclusively by charlatans and the insane. Yet, despite all of this, the Defense Advanced Research Projects Agency devoted billions in black project money to develop the technology for military applications. I was one of the researchers brought in for what Resnov insisted we call Project Raiden."

Livingston said, "After the Shinto god of Thunder."

"After some character in an old video game—note that Resnov was fifteen years old, and mildly autistic. DARPA's directive was to develop the power source and create new weapons systems around it. But Resnov had higher ambitions. He had no interest in building new weapons. He wanted to build new *men*. He steered his designs toward devices that could be grafted onto bone, woven through muscle. Devices that could power a man to do, well, *anything*. All hidden from his superiors at DARPA, of course."

"Why hide it? Sounds like that's the kind of thing they'd love. Soldiers who can fly and punch tanks in half? That's what we're talking about, right?"

"You have not thought it through, Mr. Livingston. A boy grows up, he enlists in the army, they hand him a gun. He fights the war, or doesn't, and then he gives back the gun and comes home to become a mechanic, or farmer, or criminal. A soldier, in other words, is just a man, doing a job. With Raiden, there is no putting down the gun—the man *becomes* the gun. Think about the relationship between the man—or men—who possess these powers, and those who do not, knowing what they are now capable of. At that point you are no longer talking about a new weapon. You are talking about a new *species*. A dominant one."

"But either way, you had this stuff working, right? So why are you talking to me, and why doesn't the army have death rays that can do to the Chinese what you just did to that mannequin there?"

"I shall allow Cornelius up there to explain."

Zoey actually tensed up in anticipation of the chimp turning around and talking to the camera, but that didn't happen. Instead, Singh tapped on his control pad again and told Arthur to put on his goggles.

The chimp raised his right hand once more, the lightning flew from his palm, and once more a mannequin was obliterated—this time it was vaporized, not even chunks remaining in the aftermath. As if he had turned up the power.

Singh tapped his controls again.

The chimp raised his arm a third time—

There was a blast that sent Arthur and his camera reeling. The view whipped around the rooftop, and when it focused again the last mannequin stood unharmed—but Cornelius the chimpanzee was nothing but a smoldering stain on the rooftop.

Zoey heard Arthur say, *"Christ."*

Singh stuffed his control pad into a shirt pocket and said, "Resnov's design was highly unstable. We spent seven years trying to stabilize it until, finally, there was an incident in which one of the devices exploded, killing eleven people, including Resnov. Much of the research he left behind was utterly incomprehensible. Soon, the Department of Defense got wind of his more . . . *unconventional* prototypes and quickly pulled funding."

"And you decided to sneak some designs out the door to see what the highest bidder would pay for god powers."

Singh shifted in his chair, not liking the way his whole enterprise had been boiled down to such crude terms.

"Mr. Livingston, as a man of science, I am not willing to give up on what I consider to be, not just the most important invention of all time, but the single greatest leap in human evolution since the species gained the capacity for conscious thought. I got out with six hundred gigabytes of schematics and hardware drivers. We could plug them into a nano-capable fabricator and, in minutes, start building working prototypes."

"That turn the user into a splatter of pulled pork when they fail."

"I can fix Raiden. I know I can. The flaw is in the software that stabilizes the capacitor, I was working on a fix when the project was shut down. I was *close*, Mr. Livingston. I believe if I still had access to the right facilities I would have done it by now. But I lack the facilities, because I lack the funds. So I am seeking out a partner with, let us say, an excess of funds."

"And if the government finds out you're doing this . . ."

"They will kill me, and everyone I showed Raiden to."

"Gee, thanks."

"I assure you, I have many bidders waiting, Mr. Livingston."

"You have many bidders who have fifty million dollars on hand to throw at an illegal weapon project that may not even work?"

"Yes."

"So you're talking about underground arms dealers, right? Guys who want to buy this up and sell it to third-world dictators and terrorists?"

"I also have Russian mobsters, cartel bosses, Cambodian insurgents, and Sub-Saharan African warlords. And one real estate tycoon who is most well known for showing up pantsless to the groundbreaking ceremony for his own casino. So you must understand, Mr. Livingston, that at this point I am as curious as you. I know what those other men want to use Raiden for. The fact that I don't know what you want it for actually makes me more nervous."

"Who's to say I don't just want to keep it out of the hands of those other men? Maybe I don't want a world full of flying superterrorists who can rip airliners to pieces with their bare hands."

"That is a lot to pay for a clean conscience."

"A clean conscience is expensive, it's the reason most men have to live paycheck to paycheck."

"So you are saying you're offering to pay me the money to *not* finish my research? Your goal is to bury it?"

"I didn't say that. I'll get you your facility. I'll get you the nano-whatever fabricators. Whatever you need."

"And when I get it all working, what happens then?"

"That's my business. Who knows, maybe I want to implant all this stuff, put on a cape, and go fight crime."

TWENTY-ONE

The feed went to black and Zoey started to take off the glasses. Armando asked her what the hell was going on, but another video started and she shushed him once more.

The date on this recording was about two months ago. The feed picked up inside a moving car, rolling through downtown Tabula Ra$a. Will Blackwater was behind the wheel, and the camera had started recording him in mid-sentence.

"... I guess a lot of them got moldy in storage, they're all canvas you know, and the Tenth Street warehouse flooded last spring. They're fine, they just smell bad. They'll air out by Halloween."

Arthur, who once again was unseen behind the camera, said, "And the snow, you get that all lined out?"

"Had to reserve five more machines from a resort in Park City for some obscene amount of money, but yes it's all a go. Echo has the running itemization if you want to check out what this is costing you."

"Why would I ever want to do that?"

And then, Will did something Zoey had never seen him do in the couple of days she had known him: he smiled. Will cranked the wheel and shifted into park, driving the car the old-fashioned way. They had arrived, but the camera's viewing angle didn't make it clear where they were.

Arthur said, "You do a good job, Will. All of you do. I don't say it enough."

"Yes, when it comes to party planning, you probably won't find three, four billion people in the world better at it than me."

"You know what I mean, smart-ass. I appreciate what you guys do, just, day to day."

There was a silence that Will seemed uncomfortable with. Finally he said, "That's Singh's car, right? Are we waiting for somebody else?"

"Just goin' over the game plan in my head. I need to relax, I didn't do my yoga this morning."

Will laughed. Some kind of private joke between them.

"Here," said Arthur, "do the thing with the coin."

Arthur's hand came into frame, palming the one-sided "lucky" coin Arthur had made a point of leaving to Zoey. Will took it and showed it to the camera, holding it between finger and thumb. He passed his other hand in front of it, and it was gone. He held up both hands like a magician, showing they were empty, the coin nowhere to be found.

"Amazing. Even knowing how you do it, I can't see you do it."

Will, without cracking a smile, reached down the front of his pants and produced the coin.

Arthur laughed and said, "Jesus, I don't want it back now. That was never part of the trick before, letting it touch your balls. If I'd known that, I'd just given you a regular quarter." Will kept offering it back and Arthur said, "No, no! It's all yours now."

"It didn't touch my balls, Art, it was hidden in my hand. That's the trick."

"Still . . . I want you to keep it. Seriously."

Will's face froze. He wasn't touched by this gesture, or amused, or grateful. His eyes were watching Arthur carefully, unblinking. Trying to read the man.

"Art . . . what's going on?"

"Don't make a big deal of it. The whole lucky coin bit, it was always a silly affectation. I'm not even superstitious, you know that. It was just a conversation starter. I can't even do tricks with it, not like you. You keep it: make up an interesting backstory. Tell girls in bars that you got it off a soldier in Korea or something. Then do that magic trick and you'll hear panties dropping from across the room."

Another pause. Those blue eyes watching: the brain behind them running through scenarios.

Finally, Will said, "Why don't I come with you?"

"We're not having that conversation again. Singh demanded confidentiality on this thing and I don't want to spook him. As soon as we have a working device we can take to market, trust me, you'll be the first to see a demonstration.

As for this, it's probably nothing. He called in a bit of a panic, but Singh panics over everything. He's always paranoid the government is gonna finally come after him."

"Are they?"

"I'll see you back at the house. And stop worrying. Life's too short."

The camera tracked with Arthur as he stood up and closed the door of the car—Zoey saw it was Will's Astin Martin—and a warehouse came into view as Arthur turned to face it. Presumably this was the building as it had existed before the mysterious event that turned it into a charred crater. He took several steps toward a back door and dug into his front pocket for a set of keys, but when his hand emerged, it was holding his lucky coin—Will having slipped it back to him at some point, using some bit of sleight of hand. Arthur barked out a laugh. He turned to see the Astin Martin's taillights vanishing around a corner.

The feed cut to black, then a split second later, Zoey thought the glasses were just glasses again—the view was of the bedroom, as seen from right where she was sitting. But there was still a date stamp hovering in the corner, marked as having been recorded ten days ago, and the room was no longer in disarray. She was just watching a feed that had been recorded from the very spot where she was watching it.

Zoey flinched as a hand came up into view, as if she had a phantom limb. The hand was holding Arthur's lucky coin. The other hand came into view and he tried to do Will's magic trick. The coin tumbled into Arthur's lap.

Arthur's voice said, "I hope I've done this right. If I'm heading toward, well, what I think I'm heading to, then there's a better than even chance this will be my last day. And that's okay, because if I do this right, I'll spend this last day saving the world. Granted, I'll be saving it from something I myself unleashed, so you know, don't build any monuments to me for it." He let out a long breath and said, "All right, no speeches. Let's just do it."

The view jumped inside a cavernous building, which Zoey assumed was the warehouse she'd previously only seen from the outside. Arthur strolled between rows of tall metal shelves, three stories of bags and boxes and barrels looming overhead. He passed a row of dormant forklifts plugged into wall chargers, before finally arriving at a utility closet full of janitor supplies. He issued a voice command that caused the back wall of the closet to slide open, revealing an elevator. Arthur went down one floor, then down a hall and through a full body scan security airlock—the scanner between a series of steel doors thick enough to blunt a nuclear warhead. This, Zoey realized, was the real warehouse. Everything above it was camouflage.

When the final door rumbled open, Arthur was greeted by a massive bloodstain that covered the concrete floor.

Zoey heard a sigh from Arthur. Saddened by what he was about to see, but not surprised.

He stepped cautiously around the crimson stain and the view panned over to see a toppled wheelchair that was also soaked in blood, tossed against one wall. Arthur found Singh's legs jutting out from behind a crate, then the view panned around again and found Singh's torso sprawled behind a forklift across the room. Arthur moved slowly but deliberately into the room, entering a space full of workbenches and elaborate machines, some of which were the size of houses, one shaped like a big robotic caterpillar. He crossed the room and approached one more doorway, this one standing open. Behind it came the muffled sound of giggling and wet, ripping noises.

Arthur and his camera passed into a long open room that looked like a shooting range. At one end hung four pig carcasses, dangling from meat hooks. Standing among them was a young guy who had his back to them. He was shirtless, with long flowing blond hair, wearing a backward baseball cap and jeans. He bulged with tanned muscles—he looked like he'd borrowed the photoshopped body of a model on a billboard.

Zoey would forever have to live with the fact that this was her first impression of Molech: admiring his rippling back muscles, beach-tan biceps, and a perfect butt under worn jeans. And she was sure this was Molech, mainly because he had the letters M O L E C H tattooed across his back.

In Molech's right hand was another hand. Most of an arm, actually—everything from the elbow up, as if he had severed it from someone's body and carried it around as a keepsake. For a horrified moment Zoey thought he had hacked it off of Singh's corpse, but as the view got closer it became clear that the severed limb was made of rubber, or plastic. A prosthetic. Molech was using it as a weapon—he reached back, shoved the hand through the rib cage of the nearest pig with a crunch of snapping bones. He twisted it around inside and with a series of wet, sucking squishes, pulled the hand out of the ragged wound, which was now clutching a pink and yellow mass of organs in its fist.

Molech laughed uproariously and said, "Dude, this is *orgasmic!*"

He couldn't have been any older than Zoey. There was another man watching him, a bearded black guy who looked a bit older than Molech, but who probably still hadn't seen thirty. Standing around the room were four other musclemen holding shotguns and watching Molech play—there didn't seem to be an ounce of body fat in the room. Molech turned and looked toward

Arthur and the camera. He smiled, and swung the prosthetic arm toward the floor, discarding the wad of guts with a wet slap. The fingers flexed on their own, with a mechanical whirr.

"Artie Livingston! As I live and breathe! Dude, I have to shake your hand!"

Molech extended the prosthetic limb toward Arthur, as if to shake with it. The mechanical fingers flexed. Molech giggled.

Arthur declined the shake and said, "I don't believe we've met."

"Nope, but I bet you've heard of me. They call me Molech."

"Who's 'they'?"

Molech gestured toward the black guy with the beard and said, "This is my right-hand man, Black Scott. And don't call me racist, that's the name he gave himself."

In the background, Black Scott shook his head and silently mouthed, "Nope."

"Oh, and sorry about your friend back there. It was self-defense, I swear! Dude kept tryin' to run me over in his wheelchair. And by that point, the juice was flowin' and, dude, you just got to ride it out, know what I'm sayin'?"

"Did Singh let you in here?"

Molech used the mechanical hand to scratch his chin and said, "He didn't, the ingrate. And we go way back, too! See, a while back I put in a bid for all his awesome toys, but some rich bastard outbid me! You wouldn't know anything about that, would you? Ha!"

Molech walked over to an empty oil drum, grabbed it with the disembodied hand, and watched as the fingers effortlessly tore a chunk out of the side, the metal squealing as it ripped like construction paper. Molech giggled until he couldn't breathe.

"So, who did let you in?"

"Not everybody on your team is as loyal as you think, Artie. See, there's two ways of keepin' everybody in line, they can be scared of you, or they can be your buddy. Sounds to me like you do it the second way. The problem with that is, they turn on ya the moment you piss 'em off. Me, I run a tight ship. Everybody knows the score—stick with me, you live like a king, you cross me, I put your ass in Hell."

"So, what can I do for you?"

"You've already done it, my man. You just didn't know it. Though I got to say, you got a way better setup in here than I got. Way more floor space."

"So . . . you have your own workshop? Someone leaked the Raiden tech to you. Was it Singh?"

"Dude, I'm so juiced out I can barely think straight. You ever felt it, Artie? You ever felt the juice? Or has it been so long that you don't remember?"

"I suspect you intend to kill me, Molech. But I can tell you now that I think there is more to be gained by keeping me alive. I am a man of means and even if Singh was leaking designs to you, you don't have everything. I don't think you really want to do what you came to do."

"What I want don't matter, don't you see? I serve the juice. We all do, even if we try to deny it."

"Are you trying to tell me you're high? Because that's never stopped me from negotiating before."

"Nah, juice is a *natural* high, man. First time I felt it, I was out huntin' with my daddy. See, the way he hunted, you don't pack no food for the trip. You stay gone for a month, and the hunting grounds are a two-day hike from the car. You only eat what you kill, see, that's the idea. So my first time, we shot nothin' for three days. And we was starvin' at that point, I cried and begged, out there in the woods in Montana, just the two of us, beggin' him to take me home, to take me to McDonald's. I got so hungry I tried to catch and eat some crickets that had gotten into my tent. They got away and I just cried, like a little baby. Old man heard me and beat the piss outta me. Ha!

"And he sits me down and looks me in the eye and my old man told me how it was. Told me you got to let the hunger *drive* you, to motivate you. Next morning, I'm layin' in wait up in a tree and a big ol' wild boar comes gruntin' through the bush down below. The gun is shakin' in my hand, I know if I miss, that may be it for me, I might get too weak to hunt, might die out there in the woods, in the wet and the cold. But I shoot and the shot goes true and when that thing fell over, I felt it, man. I felt the *juice*. The adrenaline, the dopamine, all that pumpin' like fire through my veins and my brains and my balls. I had *won*. We built a fire and gutted and cooked that bastard and when my teeth sank into that tough, charred meat . . . mmmm. That was the first time I'd ever really eaten. The first time I was ever really alive. I was ten years old."

Molech watched as the mechanical prosthetic flexed its fingers, mesmerized.

He continued, "My daddy told me what I was feelin'. He says, man evolved to have these juices that flow through your body to reward you for doin' somethin' good. All them hormones, the dopamine, the adrenaline—the *true* drugs. You get that high—the real high—when your body knows you did somethin' to advance survival, not just yours but the *species*, man. When you won a fight, or killed some food, or banged a chick. And he tells me how now all my friends are livin' off fake highs, smokin' meth or playin' video games or jerkin' it to porn—all these little tricks to try to trigger the juice without earning it. Fake sex, fake danger, fake victories. But if we're gonna survive, he says, we got to get back to the true juice. Get rid of all that other nonsense and live the way we was intended. Muscle. Blood. Sweat."

There was a silence in the room that was broken by Molech snorting a sudden, crazy burst of laugher.

Arthur said calmly, "We're both businessmen, Molech."

"You're a *business*man. I'm just a *man*."

"All right, how about I put it like this—I'm a realist. I know what you're capable of and I know I don't have any choice but to cooperate. A man like me doesn't survive this long without knowing which way the wind is blowing."

Molech tossed the mechanical arm from one hand to the other, grinning that stupid grin.

"Yeah, like one of them fat fish that sits on the bottom of the river and just waits for worms to float by, right? Just sittin' there and eatin' up everything that comes your way, gettin' fatter. But you know what I am? I'm a shark."

Molech swung with his real hand, and connected with a blow that landed with a sickening crack of bone. Zoey jumped.

The camera's view spun and whirled, showing floor, and then ceiling.

Molech loomed over Arthur. "Nah. You know what, I thought of a better animal for you. You're a panda. You hear about that? The way they had 'em in zoos, tryin' to force 'em to hump because they wouldn't do it themselves. See, a long time ago, the pandas forgot they were bears. Stopped huntin', stopped fightin', started eatin' leaves instead of meat. They let the juice dry up and pretty soon, the pandas were all gone, too. If it was up to people like you, we humans would go the same way. Well, I've decided I'm gonna go ahead and save the world."

Arthur gasped and tried to say, "Listen! Listen to me! It's not too late—"

Molech said, "Let's hope not."

And then Molech struck again, and again, and again, each time with that horrible *crunch* of impact.

Then he grabbed the mechanical arm and reached down. There were wet, ripping noises.

Zoey yanked off the glasses. She stood up, tried to catch her breath, then ran into the bathroom and threw up.

TWENTY-TWO

Armando appeared in the door of the bathroom with his gun drawn, because in his world even a vomiting woman was apparently a problem that could be cured with a well-placed bullet. Zoey told him she was fine and he kind of awkwardly put his hand on her shoulder, as if he had seen somebody do it on TV once. Zoey shrugged him off, flushed, gathered herself and was about to speak when Carlton appeared in the doorway and asked if all was well.

Zoey hesitated. Molech flat out told Arthur he had a traitor on his team, and he apparently wasn't referring to Singh because Singh was already in multiple pieces when he said it. If he wasn't just playing mind games, then the traitor was someone close enough to know the secret codes or keys that would get him into a structure built like a nuclear bunker. Aside from the Suits, who else would have that kind of access? Could it be Carlton?

Zoey said, "I'm fine, can you give us a minute?"

Carlton left and Zoey told Armando, "I just watched a Blink of Arthur Livingston getting murdered by Molech with a disembodied mechanical arm after the latter stole a bunch of magic weapons from the former."

Armando furrowed his brow as he tried to untangle this sentence.

"Oh. I'm . . . sorry . . ."

"No, it's fine. I mean, it was awful, but I saw Molech's face clearly."

"Everybody has left, but we can call—"

"Wait, there's more. Before he killed him, Molech said there was a traitor on Arthur's team."

"You think he was telling the truth, or just making a play?"

"I don't know. What do I do?"

"Call Will."

"How do we know he's not the traitor?"

"We can't ever know anything for sure, but I'd say he's by far the least likely to betray Arthur and he definitely wouldn't do it on Molech's behalf. I don't know Will but I know enough about him to say that with some confidence."

"Maybe Molech forced him. Threatened him into doing it."

"Ha. You don't know Will."

Zoey thought back to the beginning of the second video, Will escorting Arthur, seemingly in the dark. If he had known at the time what was about to happen, the man hid it well.

"What about the rest of them?"

Armando ran his hand through his hair, thinking. "All I know is what I pick up from the grapevine, you understand. So . . . Echo hasn't been here as long as the rest, so there is that to consider. But the thing with the Suits— you're better off assuming that everything they present to you is a mirror image of the truth. That's their game. If you want to know who to be afraid of, start with who seems to have worked hardest to earn your trust."

"Well, that's definitely not Echo." Zoey considered. "That first night, it was Andre who came and found me, to talk me down."

"Knowing what little I know, Zoey, I would not . . . well, I was about to say I would not turn my back on him. But this is Tabula Rasa. You do not turn your back on anyone here."

Zoey made a decision. Will arrived at the Casa ten minutes later.

They watched the glasses video together on the Mold Room's wall display. Zoey warned Will about the graphic nature of the ending, and offered to simply describe it to him, so he wouldn't have to watch his friend get gutted by a backward cap-wearing frat boy. But Will insisted on watching it, which didn't surprise her. Will showed no emotion, right up to and including the moment when Arthur met his gruesome end. He let the video play out, then replayed it, stopping it at various points as if to notice minute details he'd missed the last time around. After he watched the video six times, he paused it on a clear view of Molech's face, then got up to pour himself a drink.

Will muttered, "Just a kid. Looked like he had to skip a frat party to be there. After all that. All these years. Just some goddamned kid."

"Did you recognize him?"

"No, but either Budd will know who he is, or we can run him through facial recognition. Either way we'll have his real name by morning."

"The first time I watched it, I thought Molech kept saying he served 'the Jews.'"

"So did I."

"I bet his real name is Chad, he looks like one. Did you hear the part where Arthur asked him how he got into the building and he said—"

"That somebody on the team had betrayed him. Yes, I picked up on that, Zoey."

"So who is it?"

Will thought for a moment and said, "Why were you so sure it wasn't me?"

"Armando. He said you had too much history with Arthur."

"Did he tell you the story? Of how we met?"

"No."

"Good."

"So who is it?"

"Nobody in the inner circle. Not Carlton, either."

"Are you sure? Maybe somebody else who worked for—"

"No. I will stake my life on it. I'm not using that as a figure of speech. I'm telling you I am literally going to stake my life on it tomorrow. If anyone was going behind our back, I'd know. End of discussion."

"So these gadgets, this stuff that gives you murderous superpowers, Arthur is the one who unleashed it on the world."

"It would appear so."

"And you actually knew that this whole time, didn't you?"

Will set his glass on the conference table, then made like he was packing up to leave.

"Not the exact details, no. But enough to know whatever he was working on was dangerous in the wrong hands. Bodies started turning up, and it was clear Arthur was involved from the way he acted. Wouldn't talk to us about it, though, because at some point he decided he didn't know who he could trust. Including me. After everything, he still wasn't sure *I* wasn't going behind his back."

Will worked his jaw. Grinding his molars, trying to push down rage and sadness before they bubbled up to where the world could see them. He almost got his face back to that of a chiseled, impassive robot. Almost.

Zoey said, "I'm sorry."

"For what?"

"For your loss. I should have said that. You said it to me the first time you called me but that was stupid, it was your loss, not mine. I should have realized that."

Will waved her off. "No, it's . . . fine. Anyway, that's why there was such a mad scramble for his vault key, we were trying to piece together what exactly he had been up to, because it seemed so . . . apocalyptic. What we were hoping to find in there were the schematics, or some prototypes, anything. Backups. Hoping it hadn't all gone up with the warehouse. Then we finally get it open and, you know the rest."

"But that doesn't make sense, either. Molech *has* the gadgets. He's the one person who had no need to get into the vault. He should be happy, right? You saw the video—he won. He got what he wanted."

"Well, now he wants the gold."

"Whatever that is."

Will finished his drink and said, "He's apparently going to tell us tomorrow, so there's that."

"If he doesn't just kill us all first."

TWENTY-THREE

Zoey woke up and for a blissful moment thought she was back home, and was waking up from an exceptionally weird dream. Then she realized she was in some kind of strange bed that she could actually roll over in without running into either a wall or a hot-water heater. Then the dead silence registered, that eerie feeling like she was the last human on earth. Nobody arguing outside, not even the sound of her mom clanking pans around in the kitchen. There could be a war raging outside the gates of the estate and not a peep would reach Zoey's bedroom.

She had forgotten about the talking toilet, and the startled fart she gave when it spoke up was interpreted as consent to show her the morning's alarming news. The lead story was the terror threats surrounding the upcoming memorial service in Tabula Ra$a, showing video of the city's park, where crews were already setting up for what looked less like a funeral service and more like a massive winter music festival. Were they inflating a bouncy castle out there?

The next story was new to Zoey. A ten-foot-tall bronze statue of Arthur Livingston had been stolen from its perch in front of an art gallery (accepting a gaudy statue was apparently the cost of taking a large donation from the man) by a pair of muscular men with some kind of flying apparatus on their backs—neither of them were Molech, but there was no doubt who they worked for. The statue was hauled a few blocks away to the financial district, where there sat a life-size bronze statue of a bull. The two men spent the next hour using blasts of electricity to weld the Livingston statue to the bull, in a position that made it appear he was having interspecies relations with it. The task took much longer than necessary because both men couldn't stop giggling, or pausing every five minutes to flex for the crowd. Finally, their work done, the men had stuck their arms in the air and zipped off into the sky, trailing tails of electric blue light. One second later, they both went spiraling off in different directions and crashed into nearby buildings. Zoey assumed that hadn't been part of the plan.

She turned it off, and when she wandered out of the guest room she was immediately accosted by Carlton, asking to make her breakfast. Her stomach was in knots, so instead she handed off to him the job of feeding Stench Machine. If Carlton considered this task below him, he showed no sign. They headed down the grand staircase and at the bottom Zoey found Armando, who was sitting in the lotus position on the floor, cleaning a gun he had taken apart and spread on a dirty towel. There seemed to be a ritualistic aspect to what he was doing, a ceremony to calm the nerves. Zoey didn't bother him.

She wandered into the kitchen where there was a brown paper package sitting on the bar—the delivery of freshly roasted espresso beans Arthur had flown in every week. Zoey smelled them, swooned, and headed over to the kitchen's coffee bar and dumped them in a grinder. She didn't even want espresso, she just wanted to go through the process of making it. She started grinding beans and asked Carlton if he wanted something. He declined, because accepting such a thing from his employer would probably violate some sacred code of his profession. She yelled the same offer to Armando and he said yes, which almost made Zoey giddy. She started warming up the machine.

Armando strode into the kitchen and Zoey asked him, "How many people are going to be there? At the memorial?"

He shrugged. "Over the course of the night, maybe a hundred thousand? It's open to the public, crowds will wash in and out of the park all night. And a Livingston Drop party has a way of spilling out across the city."

"A what party?"

"It's a city-wide festival Arthur would throw whenever he could invent a suitable excuse. It shuts down the whole downtown area, traffic is always a disaster."

"Still, sounds pretty cool as far as funerals go."

"Unless you are trying to organize security around a known assassination target, in which case it becomes a logistical nightmare."

Zoey poured steamed milk into Armando's drink, drew a dragon into the foam (with the nozzle of the steamer, not a toothpick—she didn't cheat) and slid the mug over to him.

"There, try that."

He took a sip, completely failing to noticed the design she had etched into it, and said, "Oh, wow. That's has a . . . kick."

"It's a café mocha with cinnamon and a dash of cayenne pepper. The liquor is right over there if you want to Irish it up." She started wiping down the equipment when she had a thought. "I wonder if I should call in for work on Monday."

Armando said, "Work?"

"Well I'm supposed to open at the Java Lodge Monday morning. They're not open on Sunday so if there's a good chance I'll get killed tonight that means I need to call today to get somebody to trade with me."

Armando just stared.

Zoey dug out her phone and dialed. She got the voice mail of her manager, Arya, and said, "Hey, this is Zoey, I'm still in Tabula Rasa for that funeral, and, um, there's a chance I won't be in on Monday morning, can you see if Chel can cover for me? Tell her, uh, I'll give her ten thousand dollars. That's not a joke, tell her if she gives me her account number I can send the money at any time. Oh, and tell her to remember to change the floor sign, all the holiday flavors go back to regular price this week except for the peppermint. Good-bye." Zoey hung up, thought for a moment, then said, "I wonder if I should call my mom? Ah, I think it'd just freak her out. I mean how do I say good-bye without scaring her?"

Armando said, "Zoey, we are going to do everything we can to—"

Zoey turned her back to him and said to Carlton, "Will you take care of Stench Machine?"

"I'm sorry?"

"My cat, that's his name. If I don't come back from this thing, will you feed him? And find him a home if you don't want him? Cats were never my mom's thing."

"Well, I could—"

"He doesn't just need a roof, he needs to be with someone who loves him. He'll want to sleep in the bed with you."

Before Carlton could formulate a response to this—it was clear that he and Armando both wished they could just flee the room—Budd, Will, and Andre filed in.

Zoey asked, "Where's Echo?"

Will said, "At the park, installing about seven million dollars' worth of hardware."

Zoey asked if they wanted coffee. Will said no. Budd asked for Folgers' Crystals, black. Andre asked for six shots of espresso with three shots of peanut butter cheesecake syrup, with whip cream and chocolate shavings on top. Zoey got to work.

Will said, "I showed them the video."

"And?"

Budd said, "Real name is Chet Campbell—"

Zoey said, "Oh, I was *so close*."

"Son of Rex Campbell. Arms dealer. I ain't seen him since he was a boy, but it's him."

Armando said, "I'm not familiar."

Budd said, "Rex was before your time. Douche bag gunrunner from Oregon, used to specialize in makin' exotic guns and ammo for high-end thugs, gold-plated assault rifles, shotgun shells full of acid, that sort of thing. Crazy survivalist type, came here in the early days to flood the streets with military surplus iron. Wound up skimming from a deal with the Russian mob. They caught him and cut off his head, stuck it on the front of his Marauder four-by-four like a hood ornament. He would have left a nice chunk of change behind for Chet, though. And plenty of connections for him to pick up the family business."

Will said, "The tech he stole from Arthur will make him more money in five minutes than dear old dad made in his whole gunrunning career."

Armando said, "Frankly, I am surprised the mob left Chet alive at all. Boys in that situation tend to grow up angry. You would prefer they not appear at your door ten years later."

Budd said, "Oh, they tried to take him out. Chet couldn't have been more than twelve at the time. He not only got away but stayed gone. Everybody just assumed they got 'im at some point, but then all these years later, sure enough, we start hearing about a lot of dead Russians with exotic wounds. People start whisperin' the name 'Molech.' Little Chet Campbell, all growed up and makin' a name for himself."

Zoey said, "Exotic wounds caused by exotic gadgets that *you* gave him. I just want to reiterate that this is Arthur Livingston's mess we're cleaning up here."

Will said, "And we *will* clean it up."

Budd said, "Even though cleaning up Arthur's messes is such an unusual and alien experience for all of us."

"The point," said Andre, "is that this is *what we do*."

Candi appeared in the room and said that there were five men with very large guns at the gate insisting they were associates of Armando Ruiz, along with a flamboyantly dressed man named Tre who insisted that he was Zoey's personal fashion designer. Zoey wasn't sure which of those alarmed her more.

Andre clapped his hands, picked up his mug, and said, "All right. Let's get ready for a funeral."

TWENTY-FOUR

Andre said, "Zoey, this is Tre. My brother. He's gonna fix you up. He does all our suits, Ling's outfits, too."

They were all up in Arthur's hidden third-floor suite, standing in the massive "closet" that could have comfortably accommodated a dozen more people. Armando, as always, watched the door. Tre's own outfit was not inspiring confidence in Zoey—he was wearing a suit made of crimson leather, the shirt unbuttoned to his navel. Several gold chains were draped across a well-muscled and well-waxed chest.

He said, "Pleasure to meet you, Ms. Ashe." To Andre he said, "Damn, you was right. Gonna have fun dressin' her."

Will said, "We're going for confidence here. I don't want her dressed like she's coming in nervous, or armored, or ready to run. I want her dressed like she's going to a party without a care in the world. We want to sew doubt about why she's so confident. I'd suggest something tight, with heels."

Zoey said, "I think you're blurring the line between strategy and your own perverse fantasies, Will." He wouldn't take the bait, choosing instead to lean in one corner and engross himself in his phone.

Andre rolled his eyes. "I'm going to leave y'all to it. Now Zoey, keep in mind, Tre's not gay. Don't let him linger with the measuring tape: he's just using that as an excuse to put his hands on you. He'll act like he forgot the numbers, don't fall for it."

Tre said, "I resent that. I'm a professional."

"You resent it because it's the truth."

Andre left and Armando said, "Do you want me to close the door?" Meaning, *with me on the other side of it?*

"No, you can stay, in case Tre turns out to be an assassin. Just turn your head if there's nudity."

This prospect seemed to alarm Armando quite a bit.

Tre said, "So, I brought a selection with me and if you don't like what I've got, I'll go get more. You trust me to take your measurements without feeling you up, or has my brother already poisoned the well in this relationship?"

"Can I not just pick out something on my own? I'm not six years old, I can dress myself."

"Girl, please don't take this as an insult because you are a lovely young lady and it is people with a rich inner life and transcendental spirit who tend to neglect their outer appearance. But that said, you're wearing eight items of clothing, and at least two of them don't fit you. The other six are including your shoes and socks. Your shirt hangs like a maternity dress. You're goin' out in public, gonna be people watchin' from all over the world, you got to show off the goods."

"I absolutely do *not* have to do that. And it's not my fault nothing fits, I have a weird body. This shirt isn't supposed to be this low cut, it's just that everything is designed for somebody six inches taller. So what's a dignified neckline on a normal woman makes me look like I'm supposed to be in a parade in Rio."

"And *that's why you got Tre.* You don't got to buy off the shelf no more, that's the point—we're gonna take what I got and we're gonna make it so it fits Zoey Ashe and nobody else on earth. Only thing is, you gonna realize all at once how much all your other clothes were made with somebody else in mind. Soon you won't want to put on pajamas without pickin' up the phone and callin' Tre to tailor 'em up. Now, let's be frank, I'm obviously gonna start with them titties. See, we dress the girls first, then we can take in the bottom part. Bring out them curves."

"Wow. I don't even . . ."

"Hold still, I'm gonna measure you up."

"My mom would be so disappointed. She—"

"Hold out your arms. There."

"She used to say I should pity people who obsess over this type of thing."

"Who's obsessing? You just wanna make a splash, that's all."

"Okay, again, I absolutely do not want to do that."

"Better to be looked over than overlooked. You want to walk into that funeral and have every dude in that room whip their head around and say, 'God-*damn* them is some fine-ass titties. I got to find me a divorce lawyer in the next five minutes.'"

"Wow. I'm just going to leave . . ."

"You want every girl in that place to be murderous with jealous rage. Like, I got to get my man outta here before he sees *that,* and leaves my skinny ass. Why are you laughing? I'm serious."

"I know you're making fun of me."

Armando remained silent across the room but clearly wanted to be literally anywhere else. Will worked his phone, seeming to have completely forgotten anyone else was in the room.

Tre said, "I'm just trying to relax you, honey. I'm measuring your butt, don't be alarmed."

"I don't even know why I'm laughing, I'm probably going to die tonight. Get me a dress that won't make me look ridiculous when they show my body on the news, that's all I want."

"You got dark thoughts, girl."

Tre started sorting through a rolling rack of dress bags he'd brought and as he was grabbing one, Zoey said, "Don't give me anything that doesn't have pockets."

Tre paused, put it back, then pulled out a different bag that turned out to be a surprisingly dignified black blazer and skirt.

Zoey said, "Oh. Well that's not too bad."

"Thank you for believing in me. Can you try this top for me? I can leave the room while you change if you don't want me to see you in your bra but, for real, I am a professional here. Think of me like a doctor, I do this every day."

"It's fine." She made a twirling motion at Armando, who not only turned his head, but turned his whole body to face the wall. Like a little kid. Will kind of had his back to them anyway, hunched over his phone and muttering something to Echo's worried, holographic head. The other three people in the room could form a naked human pyramid and it'd take him an hour to notice.

Zoey pulled off her T-shirt and immediately Tre said, "Damn! Them's the type of titties they write songs about."

Zoey covered her chest with the shirt and said, "Okay, you're not actually a designer, are you?"

"Go on, I'm just playin'. By the way, make that *three* items of clothing that don't fit you. Oh—what's that? On your shoulder?"

Zoey glanced at her back in the mirror, but didn't need to see to know what he was referring to. Her rainbow scar. Four curved lines of pale knotted flesh swooping from her shoulder blade to her armpit.

"What does it look like? Guess."

"It's a scar, right?"

"Well, duh. What kind? What does it look like?"

"Like a big animal clawed you. You get in a fight with a bear?"

"No. See how it's perfectly round? Like the burner on an electric stovetop?"

"What, did you fall on the oven while it was on?"

"Sort of. One of my mom's boyfriends, he held me down on the kitchen counter with a steak knife to my throat. Shoved me on the burners, leaned all his weight on me, and turned it on. Then we both laid there while it got hotter and hotter. Burned through my shirt, burned through my shoulder. There was actual smoke. Caught my hair on fire, too. It set off the smoke alarm. And he just laid on top of me, grinning, the whole time. He wasn't a nice guy."

There was silence all around, as there always was when she told this story. Even Will had glanced up from his phone, to try to figure out what drama had stopped the room. Without turning away from the wall, Armando said, "This man, is he still around?"

"Don't know. This was several years ago. He went to jail—not for that, but for something related—but I'm sure by now he's probably gotten out and then got put back in for something else."

Armando asked, "What was his name?"

"Why? You think you know him?"

Armando shrugged. "Maybe I want to get to know him. Maybe I should drop in and say hello. Maybe show him what a hot stove feels like against his scumbag face."

"Ha, then we all go to jail."

"When a billionaire makes a career scumbag disappear, no one goes to jail. A man like that, I could do him in the parking lot of the police station and they would send me a fruit basket at Christmas."

"Anyway, that's why I can't wear tank tops."

Tre said, "Bet that saves you a lot of time shaving them armpits. You ever wear a shaping top like this? No? It's gonna feel weird, just roll that down to your hips, like you're putting on a giant rubber. It's a polyurethane blend that'll kind of shape itself to your—yeah like that."

"I . . . don't think I can breathe in this."

"Yeah that's normal, that's only because it's squishing all of your organs together. I got tights in here for the bottom half but we're not worried about that right now. See that? You just lost like twelve pounds. See, this is why us humans invented clothes, hides all the workouts we skipped. Put the jacket on. Nice—here, put your arms down so I can mark the sleeves. Perfect. Take a look in the mirror. We'll bring that in at the waist, like this. So it's got that slimming effect, right?"

"Oh, wow. That's not bad."

"Got a little bit of collar gap back here, we'll take care of that. Like Will's suit, see how everything fits smooth and flat against his neck, no wrinkles or anything around the shoulders or buttons? Here, put the skirt on."

"You're not watching this part, you've lost that privilege. Turn around."

Tre made a show of turning around and covering his eyes with both hands. She changed, gave the all-clear, and Tre said, "Yeah . . . hold still. See, we'll bring it right above the knee, like this. Probably don't want it any tighter than that or—"

"Or I start to look like a sausage."

She looked herself over in the mirror.

Tre said, "Admit I know what I'm doin'."

"It looks good."

"See? Look like a dignified businesswoman and yet still gonna have you showin' up in a hundred dudes' wank fantasies tonight."

"Tre, *please*. Armando? What do you think?"

He turned away from the wall and came up behind her.

"It looks very nice."

Tre said, "He means it, too. Don't know if you noticed, but his eyes made two stops, he looked at the mirror second but he looked at your butt first. See, that's what we're going for."

"My god, I'm going to have to go take a long shower after this."

Will approached, studied the mirror like a doctor diagnosing a patient, and said, "And you'll have her in heels, correct? I want the subconscious impression that she can't run away."

"And that would also mean I can't *actually* run away, *correct*?"

"I think any plan that relies on your foot speed is probably not a sound one."

She nodded toward his drink glass and said, "Right, just like any plan that relies on your sobriety."

To Tre she said, "Do you have a different top? Aside from the fact that this one is probably squeezing my liver to death, it seems like this is showing a lot of boob for a funeral."

"One, it's not really a funeral, it's a memorial service in the park. And two, girl, this is *Arthur Livingston's* memorial service. You'll be showing the least amount of boob there. We'll get you a necklace—maybe pearls or a nice gold cross to come down right here. It'll be classy, trust me. Even your momma would like it."

"She would not. She's a hippie, says we're ruining the world because we throw out perfectly good clothes and cars just because we want to keep up appearances. She used to say that mankind would rather look good and die than look bad and live."

Tre shook his head. "Girl, style is the only thing that separates us from the animals. A bird or a bear, all its got is the feathers and fur it's born with, but a human, we can take our crazy imaginations and wear 'em on our sleeve. The only tragedy is not everybody can afford to bring out that natural expression of beauty."

"So now I'm not trailer trash anymore, because I can afford a guy to dress me?"

"Girl, you were never trailer trash. Your circumstances just forced you to dress like it. Now take that off and let me make the alterations. Chantrell will be here in a minute to do hair and makeup."

"Wait, what?"

"Bye-bye. I'd wish you luck, but in that outfit, you ain't gonna need it."

TWENTY-FIVE

Zoey had literally once quit a job because it required her to wear a skirt and pantyhose every day. She always felt like her whole lower body was being slowly strangled, and the boobs-to-toe body-shaping garments Tre had her squeeze into were much, much worse. She shuffled toward the grand staircase and saw that below her, the mansion had become a raucous gun party full of burly men chatting in circles and guzzling hopefully nonalcoholic drinks, comparing gear, and sharing anecdotes that were punctuated with hand gestures demonstrating acts of violence. She headed down the stairs, thinking it would be hilarious if the heels caused her to tumble down and break her neck in front of fifty men who'd been hired to protect her.

Andre and Armando intercepted her at the bottom of the stairs. Andre was in a black suit that gave little whispers of purple, the colors hidden in the pinstripes and in subtle shades that revealed themselves when the light hit his tie and pocket square. Little splashes of flamboyance in his somber mourning clothes.

"Damn, Tre did right by you. You don't even got to say anything, I can tell by the look on your face, you're like, 'I know I look good, we all know it, end of discussion.'"

"You can tell him he did a good job, I'm sure he really needs the self-esteem boost. But frankly I think it's kind of weird how much you guys care how I look."

Andre held out his hands in a *look around you* gesture. "I don't know if you've noticed, but presentation is kind of *our thing*. Now admit it, that's the best you've looked since your prom night."

"I wore pajamas on prom night. Nobody asked me to the dance."

Andre looked her up and down and said, "Well, I just now found out that you went to an all-white high school."

"What does *that* mean?"

Armando pushed past him and said, "Follow me. We're going over the plan."

They shouldered past the armed men in the foyer, then had to wait for a stream of guys filing out of the dining hall, each with long guns strapped to their backs.

Zoey said, "Actually, I wonder if my ex-boyfriend Caleb has heard about all this."

Armando said, "There are people living in mud huts who have heard about this."

Andre said, "You think he'll come callin'?"

"It was an ugly breakup. He cheated on me and I stabbed him in the crotch with a pair of scissors."

That got Armando's attention. Zoey laughed and said, "No, not really. He just upgraded."

Andre said, "What do you mean?"

They shuffled into the crowded dining room, where the sprawling table was now covered in weapons—men tinkering with rifles and loading them with gleaming bullets that were as long as her hand. Did they think they were going to be attacked by bears?

She said, "He was in college when we met, in business school. I was waiting tables at Cracker Barrel. We moved in together after a year but then all of his future MBA buddies start picking out the sorority girls they were going to marry and it became obvious that a future businessman destined to make six figures needed something way thinner and blonder than me. He was actually really nice about it: he got me a gym membership for Christmas, kept buying salad ingredients to keep around the house. He really did want it to work. Offered to pay to get my teeth fixed."

Andre said, "You can't take it personal, sometimes the fire just goes out. I should know, it's happened to me with four wives so far."

They had to pause at the doorway to the hall, where a parade of four men walked in hauling boxes that were, alarmingly, full of medical supplies—wound-dressing kits, emergency burn care, disinfectant.

As they headed toward the Mold Room door, Zoey said, "But that's the thing. When the lights were out, everything was the way it was before. I don't want to get gross or anything, but there's *no way* the new girl does, you know, the things I did. My mom taught tantric sex classes, out of our trailer. Always creepy naked people with tattoos in the living room. I know my way around a dude. I learned this massage technique, I swear Caleb actually blacked out one time, I thought I was going to have to call an ambulance, his balls were—"

Zoey realized they had timed their conversation just so that everyone in the conference room could hear that last part.

She said, "Nevermind."

Andre raised an eyebrow. "So . . . *what are you doin' after the service?*"

She sighed and said, "Decomposing."

Armando went to the back of the room to grab some equipment. Will and Echo were seated at the table in their assigned chairs, examining a tiny object and muttering an argument about it. Will was in a dark gray suit jacket the color of a charcoal drawing, with a white shirt and a dark tie with the slightest silver shimmer to it, looking as always like he would clink if you tapped him with a fork. Echo had been poured into a dress that was made of exactly one piece of black stretchy fabric sewn into a tube, and looked like she could stop traffic three cities away. Zoey thought that the least Echo could have done was dress down so as not to upstage her boss, then sadly realized that she had tried to do just that.

Andre said to Zoey, "I'm just playin'. But seriously, listen up because this is important and this is where we'll leave it. Your boy, my guess is he never stopped thinkin' you were beautiful. The only thing that changed was he started worrying that *other people* didn't think you were. So now he's gonna spend his life with a gorgeous, boring woman who'll make him miserable, all so that he can wear her on his arm to parties, thinkin' that'll show other people how great he is. He'll pick the career and car and mansion that he thinks *other* people expect him to have, put all his energy into building up that front. Then one day he'll find out his life is all wrapping paper and no gift."

"Though that would be a perfect gift for a cat," noted Zoey. "So you're saying what he really wants is a skinny fashion model he can tote around at parties, then swap her out for one of me when the doors are closed and the lights are out?"

"I know half a dozen dudes got that very arrangement going."

Armando was back. He picked the tiny object off the table and said, "Ideally we would have had thirty days to work out the logistics of this operation, but . . . here, hold still."

He leaned close to Zoey, pushed her hair aside and placed a tiny, clear piece of tubing along the back of her ear. He ran his finger along her earlobe to press the adhesive backing into place.

"What's that?"

Echo said, "This will let us hear each other, and we'll be able to track you. We have equipment to detect if there is a firearm within five hundred yards of your location, but of course, we don't know that they're going to have guns. If you do get taken, just cooperate—we will be able to track you the entire time."

Armando said, "Our problem is that none of what we are doing here will be a surprise to Molech or his people—he has told us ahead of time to expect him and he knows we are going to prepare accordingly. And, unless he is a fool, he can figure out ninety percent of what we're doing. These are all standard procedures."

Zoey nodded. "Right, unless we, like, got a bunch of big catapults and tossed clowns at him or something."

Ignoring this, Armando continued, "The one thing we cannot stop is the one thing we are also assuming he won't do—come in with some kind of undetectable exotic weapon or bomb, and just take us all out. Our one advantage is that he needs something from you, and we are assuming that is not just a ploy."

"Well, that's only twice you used the word 'assuming' in that spiel, so it sounds like we're on solid ground. So, let's say he flies down into the middle of the park in a big hot-air balloon in the shape of his head, and demands this 'gold' from me. Then what? You shoot him?"

Will piped up. "That would actually be our second best option. The best would be to turn this into a negotiation. I'll be the negotiator."

"Why is that better than just shooting him?"

"Zoey. This is taking place in a crowded public park. There may be children there. In the real world, bullets that miss their targets keep traveling until they hit something. They fly through windows, and into the bodies of bystanders. And even successfully killing a bad guy creates blowback, sets off a whole chain of consequences that are impossible to predict. Guns always represent a failure of negotiation."

"So what do I do?"

"You're going to play dumb—"

"I won't be playing."

"And I'll make it clear that any conversation or confrontation between you and he is a dead end. You don't know what he wants, or how to get it.

You'll hand it off to me. Armando will get you to safety. The rest is my problem. If it goes wrong from there, well, then we do it the ugly way."

"And if he doesn't go for any of this, and just tries to stab me to death?"

Armando said, "If he makes a move, hit the deck. Go flat on the ground, don't get between Molech and the many bullets that are going to be flying in his direction."

Zoey took a breath and said, "All right. And we don't know when he's going to show up?"

Will said, "Or if he's even going to show at all."

"Well . . . how long does the memorial last?"

"All night."

"Okay. So what do I do the rest of the time?"

From behind her, Andre said, "It's a party. You're rich and famous. You mingle and have fun."

Zoey felt a sinking in her gut. "Well, let's just hope he shows up and tries to kill me near the start."

Armando put a hand on her shoulder and looked her in the eye. "Hey. You will be fine. Let's go do it."

Zoey sighed and said, "All right. I have to go say good-bye to my cat."

TWENTY-SIX

🔑

The traffic was the kind you'd expect to see five minutes before the utter breakdown of civilization. As they inched nearer to the park, they saw more and more work crews in reflective vests, sometimes dragging huge black canvas sheets across the street, or trying to direct traffic around delivery trucks disgorging kegs of beer and cases of liquor.

Zoey said, "This was Arthur's dying wish. To make everyone else's life miserable for an entire night."

Andre raised an eyebrow and said, "Not everyone. Only the few million people who aren't going to be at the party. And that's their own fault, isn't it?"

Zoey said, "Is it snowing? I mean is it only snowing around the park and nowhere else?"

"There are snow machines on top of all the buildings downtown. They run every night for the couple of weeks leading up to Christmas. Made possible by a generous donation from, uh, you."

They arrived at a roped-off staging area packed with freezer trucks and stacks of supplies. Zoey had a good view of the park for the first time and even though the celebration hadn't technically started yet, the park was already more crowded than Zoey was comfortable with. She felt social-anxiety alarms buzzing deep in her gut. She wondered if she could just hide back here the whole time, maybe make herself a fort out of beer kegs.

The most prominent feature in the park itself was an inexplicable thirty-foot-tall mountain of white near the center. Some college-age kids were digging into the side.

"Beer Mountain," said Andre. "Twenty tons of chipped ice, ten thousand bottles of beer embedded throughout. Partiers just dig 'em out as the night goes on. Can't tell from here, but it's in the shape of Mt. Rushmore, only all four heads are Arthur."

"Thank god, for a second I thought it was cocaine."

Near Beer Mountain was a pink and yellow inflatable castle, with a few kids bouncing around inside it. Nearby was the bandstand, now lined with amplifiers and roadies doing a sound check.

A flash of firelight caught Zoey's eye, flaring up from a nearby stand that was about ten feet tall, with a stone firepot at the top. A staff member was up on a ladder, he punched a button and with a *whoosh*, a dozen jets of blue/orange flame roared to life. They flashed and pulsed and danced, creating patterns and designs sculpted out of fire. The pot burped a flaming letter "A" that vanished into the sky a moment later, then the jets re-aimed themselves and a fiery angel appeared, wings outstretched. Satisfied, the man climbed down and moved his ladder to another, identical stand nearby—dozens of these firepots encircled the park.

And then, the smell of food hit her. The entire park was ringed in tents with black awnings trying and failing to signify the somber, dignified tone of the event (it didn't help that they bore the yellow Livingston Enterprises logo, which was a letter "L" superimposed over a cartoon handlebar mustache). One massive tent housed a row of barbecue smokers, a guy flipping racks of ribs covered in a glistening bark of caramelized sugar and sauce. The tent next to it had a flashy sign promising Danish hot dogs and deep-fried lasagna balls. Under the next was a guy sweating over a giant cast-iron caldron bubbling over an open fire, the man standing on a stepladder and using a boat paddle to stir seventy-five gallons of chili (Zoey figured by the end of the night, at least a gallon of that would be that man's sweat). Next to him was a stand with a series of festively colored vats, manned by a huge guy with a waxed mustache who was dipping flavored popcorn in liquid nitrogen, cold steam rising as he poured it into red-and-white-striped boxes.

"Good, you're here." Zoey was jolted out of her junk-food trance by Echo. She and the rest of the Suits were suddenly standing in a circle around her. "Welcome to the Arthur Livingston Street Obstruction Festival."

Armando said, "Security is in plainclothes, mingling through the crowd. You won't know who they are, but you don't need to. Everyone will be listening in and monitoring your vital signs. If you panic, four dozen men with guns will come running. There are spotters on the rooftops there"—he started pointing to buildings surrounding the park—"there, there, and there."

Echo said, "You see those firepots around the perimeter? Those are actually hiding backscatter scanners—unfortunately we can't pat down everyone who comes to the party since it's open to the public and crowds will be drifting in and out, but these will scan in real time for anything, uh, mechanical. We should know within seconds if something tries to slip in."

Will said, "Now, never take your eyes off the DQ, it's over there in the southwest corner. See the flowers?"

Zoey followed Will's gesture and saw an explosion of color—a dais, straining under flowers piled on top of flowers, wreathes and bouquets and arrangements as tall as a house. At the center of it all was a ten-foot-tall stack of logs, and on top of that, a body in repose.

Zoey said, "Wait, is that . . . I thought there was no body?"

Will said, "There wasn't. We had a wax replica made, getting it done on such short notice only cost a mere thirty thousand dollars. But you need it for the DQ."

It was the creepiest thing Zoey had ever seen. "Now what's DQ stand for again?"

Andre said, "You know how you get ice cream from Dairy Queen, and it's always got that little curl at the top? What's the first thing you do when they hand it to you?"

"You bite it off."

"Right, you can't resist it. Back when we were doing, uh, the job we used to do before this, the DQ was the equivalent of that, something you knew the enemy would go right for, first thing. See how we got the speakers sitting right there? We're trying to keep the crowds sparse around it, that's why."

They were starting to lose her. Zoey thought, *This is just another Saturday afternoon for these people.*

Will said, "Speaking of which, try to eat something. Do it out somewhere where you're easily visible. And laugh, make it a point to laugh during conversations, even if they're not funny. And when you're talking to people, put your hands on your hips like you do when you're angry. Yeah, like that, elbows at a ninety-degree angle. Not like you're angry, though, but like you're confident, making yourself bigger. Any questions?"

She had so many. But instead, she asked, "Where are the bathrooms?"

Echo said, "Don't use any of the public toilets. They're disgusting. We have our own, behind the first-aid tent. Armando knows where it is."

"Good, because I think I'm going to be sick."

Zoey walked away from the group, trying to quell the riot that was breaking out in her abdomen. Someone was following her. It was Echo. Zoey stopped, and tried to breathe.

She asked Echo, "Do you have cats?"

"What?"

"Do you own any cats. As pets. Or are you good with them, I guess is what I'm asking."

"I have dogs."

"Oh. Nevermind."

"Come on, Zoey, don't fall apart on us. You've handled all of this with aplomb so far, we're all impressed."

"This is just . . . it's all hitting me at once. My mom told me one time that everybody thinks they're the star of their own movie, and I don't think I knew what she meant until now, this exact moment. Because Arthur thought *he* was the star, that he would be the hero who would see this whole crazy thing to the end. Then just like that, he was gone. And it's just now hitting me that I'm probably not the star of the story, either. I'll be that girl who dies halfway through the movie to give the real hero motivation to beat the bad guy. My movie could end tonight and . . . that would be it . . . just, nothing . . ."

Zoey was hyperventilating. She bent over and tried to steady her breathing.

Echo kneeled by her. She put a hand on Zoey's elbow and said, "Come on. Stand up. Rule One, we don't let them see us like this."

"Who?"

"You know what I mean. Look around. Stand up."

Zoey stood, and nodded. "It's okay. I think I'm okay."

"Here."

Echo pressed a bright blue capsule into Zoey's palm.

"What's that?"

"Plaxodol. Antianxiety. Don't tell anyone."

"Where'd you get it?"

"My doctor, obviously. I have two other prescriptions in my purse if this one doesn't work."

Zoey swallowed the pill, along with all of the follow-up questions she had been about to ask.

Echo said, "Hey. Look at me. This is what he wants. This is what they always want. That's why he told you he was coming. It was all about making you feel like this. Don't give him that. Whatever he does when he arrives, you have control over this part. You all right?"

She nodded, let out a breath.

"Yeah. Let's do this."

Zoey ventured out into the rapidly thickening crowd, Armando right behind her. She immediately felt like a thousand pairs of eyes had all turned toward her at once, then realized that if you factored in Blink, that was probably only a tiny fraction of the real total. She considered going back to get a second pill from Echo. Zoey thought that it was like she had a bull's-eye on her back, but then she heard the sudden chatter of voices in her earpiece from the rooftop snipers announcing her movement to each other, and realized that she actually had a dozen bull's-eyes on her back.

That she knew about.

TWENTY-SEVEN

Overload.

Rushing flames lashed and danced from the firepots, perfect girls giggled in tiny dresses and garish wigs, guys screamed jokes and laughter at each other, a terrible band angrily stabbed power ballads into the night. The buildings overlooking the park were lit up so that they were like the bars on an equalizer, vertical lights pulsing up and down in time with the music. Zoey felt each beat pulse across her throbbing cranium.

Oh, and there were ghosts. They had these stupid holograms roaming randomly through the park, depicting a translucent Arthur Livingston doing ghost things—conversing with Gandhi, fistfighting Hitler, high-fiving Jesus. The projectors were mounted on little remote control buggies that rolled around in the snow, to make it look like the ghosts were mingling with the crowd—Stench Machine would have hated it. Then Zoey started noticing these weird little green, glowing orbs floating around the crowd, and finally got close enough to one to realize it was this glow-in-the-dark ice cream people were eating out of little cups. Even the food here screamed for attention—she was surprised they hadn't modified it to make a loud noise the whole time you were eating it. She was looking forward to seeing one of the drunks spray glow-vomit everywhere.

Under all of this were the electronic voices coming from the earpiece—useless cross-chatter from rooftop spotters, perimeter guards, and undercover gunmen mingling with the crowd. Spotting threats, dismissing them, throwing around jargon that imparted no helpful information to Zoey about whether or not she was about to die.

Through it all, she just kept moving, through the noise, and the little clouds of steam from people puffing on vaporizers that would probably give her a contact high by the end of the night. They say humans, and many other herd animals, will wander in a counterclockwise motion if left to their own devices—grocery store floor plans are set up to accommodate this, for instance. And sure enough, after a couple of hours, that's what Zoey found herself doing—circling the park, aimlessly, only because she couldn't stand to be still. Her feet were already killing her. She glanced behind her for the five hundredth time in the last two hours to find that, yes, Armando was still back there, following her around like a puppy. He was wearing a black pinstripe suit over a deep, blood-red shirt with no tie, sunglasses with dark wraparound lenses that flashed crimson when light hit them. She assumed they were wired up to feed him real-time security scans, but it was no accident that they also looked cool. It was also no accident that it was very easy to see the chrome-plated gun in his shoulder holster every time his jacket shifted. Armando was not undercover.

A sorority-looking girl passed them, wearing what appeared to be a fur coat and absolutely nothing else. She and a lot of the girls here had gotten that eye-widening surgery celebrities kept getting. Zoey thought it made them look like cartoon characters. Yet Armando watched her pass, apparently his glasses feeding him intel that the potential assassins were all young girls in slutty clothes (on at least three occasions, the rooftop spotters in Zoey's earpiece had called out "targets" to Armando that amounted to, "Ruiz, we got a blonde bending over in a skirt, three o'clock, good god would you look at that"). Earlier Zoey saw a size zero blonde wiggle by wearing nothing but a men's button-up shirt and panties, her hair mussed like she had just rolled out of bed. Then she saw six more girls dressed like that over the course of the next hour and realized it was a common party outfit in Tabula Ra$a. Tre had been right: Zoey's outfit was dowdy in comparison to the girls who'd come to mourn Arthur Livingston's passing with free drinks and bumps of cocaine, along with the copious party drugs that were making them think the temperature was forty degrees warmer than it actually was.

To Armando Zoey said, "This place is Slutsylvania."

"It's what?"

"Nevermind."

Zoey had noticed that when a particularly spectacular girl sauntered by, Armando would always start doing official bodyguard things—putting his finger in his ear as if to hear commands, putting a hand on Zoey's back as if to guide her through the crowd. In other words, making it very clear to the world that he was *not* there as Zoey's date.

A group of young Korean couples passed. They looked Zoey over, then gestured and laughed.

Yeah, that was the other thing: it wasn't until the party started that Zoey suddenly remembered that she was famous. Not the kind of celebrity that draws admiration or autograph requests, oh no. This was the "Hey, I saw this person in that crazy story on the news, and isn't it weird that they also exist in real life" sort of fame. Lot of glances and giggles and nudges, like her existence was one big inside joke. Zoey always felt in crowds like everyone was staring at her, but this time it was true. No one could devise a more exquisite form of psychological torture.

But worse than the gawkers were the people who knew about the assassination threat, and had come specifically to watch it play out. She could read it on their faces. They were the ones who didn't laugh, but instead had the expression of someone who was watching a movie that was just getting good. They'd point and mutter to one another, like, *There, she's the one we're going to see get killed at some point.* Like they were attending the world's most elaborate murder mystery dinner theater.

But just as Zoey had decided that *those* people were the worst, she passed a chubby boy who looked fourteen, wearing a black "TEAM MOLECH" T-shirt, the logo animated to look like it was on fire.

As he passed, he giggled as he shouted, "Say hi to your mom!"

"Oh, you've got to be kidding me. Can we kick that kid out?"

Armando shrugged it off. "Just him, or all of the people wearing those shirts? They're selling them out on the street."

"I hate this place."

"Try not to think about it. It isn't real to them. Have you ever met a celebrity you've seen on TV? That first time, it's like you're in a wax museum that's come to life. They just don't seem real."

"Are there no Team Zoey shirts?"

"I'm . . . sure there must be. Somewhere."

"Well, at least my cat likes me."

"If it makes you feel better, they have always done this. People follow Tabula Rasa's gang wars on Blink, they pick sides and track the body counts, like keeping score. Whenever there is a shootout, everyone jumps into the feeds and watches in real time, rooting for their side to win."

They passed one of the little hologram toys that had been kicked over, its holographic animation of Arthur Livingston—admiring his new angel wings and adjusting a halo—being projected sideways into the dirty snow.

Zoey said, "But shouldn't they all be rooting for me? Aren't I the good guy here?"

Armando hesitated, then said, "You have to understand, Arthur was the richest man in the city. Loud, brash, always on the news. And he was a real estate tycoon—meaning he owned a lot of property, and charged a lot in rent, and maybe did not always maintain the buildings to people's satisfaction."

"So he was a slumlord."

Armando shrugged. "No one likes their landlord. Do you like yours? But in this case, the landlord was also a flamboyant playboy who smoked cigars worth more than some of these people's wardrobes. So on Blink, the narrative frames it as the spoiled rich daughter of a slumlord versus the shirtless alpha males looking to put her in her place. Remember, it's a largely male audience."

She spotted Budd, telling an apparently hilarious story to an enthralled group of a dozen men in some kind of military dress uniforms. Old army buddies. They ran across Echo near the first-aid tent, messing with her phone while ignoring a male model-ish guy who was trying to hit on her. She was hoping to find Andre, but he must have been off coordinating security or doing some other Suit business she probably didn't want to know about.

Will, on the other hand, she found in a somewhat hidden spot back near the dais where the creepy wax corpse of Arthur Livingston was raised over the flower jungle. He just stood there in the shadows, sipping his drink and watching the crowd flow past. That wasn't a surprise—Zoey had trouble imagining him mingling.

Armando muttered to Zoey, "Watch the crowd. As it passes Will, watch."

"What do you mean?"

"Notice how no one comes within ten feet of him? Everyone gives him a wide berth. Scared of bumping his elbow. That, Zoey, is the proverbial black cloud."

It was true. The crowd flowed around his spot, like he had a force field. At one point a drunk girl stumbled close to him and her boyfriend grabbed her arm and yanked her away, as if pulling her away from a cliff.

Armando said, "The people who are from Tabula Rasa know who he is. The rest get alerts in their glasses, the facial recognition flashing up a warning saying, 'Do not make eye contact with this man.'"

Zoey approached Will and said, "You've been hiding back here the whole time?"

"I had to oversee the preparations of the, uh—"

"You are a lying fart balloon! You're avoiding the party! Ha, I knew it!"

"I'm doing no such thing. I don't know why you would think I was, or suspect that deep down I think all of these people are leeches."

"Armando was showing me how all of the people in the crowd steer way clear of you. Is it because they're afraid your liver is going to spontaneously combust?"

"What?"

"I'm making fun of your alcoholism because it's the only thing I know about you." She glanced around at the crowd. "There's got to be like ten thousand people here."

Will said, "Eighteen thousand, one hundred and forty-six inside the backscatter perimeter at this moment."

"Right. You know how many people would be at my funeral if I died? Like, four. I'd have to have Stench Machine give my eulogy." Will wasn't listening. He just watched the crowd, over her shoulder. Zoey said, "Oh, you know what you forgot to do? Show me how to do the coin trick. That was in Arthur's will."

"Later."

"There might not be a later!"

A Chinese man with a shaved head and smiling eyes walked up in a black tunic, with a katana strapped to his back. Zoey barely had time to brace herself for a kung fu sword battle, when Armando glanced at him and nodded.

"Zoey, this is Wu, my backup. I don't believe you have met him yet, you've always been asleep when he has rotated in."

"Oh, I just thought you never slept."

Wu said, "Pleased to meet you, Ms. Ashe."

Zoey said to Armando, "Why don't *you* have a sword?"

"Why don't I have a fake sword, you mean?"

Wu said, "I assure you, the sword is real. This blade is three hundred years old. When I bought it, it was covered in blood rust. When I grind the blade, the water in the bucket runs red—dried blood of men who died on the battlefield centuries ago."

Armando rolled his eyes and said, "Wu was born in Oakland, by the way—remember that when he starts dropping ancient wisdom from the Orient later. The sword is for show. I know for a fact he has never used it."

"Of course it is for show. But it is also real. Only a fool would consider those mutually exclusive."

Armando said, "All right. Look alive."

The band stopped playing, and an announcement came over the loudspeakers that they were going to be lighting the pyre. Zoey actually hadn't gathered that the pile of logs stacked under Arthur's wax body was a funeral pyre until just now, but how else would he go out if not in a stupid blaze of glory?

Will and Andre had stepped up onto the dais, joined by a group of people Zoey didn't recognize—presumably Arthur's friends, business associates, and . . . family? Zoey hadn't even thought about it, but if Arthur had a brother that would mean she had an uncle. And an aunt, and cousins. Weird.

Will now had a microphone, and asked for quiet. He said, "I would like to say a few words about Arthur Livingston. I would like to, but his will expressly forbids me from giving a eulogy at this service, for fear that it would, quote, 'bring everyone down.' Instead, he only wanted us to impart one final wish on the guests here, and I am going to hand this off to Andre Knox for reasons that will soon become apparent."

He handed the mic to Andre, who was greeted with massive applause. He pulled out a small slip of paper.

"Now, I'm gonna read Art's exact words, so no one here thinks this is coming from me." He made a show of reading off the slip. "'Those of you listening to these words are in the midst of enjoying free food, drink, and various illegal substances at my expense.'" Huge cheer from the crowd. Andre motioned for quiet, then continued reading. "'I only ask that you repay this act of charity in the same way that so many lovely ladies repaid mine—by having sex with someone several notches lower than you on the attractiveness scale.'" Laugher and hoots from the crowd. Andre gestured for quiet again. "'If you're a nine, go home with a four. You'll give them a story they can tell for the rest of their life, and be shocked at what they're willing to do once the lights are off. Do it in my memory. Thank you.'"

The crowd cheered and whistled. So loud, that it drowned out the sudden panicked radio chatter happening in Zoey's ear. She spun, scanning the crowd for Molech, then the sky. Was he in disguise? Would she even recognize him if she saw him again? She listened for useful instructions, and only heard men shouting questions and commands at each other.

Up on the dais, Will was handed a torch and he touched it to the pyre, which went up with a roar—like it had been soaked in gasoline. From the bandstand came a guitar solo version of "Amazing Grace."

Zoey caught Will as he was walking away from the inferno that was now raging behind him. "Hey. Something's happening."

Will listened, then turned back to the pyre. Armando followed his gaze and drew his gun. The spotters in her ear were yelling for them to get out of the way. Out of the way of *what*?

Then the crowd was running, and screaming. There was the sound of a massive approaching engine, and then bombastic arena rock filled the world.

Arthur Livingston's funeral pyre exploded, flaming logs flung in every direction. A monster truck crashed through it, mashing Arthur's wax body under gigantic tires. The truck was electric but had been rigged with massive speakers to broadcast gasoline engine sounds, and was playing an old heavy metal song in which a raspy singer was offering to rock everyone like a hurricane. Flashing across the grill in yellow letters animated into flames was the word, "MOLECH."

Will said, "I think that's him."

TWENTY-EIGHT

The truck skidded to a stop and out from the cab hopped a shirtless Molech, along with Black Scott, the sidekick he introduced in the Arthur Livingston death video. Behind them, four more muscle-bound dudes hopped out of the bed of the truck, not a shirt among them. They all wore suspenders that they left dangling at their hips, and each of the henchmen wore baseball caps with the bills facing in various directions.

Cheers went up from the crowd. Zoey hoped those weren't all Team Molech, and that most of them were just cheering because the action they'd come to see was finally unfolding before them. Molech, smiling broadly and thoroughly pleased with his entrance, turned and waved to the crowd.

He had stitches. Incisions that ran across his shoulders, and down both arms. She could see them on his sidekick Scott, too. She wondered if all of his men had them, the mark of the Raiden implants. The pair of them then turned and swaggered directly toward Zoey. Armando edged around to get his body between them, gun in hand. The crowd was forming a circle around them, everybody trying to make sure their camera was getting the best view.

Molech and his partner stopped a step short of a confrontation with Armando. Molech looked Zoey up and down, and burst out laughing.

To Scott, Molech said, "Dude, this is her! Like twenty years ago Art knocked up a stripper and his trailer park daughter wound up with all his money. Now Blackwater and all those guys are having to kiss her ass to try to get her to turn over the estate. Look at her! They gave her a makeover." He shook his head. "Dude, this is priceless."

Zoey said, "I know you, too. I just watched a video with you in it."

"Oh, is that right?"

To Armando, Zoey said, "These two are from *Sausage Express*, that gay porno I was telling you about. Armando, meet Miles O'Smiles and Dick Christmas."

Molech said, "Oh, look, she's funny. Hmm, let me do the math—funny girl, absent father—want me to guess which antidepressants you're on?"

"I've actually found a new form of therapy. It's watching your employees die."

"Let's see what else I can guess about you. You're too fat to be a stripper like your mom. So . . . waitress? Am I close?"

"Close. I'm a professional hunter. Been doing it since I was six. Got a wild boar on my first day. Not very hard."

This stopped Molech for a moment. Will watched them, saying nothing. That look on his face again, like he was doing calculations in his head.

If Molech makes a move, just get flat on the ground.

Molech recovered and said, "I got to hand it to whoever picked out that outfit, showing off your tits to draw attention away from your face and jacked-up teeth. How about I bend you over my tailgate, yank up that skirt, and let my boys line up and take turns?"

"Can I bring a magazine? It sounds boring."

"Come on, baby! If you didn't want it, you'd have covered up."

"And you must want to get shot in the head, or else you would have worn a helmet. There are ten guns pointed at your head right now, by the way."

That was a conservative estimate. She could see five of the plainclothes security that had edged into position among the encircled crowd, all with guns drawn. And those were just the ones she could see.

She looked Molech over. "So, how much time do you spend flexing in front of a mirror on an average day, trying to convince yourself that people still associate muscles with strength? How many hours you spend in the gym piling on mass to hide the scared little boy under it?"

Molech glanced around at the gunmen and said, "Whoa! Hey, guys, we're just here to have a conversation! I don't know what's happened with the world today when a common man like me can't come to a public park to discuss business without a small army freaking out and pulling firearms. This is completely ruining the conversational environment. Here, let me take care of that. Todd?"

One of Molech's shirtless henchmen was carrying what looked to Zoey like a fire hydrant from the year 3000—a flat black, knee-high object with a top that looked like a honeycomb. The guy sat it on the ground and a dozen armed men, including Armando, screamed at the man to step away from it. Zoey assumed it wasn't a bomb, since Molech and his shirtless band were presumably no more bombproof than she was, but the thing wasn't going to start oozing homemade ice cream, either.

The henchman smiled and held up his hands in the kind of playful "don't shoot" gesture you'd give to a toddler with a toy gun. The device had already been activated. It whirred to life and the upper part, the honeycomb section, started spinning, impossibly fast. The device started glowing, the spinning top forming a ring of bluish white light that was too bright to look at. Zoey felt a hand against her back—Armando's—about to throw her to the ground.

But it was too late. The machine went off, with a shriek that crescendoed into a thrumming *WUBWUBWUB* sound that shook the earth.

Armando fired his gun.

Zoey flinched at the sound, and went down to one knee.

Wait, no, that wasn't right—he hadn't pulled the trigger at all. The gun had spontaneously exploded in Armando's hand.

Armando cursed and yanked his hand back, flinging flecks of blood from several gashes in his palm. Smoldering shards of metal were lying between his shoes. Then there was a series of pops, like very loud firecrackers—all of the bullets were going off inside the remains of the gun, sending high-speed hunks of metal in every direction. People started running, or diving for the ground.

And then it happened again nearby—this time one of the plainclothes gunmen screamed, clutching a ruined hand. And again, and again, until it was a continuous staccato cacophony, like the finale of a fireworks display. The harsh rattle of dozens of bullets all detonating at once, ruining every firearm in the vicinity.

And then, there were fingers around Zoey's throat.

She was lifted to her feet. Molech's face was suddenly three inches from hers.

Without looking away, Molech said, "Be cool, Ruiz. We're all good here, just takin' the guns out of the equation, that's all. A few of your boys are missing fingers, but they can learn to jerk off with the other hand."

To Zoey, he said, "That gadget there was a gift from your daddy. It cooks the cordite right inside the cartridge, it uses microwaves, or ultrasound, or somethin'. Kills every firearm within three hundred yards. See, now we can have this conversation like civilized people."

He squeezed, and waited. Zoey didn't know what he was waiting for, but of course he was letting the chaos die down, and allowing all of the cameras to focus on him and him alone. He wasn't going to waste his monologue.

Molech said, "Look around you, piglet. What do you see? Same thing you see in the mirror—fat, weak, lazy slugs. The gene pool so diluted that you can barely recognize these pale blobs as human, all their juice watered down. We did this to ourselves, piglet. Back before you and me were born, all the politicians got scared about all the crime, and all the wars, so they pumped everybody full of antidepressants and soy and estrogen, trying to dull that fire, that natural fire that's supposed to burn inside all of us. They gave all the men porn and video games, to soak up their conqueror instincts. Worked like a charm—crime went way down, rape went way down, pregnancy went way down. And the only price was they turned all the men into fat little toothless blobs and the girls into arrogant, squealing little piglets, like you. Puttin' that fire out forever, that natural fire that comes from the balls. The fire that built this world. Well, I'm here to tell you, there are still some men left. So no, there's not gonna be no negotiation. The lion don't negotiate with the gazelle."

He squeezed, and lifted, and Zoey was now standing on her toes.

"I said we were going to talk like civilized people, and this, here, is how civilization works. The goods go to the strong, and the weak starve, so that the species can get stronger. When the weak hold the goods, the strong are *obligated* to take them, to propagate strength, and eliminate weakness."

From behind them, Will said, "Zoey doesn't have what you want, but I do. Will you allow me to explain, or do you want to keep choking the barista?"

"Dude, I know who you are and what you're all about. You think you can string together enough fancy words to get me to sell you my own mother. We're done talking. You hand me the gold or you shut your squeal hole."

Will said, "The gold—you're referring to the software that runs Raiden, correct? The hardware works. The software that manages it doesn't."

Molech smiled. "See? Look at all the trouble we had to go through just to arrive at this point."

Will said, "In programmer slang the rough code is the beta and the final working copy is the gold, right? So stop me if I'm wrong, but I'm thinking the gear you got from Singh had the beta code. That's why your minions keep going up like roman candles when they try to use it. Without the gold code, all of this gear is useless to you. Right?"

"So here's the part where you tell me you've got the gold in your pocket, before I pinch little Zoey's melon off and punt it like a football."

"I'm not sure you want to do that. This defect, it's common to every device, including the augmentations in your arms. You didn't know that when you got the implants, did you? How many times have you used them? Because the next time you activate those motors, the whole thing could blow, just like your friend at the train station, and who knows how many hobos you've used as test cases. So now you've got your supervillain powers all rigged up but you're playing a game of Russian roulette every time you try to use them. And that's driving you crazy, because you want to play with your toys. Don't you?"

"You don't think I'm capable of ripping her windpipe out without the aid of Singh's gadget? Watch me."

"No need, you're going to get everything you want. The gold, unfortunately, appears to have gone up with the warehouse. The warehouse you blew up. You did blow it up, correct?"

"I don't know what caused that, but it was also awesome as hell. I regret nothing."

"Anyway, we have a computer genius on our staff named Echo Ling, she built and managed all of Arthur's software. She has been analyzing Singh's schematics and code. Says she'll have your stability issues corrected within one week. You'll get your gold."

Molech barked a laugh.

"You think I'm the dumbest asshole in the world, Blackwater. I walk away and you promise to give me what I want in a week, in the meantime you spend the whole week, what, scheming to take me out? Taking all of Livingston's cash out of the bank and running to South America?"

"Well of course you'll leave here with collateral. I'm going to suggest you take me. As your hostage."

Zoey was utterly unable to read Will, and had no idea if this was a genuine offer or a con. But Molech made no show of letting go of her.

Will continued, "I'm open to other offers. Andre would be more fun, but also more expensive to feed. Otherwise, you lock me up and if the team fails to deliver the fix, you can crush my skull and do all of this again."

Molech studied Will's face, weighing his options. Finally he took his hand off of Zoey's throat, but latched it around her right wrist instead. He put his other hand on her elbow, so that he was holding her arm like the handlebars on a bicycle.

"All right. I'm a reasonable man, like I said. But there's one last thing that needs done to make it even. See, your girl here insulted me, right to my face. On top of killing two of my men. But it's really the insult that I can't abide. So as a reminder to her, I'm gonna break her arm off at the elbow. Both bones in her forearm will snap, and I'll just twist them like celery. I'll keep the rest of her arm, as a memento, in a big jar on my mantel. Meanwhile, she'll have a nice long trip to the hospital, what with traffic shut down all the way to midtown, screaming with her arm a ragged stump. And she'll have that memory to remind her that the days when weakness can insult strength are over. Everybody get your cameras in on this, and give me silence. I want you to hear it when the bones snap."

Incredibly, everyone in the crowd *did* go quiet. Zoey tried to pull away, so she could go flat and hope that somebody, somewhere, still had a working gun. There was no give in Molech's grip whatsoever, it was like her arm was caught in an industrial machine. The two hands clamped down on Zoey's wrist and elbow and pain jolted down the bone. She squeezed her eyes shut.

And then there was a terrible, meaty sound, and then there was blood.

TWENTY-NINE

Zoey stumbled back. Everyone was screaming.

She was surprised to find that her arm was still attached to her body. And in fact, Molech's two hands were still clasped to it. But Molech was not attached to his hands.

He was standing ten feet away, staring at the neat, bloody stumps where his hands used to be. Standing in between Molech and Zoey was Armando, holding a bloody, smoking katana and looking as startled as anyone. Zoey frantically pried the two disembodied hands off her arm and flung them to the ground, like they were a couple of huge, disgusting insects that had landed on her.

Molech continued staring at the two spots in his universe that for his entire life up to now had always been occupied by hands. He did not scream, or panic, or cry. He bared his teeth and furrowed his brow, then slowly closed his eyes. Frustration, like he had just busted out in a game of poker and was already trying to think of ways to get his money back.

His henchmen, on the other hand, were staring wide-eyed, like their whole world had come undone, as if they'd just seen the sky open up and a huge God poop fall out. One of them bent over and started retching.

Molech turned and stumbled toward his truck, barking at his men for help.

Zoey grabbed Armando's sleeve and said, *"Finish him."*

But Armando was staring at the smoldering katana, which had two ragged, charred notches in the blade, like a demon had been gnawing on it.

Zoey shook him.

"Hey! He's getting way!"

Armando snapped out of it. He moved toward Molech, but now Molech's henchmen had closed ranks, forming a bare-chested wall around their boss. Black Scott was dragging Molech into the bed of the monster truck, and the rest of the dudes piled in. The crowd parted as the massive truck rumbled away, its fake engine sounds droning into the distance.

There was stunned silence in the crowd. After all this buildup, the whole thing had played out in less than five minutes.

Armando put a finger in his ear and said, "Jeff? You there? We need to make sure that truck never gets where it's going. *Especially* if it's going to a hospital."

Armando watched the truck round a corner. He looked down at the katana again, then walked over and handed it back to Wu, who was standing in awe.

Armando said, "This is a genuine katana. I owe you an apology. And I will replace it, I think I ruined the—"

He was cut off by a hug from Zoey. "Holy crap! Suddenly I get why you charge three hundred an hour."

"And to think that I took this job without finding out how truly crazy you are. You got right in his face."

Andre had made his way to the scattered, flaming ruins of the pyre and found where the microphone had been tossed aside.

He picked it up, turned to the stunned crowd and said, "Uh, thanks for watching, everybody. That was of course a scripted event that, oddly enough, was laid out in Arthur's strangely specific will. Those were all actors, everything is fine. Drop party starts in thirty minutes!"

The crowd cheered. The band started playing again. Zoey found Will, who was looking down at the two severed hands at his feet, their fingers still twitching in the dirt. She couldn't tell whether he was happy or unhappy with this result. Echo appeared, and placed the two severed hands in a cooler she had stolen from somebody. They were getting quite a collection of hands.

Zoey said, "He'll bleed out, right? You can't just . . . lose two limbs like that."

After a long pause, Will said, "Probably."

"Was that a real offer you made him? Were you really going to go along as his hostage?"

"It doesn't matter. It's done. It's fine."

He turned to walk away.

Zoey said, "Hey! We won, right?"

"Sure. Go get something to eat, you did good. Go enjoy the rest of the party."

Zoey watched him walk away.

"Hey! You still need to show me how to do the coin trick!"

No response, and then he was swallowed by the crowd.

Enjoy the rest of the party. That was, in context, the most laughably inappropriate suggestion she'd been given in her entire life. But, sure enough, ten feet away the party had in fact resumed as normal. This was Tabula Ra$a, it probably wasn't considered a real party until somebody got threatened and dismembered. And the ones who had come specifically for the drama, well, they were only disappointed that it wasn't worse.

Zoey said to Armando, "Come on. I'm buying you a drink."

"I can't drink alcohol on the job, Zoey. And we should get you out of here, Molech's thugs might come charging back, especially if their boss dies . . ."

"Yep, I totally agree."

She hustled him away, toward a stand she thought she remembered passing earlier. They arrived at a dark corner between food tents, where a tiny potpourri-smelling drink tent had been wedged in. A crude hand-painted sign claimed to sell "Spirit Teas." The menu was promising "potions" that could make you smarter or happier or ease your anxiety. Heavily featured at the top was an unnamed concoction with no description—just a picture of a thermometer with the red mercury pegged to the top. She asked for two, and the hippie girl behind the counter refused to take her money. Get rich enough, Zoey thought, and you don't have to pay for anything.

Zoey handed one to Armando and said, "It'll warm you up."

"Great. Let's go."

He pulled at her elbow and they immediately ran into Andre, who had pushed through the crowd, looking mildly panicked.

"Ah, there you are." To Armando he said, "Got the three worst hand injuries into ambulances. One of the snipers took shrapnel to the face, might lose an eye."

Armando said, "We are going to get her off the grounds. Tell Wu he's in charge."

Zoey said, "Not until I get something to eat. I deserve it, even Will said so."

Armando glanced around at the crowd and said, "Zoey, I . . ."

"No. Screw Molech, and all of the people out there rooting for him. He doesn't get to run me out of my own party."

"You didn't even want to come."

"I'm getting something to eat, and *then* we'll go. I'm fed up with this victim crap." She shook his hand off her arm. "And I'm tired of being led around like a corgi at a dog show. Don't do that again."

Andre said, "So sayeth the queen. You ever had a Danish hot dog?"

"Is that food or a crude innuendo?"

"It's a gourmet hot dog, like they make them in Denmark. Sweet cinnamon bun, caramelized onions, mustard. Like a party in your mouth. Comes with a bag of donut fries."

"Lead the way."

Ten minutes later Zoey was eating the last third of a hot dog, sipping magic tea, and tromping up a flight of stairs, following Andre. They were in a hotel overlooking the park, and when Zoey asked Andre if he had a room or something he said no, and just kept going up the stairs.

Finally they reached a door marked "ROOF" and they emerged into a chilly but quiet rooftop, overlooking the chaos of the Arthur Livingston Memorial Service from twenty stories up. Below them, bright specks of orange flashed and danced in the firepots, columns of smoke and steam drifted out of the food tents, music wafted up through the chilled air. The bouncy castle was rocking back and forth from the reverberation of partiers jumping around inside, like the huge inflatable structure itself was dancing to the rhythm. The once-mighty Beer Mountain was now just a smashed pancake of dirty snow, and Zoey could see the specks of a few desperate people stomping around it, trying to fish out the last of the free beers. From up here, it looked like fun. Zoey decided this was about the right distance for her to enjoy a party.

They weren't alone on the roof, some other kids had found their way up there and apparently it wasn't a secret spot, since security guards in yellow vests were standing along the edge. Still, it was a hundred times quieter than the pounding din of the party. Zoey finished her hot dog and couldn't find a trash can to throw the wax paper into, so she wadded it up and stuffed it into the pocket of her blazer. She thought about Arthur holding his meeting with Singh atop Livingston Tower and how rich people seemed to like high places— penthouse apartments, high corner offices with a view of everything—and for the first time saw the appeal. All the little people scurrying silently below you while you look down, untouchable. She had to admit—she liked the view.

Behind her, Armando was spitting instructions to Wu that Wu was receiving with mild amusement, humoring him. Zoey got the sense that Wu had been in the business longer than Armando. He knew what he was doing.

Armando said to her, "They stopped Molech's truck, about six blocks away."

"Is he dead?"

"Still waiting for confirmation."

Wu pulled out his katana, examining the charred gouges in the blade.

Armando said, "Like hacking through a power line."

Wu shook his head. "What kind of a man would willingly implant machinery inside him?"

Armando shrugged. "My father has a pacemaker. I will buy you a new katana, but you will have to tell me where to find one."

Wu shook his head. "Nonsense. If this blade could speak, it would not have asked for a long retirement on my mantel. It met its end in battle, just as it was created for."

Armando rolled his eyes and sipped his tea.

Zoey said, "You like it?"

"It tastes like flowers or something."

"When have you ever eaten a flower?"

"You know what I mean. Also, I am not sure what the secret ingredient is, but I am starting to think it's not sugar and spice. I feel like I am getting hot flashes."

Zoey agreed, the warming effect was kind of alarming. All at once she felt like she was dressed too warm for the weather, even though it couldn't have been above forty degrees on the rooftop

Armando listened to something in his earpiece, then said, "Car is ready. Let's move." He came up to her and started to put a hand on her elbow, then stopped himself.

Zoey downed the last of her tea, and had an almost medical urge to get out of her clothes. She stood on the ledge and watched the mass of partygoers swirl in and out of the park like ants, and wondered how many of those people were going to be having sex in the next few hours.

She started to tell Armando she was ready to go, but from behind them, came soft footsteps.

Zoey had time to hear Andre say, "I really am sorry about this, guys."

And then a strong hand shoved her off the roof, and she was falling down, and down and down, through the frigid night air.

THIRTY

Arthur Livingston could not have told you exactly how many women died while in his employ, it wasn't the sort of thing a man like him kept records on. And honestly, nobody ever asked. A client looking to enjoy an evening at the club with a beautiful escort doesn't want to know how she got there, any more than he wants to go tour the slaughterhouse where his steak was made. The twenty-first-century consumer doesn't particularly care how ugly things get on the back end, as long as a beautiful piece of meat winds up on the plate.

But it was this ugly back end of the process that resulted in Arthur Livingston meeting Will Blackwater, Andre Knox, and Budd Billingsley. This was fifteen years prior to Zoey's tumble off the roof in Tabula Ra$a, right around when she was entering elementary school and, for the first time, hearing the rich kids tell her she smelled bad. Arthur had been at a bar, watching a news report about the impending war in Korea and saw a tragic story about the poor souls trying to escape the country, and the unscrupulous human traffickers who were scooping up terrified female refugees and selling them into sex slavery abroad. Tragic, that is, because Arthur wasn't the one doing it.

Fortunately, Arthur had friends in South Korea. And also North Korea. And China. And Russia. He very quickly slapped together the Arthur Livingston Foundation, a supposed international aid organization dedicated to handing out food, water, and emergency medical care to the desperate North Korean refugees. Grateful people were fed, clothed, and healed while Arthur's people wove through the camps, secretly offering the most attractive of the female refugees safe passage to the United States, complete with very authentic-looking documents.

That wasn't as simple as it sounds, of course—most jobs aren't. The entire Korean Peninsula at the time was in that proverbial moment in which you realize your nausea is going to turn into a puke and that there is nothing to be done about it. A brutal insurgency was gnawing away at the foundations of the North Korean regime and the mad dictator in charge swore that before he ever relinquished power, he would launch his cache of nuclear warheads and turn the south into a radioactive wasteland. So Arthur didn't like to visit the area himself, he'd just do a quick round trip every few months in order to get himself photographed in front of some starving children.

To be clear, Arthur's promises of safe passage and freedom for the girls were absolutely true. It's just that the type of work he had in mind for them once they reached the Land of the Free was probably not what they imagined. Or maybe it was—just because they came from an isolated police state didn't mean they were naïve. As far as Livingston was concerned, everybody won. The girls got safely away from a country that was about to turn into a meat grinder, and Livingston's wealthy clients back in America got the stunning "Japanese" girls who were constantly in demand among a certain crowd (namely, those who had made their money in the tech industry). The only downsides to this extremely lucrative trade, as far as Arthur was concerned, was that the long plane rides were very tiring and the process of negotiating bribes with three countries' worth of bureaucrats was very tedious. Well, that and the fact that if he was caught in-country, he would immediately be executed for the crime of human trafficking, and the news would trigger an international incident that could very likely result in nuclear war and a subsequent chain reaction that would render all human life extinct from the universe forever. But of course no investment is completely free of risk.

A few months in, the Chinese clamped down on North Korea's northern border, resulting in a rather ugly incident in which six of Livingston's girls were burned to death inside a truck as it crossed North Korea's hilariously named Sino-Korea Friendship Bridge. Arthur didn't skip a beat—he tracked down a friend in Nagasaki, Japan, who ran an underwater tourism business on the island of Tsushima, and asked him if he could buy his submarine. Within a week he was back in business, transporting the girls under the Yellow Sea, puttering toward South Korea past schools of exotic fish and underwater mines. He figured if the government ever seized the sub, he'd buy some big weather balloons and just float the girls across the DMZ. Or find a way across the other northern border, into Russia. Arthur Livingston, you see, lived by a very simple slogan: "There is always a way."

It's not like the authorities never caught wind of what was happening.

Livingston was useful to the regime, because it liked making a big show of how it was working with international aid groups to assist the poor refugees who were suffering under the senseless rebellion. And he was useful to every official who relied on his bribes to stay afloat. For example, at one point an ambitious young officer from the regime's Ministry of Public Security started asking after two dozen females who had vanished from one of the camps overnight. A week later, the man was found in a parking lot having tragically committed suicide by shooting himself in the head four times. Arthur didn't shoot the man, or order the man shot—at the time he was in Utah, pitching investors on the idea of a luxury hotel with an all-nude female staff. Arthur had never personally killed any man, in fact. But as far as he was concerned, if you stood in his way, you made your own choice. The market is a machine, if any man is so foolish as to try to stop the works from turning, he should not be surprised when he gets ground up in its gears.

So, it was with great alarm that, on his last ever trip to North Korea, Arthur was snatched out of his hotel in Kaesong and stuffed into the back of a waiting sedan. Three gruff soldiers drove him out of the city, none giving even the slightest reaction to Arthur's lavish offers of a lifetime of wealth in exchange for simply telling their superiors that he had not been home. Arthur was driven to an airfield that had been blasted into a cratered Hellscape by insurgents, the sedan passing between the twisted and charred carcasses of fighter aircraft that never made it off the ground. The car stopped outside a hangar so riddled with bullet holes that it looked like it was coated with poppy seeds, and Arthur was roughly escorted inside.

Waiting there, to Arthur's surprise, had been an American man in his fifties. He was not in uniform, but could be tagged as military from half a mile away—his posture, haircut, and jawline would have made him look one hundred percent marine even if he'd been wearing a dainty sundress. Arthur's Korean escorts shoved him forward and the marine asked them to wait at the entrance while he and Arthur took a walk. Together they strode into the building, pausing to step over a blackened object that it took Arthur a moment to realize was a charred skeleton, frozen in the position in which the victim had been trying to crawl away from the fire. There was a greasy pool under the skeleton—a dried puddle of melted fat.

The marine said, "Mr. Livingston, it is my understanding that if I need someone moved across the border, you're the man to talk to."

"You know my name. What do I call you?"

"Call me Randy. I've always liked that name."

"Okay, Randy. Am I off base here or are you not supposed to be in this country?"

"That depends on who you ask, doesn't it? There are three Americans being held in Kaesong. We need to get them out."

"Soldiers?"

"Not officially, no."

"CIA?"

"Civilian contractors. Doing work on behalf of our government."

The man handed Arthur a tablet displaying three photos and a list of names, along with their height and weight. There was no other information.

Arthur glanced at it. "On behalf of what branch?" The man didn't answer. Arthur asked, "Well, can I ask what they were doing, at least?"

"Preserving freedom and looking out for American interests abroad."

Arthur grunted and said, "'Will Blackwater'? That's about the fakest name I've heard. You can't let operatives pick their own aliases, Randy. You wind up with a bunch of guys named 'Max Strong' and 'Nathan Steel.'"

"The three are scheduled to be transported to Pyongyang at oh five hundred hours tomorrow, and then will be publicly executed. We intend to get them out of there before that happens. And that of course is what brings you here."

"Why do you need me? Just call in an air strike."

"The United States of America is not officially involved in the Korean insurgency in any way, and will not officially get involved until the moment a North Korean soldier, aircraft, or artillery shell crosses the demilitarized zone."

"Ah. Of course."

They had reached the other end of the hangar. Out back, a pillar of black smoke was still billowing from a crater in the pavement, underground fuel tanks that had probably been burning for months.

Arthur said, "Well, I have a vessel."

"I know. At Ongjin. A glass-bottom submarine you've dressed up like a fishing boat. Very cute."

"Bring your people to the docks and, for a reasonable fee, we'll ferry them down to Incheon or wherever you want them."

"I'm afraid it won't be that easy. We have negotiated an exchange, under the table, with the officer in charge of transporting the prisoners. The three of them will be 'killed' in an escape attempt, but the bodies he presents to his superiors will be substitutes. *His* fee is that he wants his daughter back."

"You're saying that like I know who his daughter is. Do I?"

"Sixteen-year-old girl named Choi, you transported her out of the country six months ago."

"Oh. Well, then, at this very moment she's probably currently in a club in Utah, pretending to be a geisha and laughing at some American salesman's terrible jokes."

"So you know where she is, then. We have less than twenty-four hours. You need to get her on a plane, bring her back here, get her across the border, and back into the hands of her father."

"That would be the very father she just risked her life to escape, in the country that's about to be torn apart by war."

"It is unfortunate for her, to be certain. One of a million unfortunate fates that are going to be met within the borders of this godforsaken patch of land, no doubt." The man glanced around at the carnage of the ruined airfield. "You know, my great-grandfather died here. Truman should have let MacArthur drop the nukes, like he wanted. Do we have an arrangement?"

"What happens if I say no?"

"If you say yes, you will have the gratitude of the United States government. Something a man in your position is bound to need between now and the day he is laid to rest."

"Interesting how you turned that question around."

"These three operatives are close colleagues and friends of mine. They've been doing extremely high-risk work in-country for the last year. If I have to stand by and watch them be executed on state-run television because you didn't want to give up one of the pieces of meat you buy and sell like a street vendor doling out kebabs . . ." he shrugged. "I'm not officially here. You're not officially here. And people disappear from this place on an hourly basis. Your fate will go unrecorded by history."

Arthur glanced around at the cavernous, ruined building, thin shafts of light slicing down through the bullet wounds above them.

"Do I even want to know where you're going to get three substitute bodies to stand in for your dead prisoners?"

"I forgot to mention. We'll also need you to find us three bodies roughly matching the build of the three operatives."

"Jesus."

"Freedom isn't free, Mr. Livingston."

In the end, the choice was no choice at all. Arthur made his phone calls. A lie had gotten the officer's daughter, Choi, onto a private plane at Salt Lake. When she realized where she was going, she started screaming. It took three men to restrain her. She tried to get off the plane when it landed to refuel in

Los Angeles. She tried again in Tokyo. She talked about what her father had done to her, and what he had promised he would do to her if she ever tried to leave. None of that mattered, of course. The market is a machine, and these are just the noises the gears make when they turn.

Meanwhile, Arthur paid a local man to provide him with the three stand-in bodies, and he delivered in less than twelve hours. Arthur didn't ask where they came from, or whether or not they were alive when the man found them. It was a war zone, and the price of life had dipped into negative territory—many of the citizens were simply worth more dead. The market is what it is.

The "attack" on the convoy transporting the American hostages occurred right on schedule, though maybe "attack" shouldn't be in sarcasm quotes considering that, as far as Arthur could tell, thirteen real people had been killed in the assault, and ten more had been maimed. One guy got his legs blown off. Arthur assumed that none of the victims knew that their deaths were intended to be a form of very convincing method acting to carry out a CIA ruse.

After all of that, when the deadline for him to set sail arrived, no one showed up at the docks. It would be nearly five hours before the three American captives showed up to be hustled onto Arthur's submersible "fishing" vessel, two of them with serious wounds that he did not have the equipment on board to tend to. And so as they sailed away, a gruff Texan named Budd tried to put pressure on a spurting artery that had drenched his left leg, while the blue-eyed "Will Blackwater" was wearing a shirt doused in his own blood. As the vessel sank under the waves, a strapping young black man with a goatee and big brown eyes watched nervously as the water covered the windows and said, "It's supposed to do that, right?"

Will sat next to Arthur at the controls, holding a compress against a freely bleeding head wound, and shook Arthur's hand with fingers that were slick with fresh blood.

Arthur stared down at his blood-smeared palm and said, "Pleased to meet you."

The man said, "When we get a free moment, I want to know how you managed to pull this off."

"You don't want to know."

"Yes, I do."

Arthur thought for a moment, and tried to tally up the dead bodies and ruined lives that had pried this group loose from the People's Republic of North Korea, and lost count. He surely didn't know about all of them anyway. And it didn't matter. He had a job, that job was going to get done, and that was that. You get sentimental and you might as well walk away. Go sit in a cubicle and run out the clock until you die.

Arthur stared into the murky waters churning outside the portal window, wiped off blood onto his three-hundred-dollar slacks and muttered, "There is always a way."

So anyway, no, Arthur couldn't tell you how many of the girls he squirreled away from the Korean peninsula and other parts of the world either never made it to America, or if they did, never made it to old age. Statistically, the moment a woman accepts money for sex, her chances of being murdered shoot up five thousand percent—a woman who stays in that line of work has a life expectancy of thirty-four. But, he would say, would any of them have been better off where they were? Whether they were born in Pyongyang or Pennsylvania, they didn't wind up in that life unless they were out of prospects, and Arthur kept them clean and comfortable right up until the day they stopped being profitable. The market is the market, and it's not his fault the market says young women are cheap and plentiful and spoil faster than green bananas.

And as for Zoey Ashe, well, it simply wasn't all that unusual to find a twenty-two-year-old female dead on the pavement outside some Livingston property. It just didn't happen on this particular day.

THIRTY-ONE

Zoey fell, the freezing air rushing past her ears, waves of mortal panic and terror crashing through her nervous system. Limbs trying to climb through the air, uselessly grabbing for purchase that she knew wasn't there.

Just a few seconds.

An eternity.

Her last thought was "I'm going to die with a hot dog wrapper in my pocket" and then,

WHAP!

Zoey impacted pavement that was much softer than she had expected.

Her face was crammed into something that felt like rough canvas, and then she was sinking, gently being lowered until she was resting in what felt like a gigantic hammock. A split second later Armando landed five feet away from her and sent a jolt through the cloth that sent her bouncing. Zoey thought for a moment they had lucked out and landed on an awning, but Armando was laughing when she sat up and saw it was some kind of massive inflatable trampoline thing, which Zoey believed stuntmen used when jumping off buildings for movies. This one seemed to extend forever in both directions, covering the sidewalk and part of the street. It was black, with huge yellow letters printed on it that said simply "DROP."

A moment later Andre, knees drawn up in a cannonball, landed nearby, sending another ripple through the bag. It rolled Zoey into the dent in the canvas where Armando was lying, and she rolled on top of him and giggled and poked him in the chest.

"That was some real good bodyguarding you did there, buddy! You just let somebody push me off a roof!"

"I knew this was down here. Otherwise I would never have let you get so close to the—"

She kissed him, right on the mouth. She didn't even know she was going to do it until she did it.

Armando didn't kiss her back, but was very gentle in the way he pushed her off.

Very sternly he said, "Zoey. No."

"Okay, okay."

He sat up, trying to figure out the quickest way off the high-fall bag.

He said, "Don't be embarrassed, this is a very normal reaction when you have had the kind of experience that—"

She started crawling away from him while he was still muttering his explanation and stumbled/rolled toward the edge, finding she was still six feet off the ground.

A piercing horn sounded and suddenly there was a rain of people falling from the ledges of the buildings along the park. They fell, landed on the bags, rolled off, and ran into the buildings to go back up and do it again.

Zoey rolled awkwardly off the bag. Andre was already standing in the street, which was covered in a soft mat that she assumed was there to catch people who accidentally fell off the edge of the bag on impact. He had a ridiculous grin on his face. Zoey shoved him and laughed and Andre put on an innocent look.

"What, nobody explained to you what a Drop party is? You ain't felt adrenaline until you've jumped off a tall building and seen the ground flyin' up at you. Arthur kept wanting to set it up around Livingston Tower but that's way higher than what these bags are rated for."

Zoey brushed snow off her skirt while Armando attempted the impossible task of dismounting from the high-fall bag gracefully.

She said, "Ugh, I'm all wet now." She said to Armando, "Take me back home, you need to get me out of these wet clothes."

"Zoey . . ."

"Calm down, grumpy pants. I'm just joking. But seriously, these tights are cutting off circulation to my legs and you may have to take me to the hospital if I don't get them off."

Andre said he had three prospective ladies waiting for him back at the party, so he excused himself while Zoey and Armando made their way to the waiting car. Armando checked it from stem to stern to make sure there wasn't a bundle of dynamite strapped to the engine, despite the fact that it hadn't been out of the sight of four armed guards for the entire night.

Armando slid in first, and as Zoey climbed in the passenger side he shook off his suit jacket, and unbuttoned the top tree buttons of his crimson shirt, revealing a gold cross on a chain, and a square Band-Aid on his chest, as if he'd cut himself shaving his body hair.

As Zoey settled in she said, "It's that tea, right? It makes you feel like you've got a fever or something." The second Zoey's door closed she said, "Turn your head," then kicked off her shoes, hiked up her skirt, and shoved the tights off her legs. She wadded them up and stuffed them into her pocket along with her hot dog wrapper.

"That's better. And I'm—wait—yes, I am wearing underwear. Whew."

Armando sighed, pulled them out into traffic, and hesitated as if trying to formulate his words.

"Zoey . . . I have had a lot of female clients, this sort of thing, it comes up more often than you think. It is actually covered in training, during licensing. The client is under stress, in a vulnerable place, coming down off a rush of adrenaline. They start misinterpreting their feelings. The reaction is chemical, nothing more."

"Okay, okay, stop lecturing me. I'm blaming the tea all the way."

"I cannot continue with the contract if it is going to be like this. Even if it was mutual, it is strictly forbidden by our code of ethics."

"You're right, and using the word 'forbidden' definitely doesn't only make it hotter."

"Zoey, this is not a joke."

"I get it. You're a handsome Latin action hero. I'm a trailer troll with the wrong eating disorder. Stop freaking out about it, you can surely resist the temptation of little ol' me." She shrugged out of her blazer. "Even if I'm not a hundred percent sure I can make it home before I have to get these clothes off. Are these windows tinted?"

"Just so you understand, this is the last we speak of it."

"Of course. Jeez, you're so tense. I don't think you were this tense during the actual life-and-death standoff."

Silence, of the awkward variety. They crawled through the coagulated downtown traffic.

After several minutes, Zoey said, "You know what would help you relax? A nice massage."

THIRTY-TWO

Zoey's butt was so cold it literally woke her up.

She pulled her eyes open and saw water, and she had the bizarre sensation that she was out in the middle of the ocean, drifting naked on a raft. But she was in a bed, though one where the pillows had been knocked off the side and the sheets were knotted up around her feet.

She raised her head, which weighed at least fifty pounds, and saw that the bed was on a circular island in the middle of a small indoor pool, a narrow glass walkway connecting it to the door. Was this some cheesy hotel in town? She craned her head around and saw that the wall behind her was entirely glass, looking out into the snowy courtyard of the Casa de Zoey, under midmorning sunshine. So this was another of Arthur Livingston's ridiculous bedrooms. There was a member of the house landscaping crew out in the courtyard messing with some of the Christmas decorations, and Zoey hoped the glass was tinted from the outside. She lay back down and waited for the pain to go away or for her to just die, whichever. Something black was floating in the water just off of the bed island and she realized it was her underwear. Zoey rolled over and found she was alone in the bed. She looked up and saw herself looking back from above—the entire ceiling was a mirror. She looked like she had been tossed out of a tornado.

But she lay there, on a world-class mattress, listening to the sound of water lapping gently against the walls of one of her palace's many bedrooms, and decided that she could totally live like this. This mansion was a ridiculous museum to Arthur Livingston's deranged tastes, but what difference did that make? She could have the whole place bulldozed. She could build her own. And if anyone else wanted to mess with her, well, look at what they got.

It suddenly occurred to Zoey just how badly she had to pee, and she wondered how many hundred yards away she was from a bathroom in this place. She glanced over at the pool water and had a shameful thought, when her phone rang. The tiny holographic ghost of Will Blackwater appeared on her nightstand.

Zoey frantically covered herself with the sheet, as if Will could see her through his hologram eyes (he couldn't). She grunted and let it ring through to voice mail.

"Zoey? Where are you? Come to the conference room. It's an emergency."

Zoey groaned. She again thought of how ridiculous it was to have a house so big that you had to call a person to find out if they were even in it.

She pulled the sheet around her and tried to sit up. She had no idea what part of the house she was in, though another glance out the glassed-in wall told her that the East Wing of the house was visible across the courtyard, so that meant she was in the West Wing unless this was some kind of M. C. Escher house that existed in five dimensions. The landscaping guy waved.

She wrapped the sheet around her and thought about fishing her clothes out of the pool, but saw that by the door was a folded-up bathrobe and slippers next to a silver tray offering a selection of fresh-cut fruit, orange juice, bottles of water, and aspirin. Carlton had done this before. She tried to do a juggling act with the sheet and robe that would let her drop one and put the other on while protecting some last shred of modesty, but failed spectacularly. Instantly she had the chorus to "Butt Show" stuck in her head again.

Finally, wrapped in a robe that felt as thick as a mink coat, Zoey emerged from the room and was immediately met by Carlton himself.

"Good, you found the robe. I would have come sooner but we were not sure where you had landed last night and I'm afraid a bedroom-by-bedroom search of this estate can occupy most of a morning."

"Where's Armando?"

"I do not know. His understudy, the Chinese gentleman, is here."

"Will called, he's in a state. Am I walking toward the conference room?"

"Yes, Ms. Ashe. I trust you had a pleasant evening?"

"Yeah and, uh, that room is kind of a mess. I'll go back in there later and just . . . fish my underwear out of the pool and all that."

"No need, that task was always part of my Sunday morning to-do list. Will you be attending church services?"

"No."

"Very well."

"Did Arthur do that, when he was alive?"

"He never missed. Whether he found spiritual fulfillment there or merely a prime networking opportunity, I do not know. Perhaps that's where Armando is. Maybe he needed . . . *spiritual cleansing* for something."

"Heh. Yeah. I never really thought about the religious stuff, all I know is Christians are lousy tippers. I used to wait tables at a Cracker Barrel when I was in high school and that was the first thing the other girls told me—don't expect tips from the after-church crowd. Bitter, fussy people leaving coins on the receipt."

"The foyer is just ahead. Follow the scent of fresh pine."

"Got it. Look, the way I see it, two people walk in the restaurant, a Methodist and an atheist. The Methodist says, I'm not going to tip because I just came from church and I've already done my good deed for the day. The atheist says, I'm not tipping because life is meaningless and we're all just animals. To me, they're both members of the same religion, because they're doing the same thing. Whatever little story they tell themselves to justify it is irrelevant. It goes the other way, too—if a Muslim and a Scientologist come in and both leave a tip, they're on the same team. It doesn't matter to me if one did it because of Allah and the other was obeying the ghost of Tom Cruise, what matters is it resulted in doing the right thing."

"I would say you have devoted more thought to it than most."

At the foot of the grand staircase they ran into Will, who was hanging up from a phone call. He was still wearing last night's suit, which hadn't acquired a single wrinkle or strand of lint. Had he slept?

She pulled her robe closed and said, "Sorry I'm such a mess. I got high on magic tea and had sex with Armando."

"You have a keen ability to quickly answer every question I have no intention of ever asking. We've got a problem."

"Can I put on some clothes first?"

He answered by saying nothing and hurrying across the foyer, toward the Mold Room. It was the fastest Zoey had seen him move.

"What is it?"

"Molech is about to make a public statement."

THIRTY-THREE

Echo was waiting in the Mold Room in a neon pink tracksuit, as if she had been interrupted from a morning run. Zoey asked her if she'd seen Armando.

"No, the other guy is here, he was looking for you."

"Okay. I hadn't seen him since last night. In the bedroom with the pool in it."

Echo said nothing.

"Where we had sex."

Will said, "This is it." He brought up a feed that, at the moment, was just a black screen. "Supposed to start a few minutes ago, he's keeping everyone waiting."

"Who?"

"Molech. Maybe."

"No. Stop. Back up. He isn't dead?"

"We assumed he was until ten minutes ago. His truck was run off the road by some Pinkerton contractors, between Ventura and Twelfth. There was an altercation with his henchmen, but Molech got away."

"'Got away'? He was leaving a gallon of blood behind him with every step, I can't believe he even survived the truck ride. He had no arms!"

"He fought off six Pinkertons with his feet, then ran into a construction site. Had belts tied around his forearms as tourniquets. They went in after him, never found the body. But there was no place for him to go, we were confident that . . . we wouldn't be hearing from him again. Then his publicist put out a press release an hour ago. We wrote it off as a hoax, but our sources are now suggesting it's not."

Echo said, "It would actually be an inspiring story of survival, if he wasn't such an asshole."

"Hold on, Molech has a publicist? Where's Budd and Andre?"

Will said, "They spent all night sorting through Blink feeds from around that neighborhood, to see if there's a glimpse of Molech somewhere. They wound up finding some kids who claimed they gave him a ride home. Probably a long shot, though, those are usually just boasts the Team Molech types tell each other."

Wu appeared at the door.

"Ms. Ashe, we met last night, I don't know if you, uh, remember—"

"Yes. Wu. The sword guy."

"Armando asked me to—"

Will shushed everyone. The feed blinked to life.

It was a man in a hospital bed—a nearly unrecognizable Molech, so pale that Zoey thought he looked like he'd been gang-bitten by vampires. His handless stumps were now thick clubs of stained gauze. At the sight of him, three different people in the conference room spat three different curses. Zoey was proud that her's was the most profane.

Zoey whispered, "So he *is* in a hospital, can we find out which one? Go pull his plug?"

Echo said, "We've been watching every hospital within driving distance since last night, he didn't check into any of them. He didn't charter a flight, either."

The camera settled on Molech's pale face.

"First of all," he said, "I want to say that was a lovely funeral last night and I'm sure Arthur Livingston would be pleased if he weren't burning in Hell right now. Second of all, I want to thank the Livingston crew for the new hands. See, I had been wanting to add robot hands for months now and they've finally given me an excuse to stop procrasturbating and get it done. As my dad always said, you can use space-age technology to give your joints and muscles godlike strength, but you can't punch through a wall if your fragile little hand bones are going to get turned to powder on impact. The new ones are titanium. We're gonna fit them right after I'm finished with my message here, then I'm gonna see what it's like to get jerked off by a robot. And third of all, I want to show you somethin'. Zoey Ashe, if you're out there, pay attention. This is live."

The feed switched. They were now looking at the interior of a car, two gloved hands on the steering wheel—the feed from a glasses camera. A coffee cup was raised up to the bottom of the screen. As the driver drank, he turned toward his passenger.

Sitting there in the passenger seat, visible above the curved white rim of the cup, was Zoey's mother.

Zoey heard herself say, "No . . ."

Molech said, "Say hi to your mom. She and the craziest bastard in my employ are currently driving together toward an undisclosed location in Colorado, where I assure you the local bumpkin cops will not find them. Now, don't be alarmed. My man is not going to kill her. He's just going to temporarily paralyze her with a spinal block. Then he's going to nail her into a box, and put a live cam in there. Then he's going to bury that box. I'm going to broadcast that coffin feed live, round the clock, for you and the whole world to watch. When I get you—and I *will* get you—I'm going to lock you in a room and put that feed on every wall. You'll get to see the moment your mother regains control of her limbs, and then the moment she realizes she's been buried alive. You'll watch her scream and claw and cry and beg. For hours. Until she slowly runs out of energy, and air, and hope. You'll wake up to it, you'll go to sleep to it, day after day, week after week. You'll watch her die. Then you'll watch her skin turn gray, as the fluids ooze out. You'll watch as the maggots turn up, first in her nose, in her eyes, in her mouth. You'll watch the first face you saw when you were born slowly rot, lips turning black and shredding away from the teeth, eyelids eaten away to reveal that blank stare, frozen forever in that awesome last moment of panic."

Zoey screamed, "Don't touch her, shitspider!"

Will said, "He can't hear you, it's just a broadcast."

Molech continued, "So, the box goes in the ground one way or the other. The only question is who goes in it. You got two hours until we nail her in. Two hours to bring me the gold, and that's only because I got to take an hour to install my new hands and give them a test drive, if you know what I mean. My people will meet you in the lobby of Livingston Tower. If you bring security, we'll know immediately, and the clock on your mother instantly winds to zero. If you hand over the gold, my man will walk away from your mom, we'll take you into custody, sew your filthy mouth shut, and let my fans vote on what to do with your various holes before we put *you* in the ground instead. Remember, you brought this on yourself."

The feed clicked to black, replaced by white numbers counting down from 120 minutes.

Zoey stood and dug her phone from her bathrobe pocket. "I'm calling Armando."

Wu said, "Ms. Ashe, Armando has resigned. You, of course, are free to hire protection of your choosing, but Mr. Ruiz asked me to take on his shift in the interim. If you do not find my credentials satisfactory I will take no offense."

A message popped up over her phone, telling her the user had blocked her number.

Zoey said, "You call him. Tell him the job isn't done. Tell him Molech is back. Tell him I won't show any boob, not while he's on the clock."

"I honestly don't think he will—"

"Tell him Molech has my mother. And tell him . . ." she stopped, not sure how to phrase it. "Tell him I know the truth, and that it's okay. Tell him I still trust him."

Nobody in the room knew what that meant. Wu dialed.

THIRTY-FOUR

By the time Armando arrived at the front gates, they had already lost fifteen minutes. Will was nervous—he showed it differently than other people, but Zoey could smell it on him. It was freaking her out. He was wandering around the conference table doing a trick with Arthur's lucky one-sided coin that involved flipping it, catching it, slapping it down on a forearm, then lifting the hand to show the coin wasn't there. Then he'd pull it out of his front pocket and do it all over again, and again. They were all watching the replay of Molech's announcement, trying to deduce clues about the location.

Echo said, "Pause it here. See how the oxygen tubes plug into the wall behind him? None of this is makeshift. It's not a single-bed facility, either. To the left of him is a privacy curtain, like they pull between beds in surgery prep."

Zoey yelled, "You just said he wasn't in a hospital!"

Will shook his head. "Got to be some kind of underground clinic somewhere . . ."

"Which," Zoey chimed in, "we already knew he had, because he keeps cranking out psychopaths with these Raiden gadgets implanted under their skin. He's probably lying in the exact same bed where he got his own implants done. So why don't you geniuses, with your degrees and billions of dollars, *already know where it is?*"

Zoey screamed that last part at them. She waited for someone to tell her to calm down, but she guessed that wasn't the sort of thing to say to your boss.

Will said, "Now you know why I was so intent on getting the Doll Head guy back here alive, that first night. *Unfortunately* . . ."

Before Zoey could retort, Armando rushed through the door and said, "What do we know?"

Zoey said, "We need to get to Molech before he can hurt my mom. The good news is he's bedridden, because you lopped his hands off—we think he's in a facility where they do their surgeries, for the implants. The bad news is we don't know where that is. And we need to know. Now."

"Well . . . I've heard rumors that—"

Zoey rolled her eyes and interrupted, *"Armando.* You're wasting time."

He looked confused, but not as confused as Will and Echo. The difference was *their* confusion was genuine.

"I don't know what you're—"

Zoey said to Will, "Armando has had the surgery. The implants. He has four little incisions on his arms and back."

That brought silence to the room, which was broken by the clinking of Will dropping the lucky coin. Zoey wasn't sure what in that moment had alarmed Will more—that the near-stranger in the room was now revealed to be some kind of mechanically augmented monster, or that Zoey had just figured out something before he had.

Armando said, "Zoey, that is not—"

Zoey said to Will, "From the beginning he seemed strangely uncurious about the whole implants thing. Then when I was in the car last night he opened up his shirt a bit and I saw what I thought was a Band-Aid, but I saw it closer later and it was one of those skin patches with painkillers that they give people after surgery. I had to see him with his shirt off to make sure the scars were there, but . . ."

Armando was clearly trying to craft a response, but interrupted his own thought, saying, "Is *that* the only reason we—"

Zoey said, "No, of course not. Can't a girl have more than one reason for doing a thing?"

Will said, "I'd argue that's the norm." He thought, then said, "Hold on, you saw the Raiden scars while you were getting undressed, but then instead of running out of the room and calling someone, you just *kept going?*"

"Eh, by that point, I was willing to risk it. Will, the Statue of David could sue his abs for copyright infringement."

Echo closed her eyes and groaned.

Armando seemed to weigh several options, before finally saying, "It was two months ago. I heard about it by random chance, I had no idea where the technology had come from. They did a demonstration and started taking bids. The same day I got my procedure, a patient blew up in the recovery room. Splattered himself and fried a nurse. I did some digging and found out we'd all basically implanted bombs in our bones. I literally only used the implants once—to swing that katana last night, and I held my breath when I did it. If I could have the implants removed, I would. I know now that Molech just wanted crash dummies, because he couldn't figure out why the stuff he stole wasn't working. It was a foolish decision in retrospect. The waiting list was full of crazies."

Zoey said, "I know, I've met them. But why in the hell were you in line with them? Why would you even *want* that?"

"This is not the politically correct thing to say, but only a woman would ask that question. The chance to be stronger, faster, than the predators who come after my clients . . . I suppose it would be the same if you could get a device implanted inside you that would make you young and beautiful, and keep you that way forever."

"Uh, you mean *more* young and beautiful, right?"

Echo asked, "What do your implants do? Just strength enhancement?"

"Actuators in the elbows, wrists, shoulders, braces that extend down the back for stability. Preprogrammed movements. Strength, speed, reaction time, automatic stabilization to aid aiming. Told me I could punch through brick, or catch arrows, and could download Krav Maga for an additional hundred thousand."

Zoey said, "And you showed up here that first night because . . ."

"Same reason Molech came into your life. I want the gold."

Zoey growled and made a motion like she wanted to claw out her own hair. "*We. Don't. Have. It.* If we had time, Echo could program it for us—"

Will said, "Actually, she can't. That was a bluff."

Armando said, "You do have it. Arthur told me himself."

Zoey threw up her hands in exasperation. "Oh my freaking god. When the *hell* did you talk to Arthur?"

"Two weeks before he died. He came to me. He'd heard I'd gotten the implants, said they'd made their breakthrough. Asked if I'd volunteer."

"To be a guinea pig?"

"No. He said the testing phase was over. He wanted me to become what this city needs."

Zoey rolled her eyes and said, "Another mechanized kill freak?"

"A hero."

She took a deep breath and said, "All right, that's . . . a whole other discussion. *Where did they do the surgery?*"

"*I don't know.* They had us gather at another location, down in the warehouse district, and blindfolded us for transport. We were in a vehicle for four hours, but felt like we were driving in circles for a lot of it."

Zoey cursed.

Echo tapped at the wall screen, and a map of the city and surrounding suburbs appeared. She said, "We're going to need to know everything you remember about the place."

Armando thought for a moment. "We went downstairs. No elevator. So, a basement somewhere. Clinic was makeshift, but with very advanced equipment. Big stuff—they had one of those surgery machines that did the whole procedure, looked like a robot octopus. So a large building, lot of floor space."

Echo tapped. A spray of red dots appeared. "That's every building and private home with a basement." She tapped again, about seventy-five percent of the dots vanished. "These are just the ones in commerical properties with more than ten thousand square feet of floor space."

Zoey said, "*That we know about.* He could have dug himself an underground headquarters, in secret."

Will shook his head. "He could dig an underground headquarters, but not in secret. Dirt's got to go somewhere. You'd need to rent or buy equipment to dig, get trucks to haul out the debris, pay a crew to do it . . . impossible to do undercover. It's one of these buildings, most likely."

There were still dozens to pick from.

Zoey said to Armando, "If we figure out where he is, will you go after him?"

Armando took off his sunglasses. "Even if I was still working for you, I'd be your bodyguard, not your mother's. This in no way is part of my job description."

"Not as a bodyguard, no. But as a superhero?"

"Well, for that I would need the gold. And you do have it, somewhere. Arthur knew this, or something like this, was coming. His will, all of that was done in preparation for it. He did not care about this house or the cash or the real estate, he cared about Raiden. It was his life's work, his legacy. He would have kept a backup in a safe place, and he would have made sure it found its way to you after his death. You have it. You have to. Think."

Zoey said, "The vault was empty. I don't know, maybe he meant to and forgot. Or never got a chance."

Will flipped the coin. Slapped it down. Raised his hand to reveal an empty sleeve.

She said, "It wasn't even mentioned in the will."

Will produced the coin from his pocket, flipped it, caught it, then said, "Oh, son of a—"

Zoey said, "What?"

Will tossed the coin toward Zoey. She dropped it, then picked it up and looked it over.

He said, "Press your thumb against the blank side."

She did.

Nothing happened . . . then, a few seconds later, it made a tiny beep.

A holographic menu blinked to life above the coin.

Will said, "We are the dumbest assholes on earth. It's a solid-state drive, he had it embedded in the coin. He left it to Zoey. I kept missing with the trick and thought I was just rusty. But the weight of the coin is different. I could feel it but it just . . . never registered."

Zoey said, "Then *why didn't Arthur just say the gold was in the freaking coin?*"

Will shook his head. "In case somebody else got into the vault first. It was a way of making sure that either we got it, or nobody did—nobody else's fingerprint would unlock it. He thought . . . he thought I would be smart enough to see what he had done. He was wrong."

Armando said, "Give it to me. Upload it, or . . . whatever you need to do. Do that, I'll go after Molech."

Will said, "We need a piece of the tech to try it on. Do we still have Sanzenbacher's hand?"

"Or Molech's hands?" asked Zoey. "Any of the many hands we have?"

Echo shook her head. "Sanzenbacher's mechanism was too damaged. Molech's hands were stolen out of our truck by fans who presumably wanted them for souvenirs."

Will cursed. "Oh. Wait. Call Kowalski. Tell him we need the Hyena."

Zoey said, "There's *no time.*"

Will said, "There's eighty-five minutes, assuming he holds true to his word. But we have the gold, which means we have the one thing Molech wants and, therefore, leverage."

"We don't need leverage, we need to—"

Zoey was interrupted when Candi materialized and said, "Budd and Andre are here, and they've brought a strapping young guest! I hope he likes being the meat in a manwich!"

Andre's voice came over the speaker and said, "Got a guy here we need to talk to."

THIRTY-FIVE

Andre and Budd escorted in a smirking nineteen-year-old who Zoey thought had "trust fund punk" written all over him—he had shoulder tattoos that reached up onto his neck, but they were top-of-the-line work he'd paid thousands for. He had his hair dyed and teased oranges and yellows to look like roaring flames—probably four hours in the chair and five hundred dollars for that.

The kid was restrained by a bulky pair of black handcuffs, the pacification cuffs cops use that give you a nasty shock if you try to twist out of them, and can be activated remotely to give you a knock-out injection if you get really out of control. Budd escorted the guy into the buffalo room, while everyone else huddled in the hall and got a quick rundown of the situation from Andre.

"Guy's name is Kevin Baughman. A bunch of Team Molech dudes followed the pursuit out of the park last night, trying to get it on Blink. This guy went on his feed and said he and his boys had picked up Molech a couple blocks from the construction site and dropped him off at his HQ. I think he's tellin' the truth—had video of the bloodstains in his back seat. Won't say where they took him, says he'll take that to his grave."

Zoey said, "So what, do we just beat it out of him?"

Will said, "Torture is useful for when you don't particularly care about the quality of the information you're getting, but that's about it. You want a *false* confession out of a guy, beat him up—he'll say anything. But when everything hangs on getting the *right* information . . ." Will mulled this for a moment and said to Andre, "There's a stack of metal munitions cases in the hall that

Armando's people left behind last night, empty one of them, and go get Arthur's Buddha off his nightstand."

Andre turned and jogged off to go fill this order, without a single question or so much as a raised eyebrow.

When the Suits filed into the salon, the captive was standing near the fireplace examining the buffalo head, which was still wearing its stupid Santa hat and beard. Zoey wondered, not for the first time, if in the next room over she'd find the rest of the creature's body jutting out from the wall. Kevin's face showed just the slightest alarm when presented with the phalanx of Suits that fanned out before him. Zoey knew the feeling—here's the dead-eyed Will Blackwater in a suit that looked forged from cast iron, the massive Andre in a charcoal pinstripe suit with a purple shirt and a black tie, and Budd looking like he'd just returned from a tour of his plantation. Then there was Echo Ling, now in a stern black pantsuit and narrow librarian glasses, and finally Zoey, who was wearing a faded red T-shirt that said "IDAHO? YOU DA HO!" in letters barely visible behind the smelly Persian cat she was cradling.

Will said, "Have a seat, Kevin."

Kevin sneered and said, "Why don't *you* have a seat . . . on my *funbone.*" He spat on the floor.

Andre walked over and shoved the guy down into a chair—the same chair Zoey had sat in, in fact, the first night she had arrived. So this was the interrogation chair. She noticed how low it was—Kevin was taller than her, and his knees were pointing upward. Designed so that everyone would look huge looming over you.

Will said, "I take it you know who we are."

"You're The Magician. He's Black Mountain, over there is the Regulator, Echo, and Cat Boobs."

Zoey said, *"Really?"*

Will said, "And we know who you are. Kevin Baughman. Molech's second in command."

There was a brief moment when Kevin started to refute this. Instead, he puffed up his chest and said, "I'm not telling you anything."

Will said, "Time is short. Fortunately, this won't take much time—Echo here knows torture techniques from the Orient that no human has endured for more than three minutes. So before I turn her loose, I'm going to ask you once, and only once. *What does Molech want with the relic?"*

Kevin looked nervously at Echo. Zoey could see he was torn—the easy answer in an interrogation situation is always "I don't know," and in this case that would be the truth, especially considering the question was total nonsense. But Kevin also *really* liked the idea of being treated as Molech's top lieutenant.

He said, "Tell you what. You let me go, and I'll tell Molech to take it easy on you."

Will sighed, then nodded to Echo.

She strode over to the guy, and ran a finger along his collarbone, as if feeling for some sensitive nerve cluster only advanced torturers know how to manipulate.

Will said, "Last chance."

Kevin did a disastrous job of hiding his fear, but still said nothing.

Echo pinched the man's neck and twisted, in a way that seemed like it would hurt but didn't seem particularly mysterious or torturous. Kevin growled and gritted his teeth.

Echo let go and Will said, "Talk! Tell me what he wants with the relic!"

Kevin screamed that Molech would wipe his ass with Zoey's face. Echo stepped in and twisted again.

Will shouted, "Tell me!"

"Never!"

They repeated this once more, then Echo let go, hustling Will off to a corner—away from Kevin, but not too far.

In a harsh whisper that Zoey was sure Kevin could still hear, Will said, "We're running out of time!"

Echo replied, "I've never seen pain tolerance like this. It's unreal. We could do this for weeks and he'd never break."

Will sighed, exasperated. He cursed and said, "We don't have a choice. Give him the relic."

Andre looked alarmed and said, "You sure?"

"Damn it, *we're out of options.*"

Andre hustled out of the room. He walked back in with the case Will had sent him after—it looked like a heavy-duty suitcase, built to withstand an explosion. Will set the case on an ottoman in front of Kevin and opened it to reveal the bronze Buddha figurine they'd taken from Arthur's nightstand.

Will said, "You win. Here's the Buddha. I assume I don't need to tell you not to touch it—you know how radioactive it is."

Will closed the case. Andre removed Kevin's handcuffs.

Echo said, "This case, of course, is temporary containment, Molech will have a vacuum unit waiting for it, but this will buy you about twenty minutes. So don't stop for a haircut."

Will said, "You tell Molech we gave him what he wants. Now leave us alone. And I hope you're pleased with yourself, you sick son of a bitch."

Kevin actually looked *amazingly* pleased with himself, if not a little confused. He stood, rubbed his wrist, and picked up the case.

Andre said, "Now get the hell out of here. And you tell Molech Black Mountain will see him in Hell."

Budd had parked Kevin's Camaro outside the front doors, and the Suits watched as it went squealing off toward the main gates. On the way out, he passed a plain sedan that turned out to be Officer Kowalski, the bald guy with accusing eyes who had scared the crap out of Zoey her first night. He pulled up and emerged carrying a leaking grocery sack.

He hurried up to the door and said, "Got your head here."

THIRTY-SIX

Kowalski and the Suits stood in a circle around the table in the Mold Room looking at a severed head. This was the position Zoey had caught them in that first night, and she realized that she was now officially a member of their cult. Arthur's chair at the end of the table still sat empty, and Zoey had actually considered making a big show of sitting in it, but the chair looked old, cracked, and farted-on. Instead, Zoey paced around the room, squeezing Stench Machine and trying not to look at the head, which had belonged to the man who had called himself The Hyena, among other things, but whose real name had been Lawrence Shandy.

Echo was hunched over a virtual keyboard that was projected onto the coffee cup–stained conference table, typing and pausing occasionally to swipe through menus from the coin's embedded memory.

"There's a mountain of data on here. It's not just the gold hardware drivers, it's everything. I'm seeing schematics for devices, implants, prototypes . . . it goes on and on. He saved it all."

Zoey turned her attention to the wall monitor displaying the map of the city and its scatter of red dots. They had been joined by a single, moving green dot—Kevin's Camaro, hopefully on its way to impress his idol with a fifteen-dollar souvenir Arthur had bought at a gift shop in the Incheon International Airport. Zoey had expected the green dot to steadily make a beeline toward Molech's location, then felt like screaming when she saw the car stop, then lurch forward slowly, then stop again. She hadn't anticipated traffic and intersections.

Zoey glanced back at Echo and said, "So you were Arthur's computer genius?"

"Ah, no. I knew absolutely nothing about computers when Arthur brought me on. He hired me for a position that had no job description, I just taught myself on the fly because he kept calling me every time something broke."

"Really? Your Blink highlight reel referred to you as a Chinese computer hacker. And sexy seductress."

"Well, I'm Filipino, but whatever."

Without turning away from the feed, Andre said, "Yeah and *I'm* the sexy seductress."

"And your nickname is Black Mountain? Does everybody call you that?"

"No, and that's kind of insulting in two distinct ways. Still kind of like it."

"So are you saying Will's nickname *isn't* The Magician?"

Will said, "*One time*, I get caught on camera doing the one coin trick I know . . ."

Kowalski said, "They call me Supercock."

Kowalski had been a vice squad detective with Tabula Ra$a police right up until the whole organization fell apart and all vices were effectively legalized. He was technically still TRPD, but hadn't been paid in four months. Most of the rest of the cops had rented themselves out as private security to pay the bills, but Kowalski continued to show up to the precinct every day, taking money under the table to do favors for Livingston Enterprises. Meanwhile, he continued to work cases for free because, well, he liked it.

Zoey asked, "So . . . did the coroner have some reason for taking the guy's head off, or . . ."

Kowalski said, "Nope. But they got a saw in there. Slices right through tendon and bone, I just lopped it off and walked out with it in a grocery bag. I wasn't gonna drag this bastard's whole corpse into my back seat."

"And . . . that's not going to cause any problems? It's not, I don't know, messing with evidence or something?"

"Evidence of what? Nobody is disputing the shooting, the guy's own Blink got it all. And sure as hell nobody is debating whether this prolapse had it coming. The only ones who'd have a legitimate beef would be his family, if they wanted to throw him a funeral." He shrugged. "If they call, we'll duct tape it back on. Now, if you don't mind, I'm gonna leave before you ask me to do something morally questionable."

After he was out of earshot, Zoey asked Will, "How much do you trust that guy?"

"Enough." He was watching an avalanche of indecipherable code cascade down the coin's holographic display, "What are we looking at here?"

Echo muttered, "The work of a madman. This is software written in a computer language that Resnov invented from scratch, intended to manage hardware that he invented, all of it patched by Singh, who was learning it as he went. Some of the menus are in broken English, some are in some alien language that might be code, I don't know."

"If you had enough time with it, could you figure it out?"

"I don't think *God* could figure out how it actually works. I'm just trying to figure out the commands to install it to the Raiden hardware. This menu had a picture of a stick figure man with an arrow pointing at it, so I hit it, and . . . it started uploading data. Now I guess we turn on this guy's jaw implants and see if it . . . fails."

"You mean explodes?" finished Zoey. "Do you mind if I wait outside?"

Will said, "He's turning down Fairfax."

Zoey looked up at the monitor, and soon the green dot slowed, then stopped, turning off the street into what must have been an alley or parking lot. Not far down the street were two dots, side by side.

Will said, "Is that the Fire and Ice?"

Echo glanced up from her work and said, "Yep."

Andre muttered, "Son of a bitch."

Zoey asked, "Where's that?"

Budd said, "It's a pair of buildings downtown, been closed for a couple years. It was called the Fire and Ice Casino. Twin towers, the Ice Palace and the Fire Palace, on opposite sides of Fairfax Avenue. Former covered in ice, latter done up to look like it was a volcano or somethin'. They both had rooftop pools, connected by a swim bridge that spanned the street, guests could drift back and forth. It closed down after the Fire Palace was gutted by a fire."

Zoey said, "That's ironic."

Budd said, "It's not irony when a poorly designed building covered in hundreds of decorative open flames ends up a towering inferno. And yeah, he's walking toward the Fi—"

The severed head twitched, and everybody in the room jumped back at once. Its jaw opened, then closed, metal teeth clinking together loudly—a huge amount of force in the mechanism. Then the jaw clanked together again, and again, its slack lips opening and closing like some kind of macabre puppet.

Echo said, "Let's, uh, take that out to the yard."

THIRTY-SEVEN

Forty-five minutes prior to Molech's deadline, they all stood under a portico overlooking the courtyard. The severed head had been tossed out into the snow at what they hoped was a safe distance. Out in the middle of the statues and shrubs, the jaws bit at the air, teeth snapping with that metallic *snick* that made the hair stand up on the back of Zoey's neck. They all watched, mesmerized by the head that was slowly spinning around in the snow as its jaws worked, the Hyena's blank eyes half-open, a blood-encrusted hole in his temple. Andre grabbed a shovel that had been leaned against a fountain nearby, cautiously walked over and stuck the handle into the Hyena's dead, biting mouth. The teeth snapped through the two-inch-thick wooden handle as easily as biting the end off a cigar.

Come back off the ice, sweetie.

Zoey shivered and said, "I think I'm in a straitjacket somewhere, imagining all of this."

Will asked Echo, "How long do we let this go on?"

She glanced down at a tablet screen. "That's more than two hundred repetitions. The capacitor is perfectly stable, assuming that's what this green bar here means."

Zoey said, "Yay, he successfully invented a machine that will let humans eat bricks. Now we just need to develop a system for pooping them."

Echo said, "What he invented was the most important advancement in energy technology since mankind learned to split the atom. Raiden works. The world has changed forever."

Zoey watched the severed, rotting head bite its way through the snow,

220 / JASON PARGIN

leaving behind a pink smear of blood from its severed stump. "Yeah, looks like it."

Armando said, "I've seen enough. Upload it to me and let me go end this."

Will said, "I don't see why that's necessary."

"You don't see why I'd need an edge if I am to attempt to slice my way through Molech's headquarters?"

"There's no need for you to go at all. This is what I've been saying, over and over—what we have there is a bargaining chip, the one thing in the world we know Molech needs. This is leverage. The kind of leverage that could maybe make him drop everything, take Zoey off his hit list, and end this ordeal."

Zoey said, "I think the one thing Molech needs is to not get shot in the face by Armando here. I think the coin is second."

Will shook his head. "You do that, you're playing *his* game."

"If that was *your* mother in that car, you would not be standing here calmly talking about *leverage*."

"You're wrong."

Armando said, "I respect you, Mr. Blackwater, and I am sure that you know your business. But this, right here? This is war. And that is *my* area of expertise. Wars are won by people like me, not people like you."

"Wars are *started* by people like you. The peace is negotiated by people like me. Leverage brings your enemy to the table. Guns are useful only for gaining that leverage."

"Then it's decided," Zoey said. "Armando will put a gun to Molech's head and then we'll have leverage. Echo, turn Armando into Superman. And somebody turn off the head, it's freaking me out."

Echo tapped at her tablet then said, "I'm . . . actually not sure how."

"Then just throw a towel over it or something."

Thirty minutes left. Echo was watching software stream into Armando's implants—Zoey thought she'd have to plug a cable into his head or something, but it was all done wirelessly.

Will said, "Molech demanded you meet his people in the lobby of Livingston Tower, with the gold in hand, and that you come alone. But I see no reason you can't bring your phone, so the plan stays the same—I do all the talking. Stalling is the name of the game. It doesn't matter where the conversation goes as long as it *goes*. Don't be alarmed by whatever I say. Ultimately the goal is to stall, to give Armando time to work."

While he spoke, Zoey was chewing on her thumbnail and watching the feed of her mother. The car had parked somewhere in the woods, and Zoey's mother and her abductor were drinking beers and laughing, digging sandwiches out of fast-food bags. The guy had probably found her at the bar and offered a trunk full of free beer if she'd leave with him. It usually didn't take more than that to get on Melinda Ashe's good side. Zoey couldn't stop crying.

Will said, "Listen to me, Zoey. This here—this is what we did for your father. We identified and nullified threats, by whatever means necessary. We're old hats at this. There's a process, that's all. Any good plan is just a series of branching pathways, like a flowchart. We can't predict what Molech is going to do, but his options aren't infinite and we have to have a procedure in place regardless of which choice he makes. So no matter what I say, no matter what happens, we're winning as long as we keep him talking. *No matter what.* And if he thinks he's winning, so much the better. Understand?"

Zoey nodded.

Budd pointed at the feed and said, "I know who that is with Zoey's momma. See the cigarette pack on the dash? Guy's name is Kools Duncan. Real name is Charlie. Low-level rent-a-turd, got rough with one of Arthur's girls a few years back."

Andre looked dubious. "He's the only guy in the world who smokes Kools?"

"See how he's dippin' his fries in his milkshake? Playin' Nina Simone on the stereo. Yeah, that's Kools. Gave himself that nickname. He's white, by the way."

Andre squinted at the screen. "You think he went alone?"

"No way to know for sure, but I reckon so. Kools never did get along with partners. He once stabbed a fella over whose turn it was to drive. Kools says I want to drive and the other fella says sure and Kools stabbed him in the face."

Will said to Zoey, "All right, we should get going. Just wear what you're wearing. *Don't* brush the cat hair off your shirt. And don't wash your face."

"*Why?*"

"It's clear you've been crying, your makeup is a mess. Leave it like that, that's what we want. I'd have you bring the cat, too, but he's too difficult to control."

"I'm going to have to ask you to elaborate."

"This will be the opposite of how we did it at the memorial service—we want Molech to perceive a shift in power. We can't look like we have a plan here, the more vulnerable you look, the more receptive the other person is to what you have to say. They'll take any offer as genuine as long as they think it's coming from a place of weakness. And props are everything. For instance, if hypothetically you had grown mistrustful of Andre and he was trying to get back in your good graces, he might show up here looking hungover, eating some kind of ridiculous food. It would instantly endear you to him. Remember, the most powerful impression a person can make is that they don't care if they make an impression. And whoever we're meeting with needs to take one look at you and realize you're the weak link, that you can be pushed into accepting whatever they want."

"Wow. All right."

"Now, once we meet his people in the lobby, they'll presumably try to transport you to another location, though probably not back to the Fire Palace. We'll tail you wherever you go and, quite frankly, the farther away, the better—the time they spend driving you to wherever they want to meet is time for Armando to do his thing. Understand?"

"Just barely."

To Armando he said, "How much time do you need?"

"The problem is Molech can't know I'm there until I'm in his face—the moment he knows I'm coming, he might panic and tell his man in Fort Drayton to . . . do something unpleasant."

He tapped the wall feed and a photo popped into view. It was the Fire and Ice Casino, as the twin towers had looked when they were open. Zoe thought the Ice Palace was beautiful—it really did look like a fifty-story building carved out of ice, like something out of a fantasy novel. At the top was its rooftop pool, complete with water slides and faux icebergs, the crystal blue of the glass swim bridge snaking from its roof to the Fire Palace across the street. That building had been made up to look like a charred volcano in mid-eruption, with twisting paths of roaring flames undulating down from the roof to suggest oozing lava, its rooftop pool lit from the bottom with orange lights, so swimmers could pretend they were paddling around in magma. Armando tossed up a second photo next to it, an "after" pic of the buildings as they existed today—dormant, dark, each covered from the neck down in black tarps, like they were wearing frumpy mourning dresses. The swim bridge was an empty half-pipe of filthy glass, collecting rainwater and bird crap.

Armando said, "I think the Fire Palace is essentially impossible to infiltrate unnoticed. It has three times as many guards on the exterior, and there are vehicles entering and exiting every few minutes. The Ice Palace is our way in—the entrance is guarded, but the interior is nearly deserted. I'll go up through the Ice Palace, across the swim bridge, then down to the Fire Palace basement. If all goes well, I could make the whole trip in . . . twenty minutes."

Wu said, "And where will I be?"

Zoey answered, "You'll be here, watching, and if I die you're to pack up my cat and get him to safety. And so help me god, if you laugh at me right now I will claw your eyes out."

Wu did not laugh.

Echo said to Armando, "Your implants are online. I think. The progress bar stopped. There's a message here that looks like it's in Elvish but it's not blinking red or anything."

Armando stood, and put on his jacket. Wu strode up behind him and held out a katana, handle-first.

"A gift, but only if you apologize for your previous mockery."

Armando replied, "I would, but this blade looks exactly like the one we ruined last night. The one you said was an ancient one-of-a-kind relic. This makes me think that you have a barrel full of them that you buy in bulk from Costco."

"No, this is my last one. *Maybe* I have one more somewhere."

"All right," said Will. "Let's start the game."

THIRTY-EIGHT

🔑

Five minutes until Molech's deadline.

The obscenity that was Livingston Tower loomed over the sedan, having turned from flat black to beet red since Zoey had seen it last (apparently the memorial service marked the end of the mourning period). It was frosted by the artificial snow, making the whole thing look like a cherry Popsicle that had just come out of the freezer. Will and Zoey were alone in the car two blocks away, close enough to see yellow caution tape had been stretched across the main entrance.

Will said, "We had them close the building under the guise of a bomb threat. Since it's Sunday, our offices would have been closed anyway but there are five restaurants and three brothels up there, and that's their busiest day. We can't have people coming in and out, every random bystander adds another variable we can't control. Molech could take a hostage, or even worse, someone could decide to play hero."

Zoey brought up a video feed on her phone, coming directly from Armando's glasses. At the moment he was on foot, a block away from his target. Through his eyes Zoey could see the derelict tower that had once been the Ice Palace hotel and casino, behind its faded black shroud. The view panned across the busy street, to the identical Fire Palace, the glass bridge undulating high overhead. Somewhere behind those walls, Zoey thought, was Molech. Hopefully.

The camera panned back to the Ice Palace and zoomed in toward the main entrance, which was being guarded by five shirtless men who were just barely pretending to be construction workers. And this, they had said, was the *least* guarded of the two towers.

Armando held out his hand, palm-up. Perched there was a black object that looked like a large insect—about the width of a half dollar. It whirred softly and levitated out of his hand, and buzzed off toward the derelict building.

Immediately the feed switched to the point of view of the tiny drone, bobbing through the air about ten feet above street level. It passed over the elaborate hats of three passing women in church clothes, then arrived at the Ice Palace and paused, hovering over the group of guards who were smoking and conversing in front of the entrance. Graphics flashed across the screen as it scanned the faces of the guards. Then one of the men turned to go inside and when he opened the door, the drone quickly ducked in.

The dimly lit lobby came into view, a vast expanse that apparently used to be the casino floor, before all of the slot machines and card tables had been ripped out. All that remained was a vast plain of stained carpet dotted with exposed electrical outlets. The drone performed some kind of scan of the room, a vertical blue line sweeping across the screen. It paused, as if doing some calculations, and then a series of floating red cone shapes appeared in various spots around the room. As the guard walked across the floor, one of the red cones moved with him, as if emanating from his eyes. Another came from a security camera on the wall.

Will said, "The drone is tracking the field of vision of every human and camera in the vicinity, in real time. So it can feed Armando the exact path of floor across which a person can pass unnoticed. He just has to avoid the red patches."

Zoey said, "As long as he has quiet shoes. And doesn't smell."

There was, however, no such path through the four remaining armed men gathered around the entrance. That was an entirely separate problem.

Zoey heard Armando say, "Go."

At that moment, a low, flat black car with tinted windows rolled past the Ice Palace entrance. Its engine growled with a primal sound from another time: the menacing rumble of a massive internal combustion powerplant, sixteen cylinders igniting gasoline in a symphony of synchronized thunder. The heads of the four males guarding the doorway turned to see a Bugatti Chiron crawl past, a legendary dream machine that, even in a city packed with gaudy automobiles, could drop jaws from a block away. It pulled up to the hotel next door and rolled to a stop. It revved its engine, and the pavement trembled in fear.

The driver's-side door opened and a pair of bare legs swung out. A show-stopping blonde unfolded herself out of the car, an obscenely sheer red dress appearing to be her only item of clothing—it was either designed to give the illusion the wearer didn't have on any undergarments, or else it wasn't an illusion. The woman was Echo, under a blond wig and sunglasses, sucking on a lollipop.

Will said, "I want to just note that this was *her* idea."

The plan had been for her to circle around the car and then bend over and look into the trunk, but it hadn't occurred to any of them that this car didn't in fact have a trunk. So Echo improvised and kind of just awkwardly leaned over the back as if to examine the engine, trying not to accidentally get too close to the manifolds and set her wig on fire.

On Armando's feed, the red cones representing the field of vision of all four guards swung in the Bugatti's direction, and locked in place. One of the men even got out his phone to take pictures. Armando, who was dressed in paint-splattered coveralls, simply walked up behind them and quietly slipped through the door.

He made his way inside to the empty husk that had once been the Ice Palace Casino, slipping between the red vision fields of two cameras, arriving near what had been the casino's restrooms once upon a time. He pressed his back against a doorframe and waited for a guard and his red cone to walk past, then quietly slipped into a nearby stairwell.

Zoey tapped her phone and flipped over to the feed from her mother's captor. The camera was advancing forward between pine trees to the soundtrack of shoes crunching through snow—the man and Zoey's mom taking a leisurely walk through the woods. Her mother probably thought she was having a pretty nice Sunday. Sunny winter day, pristine clumps of snow dangling off pine trees, friendly new stranger with a car full of alcohol. Her captor muttered something and she laughed.

Zoey's guts were in knots. She wished there was a bathroom nearby.

Will said, "Just breathe. Slow, even breaths, in for five seconds, out for five seconds. Breathe from your belly, like you're making an air baby. Keep going over the plan in your head."

"I've completely forgotten the plan."

Will didn't reply to that.

She glanced down at her mother's feed again, then said, "Are your parents still . . . around?"

Will hesitated. "Father is. In Virginia."

"Your mother passed away I guess?"

"She killed herself when I was sixteen."

"Oh. I'm sorry."

She flipped back to Armando's feed. He was softly climbing the stairs, making painfully slow progress. Zoey noticed he had taken off his shoes. Still, one creaky floorboard and that would be that.

Zoey said, "Are you close to your father?"

There was a long moment before Will said, "No."

Silence. Zoey looked out the windshield, scanning the pedestrians wandering around outside the entrance to Livingston Tower, looking for anyone who could be the Molech henchmen she was to meet.

She said, "I've always been close to my mom. She had me so young. I would say she was more like a sister, but most sisters I've been around don't get along."

"My father had a length of chain he would hit me with if my shirts weren't pressed to his satisfaction. And he enjoyed it more when they weren't. The first girl I ever brought home, he made her leave and told me I could do better. He told her she was too fat for me."

"Ugh. I've been there. With stepdads."

Will gave her a very brief look and said, "I know."

Zoey said, "You wake up in the morning and dread going to school because the other kids torture you, then at the end of the school day you dread going back home, because of what's waiting for you there."

He nodded, almost imperceptibly.

On the screen, Armando was quietly but forcefully shoving open a roof access door. He stepped out into harsh wind and sunlight, the flickering torsos of Tabula Ra$a skyscrapers looming silently around him. The roof of the casino was dominated by a massive empty swimming pool, containing only puddles of melted snow and various debris that had blown in over the months. Zoey saw at least one dead bird nearby.

Will nudged her and she looked up from her phone. There was a commotion outside the main entrance of Livingston Tower:

Three men had pulled up, riding tigers.

Or so it appeared. As they got closer it became clear they were on customized motorcycles, each with a snarling tiger animated across the bodywork, their feet swiping the ground as they rolled along. Incredibly, these were only the fourth most ridiculous vehicles Zoey had seen since arriving in the city. The motorcycles ripped through the yellow caution tape and parked in nearly perfect unison. Three muscular, shirtless men in leather pants stepped off, each wearing motorcycle helmets that they did not remove as they strode up to the main entrance of Livingston Tower. The revolving doors were locked, but one of the men simply grabbed one and yanked it off its hinge, tossing the four attached doors out onto the sidewalk behind them, glass shattering on the black decorative stones of the entryway. The three men vanished into the lobby.

Zoey tried to follow Will's breathing advice and said, "You never did show me that coin trick."

"You should go. There's no reason to keep them waiting."

Zoey glanced down at the feed, one last time. Armando moved across the roof of the Ice Palace—alone, as far as Zoey could see. The view bounced along as he jogged toward the arched exit that led to the glass swim bridge, which would take him to the roof of the former Fire Palace and Molech's HQ, about fifty yards away.

Zoey took a deep breath and said, "All right. Promise me that if I don't make it back, you'll take care of my cat."

"I promise . . . I will hire someone to do that."

Zoey stepped out, and tried to appreciate that she could be about to die in a way she never would have expected as recently as one week ago: spectacularly, and inside a skyscraper that she owned.

THIRTY-NINE

🔑

Molech's three henchmen were standing right in the middle of the massive lobby, directly on top of the giant gold mustache that was inlaid in the black marble tile. The lobby was silent aside from the timid squeaks of Zoey's tennis shoes.

She got as close as she was willing and said, "Hello."

They didn't answer.

Zoey pulled out her phone and summoned the translucent projection of Will Blackwater, then said, "I hope you don't mind, Will didn't trust me to do this on my own."

None of the men removed their helmets, each of their expressions hidden behind dark tinted faceplates. But then a face appeared in the visors of all three—the same face on each. The facemasks were screens, each displaying the pale face of Molech, a live feed from his hospital bed.

On three simultaneous feeds, a chorus of three Molechs said, "Well, well, well, look who brought a pussy to a dick fight. We're taking a walk."

Zoey had been prepared for this, and took a step back toward the front doors when a hand clenched around her arm. That ring of bruises flared up, that throbbing band on her upper arm that rough hands kept latching on to. Zoey bit her lip, and thought of just how very tired she was of all this.

Molech's video faces said, "Whoa, where are you goin'? Paulie, walk this ham mannequin over to the elevator."

This possibility hadn't been discussed. From her phone, Will said, "Where are you taking her?"

No one acknowledged his question. They entered the elevator, and Zoey found she was looking at the street again—the elevators were glassed-in pods that ran up the exterior of the building. One of the men punched a button and Zoey watched with despair as the pavement dropped below them, feeling the ascent in the pit of her stomach—all of the people in the world who could help her were now plummeting below her feet. Up and up they went, all the way up, until the jagged, half-finished city was like a sprawling architect's model below her, flickering towers jutting up through the haze. She imagined reaching out and just sweeping the buildings aside with her hand. Just . . . wipe it all away and forget it was ever here.

The elevator door opened on the top floor and they headed down a hall until they reached a pair of ominous black doors.

They were locked, but from the phone, Will said, "Should be updated with your voice commands, just say 'unlock.'"

She did, and the locks clicked open automatically at the sound. Inside the room was a black granite conference table, etched into the surface of which was the Livingston Enterprises logo done once again in inlaid gold, complete with that stupid cartoon mustache. And that was the least ridiculous feature of the décor.

Three of the walls formed one big wraparound aquarium full of little two-foot-long sharks (Zoey decided once and for all that subtlety was not Arthur Livingston's thing). One of the henchmen went up and put his finger on the glass, and one of the sharks came over and started ineffectually biting at it. The remaining wall was a huge curved window overlooking Tabula Ra$a. Zoey imagined Arthur and his Suits hammering out deals while looking out over the insignificant ants who scurried around the city below. It occurred to Zoey that this was where Will had wanted to meet with her two days earlier, when she had led them all to Squatterville instead. He had wanted to sit her down in this menacing black room in the clouds, surrounded by sharks. The same man she was now trusting with her life, for some reason.

From the henchmen's facemasks, the three Molechs said, "Alrighty. Since you're so big on negotiation, Mr. Blackwater, I figured I'd take us up to the room where Arthur made all of his sleazy backroom deals, dreamin' up the little loopholes designed to screw over the honest folk like me. So here's my opening offer, and there's no fine print. Zoey hands over the gold. Zoey's mother goes free. I sever Zoey's spinal cord, paralyzing her, then bury her in a coffin with a camera and ten thousand cockroaches. I broadcast the results on the Tabula Rasa skyline for the next month. I use Raiden tech to rule the Earth forever and ever."

The hologram of Will Blackwater said, "Well, I suppose we had to start somewhere. I—"

"Stop right there, lollicock. I need proof she brought the gold before this goes any further."

"Sure. It's right here." Will's hologram pointed at Zoey's head. "It took us a while to figure it out, but a few months before Arthur died, he got wind that something bad was coming his way. So he made a secret appointment for little Zoey here. She was taken to the doctor, where a series of complicated brain scans were performed. Isn't that right, Zoey?"

Zoey was completely lost, but said, "Yes?"

"What neither Zoey nor the rest of us knew was that Arthur was performing a neural etch. He was imprinting the schematics and software drivers for the Raiden exoquantum hypercapacitor right into her brain tissue. The gold code is right there inside her cranium—Arthur turned her into a living hard drive."

Zoey was pretty sure this was a lie, unless she had zoned out during an important conversation at some point, but couldn't for the life of her figure out where Will was going with it.

Molech said, "You just made that up, didn't you?"

"Think it through. Arthur did not want Zoey's life endangered—and the only way to extract the information from her neural tissue is via her willing cooperation. Kill her, and those signals go dark and the data vanishes from the universe forever. Distress her, and the emotional activity will cloud the signal and make it impossible to retrieve. This is all by design, in case of a situation just like this. The girl must be placed into a perfectly relaxed state, while conscious, while the data is retrieved. It can be done instantly with any quantum data scanner capable of reading 3-D neural etching."

Molech said, "And you brought one of these gadgets with you? Zoey's momma certainly hopes so."

"Unfortunately the only one Arthur owned was destroyed in the warehouse blast."

"How convenient for you. But *inconvenient* for Zoey and the owner of the baby hatch she crawled out of."

"But there is another way to extract the data, it just takes a bit longer. Zoey, lie on the table."

Whatever Will was going for here had in no way been shared with Zoey beforehand, which alarmed her more than anything. Still, she had to assume the man had a plan, since his brain did nothing but generate plans twenty-four hours a day. She climbed onto the conference table, then lay awkwardly on her back.

Will said, "Make sure your henchmen are close enough to record clear audio, and make no sound to interfere. I'm going to remotely activate the neural upload, and Zoey will begin to broadcast the data in the form of an audio waveform from her vocal cords. Record the sound, and decode it to binary. You'll have your data. Now, the waveform will to your ears just sound like Zoey is making a series of high-pitched screeching noises. The process will take about sixty minutes. I'm activating the audio waveform now."

Zoey stared at the ceiling and tried to figure out what Will wanted her to do next.

He said, "All right, I've initiated the process. You should hear the sound of the transmission from Zoey momentarily."

Zoey waited, in silence.

"Any moment now."

Zoey finally realized what Will wanted from her and, taking the cue, said, "*EEEEEEEEEEEEEEEEEE!!!!*"

From the masks of his three henchmen, Molech watched this happen in dull silence.

After a moment he said, "All right, while we're waiting for that, I'm going to check in with what's going on up on my roof."

The henchman on the far left's mask cut away from the feed of Molech's face, and brought up a view of a group of shirtless men loading machine guns. They were on a roof, one very similar to the one Zoey had just watched Armando cross a few minutes earlier.

Zoey stopped screeching and sat up on the table, suddenly unable to breathe. She was also unable to stop herself from muttering, "No . . ."

Responding to a command Zoey couldn't hear, the gunmen crouched and jogged across the Fire Palace roof, dodging between a pair of black and yellow cranes Zoey thought looked like a couple of robotic giraffes. Zoey counted six—no, eight—men, buckles and straps jingling and clacking as they hustled toward the glass bridge that connected their rooftop to the Ice Palace. They threw their bodies up against the curved wall of the empty pool, peering across the dry swim bridge where a single speck in a black suit and red shirt was striding toward them.

Armando, walking right into their ambush.

Molech said, "Kools, can you hear me, bro?"

The facemask of the henchman on the far right blinked away from Molech and brought up the feed from Colorado, where Zoey's mother was in mid-laugh at something her captor had said.

Kools said, "Loud and clear, boss."

"Bury that bitch."

Without a word, the man reached out and roughly yanked Zoey's mother by the wrist, pulling her toward a clearing in the woods. She laughed again, still sure her new friend was just fooling around, so very familiar with men grabbing and pulling as a form of flirtation. Then she saw the clearing, and the grave-sized hole in the ground, and the open pine box lying nearby. In mid-laugh, she started shrieking.

Zoey jumped down off the table and screamed incoherently into the henchman's facemask, as if her mother could hear her. On the screen, Zoey's mother tried to rip her arm free, but the captor's hands were well-practiced at this, effortlessly anticipating and countering all of the jerking moves of the frantic woman. With his free hand, he pulled out a little gadget shaped like a curling iron. He pressed it to his hostage's spine and it made a pop and a whine, like an old-timey camera, and Zoey's mother collapsed into the frozen mud and dead leaves of the forest floor. She fell onto her back, her eyes wide open and twitching in terror, her body a useless rag doll.

Zoey screamed again.

"Don't worry," said Molech from the faceplate of the middle henchman. "That'll just stop her from thrashing around. She'll be awake, and aware, the whole time."

Zoey said, "We'll give it to you! We'll give you the gold! It's in a coin! A silver coin! There's a chip in the coin! Will, tell him!"

Will's hologram, perfectly calm, said, "Now, let's all take a step back and make sure we understand each other's positions . . ."

"*WE ARE NOT STILL DOING THE SCAM!* Give him the coin!"

Zoey heard the muffled rattle of gunfire. The sound was coming from the facemask on the far left, carrying the rooftop feed. On the screen, four machine guns were spitting fire. The four gunmen had advanced out onto the curved glass half-pipe of the swim bridge, crunching through ankle-deep slush, brass shells bouncing and clinking off the glass walls.

Armando was halfway across, still walking toward them, apparently unarmed, strolling right into the lethal teeth of the guns. He closed the distance, never slowing down as the four men fired right into his body, *through* his body, bullets chipping the clear walls and floor of the bridge. Then Armando was right in front of them and only then did they realize he wasn't perfectly solid, and that his feet weren't exactly touching the ground with each step.

The hologram of Armando Ruiz slowly stopped a few feet in front of the gunmen, his legs still going, walking in place, a looping animation emitting from one of the little toy projection cars that had created Arthur Livingston "ghosts" in the park the night before. One of the gunmen ran up and kicked the toy like a football, sending the Armando projection flying through the sky, walking in place all the way down to the street below.

As the four men watched it go, a hand reached up over the rail of the swim bridge, holding a curved yellow gadget that for one crazy moment Zoey thought was a banana. But then the gadget popped. There was a flash of blue light, and a crack and a sizzle. The gunman in front arched his back. He spun around, his limbs tensing and clenching as if in the throes of a seizure. His machine gun roared, firing out of control, ripping off an arc of bullets that tore through one of his comrades.

Armando tossed his briefcase over the rail, then effortlessly pulled himself up and over, landing in a crouch. Suddenly Wu's katana was in his hand. He ran toward the two remaining gunmen and went to work. A flash of blade, a whistle of sliced air, a sickening sound like a crab shell being smashed with a hammer. An arm tumbled to the ground. Another flash of sun glinting off steel, another high note of gashed air, a man screaming and clutching a stump. Blood sprayed across the glass walls.

The remaining four gunmen were watching from afar. They had stayed behind on the Fire Palace rooftop and were presumably trying to figure out if this was the real Armando or another strangely convincing and lethal hologram. Armando turned his back to them and stepped toward where he had tossed the briefcase. He tapped the latch with his toe and the lid flew open. Just as the gunmen behind him opened fire, two pistols jumped out of the briefcase, as if flung out by some spring-loaded mechanism. Armando caught them in midair, turned, and without taking a moment to aim, fired four shots that landed in four skulls. On the rooftop in the distance, four men slumped over.

And then there was silence. The entire confrontation had taken just over fifteen seconds.

When the last henchman's feed went dark, the camera angle switched to an overhead view from what Zoey assumed was a passing aerial drone. Armando marched off the swim bridge, onto the roof of the Fire Palace casino. Molech's HQ.

Zoey turned back to the middle henchman and said to Molech's video face,

"He's going to kill you! I can stop him! Let my mom go, I'll call off Armando, and we'll all talk about this!"

Molech seemed unconcerned. "Those men died doing what they loved—screwing up my most simplest goddamned instructions. But why do I get the feeling that your boyfriend is using a little bit of performance enhancement there? Very interesting. But that's all right, those boys were just there to soften things up for Rodzilla."

Armando was moving stealthily between the construction giraffes, scanning for more guards. He slowly made his way toward the stairwell door, which stood atop an elevated island in the dry pool.

Armando took a few cautious steps toward the door, then it exploded into a cloud of whirling chunks of debris.

A monster stood in the ragged remains of the doorframe.

Not a monster—a man, made into a monster.

He was about eight feet tall, thanks to thick leg extensions that ended in clawed metal feet, and a helmet that gave him another artificial metal head atop his actual head, so that his real face was looking out from between the robotic monster's teeth, like a sports mascot. Across an emerald green chest plate was painted the word "RODZILLA," the last two letters smaller than the rest, as if they'd gotten most of the way through and realized they didn't have room. One of the legs was still the color of bare metal from the knee down, as if they'd run out of green paint.

Molech said, "Rod decided to trick out his enhancements a bit—it's all about presentation, you know. But he didn't get started until yesterday afternoon, so . . ."

Rodzilla stomped forward, stopping at a forklift carrying a stack of plate glass. He grabbed the forklift in his metal claws, and tossed it at Armando. He had apparently underestimated his own strength, however. Instead of squishing Armando like a bug, the forklift sailed twenty feet over his head and disappeared off the edge of the building, squares of glass spinning through the air in its wake. Armando and Rodzilla both watched it go, waiting in silence for a few seconds until it and the glass could be faintly heard crashing into the street below.

Rodzilla said, "Huh. I just barely threw it, too."

Armando looked him over and said, "Nice paint job."

"How about I repaint it . . . *with your blood!*"

Rodzilla jumped ten feet into the air, and landed punch-first into the spot where Armando had been standing, his fist actually smashing through the floor of the pool.

Armando had rolled away, then whipped out the katana and charged at Rodzilla. He jumped and swung the blade and Rodzilla blocked it with a metal forearm, the blade creating a trail of sparks and a scar in the paint.

Armando landed and somersaulted and swung back at the metal monster, swiping at a spot behind the knees. A bundle of cables were severed and there was an eruption of blue sparks. Rodzilla stumbled backward, going down to one knee.

Armando stood and said, "Man, you have exposed cables all over the back of this thing."

Rodzilla growled, "We have shielding for that! The leg wouldn't bend right with it on there. We were supposed to have like two more days!"

Armando said, "What happens in two days?"

Rodzilla stumbled to his feet, a knowing smile on his lips.

"This."

The jaws of the helmet closed, obscuring his face. The eyes of the metallic monster head glowed blue. There was a deep rumble. An electric sound, the thrum of gathering power.

Armando ran away from whatever laser or lightning bolts or other lethal magic was going to come pouring forth from those eyes.

There was a flash, and thunder.

Rodzilla exploded into a ball of blue light brighter than the sun.

Armando was thrown flat, tossed across the filthy pool. Burning debris and construction equipment flew. When the smoke cleared, Rodzilla was gone, along with the raised island where the stairwell access door had been. All that remained was a crater into which several tons' worth of beams, fiberglass, and two massive cranes had tumbled.

Armando climbed to his feet, brushed himself off, and realized he was now stuck on the roof.

From the screen of the middle henchman, Molech whooped and said, "All right, Rod lasted three minutes, seventeen seconds! Looks like Bill wins the office pool on that, as he's the only one who put money on Rod making it up the stairs before overloading. And now our hero must find a way off the roof, to fight his way down floor by floor, like the opposite of the original plot of Game of Death! Somebody microwave some popcorn!"

Armando looked around the scattering of debris and equipment on the roof, then grabbed a spool of electrical extension cord he found among the smoldering junk. He dragged it toward the ledge and peered down the side of the building. From that height the wide street below looked like a thin line drawn with a Magic Marker. Zoey felt her guts tighten up at the view, just watching it secondhand.

Armando tied one end of the cord to the railing along the ledge, measured off about fifteen feet, then looped the rest around his waist, cinching it tight. He swiped down with the katana and sliced away a section of the black tarp, exposing a darkened window, smoked to black by the fire that had ruined the building two years ago. He climbed up onto the ledge, his shoes balancing precariously on the rail, his back to the open air and the steep drop below.

Armando crouched, took a breath and muttered, "I hope to god we're getting all this on cam—"

He was interrupted by the plinking of bullets, raking the rail next to him.

The Ice Palace contingent of Molech's guards had apparently figured out they'd let their boss's assassin walk right past them, and were now charging across the bullet-riddled half pipe of the swim bridge. Armando reached inside his jacket and pushed a button.

His briefcase, still sitting open on the bridge, detonated.

A spherical shockwave rippled out in every direction, shattering the bridge as it went.

Amid the cacophony, Armando pushed off the ledge. He flew back, suspended for a moment in the air above the sheer drop to the street below, then the cord went taut and he swung toward the window as the shattered glass bridge cascaded down behind him in a crystal rain, a half dozen Molech henchmen tumbling down with it.

Armando flew toward the window, bullets pelting the wall around it. One crazy gunman was shooting as he fell, as if he would still have to answer to Molech in the afterlife. Armando crashed through the window and disappeared from view.

The feed on the mask of the far left henchman went black, then switched back to Molech's bemused face.

Molech nodded slowly and said, "Yes, I knew every single one of these things was going to happen."

Somewhere in the background Zoey heard Black Scott say, "Uh huh."

From her phone, Will said, "It's not too late. We can still call off Armando, you can still call off your man in Colorado. We can still negotiate this like human beings. My counteroffer is this. We give you the gold. You leave Zoey alone for the rest of her life. She leaves town, you don't follow. You get your crazy arsenal and sell it to the world for billions. Everyone is happy."

Molech's video face said, "Counter-counteroffer. You give me the gold.

Zoey's mother goes in the ground. I get Zoey. I sever Zoey's spine, paralyzing her, then bury her in a different coffin with only . . . *five* thousand cockroaches. I broadcast the results on the Tabula Rasa skyline for the next month, yadda yadda yadda."

"We don't feel like that's a good faith offer, because it seems more like you're just trying to save money on cockroaches. Let's put all that aside for now and agree to call off the dogs, so that we can at least have time to talk. Tell your man to let Zoey's mother go, she's not a party to this either way."

"Rather than counter that, I'm just going to sit back and watch Kools bury that jizz-Dumpster."

The henchman on the far right—the one showing the Colorado feed—displayed Kools placing the lid on the pine box, giving Zoey just a brief glimpse inside—a split second to see her mother's face, eyes wide, realizing what was happening, mouth working as she tried to form a scream with a tongue and vocal cords that wouldn't cooperate. The man pulled out a little gun gadget and fired it into the edge of the lid. A nail gun.

Zoey screamed. Again. She couldn't help it.

Will Blackwater's hologram was still completely unperturbed, however, and Zoey hated him for it, wishing that could be him in that box, about to hear dirt landing on the lid one shovelful at a time. But men in suits don't wind up in shallow graves in the woods, do they? No, they ride behind tinted windows and make conference calls and negotiate away the lives of little people like Zoey and Melinda Ashe. How had she let herself get taken by these people?

Will said, "Molech, Zoey will not negotiate with you if you kill her mother. This is actually true of most people you'll encounter in a business setting."

"Blackwater, if you say the word 'negotiate' one more time I'm going to find you, tie you down, and inject bot fly maggots into your eyeballs. This is not a negotiation. This is strength taking from weakness. I assume it's true what she said, that you got the gold on a little drive somewhere?"

"Yes."

"And I don't suppose Zoey here has it on her?"

"No, she does not."

"Do you have it?"

"Yes, I do."

On the screen, Kools fired nails around the edge of the coffin lid, finishing the task in seconds. Zoey screamed for him to stop, then she faced Will Blackwater's holographic ghost and screamed for him to give Molech the coin. No one acknowledged her. One of the henchmen chuckled.

Will's hologram sighed, glanced at his watch and said, "I can see you're not willing to discuss this in good faith, Molech. Get back to me when you come to your senses."

The hologram blinked away as Will disconnected the call, and Zoey was now alone in the room with Molech's three henchmen. She screamed Will's name. She was losing her voice. The phone's voice command actually responded to this and attempted to dial, but announced that Will Blackwater was not answering.

He had abandoned her.

On the Colorado feed, Kools pushed the coffin into the grave, where it landed with a thud.

From the other two facemasks, Molech said, "Well, looks like it's just you and me, piglet. Did you pick up the subtext of what just happened there? Will Blackwater just cut you out of the equation. I do believe that not only does he not care if I take you back to my place and grate you like a block of cheese, but that he would regard that as a favor."

"You're a dead man!" Zoey screeched, through tears that probably rendered the threat unconvincing. "Armando is going to chop your head off!"

"Did you even think to keep the gold on you? Or did you just trust Blackwater with it? When the two of you were planning this little powwow, did he even make the effort to convince you to trust him with your one bargaining chip? Or did he just take it and assume you'd be too distraught to notice? You don't have to answer, I'm just curious to hear how he works, that's all. I mean, did he put *any* effort into convincing you he was your friend? Or did he just sit back and wait for your fat fatherless ass to blindly trust him?"

Zoey didn't let him finish before she turned and ran for the door. One of the henchmen wearing Molech's video face clamped down on her arm with a gorilla-strong grip, yanking her back. Squeezing that same goddamned patch of bruises. He threw her up against the glass and three tiny sharks swam over to investigate the commotion.

Zoey tried to pull away and said, "I will give you ten million dollars to let me out of this room! Enough to start a new life, enough to—"

"Honey," said Molech from the screen, "I've spent more than ten million dollars betting on sports I'm not even a fan of."

"I'm not talking to you. I'm talking to *you*. The guy wearing the mask, the guy right here in the room with me. Same deal for all you. Ten million each. All you have to do is nothing. Just let me out that door."

She looked around at the other two, one of whom was wearing the video of Kools, who was in the process of filling in the hole where Zoey's mother was nailed into the box, burying her in a spot more than six hundred miles away from anyone who cared.

"Look!" Zoey screamed. "Look at what he's doing. You have to know this is wrong. You *have* to. You don't have to do anything but take my money and disappear. Live on a beach the rest of your life."

The henchmen didn't answer, but Molech did. "Piglet, did you not just watch one of my dudes continue shooting at your man even as he plummeted to his death? How can you still not get it? They don't work for money. They don't even work for me. They work for *the juice*. If these were the type of men who were willing to trade failure for a chance to get fat in the sun, they'd have never made it past orientation day. My men may not be geniuses—no offense, guys—but they're all *winners*. They'd rather see everyone they love turned into hamburger than give one inch to your mushy trailer park ass. My men are men of iron, you chop off their arms and they'll punch you with the stumps. And I got more than fifty of the hardest converging on your boyfriend's location above us. Maybe he'll get through five and maybe he'll get through ten. But he only has to slip up once, and he's done. I got boys up there who are ex-military. Hell, I got boys who were cops until *last month*. They know how to shoot just fine. And I'm going to bet that right about now, your boyfriend is already sprawled out dead somewh—"

Molech was interrupted by the sound of a door bursting open nearby.

FORTY

There was a commotion. The camera that had been pointed at Molech's face suddenly swung away, creating a disorienting effect as the image on the hench-man's facemask blurred and shifted.

Standing at the door to Molech's hospital room was his right-hand man, Black Scott. He was smiling. Relaxed.

Zoey did not like that look.

Scott said, "You got to see this. Patch in to T-Bone, up on the top floor. T-Bone, you hear me? Molech is on."

The view on the faceplate switched again. It was now bouncing down the shadowy hallway of a burned building, past smoke-browned plaster on walls that were rotting to pieces from neglected water damage. The camera finally arrived at a shattered plate-glass window.

Lying in front of it was a body, sprawled in a pool of blood. It had an elec-trical extension cord cinched around its waist.

The man wearing the camera approached and Zoey held her breath once again—she knew what was surely coming next. She hadn't understood Will's play with the supposed "brain code" but it was clear what was happening here—this was how they would get them to let their guard down. When they turned the body over, it would surely turn out to be one of Molech's hench-men. Then Armando would spring out with his ambush, or fly into Molech's hospital room.

The view drew closer and the bad guys were still unaware of the ruse—the body was wearing a black suit and red shirt, just like Armando's. Maybe he'd had time to switch clothes with a guard. And he'd chosen his double well—even facedown, she could see this man also had Armando's trademark five o'clock shadow.

Molech's men arrived at the body and a foot emerged from the bottom of the frame, rolling the corpse over. Zoey realized she had been mistaken about the nature of the ploy—this was in fact Armando, who was playing possum—the "blood" would turn out to be a can of paint left behind by one of the construction crews, or something. The moment the henchmen let their guard down, he'd spring up and slice them to pieces.

Molech's men gathered around Armando, snickering. Armando continued not to move. His eyes were open, staring blankly at the ceiling. His chest was not moving. Finally the man wearing the camera knelt over him and turned Armando's head, to bring the other side of his neck fully into view.

The henchman said, "Look, boss! He has gills!"

One bullet. That's all it took. One of the desperate last shots of that falling madman from the collapsed bridge, who would never know that his last shot had landed true. The bullet left a deep gouge, slicing across Armando's Adam's apple and tearing through his jugular. He had swung through the window and was probably in the middle of untying the cord when he felt the wet, hot gush soaking his black suit, turning his shirt the wrong shade of red. He probably hadn't even have time to register what exactly had gone wrong, before the blood drained away from his brain and caused the rest of his body to drop to the floor, like an action figure that some toddler had suddenly gotten bored with.

And then, Zoey heard laughter. Molech, laughing so hard it sounded like he was going to choke.

That was the last sound Zoey heard. She saw the ceiling, and then she saw nothing. She had fainted.

FORTY-ONE

A kick to her ribs woke her up, and unlike her first morning in Tabula Ra$a, this time Zoey had no moment to believe she was back home, in bed, or that her mother was in the next room cooking breakfast. No, the moment she opened her eyes she was looking at the transmitted face of Molech on the facemask of a goon looming over her, the toe of a combat boot roughly shaking her torso. The wall to her right was full of Arthur's stupid pet sharks, swimming back and forth and trying to figure out why an invisible barrier was preventing them from eating her.

Molech's face was looking off to the side of the faceplate, talking to someone in the room with him. Zoey sat up and blinked and saw that the scene of Armando's death was still playing on one of the other facemasks. Now there was a bearded man in glasses kneeling over Armando's corpse, studying it with some kind of wand gadget, checking a readout. They were continuing a conversation they'd apparently been having for several minutes while Zoey was out.

The bearded man nodded and said, "They're right. It's a perfectly stable system, across the board. Molech, Armando had the gold."

From another mask, Molech said, "Sweet. So we know it exists."

"You don't understand. I can copy the software right off of this mechanism's drive. The idiots walked the gold right to us."

"Don't tease me here, Doc. You know I been hurt before."

"I can have it uploaded to a test subject for additional trials within minutes."

"Yeah, we *could* do that. Or, you could zap that code into *my* implants and turn me into a *mythical god*."

The bearded man said, "If that's what you'd prefer."

Molech's face turned its attention to Zoey once more.

"Well, all right! I like the way you negotiate, piglet!"

Zoey stumbled to her feet and said, "There! There, you've got it! You don't need me, you don't need Will, you don't need my mom. You have everything you want, just let us go!"

Molech said, "Speaking of which! Kools, how you coming?"

The view screen flipped back to the gravesite, where the box was no longer visible under the dirt. Kools stopped working for a moment and said, "What's that?"

"I need you to stop shoveling."

"Okay."

"Go down, dig up the coffin, piss in Zoey's mother's face, then resume burying her until the ground looks like she was never there."

Kools, sounding somewhat doubtful, said, "Is that an actual order or are you just saying that?"

"Are you just meeting me for the first time, Kools?"

"Well, I don't have to go right now, boss. Can I wait a—"

Before Kools could finish his question, a new voice from out of nowhere said, "Kools? You hearing this?"

A monitor in the conference room blinked to life, obscuring a five-foot-wide section of sharks on the opposite wall. The feed was displaying three people, sitting calmly for the camera. It was Budd, Andre, and an obese woman with a butch haircut and a pair of glasses that seemed designed to enhance her scowl. The woman was wearing an aqua nurse's uniform, and the three of them were sitting in what looked like the break room of a hospital.

Andre repeated, "Kools, you can't see us but we're watching your feed."

A confused Kools asked, "Who's this?"

"My name is Andre Knox, I work for Zoey Ashe. But more important than who I am, is who I'm sitting here with."

The large woman sitting with the pair said, "Charlie? What in the hell are you doing?"

Kools froze. He said, "Mom?"

"Where *are* you?"

Kools, growing alarmed, said, "If you so much as touch her you'll—"

Budd interrupted, "We're not going to touch anybody, and in fact we just paid off her student loans. No, I reckon all we're gonna do is sit here—me, Andre, and your momma—and watch you bury this nice woman alive."

Kools's mother's eyes went wide. "What did he just say? Charlie, what have you gotten yourself wrapped up in? Show me what's in that hole, right now."

"Mom, get off here. I'm at work. I'll explain later."

"You're at *work*? What kind of 'work' are you doing, exactly? That don't look like Nordstrom."

Before Kools could answer, Andre said, "Miss, your son is in the process of burying a woman he abducted, by the name of Melinda Ashe. She is thirty-eight years old. She is from a small town called Fort Drayton, Colorado. She is the mother of one daughter and you can read her missing persons report in the news tomorrow. Unless, that is, Kools has a change of heart."

"Charlie, tell me that isn't true."

"No, no. You gotta understand, I'm, uh, I'm a hostage here. There's a man pointin' a gun at me, forcin' me to do this."

"Charlie, if you don't go dig that woman up right this minute, *I'll make you wish you were dead*. Does Jacki know you're into this nonsense? Or Justine? Does she know this is how you're paying your child support? And god forbid little Lauren should find out—"

"Oh, just *shut up*, Mom. *Jesus.*" Kools stomped over to the hole and angrily started flinging dirt out with his hands, like a teenager making a show of cleaning up his room as if to say, *See, now get off my back already.*

Zoey watched all of this in dumbfounded silence. On the nearest henchman's facemask, Molech was looking offscreen, shaking his head and muttering, "Okay, I admit there are still *some* flaws in our hiring process."

Molech was sitting up now, two people helping him stand shakily next to the bed. He was flexing new mechanical prosthetics—gleaming chrome hands and forearms, making him look like he was wearing a medieval suit of armor from the elbows down. The fingers clicked and whirred as he flexed them. He made a fist, and a blue arc of electricity flashed from knuckle to knuckle.

"See that? That's juice, Scott. Juice that can break the world in half. I don't like the finish, though. That chrome is going to get all scuffed up the first time I punch anything solid. I wonder how they'd look all black and yellow, like those warning signs they had all over the construction stuff on the roof? Make it look all scratched up and industrial."

Scott said, "Yellow and black, like a bumblebee? They gonna call you Bee Man. Bee Hands. Somethin' like that."

"Yeah. Maybe blue? I don't know—what color are *God's* hands?"

"Brown."

"We'll worry about it later. Bring me my pants."

The absurdity of the situation was making Zoey dizzy.

Molech said, "You guys over in Livingston Tower, go ahead and do an orifice search of Zoey, to make sure she doesn't have the coin inside her somewhere. I don't need it anymore, I'm just curious. After that, you can do whatever you want with her. Other than let her go, obviously. From the look of this one, I would definitely wear protection, though. Them trailer park bugs eat dicks for breakfast and antibiotics for lunch."

The feeds went dark—the visors of the three henchmen were suddenly blank, reflecting back Zoey's own pale, tear-stained face. The three shirtless thugs closed in around her. One reached around and grabbed her by the hair.

FORTY-TWO

Zoey sucked in a breath and gritted her teeth. Those rough hands on her once more, a feeling that was too familiar.

Zoey twisted away from the henchman who had hold of her and said to the other two, "You broadcasting this on Blink? Then let what I'm about to say act as a binding verbal contract—fifty million dollars to whichever one of you kills this man behind me. If you cooperate, you split the money."

There was just the briefest moment when the other two men glanced at each other, as if they were considering it. This set Zoey's captor into a blind rage. He twisted his fist in her hair, then smashed her head into the shark aquarium. The glass shattered and she tumbled to the floor under a cascade of freezing water, little sharks flopping onto the black tile all around her, blood streaming into her eyes.

It didn't matter. At some point, some out-of-control chemical reaction had converted all of her pain and fear into mindless, all-consuming white-hot rage.

She swept wet hair out of her eyes and yelled to the other two men, "This is your *one chance* to be alphas! Every guy thinks he's an alpha male until he actually meets one. Well, *here's your chance.*"

The man looming over her said, "We're *all* alphas in Molech's crew, pork-cushion."

"*No!* You take orders from Molech. He doesn't take orders from you. That means he's the alpha, and *you're his bitch.*"

The guy ripped off his helmet, leaned over Zoey, and spat in her face. He then grabbed her by the jacket and dragged her toward the window. He threw her to the floor, then reared back and punched the glass wall, shattering it. A frozen wind howled into the room, the faint noises of the city wafting up from seven hundred feet below. A curious pigeon came and landed on the jagged glass.

The henchman grabbed Zoey by the hair and dragged her toward the opening—clearly intending to just chuck her out of the window. She frantically tried to claw away from him, to drop to the floor, to do anything to halt his progress. She punched and kicked and scratched, as the wind and noise of the city drew closer. He barely seemed to notice. She desperately looked around for a weapon—anything. She found nothing within grabbing distance but a toppled chair, and three little midget sharks slapping the floor with their tails, their rows of razor-sharp teeth biting helplessly at the air.

With no plan in mind whatsoever beyond "I'll shark him," Zoey reached down, feeling her hair come out by the roots in the guy's fist. She was able to barely grab one of the baby sharks by the tail. It thrashed around in her hands as she twisted and stabbed at her captor with it, hoping to scare or distract him even if for just a fraction of a second.

The man let out a howl. Zoey was suddenly free, and dove to the floor. The henchman, now with a shark ferociously biting his crotch, flailed and stumbled and crashed through the shattered window.

There was a brief moment of peace, with only the sound of the wind and muffled traffic below. Then behind her one of the remaining henchman said, "Did . . . *did that just happen?*"

Both of the men started advancing on her, one on each side of the long conference table.

Zoey threw up her hands, as if to ward them off. "WAIT! Listen! I can pay—"

WHUMPP!

There was a deep, booming concussion from below. And then, the floor shook. Both of the approaching henchmen had to steady themselves on the conference table.

Molech popped up on their facemasks. He looked pale and sickly but also happier than Zoey had ever seen another human. He was outdoors now—in fact, he was right outside the main entrance of Livingston Tower, standing there with his gleaming chrome arms, near where his goons had parked their ludicrous tigercycles. Molech was tinkering with his new right hand, as if making an adjustment. He then held it up and the chrome hand transformed—two fingers rotated and merged and lengthened, the hand and forearm transforming itself into some kind of weapon.

Molech aimed his gun-hand at the building, and fired.

There was no crack of gunpowder, just a teeth-grating shriek like a fork dragged across a china plate. A projectile streaked forth, leaving a bright yellow trail behind it, as if it was igniting the air itself as it went. The projectile hit the building and the floor shook once again—an impact so impossibly powerful that they were feeling it reverberate through the structure, seventy stories up.

On the screen, Molech laughed, said, "Much better, Doc," then aimed and fired once more.

Again came that *SSHHHEEK* followed by a *WHUMPP* of impact. He took several steps along the foundation, aimed, fired again. This time there happened to be a car in the way, parked along the street. The projectile sliced through the metal as if the car was an inflatable decoy, smashed through a concrete column behind it, and impacted the building somewhere inside. It seemed like random, petty vandalism, but Zoey soon realized Molech wasn't just breaking glass to hear the sound it made. He was targeting specific points along the foundation.

The whole building swayed and one of the henchmen said, "That crazy son of a bitch! He's just railgunning the support beams one by one! He's going to chop the tower down like a tree! Ha!"

SSHHHEEK!

WHUMP!

Zoey screamed, "WE ARE CURRENTLY IN THAT BUILDING, MEATHEAD! We have to get out of here!"

"*You* don't, jerksock. Molech's orders."

WHUMP!

"*You need me!* I know how to get us out! There's an emergency escape!" This was a lie, but one Zoey thought would be just fantastic if it turned out to be true. "Either we all die or we all live, those are *the only two choices*!"

"Then we all die," said the henchman on the left, with no inflection. "It's kind of weird that you're just now understanding how this works."

"*What is wrong with you people?*"

Both men edged toward her once more.

Zoey watched the facemask videos, timing it carefully. She watched Molech march to the next spot, finding the next support column.

He raised his arm to take aim—

She jumped up on the conference table and started running toward the door. Both men reached for her, and—

SSHHHEEK!

WHUMP!

The building jolted so hard now that all three of them fell. Zoey scrambled to her feet and ran along the table, then jumped off and flew toward the door. One of the men threw a chair at her and it exploded against the doorframe a split second after she passed through it.

She skidded to a stop, pulled the big doors shut and said, "LOCK!"

She ran down the hall, toward the elevator.

From behind her, a woman's voice said, "HEY! ZOEY!"

She spun and found Echo Ling stumbling out of the stairwell, still in her red dress but having ditched the stupid wig.

"THIS WAY!"

Zoey ran toward her and said, "We're seventy flights up! I can't go down stairs that fast!"

"We're going up!"

Echo plunged back into the stairwell and started stomping up the stairs. The building shook and creaked and this time there was the sound of several hundred windows exploding, shattered as their frames twisted and buckled. The lights went out.

The two of them emerged onto a rooftop and Zoey had the crazy thought that they would either jump off the side of the building or ride the collapse down from the top. Instead, she found the windy roof was made windier by the rotors of a black helicopter, bearing that stupid Livingston Enterprises mustache logo.

The building now had a noticeable lean. They ran toward the helicopter. When they reached it, Will Blackwater opened the cockpit door and screamed over the engines, "DO YOU HAPPEN TO KNOW HOW TO FLY A HE-LICOPTER?"

She did not.

He motioned for them to get in anyway—Echo in the passenger seat, Zoey in back. Will poked ineffectually at buttons, and Echo leaned over and yelled suggestions as to which lever on the dash would actually cause the machine to fly.

The building shook and this time it didn't stop.

There was a cacophonous noise, like the end of the world.

They were going down.

FORTY-THREE

♟

Zoey was thrown forward, clutching the back of Echo's seat as the helicopter lurched forward. She got a nice view out of the front window of the tower collapsing straight down, as if the whole building had fallen into a trapdoor. All else was obscured under a billowing cloud of dust and flying glass.

Will was yanking back on the stick and screaming commands at the machine, neither of which seemed to have any effect on its trajectory. The helicopter kept tilting forward at an alarming angle and Zoey was sure they were just going to somersault down into the falling avalanche of rubble below. Instead, the helicopter hovered, then kind of wobbled forward, nose still pointed down. Instead of plummeting into the maelstrom, they were now lurching horizontally—directly toward an office building across the street.

Will pulled up on the stick and stomped at some pedals, and Zoey could only sense that they were gaining altitude because the windows of the building they were about to collide with were whipping downward through the windshield. And then all at once they were looking at a rooftop—asphalt and duct work looking close enough to touch, the shadow of the rotor blades flitting along the surface. A flock of birds took off from the roof, and immediately one of them got hit by the rotors and exploded in a cloud of blood and feathers. Zoey heard someone in the helicopter screaming, and then realized it was all of them.

And then they were past the building and were looking down at the streets again, still leaning forward, still out of control. Pedestrians were pointing and running, for them the sound of the tower collapsing a block away now joined by the thunderous noise of the helicopter rotors chopping the air into submission overhead. Finally the helicopter's front end rose and the horizon fell into view. It was too late—the next building filled the windshield and they weren't going to avoid this one. Zoey barely had time to note that they were going to die colliding with a gigantic Santa Claus.

He was standing inside the hole of a thirty-story-tall donut, or rather, a thirty-story-tall glass building shaped like a donut standing on edge. It was a shopping mall, judging by how many of the terrified, fleeing people behind the windows were carrying shopping bags. Will yanked on the stick, presumably trying to avoid smashing into the building and sending the rotor blades flying murderously through a Lane Bryant store, but this meant he was aiming for the hole of the donut, and that meant he was aiming right for the ten-story-tall Santa Claus statue that was standing there. It was a festive thing, animated to rotate slowly, waving and jiggling its belly with laughter to the streets below. It was no hologram.

Zoey would never forget the noise the helicopter's blades made when they started sawing into Santa's neck. The statue was a hollow structure made of something like fiberglass over a thin metal frame, and the sound of the blades ripping through it was a series of thumps and screams, like a family of elves getting run over by a lawnmower. One of the rotor blades snapped and went flying, leaving a massive scar in the glass wall of the shopping mall.

They were crashing now, tumbling through the air. Zoey was thrown sideways, dangling from her seat belt. She had a fleeting thought that she wished she'd stolen one of the henchman's helmets. The helicopter got clear of the wrecked Santa statue and now the skyline was whipping around outside the windshield. Will no longer had his hands on the stick. He, like everyone else, was grabbing whatever was nearby, resigned to the crash and trying to brace for impact.

Then there was a POP and a FWUMPH and suddenly everything outside the windows was yellow.

There was a massive jolt, Zoey bashing her head on the window next to her. There was a horrific noise like rapid cannon fire, the remaining rotors tearing themselves to pieces as they battered the ground. Then Zoey was upside down and then right side up again, thrown around under the seat belt, the remains of the helicopter slowly rolling to a stop.

An engine whined and sputtered to a halt.

And then, finally, silence.

They were sideways, Zoey and Echo on the bottom. There was muffled screaming from outside. Will breathed, ran his hand through his hair, and then nodded to himself as if to confirm the job had been done to his satisfaction.

He asked, "Everyone all right?" and, without looking to see if anyone was in fact all right, started yanking off his seat belt. He climbed out of the pilot's-side door, which was pointing straight up at the sky.

He extended a hand down for Echo and said, "We have to move. He'll be coming."

Zoey checked her limbs to make sure they were there and not jutting out at weird angles, then climbed up and out. She heard air escaping, as the whole battered aircraft was being slowly lowered to the ground, thanks to four yellow plastic airbags that had inflated around the hull just prior to impact. Zoey climbed atop the hull of the helicopter—or what was left of it, the tail had snapped off and the rotor was now just four short ragged stubs—and found they had landed on the roof of a parking garage in the shadow of the donut mall.

They had left a trail of wrecked cars in their wake, and one of the loose rotor blades had impaled an empty school bus nearby. Zoey didn't know which would be more traumatizing to the returning children: the skewered bus or the twenty-foot-tall severed head of Santa Claus next to it. It was lying on its side, one eye gouged out and its nose bashed in from having landed and rolled after being lopped off its body by the helicopter blades. The rest of the Santa was still standing next door, its headless body still slowly rotating and waving inside the giant crystal donut.

Beyond it, a cloud of dust filled the gap in the skyline where Livingston Tower once stood.

FORTY-FOUR

Zoey tried to jump down, and instead awkwardly rolled down the bulge of deflating rubber, tumbling onto the pavement. She was immediately surrounded by several dozen people frantically photographing her with their phones and blink cameras, leaning their own faces into the shots. Zoey tried to shake out the cobwebs.

Echo approached, looking oddly giddy. "Whew! We did it."

Echo held her palm toward Zoey, who looked back quizzically. Echo grabbed Zoey's right wrist, brought her hand up, and slapped her own palm with Zoey's and said, "High five."

"Oh. Right." Zoey looked around, "Can we . . . call a cab or something?"

Will said, "Hold on, I'll grab a car." Will pulled out his phone, glanced around, and tapped some controls.

A random hatchback that happened to be driving up the parking garage ramp at that moment swerved off its path, heading directly toward Zoey while the wide-eyed woman behind the wheel wondered what in the hell was going on. The driver's-side door flipped open all on its own, then the car power slid toward Zoey, flinging the driver out of the door and sending her tumbling onto the pavement.

Will said, "Get in."

Zoey stared at the car, then down at the middle-aged woman lying stunned on the ground.

Zoey ran for the car, looking back and saying, "I'm so sorry, I'm going to buy this car for five million dollars, I'll send the money tonight. I'm so sorry—"

All three of them piled in and the car spun out and flew down the ramp with abandon. They emerged into traffic to find the streets were bedlam—sirens and screams and people standing stupidly in the streets to record the collapse aftermath. The hijacked car weaved around rubberneckers and even bumped up onto the sidewalk, carrying them away from the scene of the disaster, emergency vehicles whooshing past in the other direction. Soon they were out in the suburbs and into Beaver Heights. And there, all was placid calm—this was where city problems simply . . . stopped. And then there was the gate of the Casa and the grounds with its stupid tiger enclosure.

Carlton opened the giant front doors and Zoey stumbled through, unable to feel her legs. Wu rushed to meet her, said some things that she didn't really hear, then started hurrying around talking about security, and locking down the grounds. Then Echo and Will were there and they sounded very frantic and very busy and soon they went off to presumably ready the Casa de Zoey to fend off an invasion of Molech's enhanced monsters. Zoey just shuffled past them, in a daze.

Will was talking to her now, he told her that her mother was fine, that she was at the police station in Fort Drayton but that they needed to get her away, to some place safe. He was talking about options and professionals Budd worked with who could make people disappear, and how they needed to act soon before Molech sent someone else after her. But Zoey just kept walking past him, across the foyer, past the gigantic Christmas tree where some member of the house staff was now up on a ladder fixing a string of dead lights, the poor bastard lucky enough to think he still lived in a world in which such things mattered. Zoey sat on the bottom stair of the grand staircase, put her head between her legs, and tried not to pass out.

Will stopped talking. Carlton was there now, and was asking if she needed water, or a doctor, or if he should draw her a bath. All these people, buzzing around her like bees the moment she walked in through the door. She just wanted them to go away. She couldn't hear them behind the pulsing roar of her own blood pumping through her ears. She was sweating, her heart was racing, her whole body trembling.

She saw Armando, face like a wax dummy, sprawled on the floor.

She saw the look of terrible realization in her mother's face when she became sure she was about to be buried alive, for the first time realizing that death was a real thing that could happen to her. She saw the cruel, dumb joy on Molech's face when he realized he had the power of a god. Because Zoey had given it to him.

Zoey looked and saw a pair of yellow eyes were now staring back at her. There was a meow, and Stench Machine sat down between her knees and

Zoey pressed her face into his. There was silence and she didn't know if everyone had left, or if Will and Wu and Echo and Carlton were all just standing there, waiting for her to come around. She didn't care.

After a calculated few minutes, shoes clicked toward her and somehow she knew from the robot pace that it was Will. He stood over her like a statue, in silence, for an excruciating period of time before he surprised her by sitting on the step next to her.

Finally he said, "This, all of this, is what I was trying to avoid."

She screamed at him. "DID YOU KNOW THIS WAS GOING TO HAPPEN? Did you know, and let it happen anyway, you dead-eyed fucking *robot*?"

"Did I know that Armando would get shot while swinging into a top-floor window and that Molech would emerge from amputation surgery with the ability to knock the building to the ground *with me inside of it*? No, Zoey, I did not. Did I know that this plan had a really good chance of going wrong? Yes, and I said as much."

Zoey let her head sink back between her knees, deflated.

She muttered, "I'm just going to go. I should have done that the first night. I'll take some money and my cat and I'll just disappear, I'll change my name and go to some foreign country. Me and my mom, we'll take enough money to start over."

"That's your choice."

"Shut up. Don't talk to me anymore. I don't have to listen to you, so I'm not going to. There's nothing inside you but gears and numbers. I'll spend the rest of my life trying to forget I ever met you."

Will let out a breath and that was as much as she got from him as a response. They sat there for a while on the steps, Zoey with her eyes closed, stroking her cat.

Softly, Will said, "Arthur Livingston . . . was family to me. He was your father by biology, but he was like a father to me in life. We had been through more together than you can imagine. What happened to Armando . . . I know what it's like because I've watched people die in front of me, over and over. But you knew him for three days. I spent fifteen years side by side with your father. Only now, do you understand the state of mind the rest of us were in when you arrived on the scene."

She didn't answer.

Will continued, "When I kept telling you that you didn't understand the situation, I was never insulting you. I was giving you information."

"No, I get it now. I do. I'm not . . . I'm not up to this, I never was. I'm just trailer trash, just like you thought when you saw me. I'm not one of your Suits, or whatever. I'm not a hero."

Wu passed and said he had dispatched drones to watch the surrounding ten blocks for approaching monstrosities, and that he was prepping the armored sedan for an emergency getaway, should they come. He hurried off.

Will said to Zoey, "You are what you were raised to be. If you'd been raised in an exclusive prep school with private tutors and high-achiever friends, you'd be something different. Arthur could have given you all of that, but instead he spent the money on collectible cars and high-roller suites and very expensive, disposable women."

"Yep, if I'd had all that training I could have grown up to be just like you. Sad."

"I'm saying, Zoey, that Arthur failed you. And you're a walking reminder of what kind of man he could be at times. And you showed up right when he passed and that wasn't the reminder I needed just then. But none of this is your fault."

Zoey looked over at the security monitor by the door and said, "Is Molech coming? Will he come here and tear this place apart?"

"Sooner or later. Not right now, I don't think."

"How do you know?"

"If I understand Molech, he knows the collapse of Livingston Tower is the headline and he'll want to let that play. Level the Casa now and it'll be back-page news. But Molech is coming. He'll come for you. He'll come for me. He'll come to make a statement. If you're going to go, go now."

Zoey forced herself to stand. She picked up Stench Machine and dragged herself up the stairs, feeling like she was trying to summit Everest, figuring that at least packing wouldn't take long. She made it to her room and started stuffing dirty clothes into her suitcase. Soft steps approached in the hall, and she turned to see Wu standing there. He had a new katana on his back, exactly like the previous two.

Zoey said, "Sorry, but your employment won't last long. By tonight, I intend to be somewhere far away from this nightmare."

"I am sorry about what happened. I know you had a relationship with Armando."

"I only knew him for a few days, but yeah. Were you friends?"

"We worked together for three years, off and on."

"Oh. I'm sorry. I should have said sorry first, in fact. This is my fault, I sent him and I should have known."

"No. When you were around Armando, you felt what you felt because he was a man who lived as one willing to die. If he had wished to get fat in front of a desk and then rot in a nursing home, he would have done that instead. Ultimately, Zoey, you'll find that we all get what we want. Regardless of whether or not we like it when we get it."

"Did you get any of the gadgets, like Armando had? Are there any super powers you're hiding from me?"

He smiled. "I am afraid not. I do not trust myself with more power than what the universe has seen fit to grant me. Does your cat travel in the suitcase?"

"What? No. Stench Machine, get out of there. You're getting hair all over everything."

She zipped up the suitcase, hoisted the cat, and turned to see Carlton in the hall behind Wu.

"All right," she said, thinking. "Let's see. The lady who's car I stole to get here, I need you to give her five million dollars." She turned to Wu. "I need a driver, to get me someplace safe, someplace far away. Do you do that?"

"Mr. Billingsley is actually making arrangements for you and your mother both. Will told him the situation."

"I'm sure he did."

She pushed past Wu, wheeling her suitcase into the hall. She found Will on the stairs and said, "What now?"

"Livingston's cars are all identifiable. Budd is going to bring a new vehicle. And I mean literally a new one, one we're buying, as we speak. That will get you to Salt Lake. Arthur's private jet will take off from there, but it will be empty. A decoy. At the same time you'll get on a charter flight to another city where you'll meet your mother. The two of you will go through a . . . process, with Budd's people, to erase your trail. Once he's satisfied, you and your mother can fly out together."

As he talked, he was already on his way down the hall toward the library, and its secret garage entrance. She followed, and Wu followed her.

Zoey said, "Fly out? To where?"

Will glanced back. "You're asking me? Go someplace where they have a beach, I don't know. Figure out what you want to do with the rest of your life."

He pulled the not-so-secret book on the shelf and the four of them—Will, Wu, Zoey, and Stench Machine—descended to the garage. A moment later they strode out among Arthur's collection of obscenely expensive cars, and made it a point to say nothing to each other until they heard the hum of the two doors in the garage's airlock security system. Zoey tensed up, ready to be ambushed by some mechanical monstrosity, but it was the black panel truck she'd seen parked in the garage earlier, backing in. It stopped, the rear door scrolled up and twin ramps slid to the floor. A small, deep blue BMW rolled out.

Budd emerged from the driver's seat of the truck and said, "Don't reckon I got you much of a deal, didn't have time to haggle and the salesman could smell it."

"It's a cute car." That was important, Zoey thought, since there was a significant chance it would also serve as her coffin.

"Now, it's a convertible, which normally is a big no-no security-wise but, honestly, if these guys catch you I don't think it's gonna matter what you're drivin'. San Marino Blue, reckoned it matched the streaks in your hair."

"Oh. Ha. I'm dying that out the first chance I get but still, I like it. Thank you."

"Well, I paid for it with your money, so don't thank me too much."

Wu sat in the BMW, and appeared to be familiarizing himself with the controls.

Budd said, "I don't know if Will told you, but I'm going along, make sure you and your momma get to safety."

"You have to do that yourself?"

"It's better. You got to understand, making people disappear ain't so easy when you've got millions of cameras attached to millions of Team Molech rodents, all eager to report back to him. I got a network of folks who do this kind of thing and we'll get her done, don't you worry. Lot of stops and change-overs, you might have to hide inside a barrel or two. Then once we're at the safehouse, we'll go to work on you. Blink works on facial recognition, so my boys will have to make some . . . changes. But soon enough you'll put all this nonsense in your rearview."

"What, like plastic surgery?"

"Plus voice alterations, got an acting coach to give you some new mannerisms—sometimes we'll even swap out the race of the target, if we can get them to agree. But you got to understand, even if we get you to a country where they don't have Blink yet, it won't stay that way for long. The only way to keep you safe—"

"Is to turn me into a completely different person?"

"You're only twenty-two. Trust me, in ten years you'd be a completely different person anyway."

While Zoey let that sink in, Budd hurried off toward the elevator. Zoey and Will were left alone.

Zoey considered for a moment. "Wait a second. Why were you in the building?"

"What building?"

"You know what I'm asking. Why were you in Livingston Tower when it started collapsing? You and Echo were both waiting outside, that was the plan. Why'd you come in after me?"

"You heard Arthur's will. You die, the estate gets donated to the Mormons or, whatever it was."

"Wow. That's the first really bad lie I've heard you tell. You want me to believe it was easier to race to the top of a skyscraper and attempt an escape from a collapsing building in *a helicopter you don't know how to fly*, than to hire some lawyers to hash out Arthur's assets?"

"Have you ever dealt with the Mormons, Zoey?"

She sighed in exasperation. "Anyway. Thank you. For coming back for me. That's what I'm trying to say."

He shrugged. "It was Echo's idea."

"Stop it."

They waited in awkward silence for a moment, then Zoey said, "So . . . what happens to you guys? After I'm gone?"

"What does it matter?"

Wu walked up and asked if she was ready to go. Zoey turned to Will and stuck out her hand, offering to shake. He didn't raise his in return.

She said, "Come on. There's no reason to be a dick now. I'm leaving. You're getting what you wanted."

He looked at her, finally shaking her hand, his eyes never leaving hers. He worked his jaw, something grinding away inside his brain. The last time she had seen that expression, a game-show contestant was trying to work out a puzzle clue with the clock ticking down.

Will lowered his hand, seemed to consider for a moment longer, then reached into his pocket.

"There is one last piece of business, I suppose." From his pocket, Will produced the lucky coin. "This trick is really three tricks, done in succession. The first trick has five steps. If you mess any one of them up, it's over, you understand?"

"I . . . am totally okay with forgoing the coin trick provision of Arthur's will. I was just joking about that before."

"This was his final wish. At least let me have the peace of knowing I showed it to you once."

She shrugged. "It's . . . whatever. Okay."

"All magic is just misdirection. The mark's eyes will be focused on the hand that appears to snatch the coin, while the coin is secretly stashed in the other. So to start, we're going to do what magicians call a French Drop. You hold the coin like this, so your audience can see it, between thumb and forefinger. Don't start the next part until their eyes are focused on the coin. Now, step one—and I'm going to do it real slow, so you can watch it—is you appear to be closing the coin in your other palm, but instead you're going to drop the coin out of sight, and squeeze it between your knuckles and palm. But you can't close your hand, or else that gives it away—you have to let the coin hand fall to your side, like it's not involved in the trick anymore. That's what sells it. Like this. You see?"

He waited, demanding an answer.

Impatiently, Zoey said, "Yes, I see."

"If that coin falls out of your hand, the trick is ruined. Now, what you have to do next—and this is the key to the whole trick, so listen carefully—is to take that coin and practice the French Drop over and over and over. And over, and over. Thousands and thousands of times, over hours and hours and weeks and months. Just sitting at home, dropping and catching, a little bit faster with each week and month that goes by, hearing the coin hit the floor, again and again. The improvement will be so incremental that you won't feel like you're accomplishing anything. But you'll keep doing it. And while your friends are all out drinking, or playing video games, or doing whatever you people do for fun these days, you'll be at home, practicing that coin trick. Over and over. In silence. Until one day, months or years from now, you'll be able to do that move so fast that the eye can't perceive it, even if the mark is looking right at your hand. The coin will never hit the floor. Then, after you've mastered that step, you'll be ready for step two, the Back Palm. Now—"

"No, that's enough. It already sounds awful."

"And that," said Will, "is what Arthur wanted me to show you."

"That your cool magic trick is really just a bunch of tedious repetition?"

"*Yes.* That, right there, is the difference between the heroes and the nobodies. The difference between people like you and people like me. People like me know that there is no magic. There is only the grind. Work looks like magic to those unwilling to do it."

He slipped the coin in his pocket and tugged down his sleeves.

"I get it, I'm lazy, I'm stupid, I'm—"

"You didn't hear a goddamned word I said. You say you're not a hero? Well, I'm going to tell you the best and the worst thing you've ever heard. Heroes aren't born. You just go out there and *grind it out*. You fail and you look foolish and you just keep grinding. There is nothing else. There is no 'chosen one,' there is no destiny, nobody wakes up one day and finds out they're amazing at something. There's just slamming your head into the wall, refusing to take no for an answer. Being relentless, until either the wall or your head breaks. You want to be a hero? You don't have to make some grand decision. There's no inspirational music, there's no montage. You just *don't quit*."

"What, like Armando? Charging in and winding up with his blood splattered all over the floor?"

"*Yes.* You take risks. You *get hurt*. And you put your head down and plow forward anyway and if you die, you die. That's the game. But don't tell me you're not a hero. You walk away, you're choosing to walk away. Whatever bad things happens as a result, you're choosing to let them happen. You can lie to yourself, say that you never had a choice, that you weren't cut out for this. But deep down you'll know. You'll know that humans aren't cut out for *anything*. We cut ourselves out. Slowly, with a rusty knife. Because otherwise, here's what's going to happen: you're going to die and you're going to stand at the gates of judgment and you're going to ask God what was the meaning of it all, and God will say, 'I created the universe, you little shit. It was up to *you* to give it meaning.'"

"You really think God uses that kind of language?"

"*Yes.*"

"So was that little speech for me? Or you?"

"I *don't know*. Goddamnit."

"I don't get you. I'm giving you what you wanted from the beginning. Just let me go."

"You're giving me what *I* wanted. You're not giving Arthur what *he* wanted. He wanted you to have this. I don't know why. I'll never know why. But damn it, he was like a father to me and now the same deranged fool who took his life gets to piss all over his final wish?"

"So what, you're telling me to stay?"

"I can't tell you to do anything. But if it matters, I think Arthur would want you to stay, and see this through."

"To do what? Kill Molech?"

"No, that's what he's expecting. That's what he wants."

"He *wants us to kill him*?"

"He wants us to *try*. No, what we need to do is much, much harder."

Zoey met Will's eyes.

"Here. We'll let my cat decide. I'm going to put him down. If he walks toward the car, I go. If he heads back toward the elevator, I stay."

She set Stench Machine on the floor. He flopped down onto the concrete and started licking himself.

After another long awkward silence in which all three of them watched the white cat noisily lick his own crotch, Will said, "Well, I assume you're not going to do *that*."

"If I could do that, I'd have been famous long before all this started."

Will's phone rang. It was Andre.

"Get up to the salon. Molech's about to make another announcement."

Will said, "We're on our way." He strode off toward the elevator and, after a moment, Zoey followed.

FORTY-FIVE

The Suits were gathered under the buffalo head, watching two feeds on a split screen—one was black with the words "AWAITING MOLECH" in stark white letters, the placeholder for the Molech announcement that was to start at any moment. The other was drone video of the massive crowds gathering downtown, in the aftermath of the tower collapse. Zoey noted a half dozen street vendors and food trucks had rolled up to serve snacks to the onlookers. At that moment, the synchronized skyline feed switched away from the ad it had been playing (for the film *James Bond Infiltrates a Space Station Full of Ninjas and Has Sex with Four Women*) and replaced it with a single gigantic face, looming over the city.

Molech's face was bathed in a menacing shadow. When he spoke, his voice was modulated to sound like a god calling down from the heavens, the bass vibrating the streets below. The crowd went nuts, reacting like it was a concert and the headliner had just taken the stage.

"My name is Molech," boomed the voice. "I am a man the likes of which you have never seen before. You could say that, in fact, I am no longer a man, but something more. I mean, am still a man, in terms of gender, that's not what I meant when I said I wasn't a man. I'm *all* man. More man than you can possibly comprehend. I am well endowed. I am male on a level that you . . . just won't even believe it when you see it."

Molech paused and glanced off to the right, as if someone off-screen was reminding him of something.

"Right. As you saw, I destroyed Livingston Tower, with the power from my right hand. And this is just a small preview of what is coming, as I reveal my true strength to this city, and to the world. The dirty money that built Livingston's skyscrapers and slums is collected by scheming men who hide behind gated walls and grow fat on your paychecks. Men with false power, built on weasel lies buried in fine print. Well, for them the sun has set, and now the long night has begun. And thus, their reckoning comes at noon on December 21, the day before the longest night of the year.

"In forty-eight hours I will reach out with my mighty hand and destroy seven targets, seven symbols of the false powers in this city, to demonstrate *real* power, in full view of Tabula Rasa and all of mankind. The false powers are guns, money, and superstition—the smoke and mirrors that keeps beta cowards in mansions and limousines. So first will be the home office of the Tabula Rasa Security Co-Op—big, bad guns hired by fat cats, as if they deserve police but we don't. Then, in no particular order I'm going to smash the Tabula Rasa mosque, and the Catholic church the next block over, so you can watch as neither of your gods strike me with lightning even while I take a messy burrito shit on the smoking ruins of your precious faith. Then I'm going to execute a foreclosure of the Bank One tower. And guess what—you rebuild it, I'm just gonna knock it down again.

"There'll be a couple of surprises thrown in, before my tour of destruction will culminate with the estate of Arthur Livingston, which I will reduce to rubble while on the spikes of the front gate I will impale the bodies of his piglet daughter and shitwind crew, who've controlled this city behind the scenes since before it was a city. You have forty-eight hours. To do what, you ask? Nothing. I am making no demands, I will carry out my attack regardless of what action you take. See you then."

Molech stared in silence from across the skyline, then turned and said, "Did you cut the feed? The light is still on. No. Push the—"

Molech disappeared from the buildings, and across every surface the feed was replaced by a countdown, in digits thirty stories high.

Zoey said, "I don't get it. What does he gain by warning everybody? Why not just start blowing stuff up?"

Will said, "Back up, and walk through it. What do all of his targets have in common?"

"They're all, uh, prominent?"

"And?"

"And . . . their owners aren't gonna sit back and let him do it. They're going to stand up to him."

"More than you know—he's going after Co-Op's main office—that place is a fortress, and they have some military-grade hardware they can put on the street. But—"

"That's what he wants," finished Zoey. "To be caught on camera ripping through tanks with his bare hands, to make a demonstration. So he gives everybody plenty of notice so they can all tune in to see it. Gotcha."

Budd said, "Then he'll sit back and wait for the bids to come rollin' in. Just a big, ol' infomercial, for his new product line."

Andre said, "Plus he's going to blow up this house, so there's that. Somebody should probably tell Carlton."

Echo said, "The Co-Op isn't going to sit back and wait for him to come to their door. The Fire Palace will be riddled with bullets by morning, it's not like that place is a secret any longer."

Will said, "You think Molech doesn't know that? That's not going to go well."

Zoey said, "Well, what's *our* plan? Because I was about to suggest paying somebody to go level those buildings myself."

Will said, "First, we need to assess what we have to work with. We need to go through the coin, and figure out exactly what we have there."

Andre said, "And by 'we,' he means Echo will go through it while the rest of us stay far out of her way, occasionally muttering words of encouragement and giving her shoulder rubs."

Zoey said, "What difference does the coin make now? None of us have the implants, what good is the software to us?" She looked at Will and said, "Wait, you don't have the implants, do you?"

"No."

"Like you didn't get some augmentation that lets you metabolize alcohol faster?"

Echo said, "The gold drivers are just a small fraction of the data on the coin—the rest is schematics for the devices themselves. There are two petabytes of files on there—fabricator instructions for implants, prototypes, and all sorts of other gear we can't even identify because most of it isn't in any kind of human language."

"But what good does *that* do us, considering the workshop where this stuff got built is now a giant black crater?"

Will had nodded and said, "Exactly. Budd?"

Budd put on his cowboy hat and said, "I'll make some calls." Got to be wearing the hat in the hologram, Zoey figured.

Will said, "Andre and I will go meet with the hired guns, before they do something stupid. Zoey, you'll stay here and investigate the house staff."

"*Who?*"

"Well, you've got that theory that somebody on the inside is leaking information, find out who it is. Watch the grounds crew in particular, I saw a guy cleaning the gutters yesterday in a way that was particularly suspicious."

"So after your big speech about heroism, you just gave me a clearly made-up job just to keep me safe in the house while the men go out and do hero stuff?"

Will put on his hat. "That's not entirely accurate. For one, you're definitely not safe in this house."

"I'm going with you."

He shrugged. "You're the boss." He turned on his heels and headed out of the room, Andre gave Zoey an "after you" gesture.

On the way out she asked, "So . . . what are we doing, exactly?"

Will said, "The French Drop."

FORTY-SIX

Down in the garage, Will led them to the black panel truck that had delivered the BMW earlier. He tapped a menu on his phone and LED screens on all sides of the vehicle blinked to life, the sides now covered in the dancing animated logo of a cow taking a bite out of a wheel of cheese, the words "UTAH ARTISINAL CHEESES" bouncing overhead.

Andre said, "Last time we disguised it as an ice cream truck, but it drew a crowd of kids at every intersection." He opened a side door. The interior contained what looked like a surveillance setup and, at the far end, a wet bar. "There's a sofa that folds up out of the floor, too—you can't see it right now because we had to fit the BMW in. After you."

The meeting Will had called was being held under a thirty-story-tall naked woman. It was a rectangular building downtown covered in screens displaying a 3D video loop that created an illusion of depth, making it look like the building was a hollow space in which an actual giant stripper was undulating for the passing traffic below (Zoey wondered how many men actually fantasized about three-hundred-foot-tall women, as it just seemed incredibly impractical as far as sexual encounters go). Will told her that inside the building were merely a couple hundred normal-sized strippers and escorts, serving high-end clientele who had to book weeks in advance. Scrolling across the woman were the words "THE NAKED CITY" in flashing crimson.

Getting into the basement required Will to flash a little golden membership card at the door, after which Andre, Zoey, and then Wu followed him past several giant but well-dressed bouncers. Wu had to give up his katana, as the club apparently had a no-weapons rule. They soon found themselves in an upscale lounge full of black leather furniture, being waited on by girls in tiny French Maid outfits offering sampler platters that included an array of colorful liquids in shot glasses and little glass squares bearing neat lines of white powder.

An eerie, undulating blue light filled the room from overhead, and Zoey looked up and saw dangling naked legs. The floor above them was apparently full of whirlpool hot tubs with glass bottoms that gave a clear view from the basement lounge, apparently so the people down here could watch. Six hot tubs made up the ceiling of the room they were in, bulging down like a clutch of giant blue alien eggs, each one containing a writhing pair of hairy male legs surrounded by about six female ones. She had said yesterday that Arthur Livingston's wax corpse was the creepiest thing she had ever seen, but Tabula Ra$a continued to outdo itself.

They took a seat and Zoey said to Will, "Don't tell me I own this place."

"Okay, I won't tell you."

The open invitation Will had sent out to the Tabula Ra$a security community couldn't have been simpler: "Don't move on the Fire and Ice Palace until you hear what we have to say." A half dozen men soon arrived—and they were all men—representing the largest private security firms in Tabula Ra$a. Will pointed out to her the CEO of the Co-Op, a graying, tanned ex-military man named Blake who Zoey thought probably punished himself with five hundred push-ups if he ever slept past five AM. Gray suit, no tie, smelled of aftershave. Will muttered introductions to her as each man walked in, but she quickly forgot the rest of their names. One of the guys looked like an old-time Mafia don, another was dressed in black tactical gear, like he would prefer to have crashed into the room through a skylight, another guy was barely contained in a sport jacket and tank top due to pectoral muscles tugging at his buttons. There was so much testosterone in the room that Zoey thought she was going to grow five o'clock shadow by the time the meeting ended.

Will, who was not programmed for preamble, said, "Stay away from the Fire and Ice. All of you. We're handling it."

Zoey thought that bit was, at best, a gross exaggeration.

Blake's answer was calm and matter-of-fact. "I appreciate that you needed to say what you just said, as a matter of courtesy. But you and I both know that the issue is only who is going to get to Molech first. Any intel you gained about the interior layout or any, shall we say *exotic* defensive measures would be greatly appreciated."

"'Exotic' does not describe what you're going to find there. We got a man inside only because Molech allowed us to. It was . . . just a game he was playing."

Blake shrugged. "I'm eager to examine his gear after we confiscate it. We're going in with overwhelming force, Mr. Blackwater."

"It will be like a tribe of Zulus trying to 'overwhelm' a tank with their spears. He's had months to prep the building and he has his gear working now. Seeing a glimpse of what he has, I don't think it will be a fight at all. I think he can just . . . neutralize you. Whatever you bring."

The muscle guy spoke up. "He's right, Blake, you fellas should back off that. Let my boys roll in and take care of it."

Blake said, "You'll only be in the way. You don't have the hardware, Reg."

Will said, "We're going in after Molech ourselves, early tomorrow morning." This was very much news to Zoey. "If you're bound and determined to go in, fine, but let us take the first shot. If you think we're not capable, watch us fail and let it inform your strategy. Maybe we'll loosen the jar for you, if nothing else."

Blake said, "We'll take it under advis—"

He was cut off by the sound of screams and gunshots, just outside the door.

FORTY-SEVEN

Zoey flinched at the sound of the shots, but absolutely no one else in the room did. They just seemed annoyed at the breach of protocol, turning on the door with the disapproval of a theater audience looking to see whose phone had gone off.

The door was kicked in and Zoey was looking at a red-spiked Mohawk behind a cartoonishly huge gun that she doubted she could even lift—it had at least three barrels, and a chainsaw attached to the bottom. The leader of the League of Badass led his team into the room.

"Everyone down!"

No one got down.

The guy was wearing a camouflage outfit with knee pads, elbow pads, and bafflingly oversized shoulder pads. The rest was a crisscross pattern of straps and bandoliers full of bullets. Everything else was pouches. So many pouches. His boots had pouches on them. Next to him was a pair of fake boobs trying to escape a crimson one-piece bathing suit made of leather, with thigh-high leather boots of the same color. The woman's boots had holsters that presumably had held the giant handguns she was now brandishing in each fist. If she ran out of bullets, she could resort to the four—no, five—thin daggers that were strapped to various parts of her body. The other four men seemed to be in competition to see who could fit the most pads, blades, and bullets onto their bodies while still remaining ambulatory. Yet none of them had helmets or any other kind of head or eye protection. Zoey figured it wasn't worth protecting your face if it meant hiding it from the camera.

The four hustled past the Mohawk and made a beeline for the Suits. A few seconds later, and for the first time in her life, Zoey had a gun pressed to her skull. So did Andre, Will, and Wu. Will sighed.

The Mohawk said, "Everyone be cool, everything is fine out there. We just had to let ourselves in, that's all—guess our invitation got lost in the mail. I'm sure you're all familiar with my team. This here is Vixxxen, behind you are Bonefire, Bloodstick, Stormshaft, and Crankwolf. And they've all got itchy trigger fingers."

Zoey said, "I guess it's no surprise they chose this profession, with names like that."

Blake, who was still seated and was now in the process of adding sugar to a mug of coffee, said, "Lee, *what in the possible hell* do you think you're doing?"

Andre said, "I think I know what this is about. You guys probably saw the truck out back. I assure you we don't have any cheese."

The Mohawk guy, Lee, said, "We're saving the city." He pointed his enormous gunsaw at Blake and the other security execs in the room and said, "Out. All of you."

Blake deferred to Will. "That the end of the meeting?"

"Just remember what I said. Around five AM tomorrow. Don't move before then."

Zoey tried to think of how they would put together a raid on Molech HQ with less than twelve hours to prepare, but she was having trouble focusing due to the gun that was being pressed so hard into her temple that it was making a dent in her thoughts. She wondered if somebody fired a shot into the ceiling if the hot tub up there would burst and drench everyone.

Blake sipped his coffee and sat down the mug. "I'll talk to my people."

He nodded to everyone in the room, including the gun-wielding members of the League of Badass, and calmly walked out. The rest of the armed security tycoons followed, leaving the hostage situation behind them like a boring sporting event they'd decided to bail on early so they could beat the traffic. On the way out, the muscle guy paused to glance up at a pair of brown, naked legs floating overhead, and Zoey wondered if he wouldn't just go directly upstairs after this.

Once the Suits and the League of Badass were alone in the lounge, Lee said, "We're going after Molech."

Zoey said, "Great, go do it. You didn't have to ask our permission."

"You're coming with us. See, whatever plan those other guys got for getting in the door of Molech's lair, I'm guessing they didn't figure out that all they need is something Molech wants. Which is *you*. We roll up, offering you three on a silver platter, Molech shows his face, we pop him in the head."

Andre said, "Where are you going to find a silver platter that big?"

Will said, "I think there are some important news stories you've missed from this afternoon. Popping Molech is a little harder than what you're picturing in your mind."

Lee said, "That's why you're going to give us his enhancements. We saw what Armando was doing before he went down."

Zoey said, "Wait, aren't you guy's on Molech's side? You turds are the first ones who came after me the day I came into town."

"We don't work for Molech. We work for the people in this city who can't afford those guys who just left the room. That first night, we didn't try for that contract because of Molech, we just—"

"Wanted the publicity?" finished Zoey.

"Got caught up in the chase. And we didn't know what kind of man Molech was. But it was never personal."

"It's actually never personal, for the real monsters."

"Shut up. You guys cooperate, there's no reason you can't live through this. Just play the role of the hostages, we'll demand to see Molech face to face before we make the exchange, we pop him, roll credits."

Wu said, "I assure you that we will be doing you a great favor by *not* allowing you to go through with that plan."

Lee spun on him and said, "Shut up. You're not in a position to allow anything."

Andre said to Lee, "Let me ask you, what was your job before you got into . . . whatever you call this?"

"Me? I served in the Marine Corps for four years. After that, five years as the best goddamned bounty hunter in Nevada."

Will interjected, "And what are the requirements for becoming a bounty hunter in Nevada?"

Lee said, "Superior instincts, proficiency in hand-to-hand—"

"It requires a two-hundred-fifty-dollar application fee and five weekends of classes at a community college."

"Yet that was good enough to get the jump on you."

Will turned to Zoey and said, "This is good on-the-job training. Tell me, what's the thing in Lee's hands there?"

"It's uh, a gun? I don't know the brand or—"

"And why is a gun better than a knife?"

Lee said, "Shut up. We're going out to our van, you're leading the way." Will didn't move.

Zoey said, "It lets you kill people from a long way away?"

"Correct. Now look at the men standing next to each of us, and ask yourself why would you ever take such a weapon and press it against a person's skull, putting it within easy reach of their hands?"

There was a tussle and a grunt nearby. Zoey spun toward it and found that the man who had been holding Andre at gunpoint was now on his knees, his arm twisted behind his back, his gun in Andre's hand.

Lee pointed his gun at him and screamed for him to freeze. But instantly there was another scuffle from Wu's direction, and by the time Zoey turned her head, Wu was disassembling a pistol he'd yanked away from his captor, letting bullets tumble to the carpet from his fingers. The gunman was unconscious on the floor.

Will's captor quickly backed off, getting his gun out of grabbing range but keeping it trained on the back of Will's skull.

The man said, "Don't even think about it," but sounded like he had never been less confident in a situation in his life.

Will glanced back at him and said, "You're Terry Rizzo, right? Put down that gun, go to your apartment on Lake Street, get Sheldon and Jeremiah, and get out of town. Don't ever come back. You have five seconds."

The man looked nervously at Will, then at Lee.

Will said, "My men are watching this on Blink. You'd never beat them there. Three. Two . . ."

The man hurried out of the room, apologizing to Lee as he went.

Lee said, "You like to threaten people? Well you can't threaten me. Molech is about to rain fire on you, and I'm your only—"

Zoey said, "Shut your idiocy vent. If you want to talk, tell this last guy to stop pointing a gun at my head. I don't know how to get it away from him, and I don't want to have to do some big macho thing where Wu comes over here and steals it using his karate powers. Just tell him to put it away, then we'll converse. I mean, do I have to say out loud what's already obvious? That shooting me is the same as shooting yourself? I'm getting seriously fed up with all this."

Lee studied her for a moment, then gave the slightest nod to her captor. The guy backed off, then joined Lee and Vixxxen on the other side of the room.

Zoey said, "Okay, two things. First, I think that giving people the ability to punch over buildings is trusting them with quite a bit of power, and in the course of the day today I've kind of decided that the whole thing where we grant power based on who wants it most, is *probably* what has ruined society up to this point. Second, we can't actually give you what you're asking. It's a long story, but we can't do the limb enhancements, we're not set up for it."

Andre said, "You know she's tellin' the truth, too, because otherwise my dong would still be in bandages."

"But," Zoey said, "I can offer you work. The kind of money you probably don't make in a whole year of bounty hunting. You can buy a new van and Vixxxen here will be able to afford the rest of her costume."

Will looked dubious. He muttered, "Zoey . . ."

Lee said, "I'm listening."

"Squatterville. You're familiar with it? The unfinished condos the poor people have moved into, a couple of blocks down from where Livingston Tower, uh, was?"

"Yeah."

"They need protection. If Molech goes on his rampage, I need someone to get those people out of there, and to a safe place. Even if the chaos doesn't come to their block, you can help make sure the food and diapers and all that arrives safely."

"Miss Ashe, this entire city is a target. Molech could go after the hospital, the art galleries, even the nuke plant. We're not going to sit back and let him do it."

"Right, but those targets all have security because the people who own them have money. There's nobody left to protect Squatterville. You do that, *without* accidentally murdering everyone there, you get five hundred grand. Then after that, maybe we'll talk."

"But if we take out Molech, then those people will be safe."

"People like that are never safe. Take it or leave it, but here's where you get to decide if your fantasy is to actually be a hero, or to just murder people you don't like. Because in my mind, if you were *true* heroes, you'd already be down there, making sure all those poor kids don't have to go to bed scared every night."

Lee clearly hated this plan, but not as much as he hated having to openly say no.

"I . . . need to discuss it with my team."

"Zoey," said Will. "Tell him the truth."

"What?"

Will said to Lee, "Molech will almost certainly go to Squatterville. And we need it protected. But not because of the people there. We need it because of the coins."

Zoey thought, "The *what*?" at the exact same time Lee spoke it out loud.

"Two hundred million dollars in rare gold and silver coins, recovered from a Spanish galleon off the coast of Florida about fifteen years ago. They were buried there by Molech's father, when it was still a vacant lot. Now they're under the concrete of the lobby—you can actually see cracks in the floor over the burial site, on account of the loose soil underneath. It's the real reason the building was never finished. Molech found out about it, and I have a feeling that's going to be his first stop. You keep Molech away, you get half."

Lee gave no answer, but his gaze had kind of disconnected, focusing into the middle distance where a fantasy of unspeakable riches was playing out before him.

Will straightened his tie and said, "Now, if you don't mind, *we have a lot of work to do.*"

Will headed for the door, and no one stopped him.

FORTY-EIGHT

Andre was focused on his phone as they took the elevator up to the library. Will asked, "Anything?" and Andre shook his head.

Zoey asked, "What are we looking for?"

Will said, "The assault on the Fire Palace."

"By who?"

"Everyone? I'd bet on the Co-Op first, though."

"Maybe you convinced them to stay away."

"I convinced them to go in. I told them we were moving in at dawn, there's no way in hell they'd let us steal their hero moment. I basically set a deadline for them."

"Wait, you *wanted* them to go after Molech?"

"They were going to do it either way, I wanted to make sure they did it tonight."

"Holy crap, you're diabolical."

He shrugged. "The key is that Blake probably assumed I was lying about the timeline, meaning he thinks we're planning to go in much sooner, and that the dawn reference was a ruse specifically to prevent him from getting a jump on us. So he likely went back to his people and told them they needed to be ready to roll . . . pretty much now."

"So, what do *we* do?"

"For the moment? We watch."

Andre said, "Well, I for one need coffee."

They all headed down to the kitchen, because that's where the coffee was, and Zoey flitted around the bar making drinks. Nobody had ordered anything, she just made some pretty ones and lined them up on the counter. The one she was working on at the moment had four shots of espresso, a mixture of coconut milk and whole milk, and was sweetened with bergamot syrup. She drew a "Z" in an old English font in the foam, and sprinkled it with chocolate shavings. Then she grabbed another mug and started again.

Andre said, "I could watch you do that all day. It's like a dance."

"I can do any of these with my eyes closed. Java Lodge only had one barista at a time, it was a one-woman show. I liked it when it was busy, though, felt like a challenge. But now . . . I'm just trying to keep moving. If I stop and think about all this I'll have a panic attack."

They had brought up a feed on the wall behind the bar, and Andre was flipping through locations. The Fire and Ice towers, the Co-Op's headquarters, the neighborhood around the Casa.

He glanced at Will and said, "Pirate treasure? *That* was the lie you came up with. You told them that there was pirate treasure buried under Squatterville?"

"Seemed like the sort of thing they'd believe. At least it gives them a reason to be on site."

Budd and Echo walked in.

Budd said, "We got one."

Echo said, "I smell coffee."

Zoey said, "It's right there, drink it or it goes down the drain, I'm brewing as a coping mechanism. And we got one of what?"

Before Budd could answer, Andre said, "It's starting."

The Co-Op hadn't waited long after nightfall to launch their assault. A pair of massive black helicopters sawed their way through the frigid evening air toward the Fire Palace, filmed by a swarm of following drones. When the view switched to ground level, a convoy of six hulking black trucks were shown rumbling down Fairfax Avenue, three from each direction. Planning to hit the tower from the ground and the air, simultaneously.

Zoey looked around. "Where's Wu?"

Andre said, "Outside. He found a spider in the hall. He scooped it up in a paper cup and said he was taking it out to the courtyard so it could go find its family."

The feed cut back to the Fire Palace, which seemed completely dormant from the outside—if the building had any lights, they were enshrouded by the black tarp. It was just a dark void in the skyline. If bionic supervillains were scrambling into position, they certainly weren't making a public show of it.

But then, Echo said, "There. At street level."

The Blink feeds noticed a moment after she did—they all started focusing down at the circular paved walk at the base of the tower. Blue lights lit up, one by one, forming a ring. The lights were eminating from waist-high objects rising from the sidewalk, which Zoey was pretty sure were shaped like extended middle fingers.

The trucks plowed forward, their rough tires making a high-pitched buzz on the pavement like a kicked beehive, approaching from the north and south. The first trucks were still two blocks away when the circle of the blue glowing hands pulsed in unison, like a row of camera flashbulbs all going off at once, making a noise like a giant cracking a bullwhip. The Blink cameras all switched toward the trucks, as if expecting explosions. None occurred. Still, the trucks slowed at the sight of the lights, as if the drivers were suddenly unsure of what they were barreling into.

Or rather, most of them did.

The first trucks—the ones that had been closest to the blast in each direction—continued to plow forward, unabated. The first started to swerve off to the left, away from the Fire Palace, toward the Ice Palace across the street. The next rolled on toward the Fire Palace, but weaved, as if the driver was steering the vehicle with his knees. Eventually both trucks rumbled lazily to a stop, one bumping gently into one of the glowing hands outside the Fire Palace, the other rolling up onto the sidewalk across the street. The rest of the trucks skidded to a halt, uncertain, keeping their distance.

For a moment, there was nothing. No SWAT teams came spilling out of the trucks, nothing exploded, no enhanced horrors came sprinting out of the tower. Instead, after a few minutes a dozen or so shirtless Molech henchmen came strolling out toward the vehicles, calmly. One of them was eating a sandwich. They walked up to both vehicles and opened the rear doors. Zoey gasped as a bundle of charred limbs tumbled out. The henchmen rooted around inside the trucks, gathering up the weapons and gear from within and hauling it all back into the Fire Palace. One of the henchmen pulled out a can of spray paint, and in glow-in-the-dark blue paint, tagged both of the vehicles with a drawing of a hand giving the middle finger.

Next to Zoey, Andre gave a tired sigh. Zoey kept her eyes on the feed as she started grinding another batch of espresso beans.

The collective gaze of Blink switched to the roof of the Fire Palace, where the two choppers had already dropped ziplines onto a rooftop that was still smoldering from the aftermath of Armando's battle with Rodzilla earlier in the day.

Another ring of blue hands glowed to life around the rim of the circular rooftop.

280 / JASON PARGIN

There was another flash.

A rain of flaming corpses tumbled out of the helicopters.

The choppers swerved and lurched and then tumbled down onto Fairfax Avenue, joining the dead trucks nearby. The comment bar alongside the feed went wild with Team Molech cheers.

Zoey whispered, "We should have stopped them. We should have talked them out of it."

Will said, "You still have much to learn about this world."

The rest of the Co-Op's armored column was now backing up, slowly enough to make it appear to be a strategic repositioning rather than a full-on retreat. The world waited to see what else the hired guns of Tabula Ra$a would throw at Molech, but the feeds for each of the major security services were full of stunned professionals trying to hide their terror in detached discussion of strategy. Suggestions were made about cutting off power to the building to shut down the energy weapons, but someone noted that the Co-Op had actually already done that—the buildings apparently had their own power source. Analysts tried to study and identify the defenses, and quickly came to the conclusion that they were nothing currently known to science.

But then the feed switched to a group of men surrounding a single olive green truck, parked outside of town, in the desert. It had a ramp on the back aimed toward the sky at a forty-five-degree angle, covered in a green tarp. When they yanked the tarp aside, it revealed what looked to Zoey like a miniature fighter jet, about the size of one you'd make for a baby or a small dog to fly. She assumed it was neither of those things.

At the sight of it, Andre choked on his drink.

Zoey said, "What is *that*?"

Echo said, "Remote control heavy ordinance drone. Basically a cruise missile. Looks Russian."

Will said, "They're going to try to bring down the building." He seemed mildly annoyed, as if frustrated by the amateurs' unsubtle technique.

Budd said, "Those crazy sons of bitches. That's the Black Dawn militia. Guess we know who hijacked that convoy last year—"

The missile blasted into the night sky on a pillar of yellow fire, as the men on the ground hooted and yelped, several of them drinking beers. The missile had a nose camera that was patched in to Blink, because of course it was, and the feed showed the landscape whipping by underneath, the glimmering skyline of downtown Tabula Ra$a just ahead. The radio voice of the guy controlling the device narrated its trip, announcing altitude and wind direction, a red box on the screen hovering over its target in the distance.

Zoey said, "Am I supposed to be terrified that weapons like that exist out in the wild, or rooting for it to work?"

No one answered. Everyone was riveted, eyes locked on the feed as the missile ate up the distance between it and the Fire Palace.

The pilot said, "One kilometer to target. Nine hundred meters. Eight hundred. Seven hu—Whoa, what the—?"

Suddenly, the skyline jerked to the right, as if the missile had taken a hard left turn.

"Veering off course, thirty-two degrees, trying to correct." A pause of a few seconds, and then, "Controls unresponsive."

The view turned and turned, then the horizon froze in the view screen and the missile screamed forward.

"Initiating self-destruct," said the pilot. Then a few seconds later, "No response. We've lost control of the unit. Damn it, Daryl, I told you this was a bad idea."

Zoey said, "Oh my god, is that thing just flying wildly into the city somewhere?"

Echo shook her head. "Worse. I think Molech's men took control of it."

Zoey went cold. "Where are they sending it?" The real question she wanted answered was, *Are they sending it here?*

Blink switched to exterior shots of the missile, hopping from one feed to the next as it streaked past random drones in the night and flashed in between skyscrapers. It turned once more, then arced down toward its destination.

Budd said, "Jesus."

Will said, "It's heading for the hospital."

Zoey thought that somewhere she could hear Molech laughing.

The missile screamed down, leaving a yellow gash in the night sky, the massive white building filling its view screen.

It impacted the parking lot in front of the hospital, erupting in a towering ball of blooming orange fire that could probably be seen from Fort Drayton. They heard the explosion first on Blink, then a second later it echoed in from the distance outside the kitchen window. Zoey jumped both times. She had no idea if Molech landed it in the parking lot out of mercy, or just misjudged the approach.

Will turned away from the feed and said, "Like Zulus swarming a tank."

Zoey said, "What do we do, Will? *What the hell do we do?*"

Will thought for a moment and then said, "I guess now would be a good time to tell you what we were doing before we met your father."

FORTY-NINE

🔑

Will said, "Do you know what PSYOPS are?"

Zoey made herself take her eyes off of the feed and said, "It's some kind of secret military thing, right? I think I saw a movie about it once but I fell asleep during a romance subplot."

"It's psychological operations. Mind games, with the enemy, to try to win the war without firing a shot. Andre, Budd, and I all did work with the Eighth Military Information Support Group. On the private side—we were contractors, no official connection to the U.S. government, so it'd be easy to disown us if we ever got caught. Fifteen years ago, we were all in North Korea, during the insurgency that our government was not supporting in any official capacity, while pulling every unofficial trick in the book."

"And Arthur was in on this?"

"No, Arthur was there, for . . . business."

"Right, I don't want to know." She looked at Echo. "What was your job?"

"Well, I was in fourth grade at the time, so . . ."

"At the time," interrupted Will, "the insurgency was falling apart, but the regime didn't know that. Our objective was to try to convince the North Korean government that the rebels were much stronger than they actually were, try to force them to the negotiating table. We knew they were paranoid that the rebels had gained the support of the Chinese, which if true would have spelled doom for the regime. It wasn't true, but our job was to convince them it was. You follow so far?"

It occurred to Zoey that you could really get Will talking if you turned the subject to how much smarter he was than everybody else. Andre took two of the coffee drinks from the bar, and sat down next to Will. On the feed, fire trucks were swarming the hospital parking lot.

Zoey said, "Yeah. You want something to drink?"

"Can you make hot tea? I want the simplest possible cup of hot tea you can make. Nothing fancy."

"Coming right up."

"Now," Will continued, "I don't know how familiar you are with the war or international politics in general, but the leaders of North Korea were a succession of increasingly insane and paranoid despots with a swarm of angry wasps where their brains should have been. That was our advantage—if we dropped the right hints, the regime would believe *anything*. So, the first step was to just allow a large cache of insurgent weapons to get captured. Gear left out in the rain, unguarded, so the regime could sweep in and seize it all without firing a shot. Can you think of why we would do that?"

Zoey said, "It's creating the impression you didn't need it, right? Like a poor dude blowing his whole paycheck on a date, so the girl thinks he's richer than he is?"

"Exactly. If the insurgents can afford to leave *this* just lying around, imagine what they must have elsewhere."

"But that's a huge waste if the bad guys didn't happen to notice it."

"Always assume your enemies are more clever than you give them credit for—even an animal can think several steps ahead. Which means if you want them to believe a lie, you don't need to jam it down their throat. You just leave them a trail of bread crumbs, and let them believe they arrived at the conclusion against your will. But it all starts with this one fundamental principle: find out what the enemy is most afraid of, and you'll also find what they're the most eager to believe."

Zoey slid the tea over to Will. It was a cup of her Cthulhu Tea—a clear mug displaying three layers of different-colored hot tea flavors with gold at the bottom, fading to blood-red, and then into midnight blue at the top, like a sunset. A few drops of Baileys cream were dabbed onto the surface with a thin straw, where it dripped down into the tea, hanging in the dark blue liquid like the white, dangling tentacles of an unholy creature reaching down from the heavens. It was the single most elaborate drink Zoey knew how to make.

Will said, "Thank you. I think."

Andre piped up. "Now, my favorite part of that whole operation, or rather, what would have been my favorite part had it worked—"

Will held up a hand. "We don't need to go over this part—"

Budd said, "I reckon we do."

"This is all still technically classified, I've already said too much—"

"My favorite part," said Andre, talking over him, "was Will came up with this idea to make a death ray."

Budd picked up a coffee cup and said, "Now, we gotta give you some quick context here. Not to drown you in a bunch of geopolitical rigmarole or anything, but it was right around then that the Chinese were experimentin' with high-energy weapons—lasers and microwaves and all that Star Wars nonsense. So we start spreadin' rumors that the rebels had a Chinese handheld microwave gun that could penetrate even the most advanced armor. Now, this was important because the regime's tanks were mostly a weapon of intimidation. The sound of them tracks clanking down the street, flattening parked cars, and smashin' through walls—their psychological impact was way more important than their strategic value. So you can imagine how that would change the game if an insurgent had, let's say, a handheld rifle that could make a tank go up like a firework with a squeeze of the trigger."

Will said impatiently, "Budd, none of this is helping her understand the oper—"

"I've got the floor here. So, we reckon we'll make one of these Martian death rays. Not a real one—such a thing didn't exist at the time—but one that was convincing enough to scare the pants off Pyongyang. Now in the real world, you can't see a laser—guy squeezes the trigger on this end, somethin' blows up downrange. Keep that in mind. So anyway, we start staging the whole thing, set to take place in the middle of a shopping district, where there'd be lots of cell phone cameras there to capture it all. So Will here, and remember he was only your age at the time, he finds a toy store and buys of one of them giant plastic squirt guns, the ones with the big tanks of water on top. And we take it to the safehouse and paint it, modify it, put real tactical sites on it—really make it look like something that would come out of the PLA's advanced weapons lab. Then he has an insurgent bombmaker craft for us an antitank satchel charge, but modified. It'd be full of copper sulfate—a chemical you can get from the hardware store—which burns bright green, like this is some kind of crazy alien weapon we've got here. So, we had it set up where a runner would stick the satchel charge to the tank—it had magnets inside it, see—and the bomb would be detonated by cell phone, so it was as simple as embedding the phone into the handle of the fake death-ray rifle. Then the gunman would wait for the tank to rumble up, squeeze the 'trigger,' and watch the tank erupt in a beautiful green fireball, for the world to see. Boom, instant death ray. It would've been amazing. Had it worked."

Will made a grunting sound.

Zoey said, "What do you means, 'had it worked'?"

Will said, "It's not important, what matters is you understand the importance of—"

"The gunman was the weak link," said Andre, as if remembering it fondly. "The first part of the plan worked pretty good, but remember, for this to all play out, he had to get in point blank, so the people recording it on their phones could get the 'death ray' and the tank in the same shot. So the gunman blows the tank and it burns green, looks great."

"But," continued Budd, "he then turns to hightail it out of there and immediately trips over his own feet. His super-advanced death ray shatters under him like the hollow plastic toy that it is. He gets snatched up by regime troops and within an hour, all of us were in custody."

"Holy crap! You got taken prisoner by the North Korean army?"

Andre nodded. "Uh huh. Got thrown into this holding area behind razor wire, bunch of starving POWs in there. Ain't never seen anything like it. Don't want to see anything like it again, neither."

"How'd you get away?"

Andre said, "Your daddy. He was in country on, you know, business and had connections. To make a long story short, he sneaked us across the border and if he hadn't, we'd have been hung from a bridge. Arthur tracked us down back in the States a bit later, asked if we wanted to go to work for him. The rest is history."

Zoey asked, "What happened to the other guy?"

"Which other guy?"

"The moron with the gun, who tripped and ruined the whole thing?"

Budd nodded toward Will. "Why don't you ask him? Fella's sittin' right here."

Zoey laughed, then stopped laughing and said, "We are so screwed."

Budd said, "Well, we got a special delivery comin'. I reckon it might change your mind."

FIFTY

That night, she had another Jezza dream.

This time she was back in her old greasy apartment again, in the bathtub that was so tiny that even short Zoey had to keep her knees out of the water if she wanted to get her top half under it. The door opened and there was Jezza—only now, in the dream, he was half man, half machine, his eyes replaced by tiny whirring blades like from a blender, his arms bundles of wires and gears. Looming over the tub, grabbing Zoey by the neck and forcing her under the surface, the water burning down her nostrils and flowing down her throat, tasting like soap and bath salts, Zoey clawing at his face while she drowned an inch away from air . . .

Zoey awoke and sat up, splashing water in every direction and startling Stench Machine, who went skittering across the bathroom tile. She wiped water from her eyes and spent ten seconds trying to remember where she was.

She had fallen asleep in a bathtub that was twice as long as the one she was used to, and without the other end to brace her, had slid under the surface. The tub was in yet another of the guest rooms at the Casa de Zoey, a luxurious device that kept the water heated at a constant temperature, lit the room with simulated candlelight, and generated aromatherapy scents according to whatever mood it detected you were in. The inside of the tub was covered in a layer of some kind of clear gel that molded to your body, so you didn't have hard fiberglass pressing against your tailbone if you tried to sit up. Zoey wondered if there would be a perfect mold of her butt after she got out.

It was the middle of the night, about twelve hours after the events at Livingston Tower that left it a three-story-tall pile of steel beams and concrete in the center of a ten-block-wide lake of scattered glass. The bath had been Andre's idea, something he says they teach in the army, to deal with the immediate aftermath of combat trauma. When you get a moment of safety, they say, take time to do the human basics: bathing, grooming, eating, sleeping. Oh, and breathing—that slow, steady breathing, from the belly. You stay tensed up and alert all the time, Andre said, and you wind up frying those circuits in your brain, rendering them useless ("Or slowly drinking yourself to death, like Will here.").

Zoey stepped out of the guest room (and yes, the tub did in fact have a butt indentation after she got out) and found Wu patiently standing guard outside her door.

At the sight of her he said, "Ms. Ling was looking for you. There is activity in the ballroom."

"Okay, do you mean an actual ballroom where people hold dances, or that room with the Chuck E. Cheese ball pit?" Zoey imagined Will, Echo, and the rest flopping around in there among the colored balls, like a bunch of kids at a birthday party.

"The former, I would assume."

"All right, didn't know I had one of those. Do you have any idea where it is?"

"Perhaps if we join forces, we can find it together."

At the stairs, they met Carlton who said, "Ah, Ms. Ashe. Mr. Blackwater has asked if he can remove one of the walls of the ballroom."

Said ballroom was enormous, and smelled like cookies for some reason. It was absolutely choked with Christmas decorations, as if they had done the rest of the house and then realized they still had four metric tons of wreathes, bows, candles, lights, and hundreds of other festive doodads left over, then decided to just cram them all into this room.

A group of men in overalls were already tearing out the far wall with saws and sledgehammers, so Will apparently had just asked permission as a courtesy. Andre came bounding over to meet Zoey and Wu at the door, out of breath. He was in jeans and a paint-stained sweatshirt—work clothes.

"We got a flatbed out there, too wide to get into the garage. Too tall, too. Gonna have to turn the ballroom into a workshop."

Andre then walked up to the small table near the door, broke off a corner, and ate it. Zoey stared at him, dumbstruck.

"Gingerbread. Every year Arthur did a big Christmas blowout party in here, all his rich friends and their kids. Called it a Wonka party, turned this whole room into a candy palace where everything was edible. See them snowmen in the corners? They're all marshmallow, you could go over and take a bite out of one right now. The tree over there is hard candy branches and chocolate ornaments. Graham cracker shelves over there. There's 'sposed to be chocolate fountains everywhere you could dip the stuff in. Cost over a hundred grand to have it all made. Party was supposed to be the thirteenth but, you know. Got canceled."

Zoey said, "I feel like you're trying to distract me from what's going on with the wall back there."

"Budd knew a guy who knew a guy who knew where we could get a fabricator. One like we need, I mean, capable of doing nano-level builds. Tech startup in the Bay Area owned it, was using it to make prototype Blink eyeball implants or somethin'. Now it belongs to us. Fees for the high-speed freight were obscene."

"Do I want to know what you had to do to get that thing?"

"Let's put it this way. You now own a tech startup in the Bay Area."

One of the workers along the wall called out a warning and everyone scattered. The wall collapsed inward in a cloud of dust, revealing the night sky and ushering in a blast of chilled air from the courtyard. A pair of forklifts rolled into the room, leaving muddy tracks across the black and white marble tiles. Behind them came the flatbed truck, an enormous vehicle that Zoey figured they probably used to transport airliner parts or something. On the back was a series of round lumps covered in tarps. So this was what it was like, she thought. Whether you want a pizza, bodyguard, brand-new BMW, or a multimillion-dollar gadget-making machine, you pick up the phone and a little later it comes rolling up your driveway.

The machine was the size of a freight train car. It was cylindrical and flat black—identical to the one she'd seen in Arthur's death video that Zoey had thought had looked like a huge, black alien worm, or grub. The workers were buzzing around it, staff from the tech firm they'd bought out who had been paid an obscene amount of cash to make the rail trip from Sunnyvale, California, and work through the night. They were running cables and huddling around holographic displays, tweaking settings. Behind them, a team of men were hauling out wall debris in wheelbarrows and three masons were already bricking up the giant hole with startling efficiency. She figured by sunrise the wall would look good as new, an invisible amount of money deducted from some account to cover it all. It really was like a magic trick, just slower, and noisier.

By the time they finished getting the thing set up, Zoey was sitting cross-legged on the floor and eating the leg off a peanut brittle reindeer while Andre stood over her, gnawing on a piece of antler he'd broken off, devouring their prey like a pair of candy-eating jackals. Andre had found eggnog somewhere, and had been adding an unhealthy amount of brandy to each of their glasses.

Will approached just as Andre was crinkling his forehead at Zoey and saying, "I don't understand, you're sayin' my head looks like a hamburger?"

"No, not a Whopper from Burger King. A Whopper, like the candy. Little chocolate balls? Full of some kind of industrial foam?"

Will—the only person in the room still wearing a suit and tie—gestured to the machine and said, "Congratulations, the ballroom is now a fully functional factory. Feed it the raw materials, and it can weave carbon fiber, manufacture graphene or nano-tubes or aerogel, it can build a working microprocessor or circuit board . . . almost anything."

Zoey said, "Tell it to make me a mug of hot chocolate, and a baby goat to cuddle."

"It's not a Star Trek replicator. It manufactures parts for electronics, and nano-scale components."

Zoey said, "Right, right. I think it looks like a giant alien caterpillar. Andre says it looks like a turd a giant robot left on the floor. What do you think?"

"Are you guys drunk?"

"Not yet, but we're working as fast as we can. Be patient."

Andre said, "I don't think she has your tolerance, Will. Not as much practice."

Will ignored this and said, "Anyway, this is the same model Arthur had in his warehouse, the schematics on the coin drive should be specifically written to work with it. You plug in the instructions at this end, where all the monitors are—"

"And the caterpillar poops out a gadget on the other end," finished Zoey. "Neat."

Zoey noticed Echo walking over in a cute belted sweater and tights that she probably thought was her gross-manual-labor outfit. "It's supposedly ready to go. I tried to get a crash course on how to work the machine but the lead tech insisted on talking to me like I was his four-year-old daughter asking him what butterflies are made of."

Will said, "They can't stay here, they already know more than I'd prefer, and they sure as hell can't see what's on that coin drive."

Echo shrugged. "I'll figure it out." She made a noise like she could feel a headache coming on. "I always do."

As the techs packed up to leave, Zoey nodded toward Will and asked Echo, "You ever seen him in anything but a suit?"

"I've seen him . . . not in a suit, yes."

"What was he—oh my god. I'm sorry I asked."

Once the crew had shuffled out, Will handed Echo the coin and said, "Okay, fire it up."

Zoey thought that as efficient and futuristic as the fabricator looked and probably was, it was still noisy as hell. It whirred and crackled and thunked, pushing components from one process to the next, assembling, soldering, curing, polishing, and god knew what else. It also stank, the flexible ventilation ducts they'd run to the windows unable to contain the smell of a machine that was melting and cooking various presumably toxic materials. Budd said the fabricator used enough juice to power a small city, but she didn't know if that was an actual amount or just a figure of speech. Somebody would find out when the electric bill came due.

Soon there was a ding and a green light, and everyone gathered at the mouth of the machine, just a chute onto which the caterpillar coughed up the finished product into a cradle lined with black egg crate foam. The object that had slid out was an unimpressive little thing, a little shiny metal pyramid about an inch on each side, with a plastic loop to hook around your hand.

Zoey asked, "So what is it?"

Echo shrugged. "No idea. The device schematics aren't labeled in any way that I can read. I picked the one that showed the shortest estimated production time."

"Does it go . . . *inside* you?"

Andre said, "Damn, I hope not."

Will said, "A lot of what's on here will be test devices, components, early prototypes, and so on. Looks handheld, whatever it is."

Somewhat drunkenly, Andre said, "Hell, I'll give it a shot."

Zoey asked, "How do we know it isn't a bomb?"

"It has a handle. Why would you wanna strap a bomb to your hand?"

Will said, "Still, you should take it outside. I don't want you to damage the equipment."

They took a side door to the courtyard, where a dead pig was suspended from a wooden rig that reminded Zoey of a gallows. Carlton was pulling off a pair of rubber gloves and said, "That is the last of the pig carcasses, I'm afraid."

Zoey asked, "Why did we have *any* pig carcasses here?"

Will said, "Actually, they're by far the best analog for a human body, in terms of measuring impact and damage from projectiles."

"That is a *terrible* reason to keep them around."

Andre said, "E'erybody stop arguing and stand the hell back."

He stepped out ahead of the group, strapped the gadget to his palm, and held it out toward the pig. Everyone held their breath, standing silently and shivering in the chilled December air. Zoey put her fingers in her ears, for good measure.

Andre squeezed his eyes closed, and pushed a button.

There was a deep hum, no louder than a fluorescent lightbulb that's about to go bad. For a moment it appeared that nothing was happening—the pig remained unharmed and Andre didn't explode in a blue flash.

Then, there was an enraged meow as Stench Machine went sailing through the air, flying toward Andre and slamming into his palm. Andre panicked, yelped, and shook the cat free.

He stared at the gadget in his hand and said, "So it's a magnet for cats? Hey! It's a pussy mag—"

"It's a regular magnet," interrupted Budd. "It grabbed the metal spikes on his collar. I could feel it tuggin' on the keys in my pocket."

"You sure you weren't just happy to see me?"

"Anyway," Will said with a sigh, "this doesn't seem particularly useful. Echo, see what else we got."

Andre said, "You don't think a mega-powerful magnet would be useful? You cover your whole body in these things and you'd be a superhero who could manipulate all metal. You could call yourself Magnetor."

"Yes," Budd said. "Right up until you sucked a car on top of yourself."

As they passed back into the ballroom, Zoey said, "Just to summarize, Molech already has an entire arsenal of these gadgets, already implanted in the bodies of him and his goons, all of which are presumably working perfectly. Meanwhile, we're going to have at least a week tied up in just figuring out what we've got in our catalog? What exactly are we hoping to find here?"

Will said, "I don't know, a piece of equipment that protects a person against all of the gear Molech has?"

Echo said, "You want a hypothetical protection against a railgun that can fire projectiles at Mach 15, a plasma channel device that can produce enough current to turn a car into a black stain on the pavement, and god only knows what else he's got in his toy box? I can't even imagine what that would look like."

Will said, "Fine, if the issue is that we don't have enough data about the enemy's capabilities and strategy, then we need to gather more data."

Zoey said, "Perfect. How do we do that?"

Will said, "Molech's strength has always been loyalty, nobody on the inside of his crew ever turns—it's more cult than crew. The rumors about their initiation process are . . . unsettling. But you can't build a headquarters with a bunch of meathead enforcers, you need professionals. That means he's had to hire contractors. You want to turn somebody, you shoot for one of them—they're basically invisible to a narcissist like Molech, he doesn't even see them as people. So step one would be to find out who—"

"Rob Winkle Construction," said Budd before Will could ask. "Brought in from out of town, staying in temporary quarters a few blocks away from the Fire and Ice."

"So they're never far from the job site," said Will. "Meaning we'd have to walk right to up to Molech HQ and interrogate his day laborers right under his nose."

Everyone went silent for a moment, thinking.

Andre took a long look at Zoey and then said, "You know what we need? A massage truck."

FIFTY-ONE

Andre said you could stand near any construction site in Tabula Ra$a and see the "massage" trucks crawl past, stopping to pick up clients at break time. He led them down to the black panel truck and programmed in its disguise—when the graphics faded in, it literally had "massage" in sarcasm quotes (MADAM LE STRADE'S MAGIC RELAXATION "MASSAGE"), the logo in pink letters that followed the contours of a naked woman. Prostitution was legal in the city, of course, but the fact that the trucks offered legit massages gave the customers plausible deniability for the wives and girlfriends who should notice their man climbing out of one. Vices were legal, but Blink made it damned hard to indulge in secret.

Andre said, "The construction crew walks over from a makeshift dorm every shift, we just gotta catch 'em on the way in."

Zoey said, "Guys, this is the single most conspicuous vehicle in America. It literally has a naked butt on it."

Will shook his head. "The hardest part will be fighting for space with the other trucks, we'll be indistinguishable from the rest of the ass fleet."

"Really? That many guys want mobile whores at six in the morning?"

Andre said, "Well, the construction dorms have group bathrooms. No privacy, if you know what I'm sayin'." She didn't.

A short time later they were all piled in the truck, parked about ten feet from a charred patch of pavement where a helicopter had crashed the evening before, and in the shadow of Molech's own headquarters—probably no more than a hundred yards from the man who could vaporize them with the flick of a wrist. Will had assured her that this was actually the one spot Molech wouldn't think to look for them, but Will's good intentioned lies were always the most halfhearted.

Zoey, Echo, and Will sat on a red leather sofa that ran along one wall of the truck opposite a bank of feeds that played on the other. Will had changed into a suit with the color and texture of a newly paved road, Echo was wearing a black catsuit with a series of belts crisscrossing at the waist (it was the sort of thing Zoey wouldn't have had the confidence to wear in a daydream). Wu stood guard by the door, Budd and Andre were leaning against the bar, the latter eating a leftover pork chop he found in the bar's minifridge. They all watched the feeds as they scanned the passing workers, returning facial recognition profiles in real time.

Budd said, "Now what we want is the foreman, fella named A. J. Skelnik. Tall, white, bad posture, balding in the back."

They found him three long minutes later, a pale slumped-over man who trudged along the sidewalk like he was heading to his own funeral. Zoey supposed it wasn't like there was any denying the nature of the job he had taken at this point. Echo hopped out of a sliding side door to intercept him. She whispered something in the man's ear and he made a beeline for the truck.

Zoey shook her head and said, "We're all fortunate she uses her powers for good."

Skelnik climbed into the truck, looked around the interior, and froze when he saw the Suits.

Zoey said, "We're going to watch, if that's okay."

Echo closed the door.

Will said, "Do you know who I am?"

Skelnik nodded. "I ain't got nothin' you want. I don't know nothin' you wanna know. They find out I talked to you, just this much we've talked so far, they'll kill me, and they'll kill me for days. But you know that, don't ya?"

Will, showing no sympathy, said, "These are the risks we take when we choose the wrong employer."

Zoey said, "You're working for the bad guy. The *worst* guy."

Skelnik scoffed and glanced around the truck interior, briefly making eye contact with Wu. "Not like you guys, huh? Arthur Livingston. Great philanthropist. His warehouse that blew sky high, well, he was prob'ly makin' porridge for the orphans in there, right? Spare me all that. Ain't no heroes in this city."

Zoey threw up her hands and said, "Hey, I'm not even from here, and a week ago I was working at a coffee shop. I'm just regular folk, and *I'm* telling you you're getting paid in dirty money."

"Coffee shop? So, you're a drug dealer. You think folks are payin' ten bucks a cup because they like the taste? I seen documentaries about where they grow the beans, too, some of the workers young enough to call you grandma. I don't care who you are, trace your paycheck back far enough and you find it's *all* dirty money. Lemme out."

Will said, "Fine, think of me as another employer bidding on your services. At least listen to my offer. Besides, if you leave now, it'll look suspicious—the average massage truck session is eight minutes."

Zoey said, "Our job will pay enough that you can retire. Hire your own massage truck to follow you wherever you go."

Skelnik kept his eyes on Will. "You know how *I* interview prospective employees, Mr. Blackwater? I ask 'em one question, I say, 'Show me your knife.' Man don't got a knife, I got no use for him—it's the universal tool. Even apes know to keep a sharp stone within reach. Then if he shows me his knife, I scrape it on my arm, to test the edge, see if it'll shave the hair off. If the blade's dull, I say, 'Get outta here, you only got one tool on ya, and it don't work.' But mine? It'll circumcise a fly." Skelnik reached behind him and suddenly there was a gleaming blade in his hand. "You know I got to try to kill you, right?"

Will showed so little reaction to this that it took a moment for Zoey to register what the man had said. "Wait, what?"

Wu edged forward, but Will just sipped his drink and said, "No reason you can't listen to what I have to say first."

Zoey said, "Hey! No, nobody is killing anybody!"

Skelnik said, "I tell Molech about this meeting and tell him anything *other* than that I slit yer throat, he turns me into hamburger."

Will said, "You ever killed a man with a knife? It's harder than you think. Your chances of success are extremely low with that course of action."

"So you see the predicament you put me in by luring me into your vehicle. Looks like that was a bad move on your part, 'cause my best case is I give Will Blackwater scars he's got to explain every time he takes his shirt off for a lady."

Andre said, "If Molech's people knew we were here, this truck would already be a smoking wreck. There's nothin' suspicious about any of this from the outside, you just got to listen and walk out the door with a spring in your step."

"Then you got one minute to say your piece, at which point I'm gonna turn ya down because a millionaire hamburger is still a hamburger."

Will brought up a feed on the wall opposite the sofa—a street-level view of The Naked City, where they'd had their meeting/standoff the previous evening. "You know that place, Mr. Skelnik?"

"Driven past it. Place for slick-haired cuckolds who got cash but still got to pay for pussy."

"You know who owns it?"

"Don't know, don't care."

"Molech. Through a corporate front. What you're seeing there, the visible part of the building, that's not what makes the real profit. The real money comes belowground. See, there's a rumor that you show a special little card at the front door—made of solid gold, they say—and you head downstairs. Down to the *real* club."

Budd said, "We've never been down there, but they say that with each sub-basement, the girls get younger. And there are . . . several floors, if you get what I'm sayin'."

"You don't got to convince me that Molech is a sick f—"

Will said, "Look, there. You see the concrete in front of the main entrance? Let me zoom in. You see it?"

"I see concrete, yeah."

"You see the cracks? All through the middle there?"

"Yeah, whatever."

"You know what causes that?"

"Dry Utah air, prob'ly. Leeches moisture out of the wet concrete before it can cure—"

"Gases, from the decomposing bodies. Get a jackhammer and bust up that concrete and you'll find bones. At least forty bodies, of the building's construction crew, and their families. Migrants, mostly. See, Molech couldn't have them walking around out there, knowing about those secret basements, spreading rumors about their intended purpose. So on the last day of the job, he lines everybody up, and one by one they get a hollowpoint severance to the back of the skull. Buries them out front, before they poured the concrete, like a ritual. They say it was because he heard the pharaohs used to bury the slaves in the shadow of the pyramids, for good luck. Think about it, Mr. Skelnik. You say you don't know anything, but he's not going to risk it. For every man and woman on your work site, this is their last job."

Skelnik stared hard at the screen, studying the cracks in the walk, imagining the expanse of dry bones that Zoey was pretty sure weren't there.

Will said, "Can you deny the logic of what I'm saying?"

"You're sayin' I got a narrow chance of livin' either way, only your way I stand to make more money on the way out."

"No," interjected Budd. "We can get you out. You and anyone you want to bring along. We got a big ol' people mover network—it's what we do best. New name, new start. Molech won't find you. You and your daughter both."

They had been saving the daughter thing for now, Zoey thought. She watched the man's fingers tighten on the knife he was still gripping in his right hand. Wu's eyes never left that hand.

Will said, "So to start, just tell us what you know. Even if it doesn't seem useful."

The man chewed on his lip, then said, "Job came in back in August, boss told me it was a cash-paying job for a kid who had bought the old casinos and wanted them built back up in the shape of his own head."

Andre said, "His head? You mean, literally?"

The man nodded. "Wanted both to be made of obsidian, one carved to look like the guy's own face, scowling, the other would be a giant middle finger, like he was flipping the whole city the bird. I thought it sounded shady, and said as much—I mean it's one thing to get a building made into your own face, but when you insist the face be scowling, you can't be up to anything good. Ain't nobody gonna stay in a hotel with a big angry obsidian face on the front." Zoey thought she would totally stay in a place like that, but didn't want to contradict him. "We had to talk him down from actual obsidian— you can't get it in those quantities and it's impossible to work with—"

Impatient, Echo asked, "What's your interior access like?"

"Zero, that's the point I'm tryin' to make. I came up with a way to do a facade out of a rigid polyurethane foam, we just put it up in blocks and then they got these remote-controlled grinders that crawl up the front and sculpt the guy's face into it. Then we'll do a black glaze, should do a good job of hidin' the fact that the building behind it is junk. And it is junk—we're not renovating the interior, it's a burned-out wreck. All the work has been done on the outside. It's all for show."

Will said, "Well, we need you to get *inside*. With a camera. We'll tell you what you're looking for. When you find it, we'll tell you what to do. You get caught, just say you got lost, or you're looking for some duct tape. Play dumb."

"Riiiight. And maybe I'll crawl through an air duct like James Bond, cut through a window with a laser watch. Do I fit the profile of an imbecile in your eyes, or did you just figure you had nothin' to lose by askin' me to go on a suicide mission on your behalf? Here, how about we switch clothes and *you* go into the lion's den. Your minute's up. Lemme out."

Echo was blocking the door. "Stay a little longer, your friends will be impressed with your stamina."

Will said, "We're giving you a way out. Your *only* way."

"And what about the rest of my crew? Got more than twenty guys up there, they got kids, too. You can get all of 'em out?"

"Yes."

"*If* I go inside and help you sabotage Molech's operation."

"Yes."

"And if not, then whenever we finish the job, Molech dumps me and all the rest in a mass grave."

"*Yes.*"

The man stared at the floor, then at the feed.

Before he could answer, Zoey said, "No."

Zoey felt Will staring at her now, and could somehow feel him clenching his jaw.

She said, "We'll get you and your people out either way. We're asking for your help. As a favor."

The man's expression changed—he was clearly trying to figure out if this was some good cop/bad cop scam Zoey and Will were running. But then he looked at Will, who was just barely restraining an urge to strangle Zoey. It didn't matter how hard he tried to play the robot, his thoughts might as well have been flashing across his forehead in scrolling red letters: YOU JUST TOOK OUR LEVERAGE AND FLUSHED IT DOWN THE TOILET.

Skelnik said, "I'll think about it. Lemme out."

Echo looked at Will, who nodded in resignation. She stepped aside and Skelnik stepped out into the chilled morning air, still wielding his knife. There was actually another guy waiting outside the door for a "massage" but at the sight of the knife he backed off, presumably figuring that whatever was going on inside the truck, he didn't want anything that kinky so early in the morning.

Once the door was closed, Will emptied his drink and said, "Well, that was very generous of you." He glanced toward the front of the truck and said, "Take us home."

As they pulled into traffic, Zoey said, "He said he'd think about it."

Budd said, "In my travels, that's meant 'no,' exactly one hundred percent of the time."

Zoey sighed, and stared at the wall feed. It was acting like a window now, showing the morning traffic passing by. Zoey's only sleep in the previous twenty hours had been that brief, fitful bathtub nap, and exhaustion was catching up to her. Echo was leaning in the corner, eyes closed, holding on to a rail along the wall so she wouldn't topple over at the next stop. Wu actually looked like he had positioned himself to catch her if she did. Zoey turned to Will and could see it creeping onto his face, too—just a slight drooping of the eyelids, a blankness in the pupils. They were running down, like batteries, and time was running out.

Will saw she was looking and sat up straighter, tightening the knot of his tie. It was silver and black, in a pattern that reminded Zoey of chain mail. Afraid to so much as loosen it for comfort's sake, as if his suits and ties were the source of all his powers . . .

Then the idea hit her, all at once.

Zoey said, "Andre, is there any chance your crazy designer brother Tre would know who Molech uses as a tailor?"

There was a pause, as if Andre was trying to process this nonsense question. "Your words sound like you're makin' a joke but your face is all serious."

"I *am* serious."

"Zoey, the dude doesn't even wear shirts, why would he have a tailor on staff?"

"He *doesn't* have one on staff. *That's my point.* But he's had to hire one within the last few weeks, or maybe even the last few hours."

"Why?"

Zoey made an exasperated sound. "*To make him a supervillain costume. Duh.*"

Both Andre and Will started to make some dismissive joke, then stopped themselves.

Zoey continued, "Come on, you think he's going to carry out his flamboyant terror attack on the world in ripped blue jeans and a backward baseball cap? No, he needs a suit, and I guarantee you there's nobody in that building capable of creating one that wouldn't look like a child made it. I bet whoever he hired, they've been inside the headquarters for a fitting and that Molech has talked to them as recently as last night."

Budd fussed with his phone, Echo now snoring softly in the corner.

Finally he looked up and said, "Contract's with Ballistic Couture, they work out of that shop in West Hills, one that looks like it's floating. Finished costume was supposed to be delivered this morning."

Zoey said to Will, "Okay, you have to admit that despite my faults, I am *the smartest person on planet Earth.*"

Will said, "This time, you let me do the talking. In fact, why don't you just stay behind in the truck while I go in."

"How about instead, this time you actually tell me what the plan is before we start the conversation?"

"*We won't know until it starts.* You have to find out how the person wants to present themselves to the world and work back from there. The LoB guy wouldn't have gone for the same amount of money if I'd offered it as a check—you cut that guy and he bleeds Mountain Dew, that's somebody who needs a treasure hunt. So here, Ballistic Couture is run by a designer named Aziza Richards, she's a character, and deals exclusively with clients who want designer suits that can withstand a burst of high-velocity assault-rifle rounds. We're asking her to betray the trust of a client, but she gets caught doing that *once*, she's out of business. And as soon as she's not valuable to these people anymore, she's dead."

"So *that's* the image she wants to project to the world? That she doesn't mind making a uniform for a new Hitler?"

"*Yes*, and in fact her entire livelihood depends on it."

"So how do you convince a person like that to do what you want?"

"Let's just say there's a reason I wanted you to stay in the car."

"What? No. No, Will, we don't do stuff like that anymore."

Will didn't reply.

Zoey said, "I'm going to take a nap on the way there, do you mind if I lean over on you?"

"I'll stand."

FIFTY-TWO

When she awoke, they were rolling through a row of boutiques and storefronts that seemed too weathered and dilapidated for a city in which literally everything was new. Zoey wondered if they'd been built in that style, artificially aged to imitate the feel of some artsy neighborhood in New York. The Ballistic Couture shop really did look like it was floating—the shop itself was done in olive green, to look like an armored military headquarters. The first floor, however, was a wraparound LED screen programmed to always show the view from a camera on the opposite side of the building. Zoey could see people walking past on the sidewalk behind it, as if the shop was hovering ten feet off the ground.

The first sign that something was wrong was when they turned in and were greeted by a sight that was common in every city but Tabula Ra$a: police cars. One squad car with red and blues flashing, another unmarked sedan next to it with a light on its dash. Standing next to the latter and tapping things into a tablet was Kowalski. He glanced up at the truck as it approached and motioned for it to turn around. When it stopped and he saw who was climbing out, he looked mildly annoyed, like his day had just gotten a little harder.

There was smoke drifting out of the main entrance of the shop.

Zoey stepped out and immediately thought, *Soare cu Dinti.* It's a Romanian phrase a social worker had taught her years ago—it meant a day that looks bright and inviting when viewed through a window, in which the air is actually cold enough to burn your face when you step out into it. It translated literally to "Sun with teeth," unless the woman had been lying to her. For some reason, that phrase kept bouncing around in her mind as she walked up to the squad cars, watching a pair of uniformed cops stretching crime scene tape across the building entrance, which appeared to be a free-standing door without walls to hold it up. She glanced back at the truck and noted that the current disguise was that of a diaper-cleaning service.

Kowalski looked up at the approaching Suits and said, "This ought to be good."

Zoey said, "So, are the police back in business?"

Kowalski said, "For those who pay. Aziza Richards was paying. Figure the least we could do was work the scene."

Budd asked, "Where's she now?"

"That depends on whether you believe in the existence of the human soul, Budd. Perhaps she is in Heaven, making bulletproof tunics for the angels themselves. But me, I'm pretty sure she's just a pile of guts splattered on her office wall."

Zoey let out a gasp of horror. Will let out a sigh of annoyance.

Andre said to Zoey, "It was still a good idea. Just had it a couple hours too late, that's all."

Kowalski said, "You here to see me, or were you here to see the pile of guts?"

Will said, "The guts. She was making gear for Molech, I guess he took delivery of the finished product and decided to . . . sever the relationship. Hell, maybe he just didn't want to pay."

Zoey said to Kowalski, "There you go, crime solved. Go arrest Molech."

Kowalski shrugged. "Eh, this feels like a 'self-cleaning oven' type situation to me."

Will said, "We're going inside."

"It's a room full of smoking offal, Will. You're just going to get it all over your shoes."

"Did you see a phone in there? I want to see if there's correspondence with Molech, anything that could give us an edge."

"Oh, so you're still trying to fight this guy. Got it. You have any special requests for me for when I process *your* corpse tomorrow? And don't ask us not to make fun of your dick, because we do that with every body that comes through, it's how we cope."

Will ignored him, already heading toward the front door. He turned to Zoey and said, "You don't want to see this. Watch the truck." And that, of course, meant she *had* to go in.

She didn't throw up at the sight of the charred, bloody remains—she'd braced herself for that. She also didn't throw up at the smell, though that was a close one—no one had warned her that when you explode a person's body, all of the feces spills out, and no one could have accurately described what that smells like when mixed with the stench of burning hair. No, she managed to hold it together right up until she saw the photos.

The first room was a reception area with a black marble desk, behind it was the entrance to the spacious production floor beyond. Molech, or his men, had picked up their order and then simply killed every single person on their way out, including the receptionist at that front desk. You could tell nothing about the victim from what was left, but the photos on the desk told the story. Middle-aged woman, had looked like a schoolteacher. She had a husband who looked like a chubby accountant, and they had four children. Two boys, two girls. Oldest was in his early teens, youngest was kindergarten age, and adopted—an adorable Chinese girl. The largest photo was one of those posed photographs you can get done at the mall, everyone in their Sunday best in front of a generic backdrop. Only the photo she had kept was the one in which everyone had broken their pose—the baby of the group had spontaneously reached up and stuck a finger in her big sister's nose, and the photo was a blurred mess of laughing siblings and reaching limbs. That was the photo she'd chosen to keep at work, and it was wonderful. Zoey made it outside the front door before she vomited.

But then, when it was over, she stood up and went back inside. She immediately met Will, already on his way back out.

He said, "They made it a point to destroy Aziza's phone. They knew they were tying up loose ends here. Let's go."

Zoey didn't go. She pushed through toward the production floor, a spacious room that smelled of paint and glue, with walls packed tight with finished costumes on display and a floor crowded with mannequins adorned with suits in progress—everything from bulletproof tuxedos to beautifully sculpted riot armor. Budd and Andre were looking over a pair of shattered corpses along the rear wall.

Zoey surveyed the room and said, "Their computers are still intact over there, is there anything on them?"

From somewhere behind her, Echo said, "Those are design workstations, so they can model the looks before they spend the money molding the carbon fiber. Nothing that looks like client records, but that would have been surprising anyway. This is a cash-only business, most of these clients don't want a ledger kept."

"You think the design for Molech's suit is on one of them?"

Budd said, "Reckon so, but what good does that do us?" He wasn't asking that as a rhetorical question. He was asking Zoey honestly, wanting her to tell him what good it would do.

She turned to Andre. "If we got a copy of the plans for the suit, could Tre make us a replica?"

"Tre can make anything. What's your plan?"

"Wouldn't Molech hate it if he spent weeks having a custom outfit made for his coming out party, and then somebody showed up wearing the same thing?"

FIFTY-THREE

🔑

By mid-afternoon, the ballroom was a disaster area. They had dragged in tables from all over the house, and across them was strewn a colorful scatter of random objects, some of which were recognizable (Zoey had personally seen the caterpillar machine disgorge a clock, a spatula, and what looked like a sex toy) and some of which were tangled, oddly shaped tools and/or weapons that looked like they came out of a flying saucer or a Dr. Seuss cartoon. Many of the items had been labeled with masking tape and marker, bearing the team's best guess as to what the gadget did (there was a black, vaguely trumpet-shaped device that had been labeled simply "Death Horn" that she had decided not to ask about). All of this clutter was sprawling out under the mass of hanging candy canes and mistletoe, fighting for floor space with whimsical edible floor displays. Zoey had started calling it Santa's Workshop.

The problem was that a lot of the gadgets on the coin drive turned out to be pure junk—seemingly random objects that, as far as they could tell, were just placeholders Singh had scanned in to calibrate his fabricator. Since the file system on the drive was unreadable, they were having to just frantically stamp out everything on the list, and pray they stumbled across something useful. The door to the courtyard opened and Andre and Will walked in. Andre tossed aside a device that looked like a handheld spotlight.

Zoey said, "Well?"

"No, *it's not a fart ray,* Zoey. The next one won't be, either. There's no such thing."

"Damn."

Echo, who was busy poking at the caterpillar's menus, said, "We're no closer than when we started. Fifteen hours until Molech's deadline, and that's assuming he keeps to it."

Zoey said, "No closer to what? If we're not just looking for a bigger, badder gun to obliterate Molech's army with, what exactly are we looking for?"

Will said, "I guess I'm looking for . . . the One Ring."

Zoey said, "The what ring?"

"The One Ring. Like in *Lord of the Rings*."

"I think I saw part of that on cable. It's about a little British kid in glasses who can do magic?"

"Are you seriously telling me you haven't heard of—. Okay, it's about an evil wizard who makes twenty magic rings and gives them to all of the leaders of the various tribes in the world. But it's all a scam, a power grab. The wizard kept one ring for himself, and it controlled all of the rest."

Zoey said, "And Arthur is the dark wizard in this scenario?"

"He had to know what he was doing would end up this way. He *did* know, as you pointed out. But he had no safeguard built in? This stuff just falls into the hands of the bad guys and then his plan was, what, exactly?"

"But Arthur didn't give this stuff away. It was stolen from him. Maybe he just didn't anticipate that part."

"Arthur anticipated everything."

"So again I ask, in the absence of this machine literally generating a *magical object*, what's our plan?"

Candi blinked into the room and said, "A guest is at the front gate, and it looks like *boob dong boob tittytittytitty*—audio not found please contact your system administrator."

A voice said, "Yo, it's Tre. Open the gate, I don't want nobody seein' me here. You got weird enemies, 'Dre."

FIFTY-FOUR

At three AM, Zoey trudged up to her bedroom, looking to lay flat for the first time in twenty-four hours. They had worked straight through, and her brain felt like a hunk of rawhide a dog had been chewing on.

She collapsed onto the bed in the guest room, kind of wanting to get back in that huge bathtub but not having the energy to get up and run the water. She kicked off her jeans, curled up under the comforter, and waited for Stench Machine to settle in next to her face. Then she grabbed her phone off the nightstand and dialed her mother, not altogether surprised that she immediately answered. Nobody was sleeping tonight.

"Zoey! My god. This is so crazy, right?" Her mother was stretching out the last syllable of every sentence (*riiight?*), something she did when she was high. "I've never been nailed into a box before."

"Mom, where are you?"

"I am . . . let's see. I am in a cabin, in, uh, some kind of resort, I think. I have three armed guards outside—or four, they all look alike—and they won't let me out. Budd goes and gets the food at mealtime but he won't tell me what's going on and . . ."

She drew out the word "aaaaaaand" until she just gave up on the sentence. Zoey assumed she had a vape in her hand. Budd had been dispatched eight hours earlier to oversee the logistics of getting Molech's construction crew out of the state, and then to shepherd Melinda Ashe to a safehouse in which she would, to put it frankly, sit and wait to see if any of the good guys survived. In the background, Zoey heard Budd ask what she wanted on her pizza. Zoey's mother answered "Gummy Bears" and giggled.

Zoey said, "Well, I'm glad you're all right. This whole thing just keeps getting crazier. The people who live here seem pretty used to it though."

"Honey, why didn't you just get out of there?"

(*theeeeere*)

"The bad guys can afford plane tickets, too, Mom, that's why you're out in the middle of nowhere. We have to see this through, this isn't like getting away from one of your old exes, there's no place I can go that these people can't follow."

"Are you talking about Jezza? Did you hear about him?"

"What? No, why would you bring *him* up?"

"Well, you know he was the one you had the problems with, when you burned your shoulder on the oven?"

"Yes, Mom. I had not forgotten that."

"He committed suicide, in his jail cell. They found him this morning. Isn't that craaaaazy?" Zoey started to answer, but couldn't process what it meant. "It's like everything goes nuts all at once."

"Mom, I think this is all going to be over in the next day or so. If something goes wrong, not that it will, but if it does, Budd will take you to an airport, whatever one you want, and put you on a flight. You pick which one. You'll keep using that account they gave you, it's supposedly untraceable and has, well, infinite money in it."

"Whaaaaat? Where am I supposed to gooooo?"

"Wherever you want?"

"And where will you be?"

"Come on, you know what I'm saying here, Mom."

"I'm not spending the rest of my life running, Z. I've got friends, I've got Marnie and her kids heeeere . . ."

"If you don't, they'll find you. These guys aren't the type to forget."

"*What guys?*"

"Just promise me you'll go. Promise me." And then, Zoey was crying.

Her mother let out a breath, presumably through a cloud of steam, and said, "Everything's going to be fine, things always work out in the end for us."

There was a knock at Zoey's door.

"I have to go, Mom."

"All right, honey."

"I love you."

"I love you, too. And don't forget to—"

"No, Mom. If, uh, if this is the last time we ever talk, I want that to be the last thing we say to each other. I want to leave it at that. So I guess we need to say it again. You've always been my best friend and the best, well, the best mom you were capable of being under the circumstances. And I love you."

"I love you, too, honey."

"Good-bye."

"Good-bye. And don't forget to take those cranberry pills or else you'll get another urinary tract infection."

"Goddamnit, Mom—"

She was talking to a dead phone.

A voice behind the heavy guest room door said, "Can I come in?" It sounded like Will.

"Sure. I mean I'm crying and I'm not wearing pants but who cares at this point."

A pause.

"Can you put some pants on, please?"

"I will not. I'm under the covers, get over it."

Will entered, apprehensively. "It's all set, if everything goes south, a Pinkerton has instructions to get your cat to a safe location."

"Do you think he'll actually do it?"

"He didn't take the assignment seriously until he saw what it paid. And he won't get the other half of his check until he brings proof of cat life to the attorney, so I don't see why not."

Zoey said, "It's a good thing I'm so exhausted, or else the fact that I probably won't be alive at New Year's would be seriously weirding me out right now."

"You can't focus on death, or failure. Otherwise you're surrendering greatness to all the people too dumb to contemplate it."

"There was a moment when we were all working and Andre said that thing about hot dogs and we all laughed and all at once I remembered Armando, and I felt guilty. He hasn't even had a funeral yet, and already we're working and laughing and carrying on like he was never here. His family, his friends, he's gone from their lives forever. That's so strange, and so awful, the way the world just breezes right on by without you."

"And now you're thinking about how the world will go on without *you*, right?"

"I guess so."

"This is why people get obsessed with the apocalypse. They want the world to die with them. We're all selfish, we hate the thought of everyone just . . . moving on."

"Well, I would want my mom to. Even if it meant she totally forgot me, I don't want her to be miserable."

"And Armando wouldn't want you to be. He'd want you to get the son of a bitch he was trying to get. He'd want you to finish the job."

"I can never tell if you're really talking to me or just trying to sell me on something. It's always like you just see me as one of the levers you can pull to get what you want. It kind of makes me hate talking to you."

"Unlike you, who is always honest and never has an ulterior motive. That story, about how you were home and lonely at prom? Telling it in front of Armando, who made it his job to rescue women for a living? 'Oh, I'm such a disgusting troll, no one could ever love me.' Planting that seed in his brain?"

"All right, all right. I'm Arthur Livingston's daughter, is that what you're about to say again?"

Will just shrugged.

Zoey rolled over and stared at the ceiling. "There was a guy, an old scumbag boyfriend of my mom's who gave me the scar on my shoulder. I just got off the phone with my mom and she said he committed suicide. In his jail cell."

"So? Good riddance."

"Here's the thing—I had told Armando the story, when they were doing my outfit. Could he have picked up the phone and ordered something like that done?"

"No. Armando didn't have those kind of connections. That wasn't the business he was in."

"Yeah, I didn't think so."

"I wouldn't think about it anymore. See, there's a guy who *deserves* to be forgotten."

"You were in the room when I told that story, weren't you?"

"You should try to get some rest. You'll need to be sharp to pull this off tomorrow."

"And where Armando couldn't pick up the phone and get somebody strangled in a jail cell and then have it faked to look like a hanging, *you* could."

"As I said, as far as I can see, it's just another rotbrain doing the world a favor by taking himself out. Nothing more."

"And you promise me that's what it was. If you tell me now you didn't have him killed, I'll believe you."

"I think," said Will, pausing to choose his words, "that he made the decision to die. And he made that decision the moment he decided to touch Arthur Livingston's daughter."

Zoey covered her eyes with the blanket—something she used to do as a little kid. "Oh my god. Why? Why would you do that?"

"If Arthur had heard about that incident back when it happened, Jezza Lewis would not have woken up to see another sunrise. Just collecting on an overdue bill, as far as I see it."

"You people live on a different planet. I keep having to remind myself of that. Lives just mean nothing to you."

Will let silence hang in the room for a minute, then crossed his arms and let out a breath.

"My wife. She . . . she was killed. Three years ago. Organized gang of thieves, robbed a high-end jewelry store on Lattice Drive. Private security chased them. My wife was just a passerby, walking across an intersection, pure coincidence. The pursuit blew through and one of the vehicles smashed right into her. Don't even know if it was one of the good guys or bad guys and I've never tried to find out."

"I'm sorry."

"This city . . . it's like that. The people are just background, props in some-body else's adventure. And that's all my wife was, to them. A thud and a dent in their fender, a forgotten moment in somebody else's thrilling car chase. That's the way it is here and it's always getting worse. And that can't be allowed to continue."

"So that's why you're so big on taking down Molech?"

"It's bigger than that. You know what Tabula Rasa means, right? The words?"

"Clean slate? Isn't that it?"

"I'm not going to bore you with the history, but Arthur and the other in-vestors who snapped up all this land—they'd kind of gotten run out of Las Vegas due to . . . some unscrupulous practices. So the idea was they'd just start their own Vegas, the way it used to be, back when it was Sin City and not just Disneyland for the elderly. Utah had this crazy Libertarian governor at the time—anyway, the point is 'clean slate' to them just meant 'no rules.' But Korea changed Arthur. Tabula Rasa, that phrase started to mean something different to him. He wanted it to be a clean slate, for everybody. A city that actually works. Jobs, clean air, no bureaucrats . . ."

"It sounds like the kind of idea a little kid would have."

"Arthur was . . . naïve, in his own way. And he was too late —even in those early days, organized crime had moved in, getting in on the ground floor. They had set up shop before the first McDonald's, the gangs and the black markets and human traffickers."

"The Arthur Livingstons, in other words."

"Exactly. So I think all of this, the whole project with Raiden and this stupid dream about super powers, he thought what so many guys like him had thought—that with enough money and technology you could smooth out the flaws in society like ironing the wrinkles out of a shirt. Stamp out the crime like a comic book superhero and turn this place into a utopia. But you know it doesn't work that way."

"No. Because the bad guys are just as motivated to keep things like they are."

"Probably more so. But maybe I'm naïve, too, because I can't shake the idea that the whole world is watching us. When they broke ground out here, they called it the city of the future, like Tabula Rasa really is a preview of what the world is going to look like, and everybody's just waiting to see which way it goes."

"That's a lot of pressure."

"It's the burden we took on. That *you* took on."

"When I inherited all the money?"

"When you were born. Get some sleep."

FIFTY-FIVE

Zoey managed four hours. When she woke up it was the morning of Tuesday, December 21—the shortest day, before the longest night. Her toiletbot played the news for her and every feed was covering another aspect of the same story. From various man-in-the-street interviews it became clear that the people of Tabula Ra$a fell into roughly three camps in response to the terror threat:

- A. Those who were evacuating (enough to choke the highway leading out of town).
- B. Those who were out and about, camera ready, hoping to catch some of the action.
- C. Those who were just going about their day as normal, because the city was the city and the threat of exotic violence didn't mean they could take a day off work.

One thing was for sure: for the private security firms in the city, this was Black Friday. The Co-Op was spread thin, every single customer presumably having demanded extra protection. They had even ditched their black ties and overcoats for black tactical gear (though Zoey figured they could still have had their ties on underneath) and every bank, casino, and other high-dollar target had a dozen of them at their door. But the biggest show of force was at the Co-Op headquarters itself—ranks of men and terrifying black vehicles, figuring that letting their own office get leveled would surely be bad for business.

To Zoey, it didn't look like nearly enough.

The most alarming scene, though, was the two houses of worship. Volunteers had turned out by the hundreds, supplementing armed contractors they'd pooled their money to hire. That struck Zoey as madness, not because she wasn't religious, but because she knew those buildings could be put back together inside of a week, with the technology she saw around the city. Let Molech grind them to dust, who cares? God and Allah can stay in a hotel for a couple of weeks if they have to. But, she supposed, that was easy for her to say.

She went to get dressed, and found she had worked her way back around to the same jeans, Awesome Possum T-shirt, and cardigan that she'd arrived in six days ago, though at least they had been washed. She imagined the coroner examining her body later tonight and also noting that she had died in a pair of red panties that said "SHARK WEEK" across the front, with a cartoon Great White on the butt.

Carlton was already in the kitchen when she passed, ready to launch into breakfast. She asked him if he just waited there all night, but he said he had set Candi to alert him when someone else in the house was up and around, in case they needed anything. Zoey thought this sounded like a form of slavery but Carlton seemed to take pride in having thought of it, and asked her what she wanted.

"Well, it could be my final meal . . . what's the best thing you make? What was Arthur's favorite? Make that."

Carlton busied himself making what appeared to be some kind of elaborate hamburger, while at the same time dropping parts of a whole boiled chicken, egg yolks, and various other disgusting ingredients into a hand-cranked meat grinder that turned out a horrific-looking substance that Stench Machine pounced on with a fervor Zoey had never seen in the animal. Carlton had clearly been educating himself on fine cat food recipes. The burger turned out to be a seared beef patty topped with onion jam, bacon, and a peanut butter sauce, all on a bun of fried dough encrusted with potato chip crumbs. Zoey felt like it was the type of thing a person should be arrested for eating, and consuming such an obscenity at breakfast would surely keep her out of Heaven later today. It was worth it.

Soon Zoey was heading toward the ballroom, espresso in hand, and arrived in a room that was eerily silent, smelling of fresh paint, cookies, and burned chemicals. For the moment she had Santa's Workshop to herself, the giant gadget-defecating caterpillar sleeping silently in the center of the room. Zoey sipped her coffee and wandered over to the holographic displays that were showing an endless list of objects with indecipherable names. The text looked Russian to Zoey, with its backward R's and such, but Will actually knew how to read Russian, for some reason, and told her the menus were still mostly nonsense and made-up words (the labels roughly translated to things like "Particlefrack Vapinator").

She flicked through the menu, hundreds of items, each representing a gadget. She swiped down and down through the list, until the screen stopped when it reached the bottom.

The very last schematic on the indecipherable list was simply called: ZOEY.

Her coffee cup stopped halfway to her mouth.

Was this new? It was literally the only English word on the whole list. Had Echo seen it? Or Will? Why hadn't they mentioned it?

From behind her, Wu said, "There you are. We need to go over the escape plan."

"Escape plan?"

"If everything fails, the final branch of the plan—Plan Z, we will call it—is I get you in a vehicle and drive you as far away from here as possible."

"How about we just make sure it doesn't come to that?"

"We are not gods. We do not control the universe. All we can do is be ready for what it brings us. Come with me."

They descended into the garage, where they found the armored sedan pointed at the door. The blue BMW escape car Budd had bought was now parked off in a corner, forgotten. Probably a hundred-thousand-dollar car, but they'd decided they didn't need it, so it gets discarded like a cheap toy. Insane.

Wu said, "Get in."

"I don't get what it is we need to practice here. If everything goes to hell, you'll grab me and we'll get in the car and go."

"You cannot assume I will still be available, or alive, to facilitate your escape. You need to know how to initiate the vehicle's emergency protocols. And we cannot assume you'll figure it out on the fly, when for all we know at that moment the mansion will be in flames and collapsing around you."

"Jesus, Wu."

"Zoey, regardless of what happens, you cannot be surprised. Men like me and Will who have a war background know something about the world that you do not. In those moments of chaos, everything you thought you could depend on falls away. Everything turns upside down. Heroes turn out to be cowards, and vice versa. Your best-laid plan fails, your most haphazard improvisation saves your life. Friends turn out to be enemies. In the end, Zoey,

316 / JASON PARGIN

you can trust nothing. You can only have another plan ready to go. One after another. Get in."

Zoey slid into the driver's seat. The dash and windshield display lit up.

"All right. So is there a voice command, or—"

The door slammed closed on its own.

The garage door began rolling upward.

Zoey assumed she'd said something or hit a button. She took her hands off the wheel and glanced around the dash.

"Uh . . . cancel. Stop. Stop doing what you're doing, car."

Instead, the car lurched forward, tires squealing, flying toward the still-opening door.

"Stop! Hey! STOP!"

The door hadn't cleared enough room for the car to pass, but the armored sedan wasn't going to wait—it ran through it, the rising door scraping the roof as it passed. The second door was completely closed. No matter—the armored sedan bashed through it, chunks of debris piled on the hood as it flew out and down the back drive.

"Hey! Stop! Car! Stop driving! Park! Brake! Engine off! *STOOOPPPP!!!*"

The car did not respond. Zoey grabbed the steering wheel, and hit the brake—doing either should have automatically returned control to her. It did not.

The car pulled itself into traffic, weaving in and out of morning commuters, professionals from Beaver Heights who were sipping tea and applying makeup on their way to the offices downtown for yet another Tuesday. And then they were into the suburbs, whipping past the churches and family restaurants and weed dispensaries. And Zoey suddenly knew where they were going.

And she began to panic.

She tried to scream for help, pleading for another commuter to block the sedan's path, or run it off the road. But cars were remarkably soundproof these days, each driver in a bubble that seals out the outside world, people playing music or listening to soft-spoken public radio shows, commuters worried about parking and office politics and trying to remember if they had wheeled the trash out to the curb. The comforting little concerns that let us blot out the big things. No idea that they were two feet away from a young woman slapping her window and mouthing wordless cries, trying to get their attention.

They were through the suburbs now, heading into the city. Zoey desperately reared back with both feet and kicked at the driver's-side window. The glass bounced and flexed but held. This was glass intended to withstand an antitank rocket, it would be an all-day task even if she had power tools. And yet she still tried, because this was her life. She kicked the passenger side; she kicked the windshield. Who knows, maybe one piece of glass had a minute manufacturing flaw, or an invisible crack. Maybe it would trip some alarm in the auto drive, and cause the car to stop, or deviate from the course.

It did not.

As the buildings of downtown rose into view, she saw the ominous black countdown on the skyline. She punched the dash, smashing the glass panel readouts and maps and rearview monitors, hoping to damage some crucial component that would make the car stop short of its destination, anywhere other than Molech's renovated hotel. The armored sedan smoothly hummed along despite its wounds, just as its designers had built it to do. They had done their job well—her little bubble of panic bobbed along in the sea of indifference that was Fairfax Avenue.

The twin black-clad pillars grew in the windshield. Zoey screamed, and cried, and ripped the plastic inner panel from the driver's-side door, finding only solid metal underneath. The car slowed and placidly reached the Fire Palace, turning down a ramp leading to a heavy steel door. It rolled open as she approached—they were, of course, expecting her. By the time the car rolled to a stop, the inside of the driver's-side window was a pink smear of blood from Zoey's fists. When the door was yanked open, Zoey was cradling her hands, having turned her knuckles into hamburger trying to punch her way out.

Leaning into the door was Molech, wearing the ridiculous supervillain costume he'd probably paid six figures to have designed (a black costume that had been cut to leave most of his torso exposed, featuring cobalt highlights and a huge, bright blue codpiece), and the sidekick he'd named Black Scott.

Molech looked skeptical. "I'll be damned. He wasn't lying. Get her out."

Scott reached in, and Zoey pushed herself backward, kicking at the reaching hands, pressing herself up against the passenger-side door. Then that door was yanked open and she tumbled out onto the oil-stained concrete. Someone laughed.

A boot pushed her to the floor. Her arms were pulled behind her back and she felt something metal go around her wrists.

Molech circled the car, looked down at her, and said, "This here is what happens when you put blind trust in people. You Livingston crew, you let traitors continue in your midst. See, organizations, just like men, are subject to natural selection. If your organization is vulnerable to infections of disloyalty, it'll die."

From the floor, Zoey choked out the word "Who?"

"Doesn't matter now, does it?" To someone standing nearby, Molech said, "She got implants? Anything inside her she's about to spring on us?"

The bearded man who had examined Armando's body the day he died—who Molech had called "Doc"—leaned over Zoey.

He studied a gadget in his hand and said, "No, she's clean. Or she's unmodified, anyway."

Molech shook his head.

"I don't like it."

Scott said, "Seem too easy?"

"Yeah. Our man sneaking around inside the estate, rerouting the car . . . they *had* to know."

Scott said, "Damn, man, she's a hell of an actress if so."

Zoey rolled over, and tried to sit up. Her hands were bound with some kind of wire, but it felt loose. If she could just get one hand free . . .

Molech said, "No, they wouldn't let her in on it."

"Well . . . maybe she's got, like, a bug or tracking device on her that we can't detect? Somethin' new?"

Doc interjected, "It would still have to send a signal back. This building is a dead zone, we're jamming everything."

Molech said, "And she don't have a tiny bomb up her butthole?"

Doc just shrugged, making it clear that if there had been, he would have mentioned it long before now.

Molech said, "Maybe just to be sure, we ought to reach in there with a fishhook. Pull her guts out her ass, turn her inside out."

Scott said, "Man, it's past time to go, if we're gonna get set up to coordinate with the countdown. Just stomp her head in and get it over with."

"She might know somethin', even if she don't know she knows it."

"Then stick her in the cage and let Doc work on her while we're gone. Let him reconnect some nerves, turn her own body into a torture chamber."

"Yeah, let's do that. Wait—no. No . . ." Molech squinted again, the expression he apparently made when the gears in his head were turning. "No, that's what they'd expect me to do. Whatever plan they got, it's based on getting her inside my HQ, then us leavin' her alone here. I bet that's the whole point."

Scott was getting impatient. "Man, you can sit here and second guess yourself all day. Fact, I bet that's what they want most of all. You pacing around and worrying about her instead of keepin' your eyes on the prize."

Molech nodded. "Yeah. Screw it. Bring her with us."

Zoey sat up and said, "But how do you know *that* isn't what we wanted you to do?"

Molech leaned over and punched her in the jaw. Blood exploded into her mouth. She crashed to the floor, feeling sharp chunks like broken porcelain on her tongue. She spat three teeth and a gob of dark blood onto the oily concrete, then rolled over just in time to catch a boot to the face. Zoey's nose collapsed with a gut-turning *crunch* and she had just enough time to feel a boot smash into her rib cage, bones cracking like eggshells, before she blacked out from the pain.

FIFTY-SIX

There had been a four-year window in Zoey's life in which she didn't believe in monsters. It lasted from age six, when her mother told her that the scary aliens she saw in a movie weren't real, until age ten, when she ran into a big, fat, mean girl named Bella.

Bella was the class bully and one time she cornered Zoey behind a bowling alley, apparently having picked her completely at random. She wound up sitting on Zoey's chest, her knees pinning her arms down, her bulk making it hard to breathe. And as it got harder to breathe, Zoey started to panic, and as she panicked, Bella started to smile.

It had been Zoey's first glimpse of that dark thing that lurks in people, the writhing worm in the soul that feeds on other people's pain and fear. Zoey's terror and helplessness were making this person happy to the point of euphoria (in later years, Zoey would say it was getting Bella *high*). That such a look could appear on a human face in that situation was an earth-shattering revelation to little Zoey, a lesson more profound than anything she would learn in school that year. It was then that fourth-grader Zoey Ashe realized that, yup, monsters exist, all right. Not Bella, but *the thing inside Bella*.

Call it what you want, dismiss it as an old evolutionary defect in the brain that gets a charge out of cruelty, whatever. But *don't* say that the monster isn't real—what Zoey saw behind Bella's eyes was very real, and terrifying, and utterly inhuman. It was a dark, mindless hunger to hurt that was only being kept in check by fear of some greater power—parents, teachers, cops, a bigger bully. Over time, Zoey Ashe would see how this ugly, parasitic thing lurked behind everything and everyone, like the roaches in that greasy old public housing complex that came oozing out of the walls the moment the lights were off. The history books were, in fact, nothing more than a log of mankind's largely futile attempts to keep the monster in check. Zoey knew, even then, that if a person like Bella was ever to get so big and strong that nothing could touch them, so that they could just feed that monster, unchecked . . . then that would be the end.

Zoey would, of course, encounter the monster again and again over the years. She saw it in the eyes of Jezza, as he leaned her over the oven. She saw it in the face of the Soul Collector on the train, even with his eyes hidden behind those dark goggles. She saw it in the Hyena, when he had come after her in her bedroom that first night.

But what she saw on Molech's face was different.

Over time, Zoey had found that most people know they have the monster inside them, and decent people get scared when they feel it lurching to the surface. When they feel that quick rush of guilty pleasure after hitting a child or delivering a cruel insult to a spouse, they immediately drown it in shame, spending weeks doing good deeds to push that dark, writhing thing back down into the shadows. Others will invent some fiction, to pretend they have the monster under control. Corrupt cops torturing suspects in back alleys and telling themselves they're doing it for justice, or guys getting drunk and breaking their girlfriend's jaw, then blaming the booze (desperately trying to ignore the fact that the pleasure of unleashing the monster is the main reason they drink in the first place). Medieval priests ripping the guts out of screaming teenage girls, and pretending the burst of pleasure they felt in their loins was the spiritual reward for doing God's will. Everyone dressing up their cruelty as something else, rather than admit they are the monster's slave.

But not Molech.

Molech understood the monster, and embraced it—saw the world through its eyes. Five days ago Zoey had thought that only a ridiculous man would adopt a comic book supervillain name like "Molech" for himself. But now it made perfect sense. There was no "Chet Campbell" left inside that well-muscled body. There was only the monster.

There was only Molech.

Molech didn't waste energy lying to itself about what it was. Molech knew what it wanted and knew it could get it. And it would never, ever stop.

FIFTY-SEVEN

Zoey pried open her eyes and saw her wrists were now bound in front of her with barbed wire that was encrusted with dried blood, from where it had bitten into the skin. She took a breath and felt a knife-twist of pain, a splintered rib jabbing into her right lung. Her whole face was swollen, her head feeling like it was the size of a basketball. She couldn't breathe out of her nose. She was freezing, a cold wind on her cheeks and ears.

She looked beyond her bound hands and saw she was moving, heading down a busy street with people on the sidewalks stopping and staring as she passed. She tried to sit up, and winced as barbed wire bit into her neck. She craned her head around as far as she could and figured out that she had been tied to the hood of one of Molech's monster trucks, like an animal being hauled back from the hunt. Her shirt was wet, a crimson bib of blood that reached down to her belly.

The truck was rolling downtown, and Zoey's head was too muddled to think about where they were going or what it might mean. Then she saw that several blocks down the street was an imposing alabaster art deco building whose design Zoey thought had borrowed heavily from the headquarters in the old Justice League comics. Parked in front were at least twenty menacing armored vehicles brandishing clusters of gun barrels. Black-clad armed guards crowded the spaces in between them, the men and women of the Co-Op in the best paramilitary gear money could buy, brandishing armor and guns designed for the battlefield. From the hood of the truck, Zoey imagined herself getting helplessly shredded in the crossfire that was about to occur. But if it meant that somehow, some way, they took out Molech in the process, then so be it.

The truck she was bound to rolled to a stop right in the middle of an intersection, a few blocks away from the Co-Op building and its black perimeter of bristling weapons. A second and third truck rolled to a stop on either side, the one to the right with a covered object in its bed about the size and shape of a snowman. Two muscular, shirtless men emerged from the cab of that one—neither of them Molech, as far as Zoey could tell—and whipped back the tarp. In the bed was a scaled-up version of the little fire hydrant gadget Molech had pulled out at the park—the one that had disabled every firearm within a few hundred yards.

The doors on Zoey's truck clicked and creaked behind her and Molech strode into view along with Scott, who was now holding a professional-looking camera. That seemed redundant considering there were dozens of bystanders shooting from the sidewalks (each willing to risk getting torn to pieces in a crossfire if it meant drawing huge Blink numbers in the process), not to mention the swarm of drones buzzing overhead like gnats on a summer day. But, Zoey figured, Molech was like any showman and wanted as much control of the production as possible.

Molech looked euphoric, like a man released from a long, unjust prison sentence. He was bouncing on the balls of his feet, and licking his lips. He scanned the crowds gathered along the sidewalk and soaked in their awe.

He muttered to himself, "Poor bastards don't even know what they came to watch."

He looked at Zoey and said, "You get a shovel and dig straight down, you know what you find?"

She tried to say something, but just wound up triggering a gurgling coughing fit that sent bolts of pain flashing through her entire body.

Molech said, "You find the end of the world. My daddy and I, we used to go digging for arrowheads in the field behind our house. And we'd find one and he'd say, you know what this is? This is the remnants of an apocalypse. For the Indians, the white man was their Judgment Day. Scorched all this clean and built somethin' better. Same as the Black Death before that, over in Europe. Plague wiped out two hundred million people, killed all them peasants, livin' among the rats and filth. And you know what happened right after that? Little thing they call the Renaissance. That's how this always works—like a brushfire, cleaning out all that dead underbrush, so new growth can come in."

Zoey swallowed blood and said, "Chet, listen to me. This is your last chance to turn back. What you think is going to happen today . . . won't."

Molech smiled. "I know you're plannin' somethin', you and your entourage. I don't know what, exactly, but I know you've been running around like worker ants these last couple days. My personal hope is that you've built yourself a superhero, to take me on. Maybe we'll fight it out on top of a speeding train. I mean, what could make for a more awesome Raiden demo than two augmented dudes battling it out on camera?"

Molech turned to Scott and said, "Let's do this, bitch!"

Molech positioned himself in front of the truck, Scott framing him up with the camera so the shot would have the bloodied Zoey in the background. Molech glanced up at the nearest building, where the skyline feed countdown was ticking off the final seconds.

5 . . . 4 . . . 3 . . . 2 . . .

The countdown vanished and it was replaced by the feed from Scott's camera, stretching across every structure in downtown Tabula Ra$a. Looming over everyone was the image of Molech standing in front of the grill of his monster truck, with Zoey in the background trying to breathe through the bloody foam bubbling out of her nostrils.

Wow, I look like hell.

"Ladies and gentlemen, welcome. I, as all of you know by now, am Molech. And let me just kick off the festivities by bringing an end to the thousand-year reign of the gun."

Molech signaled to the men in the bed of the monster truck to his right. They punched some controls on the fire hydrant gadget. The machine hummed, whined, and spun up to power. Then there was a thrum and a pulse that Zoey swore sent a visible ripple through the air. Scott turned to point his camera at the Co-Op headquarters, and the small army parked out front.

Zoey couldn't see around Molech's shoulders and bulging lats, but she heard explosions, and screams, and the sound of bystanders running. She peered up at the skyline feed. The armored vehicles in front of Co-Op HQ were now belching fire and plumes of black smoke, their stored ammunition erupting inside. Confused gunmen ducked away, clutching maimed hands.

Molech and his men casually climbed into the monster trucks and soon Zoey found herself rolling into Hell—roaring flames, men moaning in agony, acrid black smoke searing her eyes. She coughed and pain exploded across her chest with each spasm. The truck skidded to a stop, the momentum throwing Zoey painfully forward against her barbed restraints. Molech jumped out and strode up among what was left of the Co-Op guards, Scott filming him from behind. One of the guards drew a wicked-looking knife and threw himself at Molech. The guy was quick and skilled and showed no fear. Molech made a series of moves that were too fast to see, and tore the man in half.

He then strode up to the nearest armored vehicle, a plume of black smoke pouring from its rear. Molech made a fist, and even from Zoey's vantage point she could see the bright ripple of electricity arc across his stainless-steel knuckles. He reared back and punched the tank. There was a massive crunch of rending metal and a thunderclap of energy—a blue flash bright enough to leave an afterimage in Zoey's eyes. The tank was instantly broken in two, the ragged halves spinning away as if the vehicle had been kicked by an invisible giant. Four crewmembers were spilled across the pavement.

Molech screamed and hooted and felt the rush of a man becoming a god. Then he put his wrists together, and there was a flash of lightning so bright that this time Zoey had to close her eyes completely. Then she heard screams and decided to just keep them closed.

The terrible sounds continued for several minutes, but eventually a calm settled over the scene, leaving only the gasps and cries of bystanders. Zoey dared to look and there was now just smoke and debris and black smears of ash scattered across the marble stairs leading up to the Co-Op's stately headquarters. At Molech's feet, she saw the top half of a skeleton.

Molech kicked through the bones and found what appeared to be the lone survivor of the assault, struggling to get to his feet among the blackened limbs of his peers. An older guy, with a crew cut. It was Blake, the CEO they'd met with in the strip club basement. In full combat gear, just like the rest. He'd gone out there himself, side by side with his men.

Molech stood over him and said, "I got to tell you, man, that was disappointing. I heard you had more than a hundred guys working for you, I figured you'd circle everybody around your HQ, and I'd get to shred 'em all at once."

Blake spat blood on the steps. "My only regret is I won't get to see how you go down. But as dumb as you are, I'd say you've got about a day."

Molech smiled, then pulled out a little device that looked like a metal starfish, the little pointed arms flexing on their own. He rolled Blake over, stuck the device on his back, and the older man let out a piercing scream as it dug into him.

Molech left him there, then strode over to the third monster truck and from the bed pulled an oversized device that looked to Zoey like a cartoon bazooka. He aimed it at the arched front entrance of the building, and once again waited for Scott to frame him up with the camera. Molech squeezed the trigger, firing a projectile that burst in midair a few feet short of the structure, ejecting a massive net of thin black lines that encircled the building.

The net pulled itself tight over the walls and columns, and then tighter, until puffs of dust were spurting from hundreds of cracks. The net kept squeezing and squeezing, pillars and corners buckling under the strain. Then, all at once the building imploded, sucking in on itself like a popped balloon, the netting pulling tighter and tighter until jagged hunks of stone, concrete, and glass were being crushed together into a solid mass. Soon all that remained was a massive sculpture of compacted rubble, bound together by the bundle of thin cables. It stood in the center of a now-empty foundation, a few broken water lines spurting into the air. When the dust cleared, Zoe could see the wire had squeezed the hunks of concrete, marble, and steel into the shape of a thirty-foot-tall hand, with the middle finger extended.

Molech then threw a cable around the finger, and dragged Blake up the steps. He tied the cable around the writhing and screaming man and hoisted him up, so that he was dangling from the rubble that minutes earlier had been his headquarters. Molech then climbed the hand, past the dangling man, until he was standing atop the extended finger. Scott moved to the base of the hand with the camera, getting a low-angle shot that would silhouette Molech against the gray sky, to really capture the majesty of the scene. Molech glanced up at the nearest building, taking a moment to soak in his own magnificence as it was being broadcast across the Tabula Ra$a skyline, and all around the world via Blink.

"I respect those who fight with honor, like my friend Blake here. The rest of you Co-Op foot soldiers around the city, you've got about five minutes until the device I attached to your boss slowly fries his internal organs. Come cut him down, I'm advancing to the next level. I'm about to do a little urban renewal, I think you're gonna like it."

They piled into the trucks and soon Zoey was moving again. Behind them, black trucks soon swarmed the middle finger monument that had been the Co-Op HQ, men spilling out to come to the aid of their boss.

She faintly heard Molech say, "All right, let's go to Squatterville."

FIFTY-EIGHT

🔑

As a target, Zoey thought, Squatterville made no sense. It was a crumbling tower full of shivering poor people—leveling it would prove nothing, considering the place looked like two guys with sledgehammers could do it over a weekend. But then again, the monster didn't think that way, did it? The bullies she had known didn't take on other bullies, they got high off easy wins. Zoey tried not to think about what an "easy win" would look like when the target was a rickety concrete box full of two thousand men, women, and children.

She heard the crackling of the tires rolling over broken glass, and tried to look around. They were passing through the shadow of the mountain of debris that had been Livingston Tower just a few days earlier. All of the buildings across the street had plywood and tarps where the lower windows used to be, each having taken a cannonade of debris from the collapsing skyscraper. Zoey had to admit it: her visit had been hard on Tabula Ra$a.

And then there was Squatterville, looming over them with its tendrils of smoke drifting into the cloudy December sky. In the wake of any slow-developing disaster that hits the news—a hurricane, or a flood, or a war—there's this infuriating thing that Zoey always heard people say about the victims: "Why didn't those people just get out of there when they knew what was coming? Why are they so stubborn?" Infuriating, of course, because of the blithe presumption that everyone *actually has somewhere to go.* If you're someone to whom even a cheap hotel is an unthinkable extravagance, and all of your friends already have extended family sleeping on their living room floor, all you can do is hunker down and hope the storm takes a last-second turn. You don't have a choice. That's what it's like being poor—choices are something you sit around and dream about having, some day after you strike it rich. So Zoey was not surprised to see Squatterville still fully occupied, despite the fact that word of Molech's approach must have traveled across Blink in a microsecond. If they fled the building in a panic and somehow managed to avoid being cut down in the streets by whatever exotic weapon Molech pulled out next, where would they go? They were at the mercy of whoever happened to care enough to protect them. As always.

From where she was, Zoey could see that parked in the weedy lot in front of the decomposing building was the black League of Badass van. They had taken her up on her offer, or had come to dig up the imaginary pirate gold under the floor. Either way, this was not going to end well.

Molech's convoy rolled to a stop, almost exactly in the spot where Zoey had held her open-air meeting with Will Blackwater and the rest five days earlier. The first person Zoey saw standing in the open first floor was Lee, red Mohawk and all. The other five members were fanned out on either side of him. Behind them was a crowd—residents of Squatterville having come downstairs to see what was happening. Or, rather, to find out what was going to happen to them. Some of them had brought weapons—knives, lengths of pipe—but neither they nor their ragtag band of vigilante protectors held guns. What guns they had owned now presumably lay in pieces, thanks to Molech's gadget—Zoey assumed there wasn't an intact firearm for several miles around. There were so many drones overhead that there was now a pervasive beehive buzz under everything. Occasionally a couple of the tiny aircraft would collide and tumble out of the sky, in pieces.

Molech jumped out of the truck to go meet with Doc, intently watching something on a feed Doc was showing him. Black Scott stepped into view in front of Zoey, glancing at her briefly as if to absently make sure she was still attached to the hood. He messed with his camera.

Zoey tried to clear her throat, swallowing blood in the process. She croaked, "This is stupid."

"Shut up. Ain't nobody likes a noisy hood ornament."

"You're trying to prove these gadgets can take on armies, what does it prove if you murder two thousand unarmed women and children?"

"Actually, the customers we got lined up for this gear, they need to know it can do that very thing. They just got to be sold on the efficiency of the process. Now quiet down or I'm gonna wire your whole face shut."

"Have you seen who lives in there? *These are your people.*"

"'My people'? Yeah, talk to me about racism, millionaire white girl. Your daddy buyin' and sellin' bitches like livestock. Well, instead of makin' money off the filth of this city, we gonna clean it all out. Fumigate all the insects. Here, and all over the world. Scrape off the barnacles and get this ship sailin' right."

"I'm pretty sure in Molech's eyes, we're all insects. *Including you.* What has he told you, that he's going to sell to the highest bidder and split the cash with you? *Open your eyes.*"

"Oh, my eyes are wide open. And it ain't about sellin' Raiden to the 'highest bidder,' hood ornament. That's trailer-park thinking right there. No, it's about deciding *who gets Raiden and who doesn't.* That's how we're gonna shape the world."

Molech approached, looking giddy.

Scott said, "Help, your hostage is playin' mind games on me."

"Ha! She probably just wants to play a solo on your pork horn." To Zoey he said, "He's magnificent, isn't he? Look at him. You know, you people almost blew it. But while the whites were breeding masculinity out, you were also raising slaves and breeding masculinity into them, growing the best workers and warriors and point guards. So be thankful for slavery, it wound up preserving masculinity in the species. Isn't that right?"

Scott said, "Uh, I just want to make it clear that the views expressed by Molech are not necessarily those of the rest of his organization."

Molech told Scott he wanted a shot where he was standing in front of the crumbling building and its rows of frightened faces. Scott framed up the shot, and once more the feed spread itself across the skyline.

Molech said, "To the hundred and twenty million of you who have tuned in to watch the beginning of the end of your world, welcome. Before this next part happens, I want to warn you that if you have children in the room, well, keep 'em in the room, because they're about to learn somethin' important about the world. Behind me is a building full of termites. Oh, they look like people, but don't be fooled—everywhere they go, the structures start fallin' down around 'em. This here, this was supposed to be luxury condominiums. Look at it now. Our whole civilization, it's just like this, it's like a microcosm of a world with too many damned termites in the walls. Well, I got somethin' for that. Here, let me do a demonstration. Let's switch over to our friends back at the Co-Op."

The skyline feed switched to the finger-shaped rubble of the former Co-Op HQ, now swarming with black-clad guards who probably wished they had working guns in their hands, surrounding their boss. Someone had gotten him down from the rubble and they were huddling over the star-shaped device stuck to his back, trying to figure out how to remove it.

Molech said, "Three, two, one . . ."

A flash, and a crackle, and a spray of meat.

When it was over, a crowd of skeletons cumbled to the steps of the Co-Op headquarters.

Zoey squeezed her eyes shut. From all around her, screams. Except for Molech. Molech was laughing. Not an evil laugh—she didn't actually think people did that in real life. It was an honest, involuntary belly laugh. The way a toddler laughs when he sees a fat person fall down.

Molech said, "Fries the meat right off the bone, like ribs in a slow cooker. Radius up to fifty yards." He held up his left hand and once more, his mechanical fingers transformed and changed shape, clicking and whirring into something shaped vaguely like an eggbeater. "This has a range of a hundred."

The crumbling building in front of them was slowly draining its tenants onto the surrounding streets, some of them finally making a run for it. The rest just . . . waited. Knowing they had no hope of outrunning what Molech was about to do.

Zoey spat blood and rasped, "Don't. This won't prove anything. Don't do it."

Molech smiled. He pointed his hand-gun at her. Scott came around with the camera, to get them both in the shot.

Molech said, "Make you a deal. You can sacrifice yourself, and I'll let these people live. You willing to do that? You have my word, we're sayin' this in front of the whole world here. Here's your chance to be a hero. One life for two thousand."

Zoey said, "You'll kill all of us either way."

"So I take that as a no. How about this: I'll save all of these people, in exchange for your cat. Will you do that? Will you sacrifice a single cat to save these two thousand lives? Half of them kids?"

"I'm not playing your game."

"You know damned well what your choice would be. People like you make that choice every day. You don't care about these people any more than I do. The rest of these buildings downtown, they got armies standing guard. Them churches we're going to next? They got a thousand volunteers, locking arms around them, turning themselves into human shields. Who did these people have? Nobody. But you know who owns this building? You. And the only protection you sent were half a dozen slapdicks in a van."

Molech turned away from her and strode toward the League of Badass squad, the six of them now huddled with their backs together, weapons at the ready—crossbows and swords that Zoey doubted they even knew how to use.

Molech waited for Scott to get all of them on camera, then said, "So here's what's going to happen. I am going to air-broil the flesh off everyone in front of me. So you guys standing there in your little costumes and toys, you can either die heroically yet pointlessly in the wake of the blast, or you can walk away, and admit that you actually don't give a runny shit about these people, which is perfectly reasonable considering any of them would slit your throat for meth money if given half a chance. I'll give you five seconds to decide. Five . . ."

The LoB didn't need five seconds.

Lee screamed, "This isn't over, Molech!," then grabbed a canister off his belt and threw it to the ground. It exploded into a cloud of red smoke, which actually didn't do much to obscure the sight of the six of them running frantically toward their van. By the time Molech reached the end of his countdown, the black van with the League of Badass logo airbrushed on the side was squealing out of the parking lot.

And then it was just Molech, and the tower, and the masses trying to find cover in a building that barely even had walls.

Zoey said, "Please. It's women and kids. Look at them! Please. Scott, tell him! This won't prove anything!"

Molech put his back to the building. Scott framed up the shot so that the panic inside would be visible behind him.

Molech addressed Zoey, and the world.

"'Women and children.' That's what they say when the boat is sinkin', right? 'Women and children first'? I thought you people wanted equality. Well, if the men don't count, then nobody does. And don't give me that crap about saving the little children. Maggots turn into flies. And that's all I see here— you got people who can't feed themselves, can't clothe themselves, can't shelter themselves without squatting like rats in a barn. In what sane species can this trash behind me be allowed to stink up the gene pool? So spare me, please. I'm looking at addicts and whores raising future addicts and whores. Enough. All you watching this, open your eyes and remember what you see here. This is what's coming. Everything you think you know about power is about to be—*OW!* WHAT THE F—"

A drone shaped like a three-foot-long taco crashed into Molech's face.

FIFTY-NINE

Molech grabbed the drone and smashed it on the pavement, sending a half dozen hard-shell tacos scattering around his feet.

He flung the wreckage aside, in time to be met by another taco drone, this one white and decorated with a logo bearing a cartoon chipotle pepper. Behind it were three drones bearing the logo of a purple and yellow bell. Molech swung and kicked and slaughtered Mexican food with every mighty blow, while a quarter billion extremely confused Blink users watched.

And still they came, every Mexican food delivery drone that happened to be in the air at that moment, their navigation systems hacked and commanded to fly as fast as possible to the exact location where Molech was standing. This part had been Zoey's idea, and if it caused Molech to run over and crush her skull in a fit of rage, she wouldn't mind this being the last thing she saw.

Molech took the drones out one by one, screaming incoherent commands to his utterly baffled henchmen, until he stood victorious over the shattered carcasses of three dozen Mexican food-themed quadrocopters, breathing heavily and trying to suppress his rage. His clenching mechanical fists were covered in brown and white streaks of refried beans and sour cream.

He surveyed the wreckage and said, "*What the hell was that?*"

Scott squinted at the smears of food on the pavement. "Did somebody order a bunch of Mexican?"

"Get the camera back on me." Scott did, and Molech said, "All right, I don't know who pulled that little stunt, but I'm about to—"

Molech's face abruptly vanished from the skyline feed.

The video on the walls of the buildings downtown scrambled and pixelated

333 / FUTURISTIC VIOLENCE AND FANCY SUITS

and finally resolved into a new image. What appeared there was the face of a masked Andre Knox. Andre bellowed a comic book villain's evil laugh.

"Fools! You have fallen for my diversion! I want to thank my junior partner, Molech, for setting the stage. That boy sure does love his tacos."

The shot zoomed out to reveal Andre in full supervillain gear—the exact costume Molech was wearing, only with the blue highlights and codpiece done in red. In addition, Andre had added a rather flamboyant red domino mask, and a large-brimmed black hat with a red feather stuck into the band. He was stroking a black cat.

Molech gaped at the figure that towered over him from the skin of the nearest building.

"Who the . . . *what the hell is happening?*"

Andre's booming voice continued. "As my assistant-slash-underling Molech indicated, we are a terrorist organization. We call ourselves Fire and Ice, and Tabula Rasa, and then the world, will feel the steam of our combined passion, and fury."

Molech looked at Scott, then at Zoey, then back up at the building.

Scott was messing with the camera. "They're blocking our feed. Got to have a drone up there jamming the signal or somethin'."

"As you now know," continued Andre, "over the last few months, we have built in secret a lair right in the heart of this city. The place from which I am broadcasting is invulnerable to assault from the ground and the air—as you have seen, armies will bounce off our walls like mere gerbils off a bulldozer. And now, behold!"

The view switched to an exterior aerial shot of the former Fire and Ice Palaces, captured from a drone hovering over a street choked with traffic from fleeing citizens and transfixed rubberneckers. Simultaneously the black tarps fell off each of the two towers like a pair of dresses on prom night, settling silently on the streets below.

On the each building, Molech had gotten his volcanic glass etchings, the images vividly outlined in glowing orange, as if cut from still-hot magma. A. J. Skelnik's facade crews had done a fine job, it really did look like obsidian. The etchings, however, were not what Molech had described in the work order. That's because twelve hours earlier, a brand-new rendering had been uploaded to the grinders that had been set to carve the relief into each tower's veneer. It was the one thing they were able to get Skelnick to agree to before Budd's network got him and his crew out of the state.

On the tower that used to be the Ice Palace, there was now a detailed rendering of Andre, wearing his hat and mask. And *only* his hat and mask. Zoey had never seen the real Andre naked, and doubted she ever would, but the rendering of Andre on the building had been very, very generous when it came to how well endowed he was.

On the Fire Palace across the street, instead of the huge rendering of his scowling face that Molech had ordered and paid for, there was another full-body nude. This one depicting Molech, wearing only his robot hands. Zoey had never seen Molech naked, and prayed she never would, but the rendering on the building had been very, very stingy when depicting Molech's genitalia. The Blink algorithm, tracking the camera movements and zooms of thousands of onlookers, instantly decided this specific part of the facade was most worthy of notice.

The expression on the real Molech's face would have been hilarious, Zoey thought, if she hadn't been seeing it on someone capable of effortlessly vaporizing everyone in the vicinity. He had the look of a chess player who at the same moment realized his king had been checkmated and that the beer he'd been drinking was actually piss. This had been Phase One of the plan—a stage they had simply referred to as "Confusion." And if nothing else, Molech certainly did look confused. Zoey coughed and a spray of blood splattered across the metallic blue paint of the monster truck hood. She decided that she still didn't feel like her side was winning.

Scott said, "Is that . . . is that the design you wanted, man?" Molech didn't answer. He looked like he was going to have a rage-stroke. Scott said, "I like it. Kind of got a Greek statue vibe goin'."

Molech made a sort of hissing growl, then stormed toward where Zoey was tied to the truck and grabbed her by the neck.

"IS THAT YOU? Is this your people doing this? How did he get inside the tower? TELL ME."

Zoey actually came up with something really clever to say, but her whole jaw was now swollen shut from her busted teeth, and everything was all sticky with coagulated blood in there. Her retort just came out as a series of wet moans and grunts.

He turned toward Scott and screamed, "GET IN THE TRUCK! We're goin' to the Fire Palace."

Scott said, "Man, think! Don't you get this is what *they want you to do*? I say we move on to the next target, stick with the plan. Whatever little prank they're pullin' back at the palace, that don't matter now. Think it through—what's more important, takin' over the whole world, or having a few hundred million people think you got a baby dick?"

Molech stopped, and thought it over.

SIXTY

They rolled to a stop a block away from the Fire and Ice buildings. Zoey had slipped out of consciousness again at some point, but was awaken when the truck lurched to a stop and she felt the cold bite of the barbed wire digging into her wrists. Molech stepped out, and the crowd roared at the sight of him. He sneered up at the grossly unflattering depiction of his anatomy etched into the facade. After Zoey had floated the general idea of changing the renderings, Echo had spent four hours drawing up the designs. She wouldn't show them to anyone, and had never cracked a smile the whole time she was working.

Molech stomped toward a random car—an occupied one—grabbed it by the front end and started swinging it around like a discus. He let it fly and it crashed into the faux obsidian, leaving a massive scar where his own sculpted face had been.

Scott stood by the truck, and sighed.

Zoey got her swollen jaw loose enough to ask, "Is the anatomy right? We had to guess."

Without looking at her, Scott said, "You know why he's keepin' you alive, right? It's so he can take his time with you later. You know what Molech does in his spare time? He studies torture techniques. Goin' back thousands of years. He's a walking encyclopedia on the subject. If you knew what was coming, you'd already be screamin'."

Andre appeared on the skyline feed, bellowing a cartoon villain laugh. "As you can see, my humble servant Molech has come to join me in our lavish headquarters! He appears to be throwing something of a tantrum, probably due to having had too much Mexican."

Molech walked up to the foundation and punched it, unleashing the full force of the plasma from his fist. The wall exploded, leaving a hole like a dump truck had crashed through it. A swarm of shirtless men were scrambling out of the building, Molech's own crew trying to get clear of it before their boss's tantrum brought it down on their heads.

The skyline feed blinked away to a reporter who was standing a block from the scene. Shouting over the chaos, she said, "As you can see behind me, a lone figure believed to be Molech himself has appeared, and is destroying the tower. That's right, he is tearing away at his own headquarters, as if he has had a change of heart, a crisis of conscience if you will. We're going to try to get an interview with him, this powerful story of redemption playing out before our very—"

The noise of the collapsing tower filled the world, Zoey now watching a skyscraper tumble into its own footprint for the second time in three days. Then she saw it again when Molech strode over and did the same to the Ice Palace. The reaction from the bystanders was a bizarre stew of cheers and screams of terror. Plaster dust hung in the air like a thick fog.

Molech stomped back toward Scott and Zoey and said, "I hope that was worth it, bitch. Those buildings were junk and Andre Knox is a pancake now." To Scott he said, "Give me some good news, partner."

"How about this—approximately every remaining gun in Tabula Rasa is converging on this spot." This was relayed as if it was, in fact, good news. Almost on cue, Zoey heard the faint sound of approaching helicopters.

Molech grinned, baring his teeth. "Ain't no man felt juice like this, Black Scott. It's God Mode, from here on out."

The skyline feed switched away from the Fire and Ice aftermath to the collection of ragtag armies approaching from all four directions. And then, abruptly, the feed cut to black, and then to a laughing Andre.

Molech let out a long breath, and closed his eyes. "You freaking people."

Andre bellowed, "Aha! I see that you have fallen for my trivial diversion! As you can see, I was not in the hollowed-out shell of a casino you thought was my headquarters, but am across town, in the toppled-over ruins of the once-great Parkview apartments. But you do not dare approach! For now, I unveil the true centerpiece of our master plan! Tabula Rasa, behold what is behind me, and tremble! We are in possession of a ten megaton plasma fusion warhead—a weapon powerful enough to turn all of this city into a vast wasteland of molten sand!"

Zoey heard screams and gasps from the bystanders gathered on the sidewalks, and from at least one of Molech's henchmen. On the screen, Andre stepped aside to reveal the bomb—an olive green cone with a yellow tip, about three feet wide and ten feet long.

"We will detonate this device, vaporizing everything within a fifty-mile radius, unless our demands are met within the next sixty minutes. What demands? Stay tuned to this feed, and all will be revealed!"

The skyline feed switched to a still image, a doctored photo depicting a costumed Andre and Molech standing back to back, giving a thumbs-up to the camera. The words "FIRE AND ICE" were spelled out beneath their feet, in flashy animated text.

Molech rushed over and grabbed Zoey's face.

"Hey. Wake up. Have you ever been on fire, piglet? Do you know what it feels like to have third-degree burns over your whole body? Do you know what it feels like to then lie on a dirty concrete floor in your own filth, for weeks and months after your skin has burned away? Do you have any idea how long my doctors can keep you alive in that condition? I'm going to ask you exactly one time. IS THE NUKE REAL?"

Zoey spat the blood out of her mouth so she could sputter the word "Yes."

"YOU'RE A LYING GASH SCAB. Why would you have a real nuke?"

"Why would we have a *fake* one? We bought a machine to build Arthur's designs. That's what we made."

"So what's your plan, blow up the whole city? For *what*?"

"To stop you from getting it!"

Scott said, "All the hired guns are diverting toward the Parkview site. Looks like every Blink camera in the city is headed there, too. So, what? We goin'?"

The gears turned in Molech's head. He tried to study Zoey's face.

"Yes. No! Goddamn it, that's what they want, isn't it?"

He grabbed Zoey again, squeezing her throat this time with metal fingers. Instantly, her air was gone.

"Tell me what you're planning. You think you know what I'm capable of. I promise, you do not."

He took his hand away long enough for her to scream, "I DON'T KNOW!" This was the truth, she had pretty much lost track of the plan at this point. "You want to know, ask Will!"

"Hey, good idea. Where is he now?"

"Back at the house. He's controlling everything from there!"

Molech studied Zoey's bloody face once more.

Scott said what Molech was surely thinking. "This sure looks like an ambush, boss."

"What could they possibly ambush me with, Scott? Whatever it is, I'm kind of eager to see it. Screw it. Let's go."

SIXTY-ONE

Zoey blacked out, she had no idea for how long.

When she felt the trucks slowing to a stop again, she pried her swollen eyes open and had the sense of having come full circle: she saw the wrought-iron front gates of Arthur Livingston's estate—no, *her* estate—standing closed to all unwelcome visitors, the two stone dragon pillars standing vigilant on either side. She expected the Candi hologram to appear and tell them the gates were locked, or for a crazy array of security devices to spring into action and cut them all to pieces.

Instead, the gates simply slid open.

But of course they did. Molech, after all, had someone on the inside.

Instead of looping around the winding path through all of the statues, decorations, and the Siberian tiger enclosure, Molech just pointed his hood toward the front doors and gunned it. The truck smashed through a pair of knight statues, rumbled over bushes covered in Christmas lights, and ripped through the fence around the tiger enclosure, the sleepy beasts lazily watching them pass.

They arrived in front of the massive bronze front doors, and Molech came around and ripped away the wires holding Zoey to the hood of the truck. She tumbled off onto the cobblestones, smashing her knees and elbows when she landed. A rough hand—Scott's—hooked under her armpit and yanked her up.

She instinctively started to pull away, and walk on her own—she didn't want to be carried, or dragged, or yanked around by that freaking arm again.

She was sick of being cargo. Instead, she fell limp in his strong hands. Making him practically drag her.

The front doors started slowly creaking open, on their own.

Molech said to her, "By the way, are you curious to know who sold you out? To know who it was that you trusted, and shared a roof with, while they were tipping me off? Are you curious to know who told me Armando would be mincing along my rooftop that day?" He turned toward the open doorway and said, "Come on out here and say hi."

A figure emerged from the shadows of the foyer and strode confidently into view, standing defiantly in the afternoon sun.

The man said, "It's always the last one you'd suspect, isn't it, Zoey? Always the one you underestimate. I took abuse from your father for far too long. And now, today, I finally have my revenge."

Zoey peered at her traitor through her swollen eyes. That dark complexion, the curly hair, the goatee. The toothpick, jutting from a corner of his mouth.

Zoey said, "Who the hell are you?"

"You know who I am."

"I . . . I literally don't. I have never seen you before in my life."

"YOU SAW ME EVERY DAY!" The man spat the words, in a rage. "In the yard? Trimming the bushes? Fixing the decorations in the courtyard? I was fixing lights on that tree two days ago! You walked right past me!"

"You're . . . what? One of the landscaping guys?"

"I'M GARY! Gary O'Brien! The gardener! I worked for your father for twenty-five years! We played golf together! I slept in one of the guest rooms! Oh, I knew what you were saying. 'We don't need to worry about Gary. Gary's too dumb to think up schemes like us. Well, now you're lookin' at Gary in a whole new light, aren't ya?"

"I'm . . . sorry. I just don't remember you."

"I want to hear you say it! I want to hear you say you underestimated me!"

Molech said, "Calm down, yard-master. So, she says Blackwater is inside, is that true?"

"Yeah. Go up the stairs, there's a sitting room to the left. They're just sittin' in there. Waiting. No ambush, no nothin'. They didn't even notice the grounds security was off. All because in their wildest dreams, they never could have guessed that little ol' Gary could—"

"And that's all you know? You got no other information for me?"

"No, man, but they're right up there. Go have at them."

"Good. Looks like we're done here."

And with that, Molech stepped forward and punched the man.

There was a wet sound, like a bucket of paint splashed against a wall.

And in a blink, everything on Gary from the knees up had vaporized. Fragments of pink and white and yellow flew across the open bronze doors, spraying across the marble tile of the foyer inside. A red mist hung in the air, and then was gone. Zoey screamed, or tried to. It was just kind of a gurgle at this point. Molech hooted in celebration, a sound he'd make rooting for a contestant in a wet T-shirt contest.

He said, "God, I'll never get bored with that."

They stepped inside and Molech glanced around at the foyer.

"This is a nice place. I might set up shop here after this is all said and done. Let's go."

They stepped around the spray of gore that had been Gary the Gardener, went past the massive looming Christmas tree, and headed up the grand staircase—Molech in the lead, Scott having to drag Zoey up the stairs like a bag of trash. Doc and the other henchmen had stayed behind, maybe to make sure nobody stole their trucks—Molech clearly was not worried about being outnumbered. Below them, Zoey saw Carlton enter the foyer with a mop.

They reached the buffalo room, and Molech gestured to Zoey to open the door, presumably to take the brunt of any booby traps that lay in wait. Scott tossed her in that direction, and she tumbled to the floor. She reached up and opened the door from her knees.

There was a fire going. Soft classical music played. On the wall feed, an army could be seen swarming around the sideways Parkview building. In one of two large leather armchairs on the opposite side of the room sat Will Blackwater, looking calm to the point of boredom, swirling the scotch in his glass. As if he had been watching the whole event play out, and found it uninteresting.

Sitting in the chair next to him was Arthur Livingston.

SIXTY-TWO

Arthur smiled at Molech and said, "Dun-dun *duuun!*"

There was a long silence, then Molech said, "Bullshit."

Arthur turned to Will and said, "He's nine minutes later than you said he'd be. You owe me fifty bucks."

Will shrugged. "Traffic was worse than I anticipated, lot of people trying to flee the city, due to our little bomb threat. Have to admit, I expected more from the populace. This is Tabula Rasa, since when do we *run?*"

Molech said, "I killed you. No, I not only killed you, but *your body was vaporized . . .*"

Arthur said, "You did massive damage to my rib cage, lungs, diaphragm, and various gut parts I'd never even heard of. Required fifteen hours of surgery and two thousand stitches to repair it all. So, no, I won't be jumping up from this chair and doing a jig for you—my whole torso looks like Franken-stein. But I'm a tough old bastard and I was able to crawl to the subbasement before the warehouse blew. As was the plan."

Molech paused, feeling the ground shifting beneath his feet. Zoey thought he was trying to work out the logistics of what Arthur was saying, and com-ing up blank.

When he finally got his mouth working again, all he could do was repeat, "*Bullshit.*"

Will said, "Do you want a drink? Why don't you have a drink, and we'll talk through this like adults. That's all we wanted. I mean, look at us—we had to hold a whole city hostage just to get you back to the negotiating table."

Molech turned to Black Scott, as if looking for someone to agree that none of this could possibly be real.

Scott said, "Man, don't look at me. I'm totally lost here."

Will said, "Before we begin, let's establish some parameters, just so everyone is on the same page. This estate is well within the blast radius of the plasma nuke Andre is currently threatening the city with. If I die, it goes off. You won't hear anything, you won't see anything—you just . . . won't *be*, anymore."

Molech said, "No. You're not that crazy."

Arthur said, "You didn't leave us a choice. This patch of land was dirt and scrub brush when I staked my claim and, quite frankly, I think of it as my city, still. You don't get to have it, I'll turn it all back into desert before I'll allow that. The rest of the world, I don't care. But Tabula Rasa is off the table. The negotiation begins there. Now, are you familiar with the *Lord of the Rings*?"

Molech hesitated again, realizing he was playing someone else's game, but with no idea what else to do.

He said, "Yeah, old horror movie about a ghost girl who crawls out of a television?"

"No, this is the one with wizards and elves. Ends with the midgets fighting in a volcano? It's not important. What matters is that the rings in the title are magic rings, that grant the owner total power. Kind of like Raiden, wouldn't you say? Now in the story, the rings came from a wizard named Sauron. He makes these rings and hands them out to the rulers of the land, knowing that the greed of the people would overcome their common sense, which if they'd listened, would have told them this was clearly too good to be true. So I guess he would be like me, and Singh, perfecting Raiden to sell to the highest bidder. But see, here's the twist—it turns out that Sauron was playing a trick. The rings were not all-powerful—there was one ring he kept for himself, unimaginatively called the One Ring, that ruled aaaaaall of the others. The rulers should have seen this coming, should have known a sly character like Sauron wouldn't just give away such a prize. But in their lust for power, these rulers had made themselves slaves. Just like you did."

Molech narrowed his eyes. This clearly sounded like a lie, but the events of the last two minutes had rendered anything possible.

Will said, "We have a device, a switch, that can remotely overload Raiden. You, Molech, are a walking bomb. And we hold the detonator."

"*Bullshit.*"

"Think it through," said Arthur. "Why would I have left this to chance?

The moment we had a working device, I had the engineering team build in the Sauron safeguard in secret."

Will set a simple black box on the coffee table in between the chairs. On it was a single, oversized red button.

Arthur said, "It was destroyed in the warehouse, so we needed a little time to build a new one—had to actually install a whole new factory just to build it, in fact. But it's very simple in how it works—if I push this button, you die, along with every man in the vicinity with Raiden in his bones. But I don't want that, and not just because I don't want burning chunks of you two all over my salon. I have a daughter now, as it turns out, and my goal is for her to *not* have to inherit some mindless cycle of retaliation. No, I'd prefer to make you a deal. All I need you to do is leave town. Tabula Rasa is mine. It's my baby. Take your whole Molech act and go do your demonstration in India, or China, or the Moon, I don't care. You go make your billions and leave me and mine alone. But you don't ever set foot in this city again, or else I punch the off button on your life, and that's that. You've had your fun, you can tell the city whatever you like to save face. But then you leave us alone. That's all you have to do. The rest of the world is yours."

Molech said nothing. Zoey couldn't tell if he was considering the offer or not. These next few moments were everything. Zoey studied his face from where she sat on the floor, trying to keep her mind off her battered body. That jab of the knife in her ribs, with every breath. Sick with the blood she had swallowed . . .

To Molech, Will said, "There's nothing to consider. In this deal, all you leave here with . . . is everything."

There was a meow and Zoey turned to see Stench Machine, trotting in to greet his owner and ask why she'd left the house without permission. She reached out to stroke him, and then he froze, staring down the men in the armchairs at the opposite side of the room. As if seeing his old nemesis.

Rage and terror filled Stench Machine's eyes. The sight of an old foe who had tormented him time and time again, haunting his dreams. Then came the steely resolve of an animal who has decided that enough is enough, that he's going to make a stand.

With a meow that Zoey had no doubt meant, "This ends *now*!," Stench Machine darted across the floor.

Zoey screamed at the cat. He did not respond to her command, because he is a cat.

Stench Machine cleared the distance in two seconds. There was a moment when Will saw what was happening, and began to make a move to stop it, but was too late.

Stench Machine flung his body at Arthur Livingston, who did not react. The cat flew right through his torso, through the hologram. He bounced off the back of the empty leather chair and flopped haphazardly to the floor.

Molech's eyes grew wide.

"Yes! I knew it!"

Will tried to recover. "Now . . . this changes nothing, Molech, the kill switch is—"

Molech flew across the room. He yanked Will up by his throat, kicked the chair out of the way, and slammed Will into the wall, the wood splintering with the impact.

Zoey looked at the kill switch. She wasn't actually sure how much strength she had in her legs—she'd been dogging it with Scott, making him drag her, but she also hadn't actually tested her limbs. And this, here, was a one-shot thing.

She coiled and sprung and threw herself across the room, toward the kill switch button. She could hear Scott lunging after her—she had a moment to imagine his look of surprise, at how spry his captive was. But then she fell well short of the button and banged her chin off the floor. She frantically reached up again and swatted at the button and this time, she got it.

Molech and Scott didn't explode—the button wasn't actually a kill switch, of course (having one of those in the caterpillar would have actually saved everybody a ton of trouble). But it wasn't an empty box, either.

There was a blast and a flash that Zoey felt in her gut—impossibly loud and impossibly bright. All of her senses stopped working, her vision scrambled, her ears were filled with a mind-rending whistle. It was some kind of riot-control device, Will had said, and it really did take the fight out of a person.

Still, the fact that she had been somewhat prepared for it allowed her to recover before anyone else in the room—about two seconds before, it turned out. She scrambled to her feet—her razor-blade broken rib digging into her side as a reward—and grabbed Will's collar. Together they stumbled across the room, toward the fireplace, hearing yells and footsteps from Molech and Scott behind them. Zoey snatched up Stench Machine by the scruff of the neck and together, they dove into the fire.

SIXTY-THREE

The flames in the fireplace were not real, but hid a waist-high door that served as an escape route from the room. The house, Will had shown her, was full of them, all of them ultimately leading down to the garage. Arthur's race car bed had a button, for instance, that would dump you into a chute and take you straight down. Arthur had punched it in his sleep one night and wound up trapped down in the garage naked, until Carlton came to rescue him. Arthur never wanted to be more than thirty seconds from a getaway vehicle.

Zoey skidded onto the tiled floor of a narrow hallway. Wu was standing over her. The second everyone's feet cleared the fireplace, Wu punched a button on the wall and a metal door slammed down over the hatch. He rushed forward, picked Zoey up and got a glimpse of her busted-up face.

"Goodness. Are you all right?"

Will, who had blood running out of his mouth and was likely nursing several grave internal injuries, climbed to his feet and growled, "Move."

They stumbled/ran down the hall, which appeared to be a dead end. Will tapped a spot on the wall and a door appeared, revealing a stairwell. They stepped through, and the section of wall closed behind them once again. As they ran down two flights of stairs, they heard the sound of a mechanically enhanced Molech punching through the wall of the Buffalo Room above.

Zoey asked, "Where are we going?"

Wu said, "Down. This is Plan Z, we're getting you to a car. A manual drive one, I will do the steering myself."

Zoey said, "Oh, come on! We'll never make it. One of Molech's cyborgs is going to tear the car in half before we get off the grounds!"

Wu said, "I am an accomplished driver, Ms. Ashe."

There was another crash overhead, Molech smashing through walls, trying to figure out in which direction his captives had run.

Will said, "Different plan—Wu, you're going to get one of the cars and take off out of here like a stabbed rat. You *won't* have Zoey with you, but you will absolutely make Molech's thugs think you do. Pick a car with tinted windows, make your escape noisy, so that you get their attention."

Zoey groaned. "Oh, god. We're creating a diversion. This is my life now."

Wu looked skeptical. To Zoey he said, "I work for you, not him. Are these your instructions?"

She nodded. "Drawing them away will go a lot further toward protecting me than if you stay here and smack them with your sword for five seconds before they vaporize you."

"I appreciate your frankness in regards to my abilities. Will, I'm leaving it to you to get her to safety. Do you want me to take the cat?"

Zoey thought then said, "No. He would just worry about me."

Wu hurried off. Something crashed overhead, another brick wall being punched into dust. Will led Zoey toward a row of three doors at the end of the room—the one in the middle was the elevator that brought them down from the library the other day, the other two were stairwells leading down from other parts of the house, the convergence of numerous escape routes.

"Damn it, Will, *why in the hell did you think the Arthur hologram would work?*"

"There was no reason it wouldn't. How many conversations have you had in your life where you felt the need to go touch the other person to make sure they were solid? We just didn't anticipate the cat. The lie about the kill switch was plausible enough—"

Even before he finished saying those last few words, a light went on in Zoey's brain. She felt so stupid, like when she found her car keys in her pocket after spending half an hour tearing her room apart looking for them. In the terror of having been snatched out of her home by her own car, she had forgotten what she already knew.

She said, "Wait! Stop. Can we get to Santa's Workshop from here? The, uh, ballroom?"

"Why?"

"It's not a lie! Our stupid made-up story is true! We need to get to the caterpillar!"

SIXTY-FOUR

Will led her to the stairwell on the far right. Up a flight of stairs, down a narrow windowless hallway, both grunting as each step aggravated at least one source of internal bleeding. Finally Will pushed open a wooden door to reveal shelves full of foodstuffs—they were inside the pantry of the kitchen, still one floor below where Molech's goons were conducting the world's most destructive search for their missing hostages. Will hurried out, trying to help haul Zoey along, her body feeling like she had been cut open and stuffed with broken glass. Will ran over to the room's one, large window.

"We'll cut across the courtyard. Stand back."

He grabbed a barstool and smashed the glass, then jumped up onto the sill—the man was actually as agile as a cat, when properly motivated. On the other hand, it took a lot of help to haul the crippled Zoey up and over, with Will's hand clamped over her mouth to suppress her screams when shards from her splintered rib started grinding into her lung. They emerged into the cold of the snow-covered courtyard and Zoey had to stop and cry for five seconds before she could move again. She sneezed, and flecks of blood flew across her shoes.

But soon she was lumbering along like a zombie, the two of them making laughably slow progress across a diagonal path toward the ballroom—Zoey could see where the shrubs over there had been flattened by the flatbed truck the other night. She fought to suck in each harsh, wheezing breath.

There was a blast behind them, and a row of windows exploded on the second floor.

Zoey said, "Who the hell is Gary? Or . . . was Gary? And *why the hell didn't you know about him?*"

"You ever run into a new coworker, ask them their name, only to have them tell you they've worked there for five years? That was Gary, a man so dull and forgettable that he never appeared on your radar. It's like that was his superpower. A stealth human being. We never stood a chance."

They entered Santa's Workshop and Zoey shuffled over to the console on the caterpillar.

"Here! Take Stench Machine!"

She shoved the cat into Will's chest, who immediately set him on the floor. If he got cat hair on his suit, he would probably shrivel up and die like a salted snail. Zoey started swiping through the menus.

"How do you work it? How do you tell it to make the thing on the list?"

"Which 'thing'?"

"Arthur *did* create the One Ring. It's on here. I saw it earlier."

"Zoey, nobody even knows what these—"

"No, listen. He left it to me. Arthur left me the One Ring. That's why he left me the coin. Look."

She scrolled down, and down, until she found the very last entry in the list, the one marked with her name.

"See? It's literally the only thing on here in plain English. Because he assumed we wouldn't be so dense as to not browse the whole list right away."

Will looked at the listing and scrunched his face ever so slightly, his mind working.

Zoey said, "Come on! How do you make it go?"

"You tap that symbol, the one that looks like an owl that's on fire. But Zoey, we don't even know—"

She poked the owl. A row of numbers popped up, and started counting down.

She asked, "What does that mean?"

"It's the production time. It's going to take fifteen minutes."

She groaned, and kicked the machine.

"We *don't have fifteen minutes.*" The house wasn't *that* big, and they'd just left an obvious trail behind them consisting of a broken window and a clear line of snowy footprints.

But Will was already on his phone, swiping through what looked like security camera feeds from around the grounds. He found one with a view of the rear of the house. They watched together as a low, flat black sports car went roaring down the drive, having emerged from the garage door Zoey had smashed a few hours ago.

Will said, "The son of a bitch took the Bugatti."

"Well, you told him to make it noisy."

A moment later, two of the Molech crew monster trucks went rumbling after Wu. They kept watching, but the other truck never joined the chase.

Zoey cursed.

"All right," said Will, "this is why your plan has layers. We still have a big card to play with Molech, and that's Andre's bomb threat. All we have to do is—"

He was interrupted by a call—Echo's hologram face popped into view and immediately said, "Will! Everything is about to go to hell here."

SIXTY-FIVE

Zoey said, "Oh, really? Because we've got everything under control on this end. We're breaking for lunch."

"They're breeching the building. Tune to the LoB feed."

Will brought it up. The League of Badass team was piled in their van, barreling toward the sideways Parkview apartments where Andre was holed up. It appeared they were looking to redeem themselves for abandoning their post at Squatterville, by recklessly charging toward a man with a weapon of mass destruction that could destroy the entire city, Squatterville included. Hey, they weren't called the League of Geniuses.

Will said, "Well, it's too late to go back in time and stop their mothers from drinking, so can you move the bomb?"

"Not before they get here, no."

"All right, get out of there."

Andre's voice piped up, shouting from somewhere in the room with Echo. "You need us to try to hold 'em off?"

"Do what you can. But don't get yourself killed."

They watched as the LoB crew spilled out of their van, hustled through a low sideways window and started rappelling up a vertical hallway, their crossbows and swords strapped to their backs. Lee was in the lead, and soon pulled himself up through a sideways doorway. He found a steep drop in front of him—when horizontal, this was to be a large conference room for parties and conventions. Turn it on its side, and it became a sheer drop of about thirty feet straight down, to the wall that was now serving as a narrow floor.

Standing down there, next to his nuclear bomb, was Andre. Prowling around his feet were lots and lots of cats.

The view from Lee's camera lurched over the opening, as he awkwardly tried to climb into the room without tumbling down and breaking his neck. He tried to bring his crossbow to bear on Andre—difficult to do, while trying to simultaneously straddle the edge of the sideways doorframe.

He said, "Disarm the bomb! Do it now, or we'll . . . turn you into . . . a cactus."

Zoey thought the man would regret not having a better line ready, once he found out that more than five hundred million people had heard him say it. Down on the wall/floor, Andre put his hands on his hips.

"You fools! This device is armed with a tremor-sensitive timer! If any one of you even gently touch the floor, you and the entire city will be vaporized instantly!"

Lee raised the crossbow and said, "Disarm it! Now!"

Andre laughed his supervillain laugh and said, "The world is watching you, mohawk! Let us test what you are willing to do to stop me!"

Andre pushed a button on his belt. With a howl, a cat few up from the floor and stuck to Andre's thigh, its metal collar clinking as it contacted his armor. Then another cat twisted across the room and clanked to his chest. Then another, then another. Within seconds, Andre was covered from the neck down with writhing, meowing felines.

"Ha ha!" bellowed Andre. "Go ahead! Skewer an adorable kitten while your fans look on! Now you know why they call me the pus—"

Suddenly the view was plummeting down, toward the wall—Lee had jumped, or more likely, fell. He crashed to the floor, cracking the plaster under his boots, then the view from the camera spun as the man rolled and trained his crossbow on Andre.

"STOP! And drop the . . . cats!"

But Andre was already on the move, ducking through a sideways door behind him. Lee pursued, carefully giving the nuke a wide berth. The view spun back around to the entrance, where Vixxxen was rappelling down the vertical wall after him.

Lee ran through the sideways door and found Andre had disappeared through a door-sized hole that had been sawed into the ceiling tile, allowing him to pass to the next vertical floor of the building. Lee ducked through, and found Andre running along a hallway, leaping over doorways. Lee aimed his crossbow, trying to get a clear shot. Impossible, without horribly skewering an adorable kitten in the process, utterly ruining the hero moment he would want to be played over and over again for the next century. Nobody would want to replay the video of a cat getting kabobbed onto a fleeing terrorist.

So, Lee watched helplessly as Andre bounded down the shadowy hallway, the occasional cat jiggling free and flopping to the floor as he went.

Will shook his head and asked, "Was that part your idea, or Andre's?"

"I don't even know. We were so sleep deprived at that point."

Lee doubled back and joined his team, who had gathered around the bomb. They discussed it and decided they would try to get in contact with a bomb-defusal expert and, hopefully, get kick-ass video of them cutting the red wire at the last moment and thus saving the city. But, as they were examining the nuke to try to find the trigger mechanism Andre had threatened them about, Lee got a quizzical look on his face. He reached out, gave the bomb a gentle push, and watched it topple over. It wasn't difficult, since the whole thing was a hollow shell made out of plastic.

Will sighed.

At that moment, a news alert popped up over the feed. Hovering above the screen was a scrolling headline:

LIVINGSTON DAUGHTER BELIEVED DEAD

Will brought up video of an enormous fireball, at the bottom of which was the tiniest hint of a blackened, twisted automobile.

Zoey gasped. "Oh my god. Is Wu . . . was he in there?"

Will found video of the car chase that had preceded the disaster—a black Bugatti Chiron roaring through an industrial park, chased by a monster truck, both followed by a cloud of camera drones buzzing overhead, as if they had disturbed a giant beehive and were now being pursued by the swarm. The car left the road and smashed through a chain-link fence, slicing across a field and leaving a stream of dust like a contrail. The car streaked like a guided missile directly into a row of white spherical tanks that, apparently, were filled to the top with some kind of amazingly combustible gas. The gargantuan orange and black plume rose so far into the air that it consumed half of the drones. The monster truck, unfortunately, had stayed out of the blast radius.

Zoey said, "He did it on purpose. He drove right into it. Did he . . . sacrifice himself? For me? Was that like a kamikaze thing?"

Will said, "Well, he was a man from California raised by Chinese-American parents, so the kamikaze would surely be a treasured part of their heritage. You should hide. The henchmen are going to be calling in to report what happened and if I can convince Molech that you went up with the car, then all you have to do is stay out of sight. So you at least can make it through this."

She shook her head. "I'm in no condition to run. I can't breathe. I think my lung is punctured, I'd get two steps outside that door and then it would pop and go whizzing around the courtyard like a balloon. No, the One Ring is real, and the caterpillar is going to spit it out. We just have to make it until then."

"We *don't know that*. And this is coming from someone who knew Arthur better than you. It doesn't say 'Kill Switch' or 'One Ring' or 'Master Key' or anything else—it just says 'Zoey.' It could be a little Zoey Ashe action figure for all you know. It could be a plaque telling you how much he loves you. And if we go this way, we don't have a backup plan."

"No. If *you* want to go, go. But I'm not doing this anymore. I'm not running from men like him. Win or lose, I'm not doing that."

They watched the countdown on the caterpillar, a progress bar shrinking so slowly that Zoey was starting to think it was getting longer.

Zoey asked, "Did you know?"

"Know what?"

"Did you know I was going to wind up at Molech's headquarters? Did you know Gary was a traitor, and that he was going to rig the car and all that? Was that all part of your plan?"

"No."

"If it was, I want to know. No more lies. I know that's what you do, and that's what you're good at, but this one time, I want to know."

"No. I wouldn't do that."

"Because it would put everything at risk, right? I could have broke down and told him everything."

"No. *I wouldn't do that.* I wouldn't do that to y—"

The door to the courtyard exploded off its hinges.

SIXTY-SIX

It was Black Scott who had found them first. He strode into the room, glanced at Will and Zoey, then looked over the random collection of objects the machine had spat out. He absently picked up a narrow hunk of pipe to examine it. Will walked to a nearby table and poured himself a drink.

"You want one?"

Scott said, "Man, you got a drinking problem. You people know you got a living severed head out in your courtyard? Thing is out there chewin' on the snow. Gonna give me nightmares."

Zoey said, "It's been a weird week."

Into some unseen communicator, Scott said, "They're here. Ballroom." Then he looked at Will and shook his head. "A fake bomb? What, did you make it out of papier-mâché? You know, you guys seem to have spent a long time on this plan and I got to say I got no clue whatsoever what it was tryin' to accomplish."

Will shrugged. "It looked better on paper." Will made a show of looking at his watch. "Speaking of which, we should go stand somewhere else. Sooner rather than later. Like, say, in the next six minutes."

Scott said, "I sense you're just *waitin'* for me to ask you what happens in six minutes. So . . ."

"A very big boom. The nuke was fake, of course, the fabricator doesn't have the ability to create a city-destroying device. But the blast that vaporized Arthur's warehouse, we can both agree that was real?"

Scott said, "Mmm hmm."

"That's because the fabricator does have, in its memory, the ability to fabricate a self-destruct device—one big enough to turn a city block into a crater. After Molech broke into his warehouse, Arthur set his machine to make just such a device. Well, about ten minutes ago, we set this machine to do the same."

Zoey studied Scott's face. It was interesting to watch all of the various stages of emotion wash over it. On one hand, the guy knew for a fact that Will Blackwater was a world-class liar and con man. He had no doubt been told by his own boss to automatically dismiss anything Will said as a false-hood or some other attempt at manipulation, no matter what it was. So the first expression was mild amusement, the way you react to the clumsy lie of a child.

But here's the thing—lying would have become useless thousands of years ago if countering it was as simple as dismissing the liars completely. The really good liars were like chemists, brewing formulas that were mostly truth, the toxins undetectable in the mixture. So in just three seconds, Zoey watched Scott's face transition from amusement to concern, as he started to weigh the possibility that Will was in fact telling the truth—after all, it was perfectly possible, and even logical, to do what he was claiming to have done. It would prevent the mansion from falling into Molech's hands, along with whatever valuables or secrets were stored within, and would force Scott to make a call about what to do with his hostages. It was totally the kind of thing Will Black-water would do.

To help drive it home, Will said, "I'm not going to let Molech move in and sleep in Arthur's bed. Five minutes from now, this is going to be a crater, no matter what we do. So let's not be stupid. Let's get out of the blast radius and plug our ears. I liked Arthur a lot, but I have no intention of dying the same way he did. But I will, if you insist—as you said yourself, the alternative is months of slow torture at the hands of your rotbrain employer. An instant death that I don't even feel? That's pretty much my best-case scenario at this point. So which of us has something to lose?"

Scott shook his head, grinning. "I mean this with all honesty. People say Molech is bad, but you, Blackwater, you're ten times worse. We may burn in hell but the devil gonna greet you like an old friend."

Will sipped his drink. "You're a smart man, Scott, and I respect you. You could have probably worked for us, under other circumstances. So I say, for-get Molech. Let's you and I work out an agreement to—"

Scott swung the pipe, and smashed it into Will Blackwater's skull.

Blood sprayed across a nearby marshmallow snowman, and Will Blackwater collapsed to the floor with a sickening thud.

He did not move.

Zoey screamed.

SIXTY-SEVEN

She ran toward the caterpillar, or as much of a run as she could manage, anyway. Scott grabbed her by the back of the shirt, yanked her and threw her back across the room. She crashed into a peppermint elf, her shattered ribs sending jets of fire across her torso. She coughed up blood.

Scott said, "Why don't you just sit tight for a sec. We're gonna wait for Molech to get here, right about . . ." Scott held a finger in the air. "Now."

The wall behind them exploded. Chunks of plaster rained down on Scott and Zoey, and a cold wind rushed in from the courtyard. Molech strode through the dust cloud, brushing bits of plaster off of his superhero costume. At least five henchmen had followed him, all of them looked greatly amused.

Molech glanced down at where Will was sprawled, then looked at Scott.

"What, you started without me?"

"What can I say. Juice don't wait."

"That it does not."

Molech loomed over Zoey. She tried to back away, scooting backward on her butt, nowhere to go. Molech watched with annoyed disdain.

"Tell me, piglet, what story were you telling yourself up to now? What world did you think you were living in? Don't you get that I've been preparing my whole life for this? What have you been preparing for? Don't bother—I actually know the answer to that question, and you don't. See, a gazelle goes out and eats grass because it thinks it's feeding itself. But it's not. It's feeding *the lion*. It's fattening itself up, to be food. It doesn't know it, but it was born to be prey—that is its only purpose. So what purpose do you think a dumb trailer turd with no self-esteem and big tits serves, in a world of true men? Maybe I'll let one of my boys show you. Maybe I'll let *all* of them show you."

Zoey said, "It's like you have Rape Threat Tourette's Syndrome."

"My favorite part? It's that exact moment when the defiance turns into terror. About fifteen seconds from now, I'd say."

Zoey reared back and kicked him as hard as she could in the groin, but it appeared the codpiece wasn't just decorative. Molech didn't even flinch.

"Well," he said, "just for that . . ."

Molech raised up a boot, brought it down, and effortlessly snapped Zoey's right leg below the knee. Both bones splintered, jutting out of the skin. Zoey was unable to scream, she had torn up her vocal chords too much. She could only lay there, and squeeze her eyes and try to block out the pain. To block out everything.

On the other side of the room, the caterpillar clunked and hissed and wound down. A beep announced its production of object "Zoey" was finished. A little late for that, she thought.

Zoey forced herself to look down and, for the first time, saw part of the inside of her own body, white bone jutting out around ragged muscle and fat from her lower leg, blood soaking through her ripped jeans. She felt herself about to pass out, when she heard a soft meow. Stench Machine had arrived, having tracked down his wounded owner a second time, there to offer whatever assistance he could. It didn't amount to much.

Zoey hugged him and Molech said, "T-Bone, kill that goddamned cat."

Zoey's scream of protest was barely a sound, but she couldn't stop it. The henchman known as T-Bone reached for Stench Machine, but the cat slipped out of his grasp, streaking away through the ragged hole in the wall Molech had punched open.

T-Bone giggled as he watched him go, but Molech said, "No, go get it. I want you to pull it apart in front of her."

Zoey said, "Please don't. Just . . . please."

"*Go get the cat.*"

T-Bone obeyed, chuckling as he ran into the courtyard.

To Scott, Molech said, "You got the camera? Good. Frame me up. This is about to become the Zoey Show."

Scott brought up the camera, and they arranged the scene to get Molech in the foreground, with the shattered Zoey in the background. They had to pause to move a table out of the way. Then Molech insisted on getting the feed to play on the wall, so he could check it from time to time, see how it all looked.

Finally they got it arranged to Molech's satisfaction and he said into the camera, "All right, everybody, we got a little off track with our show, but's all good now. I'm glad this happened, really. I prefer things to be a bit more intimate, if you know what I mean."

T-Bone reappeared at the ragged hole in the wall and said, "Man, there's a bunch of trees and stuff out there. That cat is gon—"

There was a roar, and a white blur, and suddenly everyone was shouting.

T-Bone was on his back, with a white Siberian tiger on top of him, ripping his throat out.

Amidst the chaos, Zoey rolled over, and tried to move. Black spots danced in front of her eyes. The pain had blown out the circuits in her brain, she couldn't even tell if she was feeling it anymore. She dragged herself on her elbows, toward the caterpillar. One of her splintered leg bones got caught against a chair leg, and she passed out.

She had no idea how long she was out. Maybe a few seconds. When she woke up again, it was to the sound of screams, tiger roars, and heavy, meaty punches. She dragged herself again, toward the caterpillar, toward the chute at the end. Nothing on her body worked other than her arms—everything was either numbness or blinding pain. She pulled herself along the black and white checkerboard tile, so slowly, the second time in this ordeal she had felt like she was living one of those nightmares where you run and run and never reach the end of the hall, some horror lurking behind you.

Zoey reached the chute, stopped to breathe, and to try to focus her eyes. Behind her, she heard horrific sounds of a man killing a wild animal. She glanced back and saw Molech stand and laugh, blood on his metal fists. She didn't have much time. She had no time. They would notice her; they would be on her in one second.

Zoey pushed herself up on her hands, unable to stand. She pulled herself up so she could reach into the into the caterpillar's delivery basket. She reached in, blindly, and grabbed the object the catalog of schematics knew only as "Zoey."

It was a football helmet.

Zoey thought, *that bastard*, and blacked out.

SIXTY-EIGHT

🔓

She forced her eyes open. Once more, she had no idea how much time had passed. She looked over and found Will Blackwater on the floor, limbs askew, his head oozing blood. Not far away, the white tiger lay dead, along with two shirtless men. Molech's numbers were only increasing, though—ten or so henchmen had joined the party. Not that Molech needed their help.

Zoey sat up, her back to the caterpillar, the stupid football helmet in her lap. It didn't even look like a real, regulation helmet. It was like a toy one, for a kid. She wanted to cry, but didn't have it in her.

Molech noticed the movement and strode up to her, clenching his bloody robot fists. Scott was tracking him with the camera.

"I want to thank you and your tiger-owning father for giving me the most amazing piece of highlight video I'll ever make. I'm probably the first human in ten thousand years to punch a tiger to death. Now, I hope you'll forgive the delay, while you were out, I let my fans vote for what I would do to you. Want to guess what the overwhelming majority voted for? Because it's winning by a ten to one margin over the next choice."

A couple of the henchmen laughed. Zoey's looked down at her ruined leg, transfixed by the sight of the leg bone's exposed gooey pink center. Her vision was pulsing red, blooming with each heartbeat.

Scott said, "Skyline feed is back, too. We're now live, everywhere. All the feeds consolidating right here, right now. Audience is sitting at one billion, with a 'B.'"

Zoey tried to think, but the thoughts were shadowy figures barely glimpsed in a thick fog of pain. She could think of nothing else but the original plan. The one that so far hadn't exactly been a raging success.

She swallowed a pint of blood and said, "We have . . . a kill switch."

"Piglet, if that existed, you'd have punched it already. Now, I have a strangely specific request from my fans here. I'm going to need you to roll over."

"Wait!" Zoey jammed the stupid football helmet on her head. It was still warm, from the machine. "This, uh, helmet! It's the magic protection helmet! You can't hurt anybody wearing this!"

Molech held out his metal hands. "Come on. This is just sad."

He reached down, grabbing her blood-soaked shirt, as if to tear it off.

"No! Stop! STOP!"

Zoey squeezed her eyes shut, and waited.

And waited.

For a moment that never came.

After ten seconds she pulled her swollen eyes open again, and Molech was standing there, completely frozen. Every part of his body, save for his face, which was contorting itself in rage and confusion, fist still clutching her shirt.

Scott, sensing his boss was in distress, rushed over.

Zoey turned toward him and again said, "Stop!" and he, also, stopped.

She backed up on her elbows, pulling her shirt free of Molech's frozen fingers.

"Oh. Oh, wow. Oh my god. It works. The helmet . . . oh my god our stupid lie was true. It really was. Okay. It's voice operated. Um . . . everybody freeze."

The dozen henchmen froze, almost comically. One guy was frozen in mid-run, like a living sports poster a kid would have on his bedroom wall, and immediately toppled over. One guy's hand was frozen on his crotch, like he'd been in the middle of scratching himself.

Their mouths still worked, as crotch guy squinted and said, "Am I the only one who's paralyzed right now? Is there a reboot or something I need to do here . . ."

Zoey said, "Okay. Um . . . everyone start spanking yourselves."

There was no response to this command, as that one apparently hadn't been programmed into the system. Zoey was deeply disappointed in Arthur but realized she needed to keep her eyes on the bigger picture.

Molech said to her, "Just deactivate the implants. Just turn them off completely. I'll take on everyone you've got with my own body, my own brain. Come on, me against whoever you can summon with your daddy's money. Take away the gadgets, I'll show you who the better man is."

Instead, Zoey said, "Scott, throw the camera."

He didn't. Another command that his body apparently didn't understand. "Uh . . . throw your left arm forward and open your hand."

That worked. He chucked the camera past Zoey, where it crashed against the caterpillar. Up on the wall feed, the view scrambled and went to black. Blink immediately switched to the second most popular feed—incredibly, it was inside the League of Badass van, which was at this moment rumbling toward the courtyard. These idiots just did not give up.

The van slid to a stop near the gazebo, the group bumbling out of the sliding side door with their medieval weapons in hand. Zoey saw for the first time that they were chasing two figures—Andre, still in his stupid costume, and Echo. They had led them back to the estate, either accidentally or on purpose, and had ditched their escape motorcycle outside the fence. Andre, Zoey noted, still had a single cat stuck to his back.

To Molech, Zoey said, "What would you do, if you were me, right now? Command your robot hands to rip out your own throat? Pull your head off? Maybe do it slow, have you pull your own guts out of your belly? Spread the video of it far and wide, so everybody knows not to mess with me?"

Molech said nothing. His muscles were flexing, veins popping, trying to move the frozen machinery in his joints. At best, he could just wiggle his shoulders slightly.

Zoey continued, "And then some cohort of yours, some 'roided up lizard brain who's sitting on his sofa right now cleaning his guns, he sees that video and he comes to get payback. And then the whole thing starts all over. Forever and ever, blood on top of blood, until somebody finally takes a breath and decides to just . . . let it go."

There was a ruckus behind Molech as Andre stumbled through the hole in the wall, eyes wide, trying to make sense of the bizarre, frozen standoff taking place between Zoey and the array of shirtless men menacing her. Echo popped through immediately after, but there was no moment of confusion on her part. She saw the injured Zoey and flew toward her, actually skidding the last few steps, sliding on the tile floor and gracefully ending up in a kneeling position next to Zoey. The bitch trying to upstage her.

Echo said, "We have to get a splint on this—"

Zoey waved her off. "All right," Zoey said to the frozen Molech, "we've got a brief window of privacy before the audience joins back in. Here's what's going to happen. Those dumb people in the van are going to pile through that hole in the wall at any moment. At that point, you can surrender and apologize, or threaten them and get shot with arrows. But it's your call. Each of you. Stand down and live, or go out in a blaze of supervillain glory. I don't care either way. I'm going to pass out now."

Zoey lay back, wondering who all had been watching this ordeal. Her mother? Caleb? Bella? Carla Dubois, the slut who had stolen her boyfriend in eighth grade? Stench Machine sauntered up, sniffed her mutilated leg, and curled up and went to sleep at her hip.

As she slipped out of consciousness, Zoey heard the faint sound of shouted warnings, angry threats in reply, and primitive weapons impaling flesh. The last thing she heard was Black Scott saying, "Nah, man, I don't even know these assholes."

SIXTY-NINE

🔑

The cast on Zoey's leg was always gently vibrating, something about using ultrasound to stimulate the growth of bone tissue, they'd said. It was barely noticeable unless you laid your hand right against the cast, but the effect was still maddening. The leg had needed one six-hour surgery, her rib another. But her face and teeth had needed three times as much work—everything from the neck up was bandages or purple bruises. But at least her face wouldn't require six weeks of physical therapy, as she was told the leg would.

She was doing her recuperating at the Casa De Zoey. They had turned one of the guest rooms into a hospital room—complete with adjustable bed, monitoring equipment, and a handsome around-the-clock nurse named Abel. Which wasn't as sexy as it sounds, considering he had to help her to the toilet six times a day.

Otherwise, Zoey was keeping to her New Year's Day tradition of watching nine straight hours of basketball. It was the third quarter of the first game of the triple-header, Zoey's Denver Nuggets on the road versus the Chicago Bulls. Andre was in a chair next to her, his feet propped up on her bed. Andre was eating a burger Carlton had made for him, one whose bun was somehow constructed of two flat lumps of fried macaroni and cheese. Zoey, fresh off of two rounds of oral surgery, was on an all-liquid diet, and had somehow gained three pounds as a result. Right now the liquid was some Russian imported beer Andre had brought with him.

Andre nodded to the wall to his left and said, "Oughta have that framed."

He was referring to a six-foot-wide stretch of white butcher paper that had been thumbtacked to the wall, covered in doodles and notes in Zoey's handwriting. Much of it was illegible, and one corner was obscured by a dried coffee stain. But in the middle was a clear to-do list under the scrawled heading "OPERATION Z-DAY."

With virtually no explanation other than crude stick figure drawings next to each, the list went:

- TACO STORM?
- ~~FAKE ALIEN INVASION~~? NUCLEAR BOMB?
- ECHO HACKS AND/OR SEDUCES SOMETHING
- DEFACE THE FIRE AND ICE (DONGS?)
- CATS CATS CATS
- GET MOLECH BACK HERE (FART RAY?)
- WILL WORKS HIS MAGIC (LIKE IN "THE RINGMASTER")

It was her initial notes from the hours-long planning session the night before the Solstice, Zoey sketching it out on her knees on the floor of the ballroom.

She grunted. "Somebody should have taken the Sharpie away from me."

"What are you talkin' about? Your part worked perfectly, it didn't fall apart until we got to Will's bit. Though all agree that my performance as Arthur Livingston's voice was perfection itself."

"*We could have gotten everyone killed.* None of it played out the way I pictured. It was like were trying to corral a rabid wolf that had wandered into a daycare. There was *so much* that could have gone wrong."

Andre shrugged. "Eh, that's par for the course. This was actually one of the smoothest operations we've ever had."

They sat and watched basketball for a moment, while Zoey let that sink in.

She took a drink and said, "When we started, Will asked me what Molech's weakness was, and that's all I could think of. He was a diva. It wasn't just that he couldn't stand to lose, he couldn't even *appear* to lose, not in front of a crowd. I figured a diva would rather die than be upstaged."

"Like I said, should be framed for posterity." Andre squinted at the screen. "I don't understand, why is it a foul to stand in the lane for three seconds?"

"You really know nothing about basketball?"

"I know the general idea. They get points for putting the ball through the hoop, right?"

"Don't mess with me, Andre, I'm on painkillers."

"That's usually the perfect time to mess with somebody. Anyway I'm more of a hockey man myself. I mean, the fouls don't make any sense. Two dudes run into each other and half the time they call it on the guy with the ball and the other half of the time they call it the other way, there's no rhyme or reason."

"Yeah, I admit that one is random."

There was a knock at the door and Wu let himself in, carrying a bouquet of Get Well lilies in what looked like an antique vase.

Zoey said, "Ooh, who are those from?"

Wu said, "They are from me. The flowers are to get well, the vase is an apology, for what I did to your car. I actually did not know it was so valuable, I picked the one that seemed most capable of speed. The explosion was, in retrospect, probably an excessive touch driven more by ego than practicality. I do succumb to a flair for the dramatic, from time to time. I believe your people had rubbed off on me."

Zoey said, "Well, it looked awesome, I'd say it was worth it. So I never asked, did you jump out at the last second, or what?"

"Uh, no. That is actually not possible without putting yourself in a wheelchair. Early in the pursuit we got stalled in traffic, and I ducked out of the vehicle and continued operating it remotely, from a nearby café. That was the reason for the fiery finale—I wanted to delay the time it would take them to realize that the interior of the car contained only marshmallow."

"Contained *what*?"

"Oh. Well, I needed to put something in the passenger seat so it would appear you were with me, if we were captured on camera. I had no time to construct an accurate analog of your body, of course, so I found one of the marshmallow snowmen that had been stored in the garage, and dressed it in your denim jacket."

Zoey stared hard at Andre and said, "Do *not* say what you're thinking right now."

"You do *not* look like you're made of marshmallow, Zoey."

"Exactly. You're employed another day." She examined Wu's gift and said, "That vase is beautiful."

The room was full of flowers, and Zoey was trying to figure out the minimum amount of time that would be polite to let them stay before having them cleared out—she hated the smell, they reminded her of funerals. But the vase with Wu's bouquet *was* cool—ancient-looking turquoise with threads of gold running through it.

Wu said, "They call it *kintsugi*. The pot is shattered, then carefully reassembled with a resin mixed with gold. It symbolizes how we must incorporate our wounds into who we are, rather than try to merely repair and forget them."

"Wow. It's really pretty. And it looks like a pain in the ass to do, trying to remember where all the shards go."

"It wasn't easy."

There was another knock and Will Blackwater was at the door, carrying a small paper bag. It was like some announcement had gone out to have everyone converge in Zoey's room.

Will said to Andre, "You know Zoey's having to live off protein shakes because of her jaw, right? And you're making her watch you eat a macburger in front of her?"

"She said it was okay!"

"Right. So just the four divorces for you, then?"

Carlton appeared behind Will at the door, apparently having rushed to the scene of a bunch of guests who all might potentially need something to eat or drink. The room was suddenly crowded, all of these people looming over Zoey. You try to watch one basketball game and suddenly your room turns into Grand Central Station. Somebody's phone was ringing.

Wu sensed her discomfort, set down the vase and volunteered to go take up a post out in the hall. He assured Carlton that all was well, and guided him away.

It was Andre's phone that had sounded, and Zoey caught that the floating display said "MELINDA."

Andre stood. "I've, uh, got to take this. It's a customer."

"It's my mom, I can see it on the display. I don't want to talk about it. Go do whatever, you're fired from watching basketball anyway."

He exited, shuffling past Will, leaving the two of them alone.

Zoey let out a grunt of relief. "Too many people. I get that many people squeezing around me in a room and I feel like—"

"Like you can't breathe?"

"Ugh. Exactly. I got a message from Echo saying her gift to me was that she wouldn't bother me for the duration of my recovery. It's the most thoughtful thing I've gotten so far."

Will's bandages were visible under his hat, and Zoey could see where they'd had to shave that whole side of his head to operate.

She asked, "When did you get out? Didn't they have to put a metal plate in your head?"

"It's not as bad as it sounds."

"Still, you had skull surgery and they let you out after a week?"

"I let myself out. No point in lying there on painkillers when I can be out getting work done, on painkillers. Speaking of which, are you supposed to be mixing yours with alcohol?"

"Whatever, *Dad.*"

"If I was your dad I'd be asking you to share. I heard back from the lawyer yesterday, the insurance company is going to fight you on the tower. They're saying this doesn't fall under the terrorism clause, they're calling it vandalism. Oh, and tomorrow the League of Badass are having their ceremony at the White House. Where they're being honored. For single-handedly saving the city."

On the TV, the seven-foot-five center for the Denver Nuggets pulled up and took an improbable three-pointer from around half court. Nothing but net. Will groaned.

Zoey said, "What, are you a Bulls fan?"

"No, I have money on the Nuggets. But I cringe when McClaren hits a three because—"

"Because now he's going to take five more, and miss them all."

"Right, he's fooled himself into thinking he can make that shot."

Zoey said, "Hot damn, have a seat. You're now my basketball-watching partner."

"I really can't, I have work I need to—"

"*You work for me*, and I'm assigning you the task of watching a bunch of New Year's basketball with me. I had Andre in that position but he failed miserably and was demoted to having sex with my mom."

Will paused long enough to demonstrate he was trying to think of an excuse, and then relented and took Andre's seat.

Zoey said, "I figured we'd be under martial law by now. Like the government would send in the army to make us all behave."

"The government is more than happy to cover up the fact that their weapons systems are now useless in the face of arms you can buy off the street. There are about four different insurgencies in the world who'd love to know that."

"I guess what I'm asking is . . . how long can Tabula Rasa be allowed to stay like this? The government isn't going to let things stay crazypants here forever."

"Well, there are thousands and thousands of wealthy political donors in this city telling them to keep their noses out—Tabula Rasa has a hundred and twenty billionaires, at last count. But no, they won't let it stay lawless forever. A city full of thriving black markets means there's a whole lot of taxes that aren't being collected. Oh, nice defense, *Raj*."

"He pouts when he doesn't get the ball." Zoey nodded toward Will's brown paper bag. "What's in the bag? Liquor?"

"Oh, right." He dumped the contents of the bag into his hand—a green rubber mouse. "It's an old cat toy. My wife used to have a cat. It has catnip inside it. I don't have the cat any more but then I thought I remembered you had a cat of some kind."

Zoey took it. The mouse smelled like new rubber, it was clearly just off the shelf. So Will had bought it, took it out of the package, put it in a different bag, and then claimed he had just found it, so she wouldn't know he had made a special trip to buy her cat a toy. Zoey thought the best gift she could get Will was years of therapy.

Zoey dropped the mouse on the bed near where Stench Machine was curled up.

"Well, we'll know right away. If he bats it away with his paw—yeah, like that. He hates it. Oh, he likes the bag though. And . . . now he has his head stuck in it. It's a disaster. Anyway, that was very sweet of you. And it's the thought that counts."

"I can't even imagine a world where that's true."

Will glanced at his watch.

Zoey sighed. "Why do you have to pretend like you don't want to be here? You could have called to tell me about the insurance, or not even told me about it at all, because I clearly don't care. Instead you made the trip all the way here. It's okay. You can just say, 'I wanted to check in and see how you were doing, Zoey, because I'm a human being and not an android.'"

That created an awkward pause, which Will broke by asking, "So how *are* you doing?"

"I'm agitated because you're acting like sitting down and watching a basketball game with me is a chore on the level of cleaning out a sewer."

Silence. They watched the game for a bit. McClaren chucked a three-pointer that missed the rim entirely.

Will said, "So what happens now? After you're all healed up, I mean?"

"I think I'm going to go on vacation."

"And then?"

"I don't know, Will."

"You're not thinking about staying, are you? After everything that's happened?"

"Didn't you *want* me to stay?"

"Didn't you *not*?"

"I don't know. I've grown to like having my toilet talk to me. You think more supervillains are going to attack?"

"Even if not, I don't think you know what you're getting into. Just living this life. Up to now, you've spent your life trying to keep your little financial raft afloat. Patching holes, bailing out water. But once you get into a nice boat with a motor, and a bunch of passengers, there's this terrifying moment where you look at the ocean around you and say, 'Okay, so now where am I actually *going*?' It's a question most people can't answer. They're just . . . not up to it."

"Wait, are you doing a reverse psychology thing on me?"

"Maybe I just want you to think I am."

Zoey tried to puzzle through that, then said, "I'll make you a little bet. If the home team wins the next game, I'll turn over complete control of the company to you and the Suits. I'll leave town and I'll be out of your hair forever."

"And if they lose?"

"I get to take a black Magic Marker, and draw whatever facial hair I want onto your face, and you're not allowed to wash it off or cover it or anything else for thirty days. You can take control of a billion-dollar empire, but you have to risk looking foolish for a single month. Oh, and at noon on the last day of that month, you have to shove the marker up your butt. Then, with the marker wedged between your butt cheeks, you have to go down to the train station and write 'Zoey is our queen' on the floor. With your butt."

Will shook his head and sighed. "You are Arthur Livingston's daughter."

"Oh, and just for that, you also have to permanently change your name to Fartt Dongman."

"This game is about over, isn't it?"

"Yep. Then it's the Hawks versus the Celtics. You've got six more hours of basketball to watch, so settle in. This is your life now."

"All right, hand me a beer."

"Get it yourself, they're in the minifridge down there. Here's something that I've been thinking about, since I've been bedridden. I don't know if you picked up on it, but Molech really didn't seem all that smart to me."

"There were subtle clues to that effect, yes."

"So . . . I got to thinking about what you said about magic tricks, and how it's all misdirection. Is it possible that Molech *was* the misdirection, for someone else? Somebody . . . behind the scenes, or whatever?"

Will, not showing any expression whatsoever, said, "Why, that would suggest, I don't know, that there's a bigger game being played here."

Zoey said, "Well, now I *have* to stay. Oh, look! The cat's playing with his mouse."

Will sat back with a beer and said, "Well, there you go. Mission accomplished."

AFTERWORD

Six frequently asked questions about *Futuristic Violence and Fancy Suits*, answered six years later:

1. Are there other books in the series?

Yes, at least one. The second is enigmatically titled *Zoey Punches the Future in the Dick* and was released in 2020. If you're reading this several years after that, there may be even more! Go check via whatever wondrous technology you use to buy books now, or venture into the wastelands to barter with the warlord who hoards the book supply—I don't know what your future looks like. I'm writing this in the spring of 2021 and all I can say at the moment is that I definitely have more ideas. As to whether they're *good* ideas—I mean, they all look good inside my head. Once I let them out, I just have to brace myself and hope for the best.

2. What real-life person is Zoey Ashe based on?

I get this question more than any other, and I honestly have no idea why. At least three readers have messaged me to say they've guessed which real acquaintance of mine "is Zoey," each suggesting a different woman. All of them were wrong because grabbing a real person and shoving them into one of my novels seems like a deeply weird thing to do. Wouldn't that make it awkward when they finally read the book? "Jason, I just want to thank you for your detailed descriptions of my boobs, terrible diet, and constant farting. My family and coworkers have been quoting those passages to me on a daily basis." And how would you write, say, an explicit sex scene with that character, especially if their partner is also based on a real person? Aren't you doing real-life erotic fanfic at that point? Is that even legal? ("And then my yoga instructor stepped out of her dress, gazing hungrily at my landlord's engorged manhood. . . .")

I'll just say it now: none of the characters I've written are copied entirely from real life. That would feel creepy and invasive to me, unless it was some famous public figure inserted for the sake of allegory. Hey, speaking of which . . .

3. So Arthur Livingston is Donald Trump, right? And this story is an allegory for the Trump years?

Oh, *hell* no.

I mean, I get it. Arthur is a flamboyant casino and real-estate tycoon obsessed with image and branding. Despite vast wealth, he has stereotypical "low-class" tastes (fast food, gaudy decor), which may or may not be part of the act. He attempts to parlay his fortune and celebrity into another kind of power, potentially altering the trajectory of world history in ways no one, least of all Arthur, could predict. I doubt any reader after 2015 has missed that connection.

But *Futuristic Violence and Fancy Suits* was conceived in 2012 and finished in 2014. When I created my character, Donald Trump was clinging to fame like a grasshopper on the windshield of a speeding car. Back then, he was still hosting *Celebrity Apprentice* on NBC to steadily dwindling ratings (that season featured Arsenio Hall, Penn Jillette, and Dee Snider as contestants). It would have been a weird time to fictionalize Trump as a dangerous visionary out to upend the establishment.

Here, I could pretend that I saw what was coming years before any expert did, or I can just point out that the actual inspiration for Zoey's father is already referenced in the story: Gangster Benjamin "Bugsy" Siegel. He, like Arthur, made his fortune in organized crime (including trafficking sex workers). Roughly a century prior to the events of this novel, Siegel wormed his way into the somewhat legitimate world of business by opening the Flamingo Las Vegas casino and hotel at a time when Vegas was still an unassuming little town in the desert with fewer than thirty thousand inhabitants. Like Arthur, Siegel was justifiably paranoid—his home was rigged with trapdoors and secret escape routes, one leading directly to his garage, where a getaway car and driver were waiting around the clock. Like Arthur, Siegel had not modified any of his body with cyborg parts.

In the end, Siegel would, like Zoey's dad, eventually cross the wrong people and wind up brutally murdered. In fact, it was his spectacular death that would turn Siegel into the stuff of legend and, I believe, make him the template for future casino moguls as brash, bombastic, media-savvy tough guys with shady connections to the underworld. If you see a resemblance between Trump and Arthur Livingston, it's because you're seeing the resemblance between Siegel and Trump. They're now a cultural archetype, men with acute instincts for working the system, learning early on that manipulating public perception is the real-world equivalent of a cheat code. They're the ones who pour so much energy into creating an intimidating persona that it's not clear if there's still a real person at the controls or if the persona is just running on autopilot.

4. When writing a story that takes place in the future, do you worry that it will seem dated if the reality unfolds differently?

No! I'm not trying to predict the future. If I had that ability, I wouldn't constantly be blindsided by, you know, every single thing that happens in my life. I do understand why we marvel when some old-time author successfully portrays our present, like when Jules Verne baffled the world with his 1899 novella, *Fast & Furious Presents: Hobbs & Shaw*. But successful forecasting is never the point; it's just a by-product of keen observation and prescience (which, you'll note, are the traits any author needs to make their work ring true, regardless of genre).

As for me, there's a chance I'll still be cranking out Zoey novels in the actual year this one takes place, and I'm guessing the technology to turn yourself into a cybernetic superhero probably won't be nearly as far along as I predicted. The Blink network, on the other hand, may exist by the time this afterword gets published. Twenty years from now, the idea may seem downright quaint. It'll be like those 1960s sci-fi novels where characters in "the future" send "electronic letters" over the "Data-Net system," and you just roll your eyes like, "Not even close, *idiot*."

5. The societal impact of social media is a major theme of this series. Do you think social media will break society?

I actually have little tolerance for scaremongering about new technology. It's not because I think every advance is good (it should be illegal for cars to have touch screens instead of physical buttons, damn it) but because fearmongers tend to monger the wrong fears. Sci-fi movies in the 1950s seemed pretty convinced that the biggest danger of nuclear power was turning animals into giants. Not only is that a thing that hardly ever happens, but it'd be delightful if it did. A twenty-foot-long otter would have thirty million followers on Instagram.

I personally think science fiction is at its best when it's examining human nature by viewing it through the lens of radical change. It's easy to predict technical advances (Computers will get more powerful! Everything will have screens on it!) but much harder to forecast how human behavior will be altered in response. Plenty of writers guessed the future would have something like the internet; some even foresaw a version of social media. But who could have predicted the ruinous effects on local journalism, the addictive nature of drip-fed outrage, or the sudden shift toward polarization and authoritarian ideologies? Who foresaw children getting paid millions of dollars to unbox toys on YouTube? And that's just the stuff we know about. What are the long-term mental-health effects on kids who spend their formative years with a device that instantly grants total access to all of the world's horrors and porn? Maybe there are no major effects! Who knows? It's essentially a massive social experiment conducted with no parameters or control group.

Look, I'm not an expert in this or any other subject, but I know that the human brain is just an organ. It can be damaged by the information it's asked to process the same way your liver can be ruined by too much alcohol or your eyes can get fried if you stare too long at an eclipse. I also know that many of you will go to bed tonight feeling like a battery that is somehow both utterly dead and also on the verge of bursting into flame. Go hide a teenager's iPhone and see how they react. It also seems indisputable that life in the public eye demands a certain amount of additional brainpower that can feel even more exhausting. Think about the vigilance required to maintain appearances, to tailor every form of expression for mass consumption out of a fear that missteps or embarrassing moments will spread around the globe at the speed of light.

Suddenly, everyone is a celebrity in a world in which celebrities aren't exactly known for being emotionally well adjusted. Hell, I can tell you from experience that life gets weird when your personality is shaped by the fickle tastes of a faceless crowd of followers you'll never meet. Just like Arthur, you can wind up devoting so much energy to the facade that the facade starts to take over. Now imagine a whole society doing that and you get, well, *Futuristic Violence and Fancy Suits.* Or not! We'll see!

6. So do you think we're all doomed?

Nah.

I've seen multiple reviews refer to *FVaFS* as dystopian science fiction, but I never intended it to come across that way. The world depicted here doesn't seem any better or worse to me than the one we know (if anything, I think it's slightly less weird than what I've seen over the last few years). But let's not lose sight of the big picture: the vibrating little supercomputer in my pocket also grants me immediate access to all of the world's great works of art and literature, along with instant communication with friends on the other side of the planet whom I'd otherwise never have encountered. I started reading science fiction around 1985; if a book written back then had predicted the invention of Google's search engine and Wikipedia's all-knowing database, including the fact that both *are completely free to use,* I'd have seen it as hopelessly utopian. They didn't even have that in *Star Trek*.

Now imagine if that same story from the Reagan era portrayed a 2021 in which:

- we not only have avoided a world war with the Soviets, but have seen no wars between superpowers for one of the longest stretches in the modern era;
- the number of people living in extreme poverty worldwide has *dropped by 1.3 billion*—the fastest reduction in poverty in human history;
- more than 2.6 billion people have gained access to modern sanitation and electricity for the first time;
- child and infant mortality has dropped by more than half, as has global illiteracy;
- thirty countries and territories have legalized same-sex marriage for more than 1.1 billion citizens.

Such a story would have been treated as almost childlike in its optimism, and yet every single item on that list has come to pass over the last few decades. We are, by every method in which we know how to measure human well-being, living in the golden age of civilization. It may not look like it from within your neighborhood, as a lot of that miraculous growth is occurring in India, China, and other parts of the world where my books aren't as widely read. But it is happening.

As for what's next, I believe we're in for a period of rapid societal change, which I admit isn't exactly going out on a limb. Exposing a population to a tsunami of new information has a tendency to shake things up. The invention of the printing press triggered the Enlightenment, a bunch of brutal revolutions, and (eventually) the birth of modern democracy. The adoption of television drove the 1960s antiwar movement. We're seeing the beginnings of something similar with the internet and social media. If you're in the USA, you've watched the trends play out in recent headlines: the xenophobia and "economic anxiety" fed by social media algorithms, the ubiquitous cameras capturing acts of police brutality.

But even beyond that, I feel like we're experiencing a sort of across-the-board class shock as social groups who'd have previously avoided one another are suddenly forced to coexist in the same psychological space. The United States is full of rigid social classes that are usually acknowledged only in the form of jokes and fish-out-of-water comedies. Imagine electing a president who is missing two front teeth or speaks with an Appalachian accent. Imagine a young ballet dancer from New York driving a huge pickup truck decorated with an American flag and NRA stickers. Imagine going to court and finding out the judge has face tattoos like Post Malone. Imagine that in the next James Bond movie, they depict him dressing up in a furry wolf costume to have sex.

Those examples make you chuckle precisely because they breach barriers we like to otherwise pretend don't exist. It's only when you're suddenly exposed to the world outside of your class that many of your supposedly timeless and sacred norms are revealed to be nothing but arbitrary tribal customs. Have you ever felt ambushed when traits treated as cool and sexy within your group made you a laughingstock to outsiders? Well, imagine hundreds of millions of people all experiencing that at once.

In the events prior to this novel, Zoey's life was upended by her high school sweetheart realizing that if he wanted to jump to a more prestigious class, it meant leaving Zoey behind. He glimpsed another world in which she would be sending off all sorts of embarrassing signifiers—the wrong sense of humor, the wrong body type, the wrong tastes, the wrong pet. He knew that any mortifying faux pas would spread across Blink before he could even finish apologizing for it. That's the kind of thing the Zoey novels are about: not whether these paradigm shifts will be good or bad for the world (how would I know?) but rather the effect they have on everyday humans who feel like they've been dropped into a sausage grinder designed to make everyone and everything fit neatly into some weird new bun.

So anyway, that's why I wrote a novel in which a man sticks a bunch of cats to his body and calls himself "Pussy Magnet."

—Jason Pargin
March 2021

twitter.com/JohnDiesattheEn
facebook.com/JohnDiesattheEnd.TheNovel
instagram.com/jasonkpargin
johndiesattheend.com

JASON PARGIN is the *New York Times* bestselling author of the John Dies at the End series as well as the award-winning first book in the Zoey Ashe series, *Futuristic Violence and Fancy Suits*. His essays at Cracked.com have been read by tens of millions of people around the world.

Note: Jason Pargin's novels were previously published under the pseudonym David Wong, the author initially adopting the name of the main character in his first book. As of 2021, the novels have been published under his real name.

READ ALL OF
JASON PARGIN'S
BOOKS!